THE NEUROSURGEON

THE NEUROSURGEON

TRAVIS ROBERTSON

iUniverse, Inc.
Bloomington

The Neurosurgeon

iUniverse books may be ordered through booksellers or by contacting:

iUniverse
1663 Liberty Drive
Bloomington, IN 47403
www.iuniverse.com
1-800-Authors (1-800-288-4677)

ISBN: 978-1-4697-0028-1 (sc)
ISBN: 978-1-4697-0030-4 (e)

Library of Congress Control Number: 2011963577

Printed in the United States of America

iUniverse rev. date: 02/03/2012

ACKNOWLEDGMENT

The author is indebted to Keith A. Runkle for the cover drawing.

PROLOGUE

And since you know you cannot see yourself,
so well as by reflection, I, your glass,
will modestly discover to yourself,
that of yourself which you yet know not of.

Shakespeare
Julius Caesar

Annapolis, Maryland, October 1961

Stephanie DeLeon leaned forward against the bitter wind while she crossed Church Circle, leaving St. Anne's on a Sunday. She had prayed so hard that her head ached and her hands throbbed from her fierce grip on the Bible. Tears had dried, bits of mascara streaking prominent cheek bones. Steffi wished that her younger sister were here, but Stella, fearful of their father, had traveled by Greyhound to stay with Auntie in Baltimore.

Father—Frank—had forbidden her to apply any makeup, especially lipstick. She reflected on his edict: "You're only a child, Stephanie. No more than seventeen." She flinched, recalling his tirade about purity and chastity. "I don't want any young whippersnapper tryin' to get into your pants, goddammit." And that was when he was still half sober.

She grieved for her mother, Trudy—Trudy Ross before she got pregnant again with Stephanie and married Steffi's father, Francis DeLeon. Of

1

course, the wedding had to be at Frank's Catholic church across town, not at Trudy's Episcopal chapel. Otherwise the pope wouldn't send his blessing, according to the stories Steffi had heard.

Suddenly, a wet piece of placard whipped through the air, smacking her, stinging her neck, causing her to scream. She peeled it away. HAVE YOU SEEN THIS CHILD? read the caption below a photograph of a waif of seven years. Steffi made the sign of the cross, involuntarily shook her head, and tossed the paper back into the elements. She gazed at the notice tumbling away. HAVE YOU SEEN THIS CHILD? Stella, probably in Baltimore now, crossed her mind once again. Something else struck her: the odor of fish in the salty air.

The teenager, wrapping a frayed woolen coat tightly about her torso, forged her way southward down Franklin Street toward the Anna Rundel Hospital. Her waist-length honey-blonde hair flapped in the wind, parallel with the nearby American flag. As she climbed the steps, her fingers rubbed the mascara stains from her cheeks. She guessed she was pretty. Her friends at school had said so. But Frank—she refused to call him Father—made it clear that she was an ugly piece of shit, that no man in his right mind would ever want her, a bastard conceived before the holy vows of marriage were exchanged.

She stopped at the information desk. "Could you tell me where Trudy DeLeon is? She's a patient. I'm her daughter." Steffi, though out of the chill, continued shivering, knowing what she would find.

"Let me check the patient files ... Hmm ... Oh, here she is. Room 354. Take the elevator two flights up and turn right." The clerk twirled her number two pencil between thumb and forefinger and then stuck it into her brunette bun. She pointed her index finger toward the hall.

On the third floor, Stephanie, with some trepidation, approached the nursing station. She stepped over a shadow stretching from a disabled gurney, paused to take in the scene, and then wrinkled her nose. Someone had just emptied a bedpan. Three doctors conversed in hushed tones, one letting out a low whistle. An orderly pushed an occupied wheelchair with its intravenous stand, wheels rattling. Its client, a pale and frightened stick of a man secured by a hospital gown and safety straps, clung to the chair's armrests as he was ferried toward God knew where. Steffi wondered if he had cancer. She had an urge to go to him and hold his hand. To tell him he would be safe. To … help, somehow.

Stephanie approached the nursing station.

"May I assist you?" A pleasant smile warmed an Indian face. She wore a nursing cap and spoke with a Bombay accent.

"It's Trudy DeLeon, my mom. I … I came to see her. If that's okay." Steffi struggled, torn between running away and facing what was left of Trudy.

"Of course, miss. The patient has taken a sedative, but she will still recognize you. Uh … you have been here before? I mean, you do know what to expect?"

"Yes, ma'am." Steffi lowered her head and shoved her hands into her coat pockets. Her fingers felt a movie ticket stub from *The Intruder*. She noticed the gold hoop earrings the nurse wore. *Frank won't let me have those. Someday I will have my ears pierced and put big, gold hoop earrings in my ears.*

They entered Trudy's dimly lit room. Steffi held her breath. The smell had altered, now a different antiseptic. A human form moved under white sheets, reminding Steffi of white sand shifting on a nearby Chesapeake shoreline. The right arm in a plaster cast hung from an IV pole. The patient wheezed as she breathed, erratic sighs, really. Steffi knew that Mommy's ribs had been fractured, and the pain just to inhale oxygen required large quantities of morphine.

"I'll leave you with her. Call me if you need anything. My name is Deena Patel."

"Thank you, nurse." Steffi clutched her Bible and tiptoed toward the bed.

"Steffi?"

"Yes, Mom. It's me." Steffi removed her coat and laid it on a recliner chair, moving quietly, slowly, as if she were living in a world of breakable glass. Lips trembling, she gripped Trudy's good left hand, stroking the back of it. Stephanie had promised herself she wouldn't cry, but filial tears dripped from long, brown eyelashes.

"Is that really you, baby?" Trudy gave her a weak and shaky grip. "The doctor ordered a shot for me, so I can't sit up, you know. Where's your sister? She didn't come?"

"Stella is ... is at the grocery store. She might come later. She sends her love."

"I can't see so good. The doc says I lost the vision in my left eye. A retinal hemorrhage."

"Oh, Ma." Steffi lay on the bed next to her mother, her hand smoothing the sheets, the wind-whipped layers of sand. "It's got to get better. It just has to. You'll leave him now, won't you?"

But Trudy did not answer for a while. "You and Stella need your pa."

Only if we want to go to hell. "I went to St. Anne's and prayed for us," the girl said, ignoring her mother's response. "If Jesus hadn't told me to love my enemies, I would have killed him, Ma. For certain, as God is my witness."

"Maybe I can get Frank to stop drinking, see a psychologist or one of them social workers, maybe. I took my vows, you know."

Steffi shook her head, her mind recoiling. She knew Frank would never change, but neither would Mother.

"Frank took all the money from the kitchen, Ma. Otherwise I'd have brought you some nice flowers." Steffi stood up and kissed Trudy on the undamaged cheek.

"God bless you, dear. Come and visit tomorrow." Her mother lapsed into a fit of coughing, flecks of blood landing on her pillow.

"Should ... should I fetch the nurse, Ma?"

"No, dear," Trudy rasped. "It's just a little catch in my throat. Love you, my honey-bun."

"I love you too, Ma. Bye." Steffi gathered up her coat.

"Steffi?"

"Yes, Ma?"

"Don't believe a word your father says. You are growing into a most beautiful woman." She blew her daughter a weak kiss and then closed her eyes.

At the nursing station, Deena Patel waved at Steffi. "Will we see you tomorrow?" A worried look had replaced her friendly smile.

"Yes, after school," Steffi promised. "Uh … do you like being a nurse?"

"I love it, helping people and all. Never a dull day." Deena closed a medical file and racked it. "Are you thinking about a career in nursing?"

"Maybe. If I can land a scholarship. Thanks for taking care of Mom. Bye." Stephanie cut to the elevator and mashed down on the button. Cables squeaked, and the lift doors separated.

*   *   *

Steffi cringed at the thought of going home. Frank was out in his fishing trawler, most likely, drinking with his buddies on the Chesapeake Bay. Steffi had nowhere else to go. Nowhere. And her dog, Missie, would need feeding. A rusty chicken soup can bounced and clattered over wet pavement. Listening to the rumble of distant thunder, she remembered that her pet was chained up in the backyard. "Maybe Frank's boat will capsize." A twinge of hope laced with shame spiked her mind as lightning streaked the eastern darkness.

A church steeple tolled eleven. Stephanie turned into the wind, pulled her wrap more closely around her, and then pushed open the front gate. Wrought-iron hinges creaked painfully with rust, and then the portal clunked against a fence post. Denuded weeping willow branches undulated with the wind. Steffi heard Missie's plaintive bark from the other side of the gray clapboard bungalow. A skirl of briny air reverberated through a clothesline, like a bass violin auguring a symphony of death. Steffi rounded the house as drops of rain pricked and danced on fallen maple leaves.

"Oh, Missie. I'm so sorry. Let's get you inside." The black Labrador puppy licked Steffi's face at the release of the tether, a rusty iron chain linked to a steel spike driven into the soil.

Steffi glanced across a flower garden, toward the Severn River. Mooring lines from a neighbor's sailboat squeaked and clanked in rhythm with the onrushing waves. Curls of foamy water battered the wooden dock, the pilings groaning with each lash. Frank's boat was not in sight, and Steffi breathed a sigh of relief. Aiming toward the back door, she nearly tripped over an upturned garbage can, its contents strewn about by nature. Or by Frank.

Inside Steffi clicked on the oil heater and then wiped the damp from Missie, her drooped tail wagging.

Suddenly, a burst of rain slammed into the rear kitchen window, knocking it open. Steffi stifled a scream, feeling her heart skip a beat. She jumped up, shoved the window closed, and secured the lock. After catching her breath, the teenage girl drew her pet close to her, its wet hair clinging to Steffi's cheeks.

"Oh, Missie, I love you so. Frank forbids your staying in the house. But I can't send you back into that weather. If you keep quiet, you can sleep with me." She wrapped a hug around the grateful dog. Her wet tongue lapped and kissed Steffi's face.

The puppy trailed after Steffi as they headed down the hall. The two passed by a closed door, and Missie sniffed the carpet of Steffi's parents bedroom. Steffi had seen it this morning. She couldn't bring herself to go in there again. Tomorrow Frank would make her clean it up. If she didn't, then … Steffi wondered if other families were like hers. Her friend Trina seemed to have nice parents.

Steffi hesitated and then entered her bedroom. No pictures. Frank had destroyed them all, even the snapshot of her in a blue and gold cheerleader's uniform. She had hidden those photos that remained. Another thunderclap followed, sheets of Chesapeake rain hammering at loosened shingles. The room echoed the sizzling *rat-a-tat-tat*.

Stephanie set Missie on one of two roll-away cots and warmed her pet with a blanket. The shades, stained from earlier days of rum-and-Coke parties, remained down, protecting passersby from such a dissolute world. A single caged bulb burned in the center of the ceiling, not far from where spots of water formed. The air smelled musty, in part from a chamber pot. Steffi and Stella preferred to use that at night rather than risk waking Frank.

On an old oaken table next to the window sat an aquarium stocked with half a dozen tiny fish, plastic coral, and small sea urchins. Sometimes she would spend long moments gazing at the fish darting here and there. The only nice piece of furniture was their cedar dresser with a large mirror, its left support footing chipped from a crowbar, a missile fired last week.

Tucked in at the edge of the looking glass was a photo—Stephanie and Stella hugging each other. Steffi lowered herself onto a chair and stripped wet clothes from her skin. She heard a sound. Was it the front gate? Then silence, except for the rain and a faint growl from Missie. *It must have been a gust of wind.*

Steffi sat naked. The frail beauty gazed at her silvered reflection, her eyes with huge raven-black pupils, a placid sea shielding pregnant, teeming depths. Thick brown eyelashes. Graceful brow. Full lips. Generous mouth. Sculpted nose. No blemishes, though a beauty spot, a brunette mole, reposed on her right cheek. Delicate fingers lifted a comb and drew along honey-blonde tresses, freeing her hair from knots. The same hand then cupped her developing left breast. *Mommy said she was a late bloomer too.*

A faint approximation of a smile washed over Steffi's face. Her expression turned almost coy. *I hope I will be as pretty as Mommy when I start college.* Her golden-brown doe-eyes traced her form in the mirror. At first, feeling embarrassed, she averted her gaze, the dark amber gems then drawn, as if by a magnet, back to the looking glass, a silver pendulum swinging in the darkness.

"Frank likes you better than me, Stella. Wonder why? Maybe it's your strawberry-blond hair. Sometimes I hate you. Mama says we should not hate others, only love them. But I cannot help this feeling, when it happens."

A floorboard squeaked. *Tap-thud, tap-thud.* Trapped. *Oh God, oh God, oh God!* Her horrified eyes flew wide open, her mouth attempting to scream, but a man's hand, its thick hair reeking of fish oil and Jamaica rum, clamped down, strangling all breath. Burly arms hauled her off the seat and against his heaving chest. Her father's claws raked down to her throat, encircling her neck.

"Well, my little slut. I finally got you alone." His round face, ridged by fat and pockmarks, dripped sweat and rain water. "Trudy won't be around to protect you now. I fixed it so's she'd spend time at our hospital, away from my little Steffi. Now it's just me an' you, where no one can interfere." He uncovered her mouth.

"Please, Frank," Steffi begged, her nakedness twisting, long legs crossing. "I'll be good. I'll clean the whole house. Even wash your clothes. *Please!*"

"I only got one leg, Steff. Remember how I lost t'other? Do ya, ya fucking cunt? 'Twere crushed by that fancy launch slipping into my dock. The very craft bringing you back home from some outlandish party with the mayor's daughter. I han't gave any permission for you to go off like that, showing up your pa."

"Pa! You were sleeping, one leg over the edge. It wasn't anyone's fault."

"And of course you will be good, Steff. Iron my shirts. And more." He kicked Missie away and hauled Steffi onto her bed, his grip pinning her arms in a spread-eagle fashion. "But now I need to teach you some of the facts of life."

His fist reached toward the sky, paused, and then whipped downward in a pique of rage. The hammer-blow cracked her lip open, blood seeping onto the pillow.

"Where'd you get them small tits? Not from Trudy, that's for sure." He grabbed Steffi's hair and yanked her head back to the pillow. "Just be good to me, and I'll leave the mutt alone, okay?"

"Please, not Missie," she pleaded. Terrified, Steffi tried to break free, twisting her body, but her struggle merely whetted his sadistic appetite. "Frank, I ca … can't breathe so well. *Stop! You're hurting me!*"

"See, Steff. You called me Frank. That's a real good sign of our future relations." He unzipped his fly.

She screamed again as Francis DeLeon raised his right fist, again smashing his daughter's twisted face, this time his glass ring ripping the skin from left cheek bone to the corner of her mouth.

"Spread your goddamn legs or, by Jesus, I'll strangle you and that fucking dog now."

Her vision blurred as a film of blood seeped over her eyes.

"Bitch, are you listening to me?" She heard his words as if coming out of a fifty-gallon barrel, the odor of garlic and rum spilling from his mouth. "Your sister Stella sure fucks better than you," he grunted. "But I'll learn ya!"

Steffi's entire body froze, rejecting the deadly scourge as the image of her father ran in and out of focus. She shrieked from the pain of his hard prick driving into her vagina, the birth canal recoiling in tortured spasms. The last thing she remembered was his cold, wet body lying on top and smothering her. He was a three-hundred-pound hammerhead atop little Steffi at ten fathoms. She squeezed her eyes shut, commanding her mind to send her somewhere else. *The aquarium!* The shark was no longer fucking his daughter. He was raping a surrogate body while Steffi floated with the colorful fishies. She drifted away, a dead woman trying to leave her memories behind. *Bitch, are you listening to me? Your sister Stella sure fucks better than you! I'll learn ya ... I'll learn ya ... I'll learn ya ...*

The black Lab puppy cowered in a corner, her tail between her legs, as the moving shadows of the master plied an awkward rhythm, rusty mattress-springs scraping together, a discordant sound against the crash of the waves outside. The telephone rang.

CHAPTER 1

God enters by a private door into every individual.

Ralph Waldo Emerson

Chapel Hill, North Carolina, March 2003

Sounds of a gut-wrenching battlefield thundered through our living room. My wife, Monica, desperate for some measure of tranquility in her life, had been praying for my redemption and understanding.

"Ira! Listen to me! What happened to your brother was *not* your fault," she cried after me when I slammed the door. "Ira, *please* come back."

Fear had closed my mind to her entreaties as I sank down onto the divan. For me, the consequences were horrifying, guaranteeing me a place in Satan's dungeon, and there was only one way to alleviate the pounding of my heart. A white icy dread grabbed hold of me. My limbs, quailing, felt wobbly, unable to keep me from falling. *Dear God, someone help me!* Monica couldn't. She did not know the whole story.

I had to escape. My trembling surgeon's hand poured another amber stream of whiskey. I gazed at my only friend on this earth. Swirled her around. Spun the ice. Drank. The alcohol felt so damn good as blue flames spun down my gullet. That craving vanished into a smoky shadow, but I knew deep down that she patiently waited, lingering, only another evening away.

A noise. Someone rapped on the side entrance of the kitchen. I awoke in the den, steadied myself, and then, with shirttails hanging out, shuffled toward the sound. My hand managed to open the door. No one was there! Not a damn soul. I returned to the den, back to my liquid mistress. After an hour of recruiting wayward resentments, I drifted back into that unstable dreamland.

The next day Monica asked me if I knew that Garth, our son-in-law, had been at the door the night before.

"Dammit!" My fist slammed the kitchen table. "I don't keep track of Garth's comings and goings."

"Come on, Ira. Be serious."

"I remember someone knocking, but I didn't see or hear anybody."

"Ira Stone! Garth stood right in front of you! He said that you just shuffled your feet and stared at him. What is going *on* with you?"

"Christ, he must have been seeing things." I turned and walked away, but with the strangest feeling that *someone* was there. More and more I felt like a slavish marionette manipulated by the strings of a puppeteer, my knees jumping up and down, driving me toward that terrible smoky and accursed destiny.

One month later

I sat in the living room with the TV on. Neither Fox News nor CNN held any interest for me. A wet stain on a doily regarded me while Monica perused the *Chapel Hill News* and twirled a lock of raven hair in her forefinger. She looked up.

"You seem to be spending an awful lot of time at work, Ira."

"Hmmm …"

"Do you love me?" The earnestness in her expression eluded me. "You never touch me anymore. Please, if you truly love me then … then …"

"For Christ sake, spit it out! Then … then …?"

"Sometimes I just need you to *hold* me, Ira."

"Okay, okay, I love you."

She sighed. "That's it? Are you going to join me in bed tonight?"

"Sure." But I found reasons not to, preferring my own bedroom. "But I need to rest for my surgery tomorrow. And you always have your grandkids over."

"They're your grandchildren too." Tears welled up in her deep brown eyes. "All of them call you 'Poppa.' Do I need to make an appointment for sex with my husband?"

"*Shit!* Leave me alone! I just want to be left alone! I'm tired, tired, *tired!*"

"Must you swear so ...?"

A letter opener lying on an end table caught my attention. Sometimes I just wanted to ...

"For God's sake, Ira!" Monica stood up and backed away.

My heart rate accelerated. I inhaled deeply. Something felt wrong, terribly wrong. I was scared. Angry. I shut my eyes and saw my life corroding, dissolving, shrinking away.

"Maybe we should see someone. A priest, perhaps? Let me ..."

"Damn! What is this? I don't like church, especially your goddamn Catholic church. Next you'll want a divorce."

"You know darn good and well I will never divorce you. I simply want us to get help. And you *must* cease that drinking."

"What are you calling me? A drunk. A fucking souse? I can manage my drinking as well as the next guy!"

"Of course not. It's just that ..."

"I'm out of here!" My fist slammed against the end table, knocking the letter opener and my drink to the floor. "Now look what you made me do!"

Mumbling to myself like a madman, I jumped up, ran to my bedroom, and popped a Valium. *Sleep!* I needed sleep. I had surgery early the next day. I was *not* a lush. *Not like Uncle Barley!*

Lying on my bed and shriveling up into myself, I fell into the now unkind arms of Morpheus, dreaming darkly of my uncle slipping beneath the raging sea. Nearby, a cruise ship discharged garbage into the ocean.

The fire fed upon itself all night. In the morning my body dripped wet, my mouth terribly parched.

*   *   *

The more my own life became unmanageable, the more I tried to manage the lives of others. I was having more blackouts and failed to realize it. I even considered carrying a nine-millimeter sidearm, but I was not sure if it was for me or someone else. The evening taverns now saw more of me than my wife did. The more I drank, the worse I felt about myself. The more disgusted I felt, the more I swilled the bottle. I felt weak, shy. I didn't fit in.

My surgeries and clinics went smoothly, but by late afternoon I kept glancing at my watch, waiting for five o'clock. Waiting with nervous anticipation. I needed to reach home by 5:30 and my whiskey by 5:45. Mr. Hyde wanted to be released, and he would *not* be denied. I could actually feel the fucking hairs pushing out.

Soon my stomach rebelled, molecules of ethanol eating away within me, piranhas feasting on my gut. I ate Rolaids to soften the distress, believing that would protect me from a gastrointestinal bleed. After all, I *was* a doctor. I found another brilliant method to keep my drinking safe— toss two antacids in my mouth before tipping the Waterford tumbler. I was so damn clever.

At times I fancied that women were dying to get in bed with me or that men reviled me, which drove me to more booze. But the sought-after serenity had made itself scarce, hiding, and that terrified me. I plunged ever deeper into that rabbit hole of no return. I needed a road sign, Saint Michael and a fingerpost to point the way out, but the path eluded me. I kept hiding from it, fearful of what might be revealed—that I was, indeed, an alcoholic.

In our kitchen one day I sensed Monica's eyes running up and down me.

"Ira, I know it is the weekend, but do you need to drink in the morning? You're going to ruin your health. Please put that away."

"*Frankly*, dear, I fail to see a problem. Don't you worry, I'm taking vitamins." Recent blood tests had shown further elevation of my hepatic enzymes. Should that continue, I would need a liver transplant—or worse.

"Slick," the intrepid manslayer as I would later learn, had become the usurper of my neural pathways. The consequence? Even yet, I remained unconcerned, hypnotized, survival too abstract and my desire for alcohol too real. *One has to be insane to live like this, truly insane.*

"You look a bit pasty, honey. At least please see a doctor. I have a feeling something is wrong. Terribly wrong." Monica rung her hands, and then her fear burst forth. *"Ira! I love you. I don't want to lose you!"*

*   *   *

How did I get to that point in my life? I was a surgeon, a respected member of the community and the profession. I was *not* an alcoholic, damn it! Not like Uncle Barley.

Monica, who knew better, somehow got me to the airport, my heels dragging, digging in. I was more frightened than I had ever been in my entire life. What awaited a sinner for whom redemption was beyond his reach?

CHAPTER 2

You who would begin to conceive of kings, living or dead,
must change yourselves to do so. Must unlearn all to learn again ...

George Garrett
Death of the Fox

Appleton Recovery Center, San Francisco, May 2004

That spring day, a Saturday, I was a shaken and shattered man gripped by a centripetal force of unkind fear, her loosened cries screaming within. I bought myself a ticket from North Carolina to the West Coast. Monica drove me to the Raleigh–Durham Airport. My procession through security felt as if I were being strip-searched and mercury torn from my dental work. I caught a Delta flight via Salt Lake City to San Francisco, once my home. While changing planes in Utah, the hum of my wheeled carry-on trailed behind. The familiar odor of watering holes led me into the SLC airport taverns, where I watched televised war clips from Afghanistan. I had already drunk two whiskeys on the first leg.

En route to my gate, I caught sight of a small crowd gathered over a figure lying on the floor. I edged closer. An elderly man was shaking all over, his eyeglasses fractured, blood seeping from his lower lip. His legs were spastic, arms flexing.

"My husband! Joshua, Joshua! Someone help!"

I rushed over, pulled out my wallet, kneeled over the epileptic victim, and pushed the billfold between his chattering teeth.

"You're choking him! *What are you doing?*" cried the frantic wife, hands clasped at her own throat.

"I'm a doctor, ma'am. I'm trying to keep him from biting his tongue." I rolled the man on his side and then cradled him in my cross-legged lap. "Has someone called 911?"

"Yes, sir," a nearby passenger responded. "Help is on the way. Anything I can do?"

"Check with the missus here, see if he has any seizure history or is taking any medication. I need to keep this guy from injuring himself."

The shaking diminished and his breathing improved as the medics arrived. I would have stayed to see him and his wife to the airport exit, but I did not want my own affliction to become apparent. And that made me ashamed.

*   *   *

Four more whiskeys on the Boeing 737 assuaged my fragile nerves. The plane arrived in Frisco late in the evening. Even after all that sedation, I was still scared and had never felt so alone in my entire life—a patient, no longer a surgeon.

The Appleton Drug and Alcohol Recovery Center sent a minivan to pick me up. As I stepped into the back seat I found myself sweating, digits twitching, eyelids in rapid blink mode. Efflux was imminent at both ends though fear tightened my nether sphincter. Bile and acid burned my stomach, throat, and tongue. I took in a deep, ragged breath. The air felt damp, cold. To make matters worse, music with a sledgehammer beat shot from the console.

"Could you quiet your radio?" I begged the driver. "My head is about to fucking explode."

"Sure thing, friend." His hand twisted the dial.

"How long will it take us to get there?"

A large head barely reached above a steering wheel gripped by brown-stained fingers. Here was my first face-to-face contact with Appleton.

"Hour and a half."

He appeared to be a likeable fellow, wavy sable hair in crosscurrents, corduroy jacket, cheeks like cracked leather, and the blackest eyes I'd ever seen. The Dodge Caravan gathered speed through the slipstream of dying traffic as we traveled north into fog. "Ever been there?"

"No," was all I could say. That seemed an odd question. I focused on the thick fold of flesh lining the back of his neck. My forefinger tried to find an irritating stone in my shoe, but I was too lazy or too drunk to assist.

"I was a patient in Appleton a few years back. They saved my life. Most of the medical people … the therapists I mean to say … are recovering addicts themselves." An unlit cigarette bobbed up and down on one side of his mouth. "Just keep a tight asshole, and you'll do okay."

Tight asshole? My lids shot up. "Good God! Another drunk is going to treat me?" I blurted out a bit too loudly. I knew my wretched mind had regressed into its egoistic self, but I was a doctor, dammit! A brain surgeon, for crissake! I deserved better than this. "Turn this fucking thing around!"

The driver, who took on the appearance of a gnome, did not seem to hear me as lampposts, exit signs, and trees loomed up and shot by. A fork of lightning appeared in the dark and murky marrow of western skies. Windshield wipers delivered their slow *thump, thump* drumbeat.

I felt certain that Lucifer's minions waited at the end of this ride. What had I got myself into? I had to have a drink! Jesus, how I wanted my Crown Royal. Balls, even a Four Roses would have worked. I needed that amber antidote for snake venom—I was holding a bag of vipers, knowing I would have to reach inside soon. *Thump, thump. Thump, thump …*

*   *   *

My marinating brain, fleeced of all common sense, was too distraught to take in the buildings and grounds of my asylum. Luke led me through the door to my future. I remember his bringing me into a large reception area with a substantial circular counter enclosing a combination nursing and clerical station, the devil's disciples within and safely separated from us more dangerous patients. Thank God my liquid tranquillizer on board was working.

"Ira Stone! We are ever so glad to see you. Sorry to greet you with our usual misty weather."

Like hell. "Yeah. Thanks."

My bag thumped down on the tile. All I wanted now was to slip into a nice warm, cozy bed. My head pounded, and the hands on my wristwatch converged at midnight.

"Why don't you rest over there on the couch? There are some magazines and a TV." Delores Something-or-other, RN—I could not focus on her name tag—pointed toward the divan. I was certain evil lurked behind that pleasant smile. "We need to search your bags and then complete an intake questionnaire."

See? Evil! Shit. I had to cipher some way to save my neck from the gallows. My brain continued to hover in suspension like dust floating between two worlds.

"Please have a seat." She grabbed a clipboard and pen, eyed me, and then jotted down initial data. "Let's see. Caucasian, brown hair, blue eyes, thin but solid build, anxious …" The nurse continued writing while mumbling to herself.

I found myself bouncing my foot against the carpet as I focused my anger on the creature before me.

CHAPTER 3

You need chaos in your soul
to give birth to a dancing star.

Friedrich Nietzsche

Appleton

I found myself trapped in a small room at the recovery center, the brutish and sickly green walls moving ever closer. Boiling and heaving, I jerked off the covers. Thunder and gusts of angry wind rattled the lone window. *What the hell am I doing here? I need my Valium. Don't they understand that? It was prescribed for me by a psychiatrist!* The facts that the prescription for this benzo had been written twelve years ago and that I had been receiving it through a means frowned upon by the DEA were irrelevant, of course.

One of my least favorite nurses arrived with two syringes. "Ira, we have some medicine for you."

"Valium?" My voice shook with agitation.

"Sorry. You know how addictive that is. You might discuss this with your counselor."

"Well, what the fucking hell are those in your hands?"

"Your doctor will make rounds shortly." She smiled. "He will review the treatment plan with you."

"Thanks." *Bitch. What kind of a hospital is this anyway? I hate everyone! Fuck all of you!*

After my backside endured the needle sticks, the RN disappeared. God, was I glad my family could not see me now.

*   *   *

Seven days of misery followed that devouring nightfall. Luke was right. Almost everyone on my treatment team had gone through a recovery program for addiction—inpatient, outpatient, AA, NA—one or all of them. I could not argue that they did not understand me or that they did not realize the pain I endured.

The pressurized nights and days in my charnel pit became a dim sepulchral blur, eating themselves out and running together, like living at the Arctic Circle. I shook as if chilled by those ice cubes known all too well to me. I wrapped myself in damp sheets, only to kick them off as my legs defended me from snarling, writhing, fire-breathing dragons and tri-headed serpents.

"Get me the fuck out of here! Get me—"

I felt a pair of warm hands sooth my brow and then push a needle into my thigh. The overhead lights dimmed, and a strange sort of unconsciousness overcame me.

I lived in a thickening twilight zone of Never-Never Land, an infant once more as the nippled bottle gave way to a slippery liquor flask. Like fractured egg shells, my dislocated emotions scattered and fell to the ground. The shrieking from deep in my throat frightened me even more than the monstrous storm raging in my head. I trembled, waiting for lightning's scimitar.

Then one day I fell into a tenuous serenity and gazed about. Life slowed from seventy-eight to forty-five rpm. My arms felt warm gentle sunshine stream through the window, flowing around the room like water. The mist had evaporated along with the toxins. Snippets of music from a television slipped under the door.

That first day out of intensive care I found myself standing at the nursing station, swallowing prescribed meds. I steadied myself, leaning on the counter, and a white skirt approached, grinned pleasantly and spoke.

"How's it going, good-looking? Feel up to me describing some of the procedures here?"

I nodded; I did not have a whole lot of choice. I struggled for composure yet saw a ray of hope. As my right hand strove to hold a cup of coffee, my eyes scanned the lofty hills pressing against her sweater. I could not help it. There ought to be a law against eye-stopping RNs. I felt a brief twinge in my neglected private parts. This nurse, with untamed and perfumed hair, scarlet and electrified like short tongues of flame, tossed me a guarded smile.

"Presently we have about forty men and women undergoing therapy. It is mandatory that there be no contact between the sexes. No hellos, no assisting in carrying laundry bags, no meals together, no dallying on the sidewalks. If you pass each other in the hallway, just pretend she doesn't exist." She winked, drawing me to her vivid emerald eyes. "No matter how charming you think she is."

"You will eat at the cafeteria in another building, with the gents in one section and ladies in another. The closest you will get to a woman, yours truly excepted, is during lectures, when you will sit on one side, the ladies on the other. Further allowances will be made later when you attend some community AA meetings."

"AA again? I thought I was finished with that."

She raised her carefully plucked eyebrows and then prepped my arm and pushed a needle into it, bursting my alcoholic bubble. The white skirt just shook her head as if to say, *My friend, you ain't got a clue, not a goddamn clue.*

"Any questions so far, Ira? If not, you have an eleven o'clock appointment with our psychiatrist." She pointed to a corkboard. "The clerk posts the daily schedule. We have assigned a buddy to you, and he will help you get wired into our program. And welcome again."

Jesus. What have I gotten myself into? "Phone calls?" *She has the reddest lips and the greenest eyes.*

"Three times a day for ten minutes each."

Amelia Levinstone walked away to attend a willowy twenty-something girl with a cloud of fair curls and sparkling tears pooling in humongous, puppy-dog eyes. On her ring finger glittered a dazzling diamond reflecting ceiling lights. The young patient, dressed in a riot of textures and colors from skirt to bandanna, shivered and made strange grunting sounds. *She certainly belongs here, but I fucking do not. Fucking do not ... do not ...*

On wobbly legs I shuffled to the bulletin board. *Let's see. It's nine. Home group meeting in Men's Library. Just down the hall I think. Where is my "buddy"?*

"Ouch!" I felt a sharp pain in my foot. My fingers grabbed the right shoe and shook it. A piece of gravel fell away.

*   *   *

"Ira, if you don't mind, would you come into my office? I need to get a bit of history from you." My personal counselor bagged me as I came down the hallway. "My name is Betsy Greene," she said, extending her hand, which I took with some hesitation.

"Again? I already explained everything to you guys." *I do not need to be treated like this. Even she does not know I am a world-famous brain surgeon!*

We passed into a comfortable twelve-by-twelve space. Betsy beckoned me toward a rosewood chair. A burnished brass lamp on a mahogany desk threw light and shadows about a room lined with books, a wall clock, and various certificates and awards. Yellow roses in a Ming porcelain vase brightened the surroundings. A copy of *Alcoholics Anonymous*, Robert Bly's *Iron John*, and a year's supply of three-by-five index cards lay on her desk. Four Dugal paintings hung on the walls, creating the impression of a bygone era. On a corner table sat a small mountain of pamphlets and manila file folders appearing to await adjudication. Betsy seemed quite at home and relaxed in her brown cracked-leather throne.

"You likely will repeat your story to many of the staff here as days go by. Each of us may have a different perception of your background and character, especially as the drugs clear out of your body over time. We compare notes at our daily meetings and search for the best treatment program." She smiled. "After all, Ira, 'to make an omelet, one is obliged to crack the eggshell,' as they say."

Big deal.

The counselor grabbed a clipboard. She clearly bore the weight of about seventy summers. The woman had short gray hair, a gold necklace with the Star of David, and a prim and proper demeanor. Her scrubbed Slavic face, reminding me of an old leather purse, was lined by the ravages of a tough existence, a life bruised by alcoholism—and something else, was my guess. Somehow I begrudgingly liked Betsy, even without really knowing her.

"Hmm. Married four times, I see." Her reflective diluted blue eyes held mine.

"Uh huh."

"And I gather you are a physician, a neurosurgeon. A noble profession."

"Nobility transformed into a fool, so you guys tell me." I glared at my spread fingertips.

"Sometimes we perceive meanings and intentions too harshly, Ira. You are highly intelligent, as the psych tests showed, and certainly you could have had any woman you chose, from the looks of you. You have much to be thankful for." The counselor picked up her pen. "Now, start anywhere you like. We are in no hurry."

What am I doing here? Where did it all begin? The first thought that came to mind was the crisis upon which the direction of my future had turned. Michael. I suppose that one must begin at the beginning of this insanity. I found myself speaking slowly, my throat tight with a terrible guilt, guilt and fear clinging to me like cobwebs—sealed off and protected by a deep, calcified anger.

CHAPTER 4

Put your hand on a stove for a minute, and it seems like an hour.
Sit with that special girl for an hour, and it seems like a minute.

Albert Einstein

My brother, Michael, was especially close to our sister, Jocelyn. Of all the Stone siblings, those two in many ways were like peas in a pod. Michael Jacob was four summers younger than her. Jocie, as we called her in her childhood, trailed me by six years. Jocie and Mike were delivered after the more Victorian era of my family history—after our Grandma Stone of Helena, Montana (my birthplace), released her caustic sway over Mom's infant-rearing management.

Radnor, suburb of Philadelphia, 1951

Winston Churchill became the British prime minister a second time. Rachel Carson published *The Sea Around Us*. And I had a date with Nadine Simpson! It was near the end of July. I was nearly a senior, and she was about to enter tenth grade in Radnor High School. That was our first date alone, and from that point on, sugarplums dancing in my head, nature took its rapid course.

One evening after a school prom, the two of us were sitting in my folk's car, a big Pontiac. Nadine and I had snuck some of her parent's Sauvignon Blanc on board, and we were becoming a bit giggly. No one but us existed on this hillock overlooking the lights of the big city. A dog barked in the distance.

"What are you thinking, Nadine?" Prickling with nervous energy, I held her hand, stroking skin as soft as swan's down. I could not remove my eyes from her bosom—figuratively speaking, of course. Thank God it was dark, though I could not hide the sense of urgency in my voice.

"Ira, you are the most gorgeous guy in Radnor." The stars were winking as she cast her luminous eyes downward and sighed. "Your hands are so strong ... and well formed, like those of a surgeon." She drew my name out like a caress, and I found myself lost in the yearning stillness that followed.

"Hmm ... hands that long to hold you, baby." *Is that me talking?* I leaned close to her.

She tilted her head. The pressure was too much. Her willowy blonde hair fell back, and moonlight reflected from those soft, wet lips. Silence, then mine covered hers, lightly at first, then tightly. Jesus, I was suddenly out of control, my heart beating faster than a small bird's. She broke for air but, shit, I wanted to die of asphyxiation! Right then and there!

"Ira, I think we had better ... mmfff ..."

Our breathing crescendoed. I wished—no, needed—to learn about that heaving female breast, so nicely exposed by the cheerful cut of her blouse. Passionate kisses did not go unanswered. Even though the concept of French kissing was foreign to us, or at least to me, such ignorance failed miserably to quench the tide of ardor, my own desire now one of symphonic intensity.

"Ira! Please, don't ..."

My left hand launched its way under Nadine's silks. The other five digits, also pressed into service, curled behind her back to fumble with the bra fastener. Which fell loose, thankfully, for my hands trembled so. I thought my zipper would rupture, and I knew right then that Nadine would be the mother of my offspring.

I can recall my very first drink of alcohol, a year previously at my parent's Eli Lilly party. It was scotch, and I hated the taste. And I haven't forgotten my first encounter that night with the female bust, excepting infancy, of course. In a Pontiac. July 1951, my left hand against Nadine's receptive bosom. Her response was a sudden intake of air as my golden finger found the nipple.

Chapter 5

Alas, poor Yorick! I knew him, Horatio.
A fellow of infinite jest, of most excellent fancy.

William Shakespeare
Hamlet

Appleton

Still a bit wobbly, I was entering the cafeteria for lunch when a plastic dish sailed over my left shoulder.

"Listen, you fuggin' bastards! I ain't staying here any longer. Fug the judge! *Fug all of you!*" screamed Rabbit as he grabbed his half-filled milk carton and fired it at one of the lady counselors. Straw-colored hair flew about his head, and sweat poured down his red face and neck.

Two guys and I rushed to restrain Rabbit, pinning his arms and chest. He glared at me and then spit. Coffee-tinged sputum slid down my cheek.

"Easy, Rabbit, let's calm down. What's going on with you?" Chester, the counselor, jumped away from a boot coming his way.

The patient struggled, his left arm breaking loose. The fist landed on my jaw, sending jolts of electricity through my head. Rabbit's legs flailed out again, kicking at the nearest knee. He was like a scorpion just caught in a bottle. But he was no match against the six-foot-five, two-hundred-and-fifty-pound former Viking tackle, now fiercely gripping Rabbit's chest.

"Let me go, goddamn it! I got to get home. Maryanne is leaving me. I got to tell her to … to … *Let me go!"* Hot tears welled up, rolling down his face as his body fell into a slump. "I love you, Maryanne. Don't leave me, please. I've stopped using that stuff, and I'll never touch it again. Can't you see … Don't take the kids. *Don't take m'boys!"*

The floor was littered with fragments of a letter Rabbit had received from Toronto, his home town. We finally got him into a chair. He kept shaking his head, *"No … no … no …"*

I relaxed my hold on his forearm and then gripped his shoulder. "Hang in there, Rabbit. We have all been there." The Lord knows I had—at both the receiving and the delivery end.

We all had families broken up by drugs and alcohol, my own included. With Rabbit it was that psychedelic methamphetamine relative, a drug called Ecstasy. He needed to be healed. And so did I.

We had nicknamed him Rabbit because his ears rose up vertically, and he sported a pug nose that would twitch while he talked.

Counselor's office, same afternoon

"You say that neither your mother nor your father were alcoholics." Betsy glanced at her notes. "Tell me about Uncle Barley. Did you actually witness his drinking?"

I stared through the window, gripping the sides of my armchair. Internally, I still harbored resentment at finding myself in this … this prison.

Helena, Montana

Barley Stone was my uncle, our father's brother, a gravelly throated and bow-legged caricature. After years of punching cows and then working on ships while in the US Merchant Marines during World War II, Barley had plunged into a state of profound depression. This likeable introvert suffered fear and degradation, which led him to numerous seaside pubs. Beer and ale in the beginning, but evil begat evil—and drink begat drink. Thus my uncle slipped further and further toward the bottom of the human food chain, finding comfort in cheap bottles and bordellos.

Barley became a driftwood derelict, one of those poor souls always on the narrow edge of death, sometimes perched by a gutter while nursing a bottle and often plagued by thoughts of suicide. He was an inconvenience, a family embarrassment. Our father supported him in later years while Barley lived out his existence in the old family homestead, a white clapboard house in Helena, Montana. Listening to our parents talk, we children found ourselves ashamed of our uncle, a man with no will to cease his drinking, they said. Yet he was a quaint recluse, an enigma—the true nature of his affliction had been carefully sequestered from us kids.

*   *   *

During the summertime of my college years, Nadine and I saw each other when I was home from Princeton. We continued going steady, looking forward to our passionate encounters, coming to a screeching and breathless halt just before coupling.

I worked various jobs to make extra spending money, and that allowed me to join my robust college compadre and high school friend, Neal, on a trip around America one exciting July. He supplied the car and the jokes and I, gas money and lodging with various family members. One of the latter lived in Montana, at the homestead of my charming but deceased grandfather, Ira Jefferson Stone (after whom I was named) and my strict, red-haired grandmother, Loreen, also long gone. They had two sons, Albert and Barley. Albert fathered me. But Uncle Barley, the opposite side of the same coin, was to have an equally profound influence on my life—a double curse. Back then I remained completely ignorant of his strange effect. Barley had never married and lived alone in Helena.

*   *   *

"Ira, are you feeling okay? You seem quiet and distant, a bit irritable. What's up, Hoss?"

"I'm fine. Pay attention to the driving, Neal."

"You sure have been a hard-ass today."

And I was. The angst was building, overlaying my usual compulsive personality. Every detail on this trip had to be perfect—the mapping, receipts for gas and lodging, planning for the next day's travel. And I needed some anger management therapy. Neal's roguish attitude brought a breath of fresh air, but today my thin skin seemed to reject his devil-may-care congeniality.

My friend, impeccably shabby and blessed with short blond hair, an engaging all-weather smile, and a bumptious appetite for the opposite sex, powered his arthritic Chevy into the city of my birth. After traveling through the tumbling great plains and the yet unsettled Rocky Mountain foothills, we descended into Helena, the town I normally loved to visit. It had been a number of summers since I had set foot there.

"Okay, Hoss, where do I turn?"

"Go right on Flowerree Street, just up ahead."

My heart accelerated as we traveled along familiar haunts, passing red maples, tulip poplars, and giant Thuja evergreens. "There it is."

The Chevrolet gave a tubercular cough and stuttered to a halt as Neal shifted gears and pulled up in front of a small white clapboard house with its enclosed front porch, one of many in the unpretentious neighborhood. I noticed a row of blackbirds sitting on a telephone line, all mysteriously facing the same direction, looking straight at us. Barley's double-window blinds remained pulled down, like slumbering eyelids. We exited the auto and climbed those oh-so-familiar stairs, the ancient boards creaking underfoot.

"Uncle Barley?" My nervous knuckles rapped on the door. "Uncle Barley, are you there? It's Ira Stone."

"Maybe …" Neal fished a pipe from his jacket pocket. "Hey, Hoss, maybe we should just go on."

"Cool it, man. We came this far."

After a few long minutes, the door shook a bit and then opened a crack. Bleak eyes peeked out. "Ira Stone died years ago. Go away."

"Uncle Barley, it's me, your nephew. Let me in. I have a friend with me."

"Oh, *that* Ira."

A bow-taut stillness followed, ratcheting up as if my uncle were gauging the wisdom of letting us cross the threshold. The entryway slowly squeaked open. More than a little anxious, Neal and I walked in and surveyed Barley and the living room.

A sick feeling washed over me. Standing before us was a man I hardly recognized. Thin and gaunt, a threadbare and stained shirt hanging as if on a coat rack. He weaved slightly, cheeks sucked in, hollow and sunken eyes rimmed in raspberry red, not truly recognizing me. I knew he had once undergone stomach surgery for some sort of bleeding problem after leaving the merchant marines, so I thought that was the cause of Barley's condition. Of course, it wasn't.

Then he muttered, "Oh, yes, it's Ira." Silence followed. "Sure. Of course. Come on in," he added in a high-pitched and raspy voice. "Well, I reckon you *are* in."

He swayed half apace backward, perhaps confused, and I wondered if he had forgotten the letter I had sent. It felt as if I were speaking to a skull, one rounding toward me with an agitated, gun-stapling frown exactly like Grandmother Loreen's.

"Is it okay if Neal and I bunk here for a few days? We won't be in your way."

"Well, I s'pose. You'll have to find some blankets and get your own food. I don't have much here."

He simply stood there, perhaps in another world. I was just a college guy ignorant of serious medical and social issues. There was something incongruous, however—a fleet of Sheaffer fountain pens lined his over-bleached shirt pocket. One instrument appeared to be leaking, forming a blue waterfall in slow motion.

"Hey!" Uncle Barley's eyes rapidly blinked as my buddy fired up his Zippo. "You aren't going to smoke that thing, are you?"

"No, sir!" Neal snapped closed the lighter and then slipped it and the pipe back into his pocket.

We remained in Helena five days, during which time Barley made himself scarce. He was a loner, and I noticed a numerous empty cans of beer and an occasional Jim Beam bottle lying and rolling about. The faint odor of paint thinner and a taint of carrion—dead rats—assaulted our nostrils. Yet a row of clean, erudite book bindings lined a library shelf among a confusion of cobwebs, discards, and dust. My friend and I scoured the kitchen and cleaned up the place as best we could, picking up containers, the dead rats, and nearly dead cockroaches.

Our greater interest lay with two girls we dated, one of whom I had known since childhood. The four of us would end the evenings atop the foothills gazing over the wondrous lights of the city below. In animated conversations my lady friend and I recalled the days of yesteryear while Neal, a man who attracted girls like priests do gold, demonstrated great form in the backseat. I was irritated and jealous of him in the same moment.

Before leaving Helena, I gave Uncle Barley a hug. He was a sad and tearful skeleton backing away from my grasp, the familiar bouquet of alcohol escaping on his breath. And then he again stepped back and appeared to be looking inside his own head.

"Take heed, Ira," he muttered. "We fail to see it, but the wind is so very strong."

He tottered away to the kitchen. My dad's brother had seemed confused, unable to put two coherent thoughts together. But now I wondered.

I was mortified and embarrassed for Neal to see this. Even so, I sensed that Barley felt even more ashamed and humiliated than I. While driving from Helena, I vowed to never find myself in such a depressing condition. Never. But I had this eerie feeling, like footsteps that follow you home at night—the feeling that I had been looking at myself.

* * *

I entered Georgetown University Medical School in September 1955. I married Nadine at her Presbyterian Church in February of 1957. While avoiding intercourse, we had canvassed every inch of our mutual bodies, and on the evening of the sixteenth, the marriage was consummated in one divine encounter. I remember. She cried when it happened. We both were so happy, and I felt as if the milk and honey of life had found me at last.

Bone of my bones and flesh of my flesh, she was, but I ... I was wishing on the moon. Father's strictures and Uncle Barley's genes were hatching other plans, and I had not a clue.

When I embarked on the field of medicine, which I also had promised to love, honor, and obey, I did not understand the precarious path lying before me. The blending of brain surgery and a new family, like the joining together of potassium permanganate and hydrogen peroxide, threatened to ignite into an explosive state of affairs.

One evening during my internship at the University of Southern California, I slipped into bed, late as usual. I had assisted on an emergency cholecystectomy. Soft strains of "Spanish Eyes" drifted from my neighbor's turntable. Next to me lay scattered pieces of a disarticulated skull, which I had named after Shakespeare's famous jester. Its sphenoid wing appeared like a lunar moth, the calvarium now split asunder. My Golgotha. I remember a shudder coursing through my young body as I picked up this piece of Yorick's head and rotated the curious sphenoid held aloft by my hand. I wondered who its true owner once was. And I wanted a drink. In ancient Nordic fashion, I hefted the inverted skull-plate filled with imaginary ale. *"Skol!"* I shouted to no one in particular.

Though I was brought up in the Episcopal Church—I was even an acolyte—it was about that time God and I began to drift apart. I certainly did not need *Him*. I was just too busy with more important issues in my life.

My hand grabbed an empty bottle of Black Velvet decorating an end table. Gently fingering the brand name of the whiskey as if it were stamped the Shroud of Turin, I slowly and deliberately stripped away her label, leaving my lady buck naked, my body hungry for more of that cup of suffering and salvation. I *owned* that bottle. In truth, the bottle owned me.

The Victrola needle was stuck—*your Spanish eyes ... your Spanish eyes ... your Spanish eyes ...*

*   *   *

In San Francisco, Nadine eagerly awaited my plane from LA. I had been accepted into the residency program at the University of California at

San Francisco. Starting in July 1960, I immersed myself in the trials and tribulations of high-powered neurosurgical training, risking a torturous disembowelment of married life.

In August 1963, our first daughter, Denise Anne, was born at the UCSF Hospital. God, she was a darling, cooing and staring up at me with her mother's eyes, so trusting. So trusting, so blissfully unaware of a tangled and precarious future.

CHAPTER 6

God, grant me the serenity ...

Reinhold Niebuhr

Appleton

Rabbit and I sat together on an outdoor bench, lungs heaving after jogging together around our elliptical track.

"Any word from home?" I asked.

"My fuggin' counselor called my wife. She's coming for family week. And I think Maryanne also will go to Al-Anon in Toronto. I hope she can convince the boys to join Alateen."

"That's great, Rabbit. I hear family week can be rather intense. Monica won't come. I think she's scared, being an addict herself—prescriptions." I hesitated. "Betsy tells me the spouse and patient really get into it at their meetings. I'll wager Maryanne will give you hell."

"That's what some of the guys have said to me. It might help. I can give her my amends. And Ira?"

"Yeah?"

"Thanks for listening to me the other day."

"You bet! Ready for home group meeting?"

* * *

"Hello, my name is Fletcher, and I am an alcoholic and drug addict."

"Hi, Fletcher," eight voices replied.

"Everyone may call me Fletch." The chiseled face of our group leader was the bronze color of a man often exposed to the weather, one in constant conflict with the elements. His eyes were clear, deep, and maple-sugar brown, arms corded like weathered wood. While rubbing his left earlobe, he announced with a solid resonance, "For those of you who are new…" He nodded in my direction. "This is your home group. After a moment of silence let's begin with the Serenity Prayer."

Everyone bowed their heads, so I did likewise.

"God, grant me the serenity
to accept the things I cannot change,
the courage to change the things I can,
and the wisdom to know the difference."

"Now each of us states how long we have been sober. For me is has been fourteen years. Start with Ira on my left."

"Uh …" I struggled to think back to the day I came into Appleton, my still-chained mind refusing to cooperate. "Ten … ten days." It could have been ten seconds or ten years.

And so it went around our circle of facing chairs, each of us giving only our first name followed by, "and I am an alcoholic," or "I am a drug addict," or "I am an alcoholic and drug addict." And an occasional "and I am a sex addict" thrown in. My anxiety level slowly faded as I realized I was not alone in my struggle. My egoistic *it's all about me* was taking a rear seat to a wider view of life, but the ever-present beast was still a back-seat driver. This resentful part of me rebelled, still determined to return to my counterfeit lover, that amber sea in a crystal glass.

God, grant me the serenity …? I did not really believe in God. Hadn't since … since before Nadine and I separated. I studied my fingernails. *Oh well, I'll just mouth the words and …*

"Ira? Are you with us"? A lock of coal-black hair tumbled into Fletcher's eyes as he cocked his head toward me again. "I was asking if you would tell the rest of us where you live."

"Yessir." My face twitched. "North Carolina. In Chapel Hill."

"Thanks, Ira. Gentlemen, we are here to separate ourselves and our warts from the scourge of mankind—drugs, legal and illegal. We are sending millions of dollars to overseas drug lords in exchange for this pestilence that enslaves the opiate centers in our brains. A chemical warfare has been unleashed, and many—especially our youth—are falling to its attack. It is up to all of us to return to society and help plug the hole in the dyke. But first each of you must fall on your own sword before healing begins ..."

My mind wandered, Fletcher's voice somewhere "out there." My nervous eyeballs gazed around the table, noticing the facial expressions of my fellow inmates stretching into strange and contradictory caricatures, my kamikaze psyche still playing tricks on me in my postwithdrawal state.

"So, until now, you have solved your problems with self-medication— if two drinks helped a little, then twenty-two would help a lot. But that was like our attempting to repair a loose electrical connection by pushing more voltage through it. Here you will find a better way."

"Bullshit," came from someone who looked like a Redskin tackle.

Ignoring Lester's comment, Fletcher continued. "And now your assignments. For the newer guys, you will be working on Step One. There are two additional projects prior to this task, and these will provide a better understanding about drugs and the drug culture. Sebastian, remind the rest of the group what Step One tells us."

I clapped my eyes on the older man taking center stage. He began flicking the nail of his middle finger back and forth against the thumbnail. A mess of thick sable hair shot with gray covered his head. A whipcord secured his ponytail behind. He was a savagely handsome, rough-appearing sort, ridges blanketing a gnarly and tanned face, half-glasses perched on the slightly-hooked arc of a Roman nose. He raised his eyebrows and rolled muscled shoulders, stretching a Harley-Davidson T-shirt.

"Hi, my name is Sebastian, and I am a drug addict."

"Hi, Sebastian," came the answering chorus.

"The First Step states, '*We admitted we were powerless over alcohol— that our lives had become unmanageable.*'" His voice rumbled as if lightning should precede it. Obsidian-black eyes delivered me a hard and imperious stare.

"Thank you, Sebastian. All of you know that whiskey and gin make bad ideas seem okay, but once the idea takes root, it spreads, taking over, blossoming as we water it with our favorite spirit. And then our life of addiction becomes truly unmanageable.

"Ira?" Fletch turned toward me. "Sebastian will show you where the worksheets are. I know you need a few more days to get rid of those sea legs. When you are up to tackling the assignment, come and see me.

"The rest of you roosters, stop feeling so fucking sorry for yourselves. Since you all appear quite bored today, you will be pleased to know that tonight is *feedback* time."

A chorus of groans, moans, and mutters arose from the gathering. "I think I will be too sick," growled a bowlegged cowboy known as Derrick. "I feel this damn stomach virus coming on."

Paying no heed to the complaints, Fletcher continued. "Okay, when talking in our recovery groups we use '*I*' and '*we*', not the '*you*' word. We only speak about ourselves, not our neighbors—feedback sessions excepted, of course. We neither give advice nor hand a weeping buddy a Kleenex box. No finger pointing and no cross-talk. And what you hear here, stays here!"

"Hear, hear!" came the loud refrain of male voices.

"Any questions? No? Okay, head to your assignments."

We all stood up, and the group formed a circle. *What's going on?* I wondered. Then everyone joined hands and bowed their heads. I felt a strange comfort as communal warmth seeped into my palms. "Our Father, who art in Heaven …" Somehow the Lord's Prayer felt a bit more meaningful now. I did not understand why.

"Hey, Kemo Sabe." I was about to leave when someone tapped my arm. "I'm your buddy. Would this be a good opportunity to show you around?" A big grin stretched Sebastian's ruddy cheeks. "With that hangdog face, you look like you could use a little help. Don't mind Fletch. He's a bit rough around the edges and tends to sermonize at times, but we all like him."

I had just come down off detox. Ponytail, for all his bravado, was to become one of my closest friends. Necessity makes strange bedfellows, but never in all my born days would I have thought that a tattooed biker and I had more in common than not. Indeed, this was the first of many ingrained ideas that began to shake loose ... shake loose with a vengeance.

We were taught that *anonymous* here meant no one in your groups knew your family name or any circumstance one did not wish to reveal. Anything said in those rooms would never be repeated outside. The source of any donations would be nameless. And we often would not know if the man sitting next to us was a wealthy banker or an unemployed truck driver. We were all equal sons-of-bitches.

In those meetings and home group gatherings I sensed a kinship I had never felt before. Admitting to dark deeds not even your wife, or wives in my case, would know was immensely painful. Yet not only was the telling cathartic but we felt safe in these chambers, safe and secure since we knew that our chronicles never found their way beyond these walls. We had the mutual affection of old campaigners whose trench injuries could never be shared with anyone outside.

After my release from intensive care I was put in a room with one other mate—my biker buddy. One day, while resting on my bed after jogging a mile around a gravel track, Nadine's image returned. I closed my eyes. How on earth could I have left her and my two girls, my children whom I loved so much? Nadine's lovely face was replaced by my father's unkind scowl.

CHAPTER 7

For aught that I could read,
could ever hear by tale or history,
the course of true love never did run smooth.

William Shakespeare
A Midsummer Night's Dream

Napa, California

Our father, Albert Stone, not only helped his brother Barley, he provided my siblings and me with a much-appreciated education, medical school in my case. My lot was to be a surgeon. Early on I did not trust in spirituality, only hard scientific facts. At the time, I never considered a spirit to be anything other than a ... you know, a ghost, something in our imagination. But there were spirits—and there were spirits, as I was soon to discover.

Many viewed the life of a surgeon as one of entitlement—wealth, hard work, excitement, and glamour. And as a medical student that was exactly what I thought. The hard work was not new to me. Excitement and glamour? Those evaporated after the first day of residency. Lots of cash was a state of existence devoutly aspired to, for one needed money to keep friends, I had been told. And I was a believer. After all, I had become a wannabe brain surgeon, near the top of my class. Nothing, but nothing, could drag me under.

Yet the waters below were dark and silent, and sailing forth I failed to recognize the dorsal fin of a shark, a rapacious predator by the name of Slick, a conquistador dwelling in my brain and separating me from the word of God. A most evil cutthroat I would have to bury alive.

* * *

Albert Edward Stone, raised in Helena, Montana, under the umbrella of Victorian authority, was our father. He'd always wanted me to be the doctor he had never become. By the time I traversed halfway through my residency, neurosurgery was my universe. Nothing else existed. Yet something deep and dark was gnawing at me. I carried it with me, more or less unconsciously, like a disembodied spirit.

On one of those few summer weekends on which I could escape from the hospital, my wife and I paid a visit to my family. Mom, I wanted to see. Dad? Not really. It would be the usual high-wire tension. And Nadine was not helping the situation.

"Well, Ira, what do you think President Kennedy's going to do about the Cuba problem?" Albert waved the venerable *San Francisco Chronicle* at a honey bee. With consummate skill, the mischievous insect dodged the weapon and landed on Dad's perspiring water glass.

"Castro will—"

I stopped in midsentence. Michael, at one-hundred-seventy-five pounds, his dark-brown mane flying back, leaped into the air, grasped his knees, and cannon-balled into the pool at the Green Valley Country Club, its fourteenth fairway bordering our backyard.

"Michael!" bellowed Dad. "See what you just did to my newspaper? How about a little consideration, m' boy." His attention distracted, Albert reached for the tumbler, melting ice bobbing about with a slice of lemon.

Mike, still under water, swam to the end of the pool and popped his head up, a look of innocence on his face. "Hey, Pa, come on in. Let's see if you can still tote me on your shoulders ... or allow me to carry the burden of Your Worship. We can battle with Ira and Nadine. The old beach ball technique."

"See this newspaper? I ought to paddle your behind with it." Father stifled a grin, though I could see his jaw working. No one could get mad at Mike and stay that way very long.

Albert, wearing his tricolored swimming trunks—Sophie, my mother, had judged her husband dashing in that swim wear—jumped in feet first. Small splotches of pigmentation covered his snow-white skin. Arthritis in his thumbs gave the man considerable pain. His fifty-four-year-old belly cried out for exercise. He was not overweight, just a bit bald and unconditioned—a prime target for a heart attack, I had once warned. But the West Coast manager for Eli Lilly & Company was more in the habit of dictating opinion, not receiving it.

"Okay, Michael, where be our challengers, pray tell?" Dad riveted stern eyeballs on Nadine and me, sitting in lounge chairs, our hands locked together. Nadine balanced a hanging sandal on her toe.

"Are you up for it, dear?" I turned to my wife. "Let's hop in. You climb up on my shoulders."

My bride stared straight ahead, fuming, distancing herself from the family festivities. She quite nicely filled out her two-piece bathing suit—38C on top. Green and orange cotton adorned smooth, tanned skin. Her blonde hair, normally in flowing waves over her shoulders, was wet after an underwater swim (she claimed swimming caps were passé). Normally outgoing and fun-loving, more recently she seemed reticent. Even depressed.

"And then what, _my liege?_" Nadine jerked her hand away from mine, suddenly unleashed emotions gathering momentum.

"Be a sport. See if you can unseat Mike from Dad's shoulders. We try to knock each other over with beach balls." I stood up, anxious to enter the jousting, maybe even show Father up, though Mike would more than make up for any paternal deficiencies in the paired-man contest.

Nadine's knuckles turned white as she gripped the armrests. Her sun shades hid the tell-tale signs of irritation, yet frown lines were setting up camp at the corners of her mouth.

"Sometimes you can be a real bitch!" I quietly hissed to my wife.

Albert harrumphed and then piped, "We'll organize a new game here. Nadine, you might go home and assist Mother with our dinner." A command, not a request.

Nadine, her cheeks burning shades of scarlet, refused to budge. Muscles flickered under the skin of her clenched jaw. She lay back and squeezed her lids shut, fingers now in a steel grip on aluminum.

"Dad ..." Feeling nailed between a rock and a hard spot, anal sphincter quivering into spasm, I didn't know which way to turn. "Uh, Dad ... Nadine is tired. I'll run over and check on Mom."

"You'll do no such thing! Ira ...? *Ira,* come back here! You better *listen* to me, son, or you will never amount to anything! Ira!"

"Okay, okay!" I yelled way too loudly as I spun away, but not before I saw Nadine's third finger surreptitiously raised and aimed right at me.

The burning in the pit of my stomach accelerated. I was unable to ferret out whether Rolaids or Jack Daniels would guarantee the fastest relief. I chose Jack. A double. Nadine was driving me crazy. Didn't she understand where I was coming from? I hadn't seen my parents for two months. The stress and hours at the university hospital were part of a resident's life. She *knew* that. *Shit!* I'd certainly explained it all before we tied the knot—as I, ill-advisedly perhaps, had reminded her again.

*   *   *

"Damn you!" she had cursed last week in the kitchen. "What about *me?*" Nadine railed on, lurching up and grabbing me by the arm. *"Don't I count for anything?* You are controlling and selfish *beyond reason!* Only your job and your ... your *fucking* ambition mean anything to you. Our first weekend alone together in weeks, and we have to spend it with your *parents! Damn!"*

"But, Nadine, I told you what it would be like married to a neuro resident. And you said no problem. Just come home to me," I replied, my own blood beginning to curdle. "And stop getting your panties in a twist. Get a goddamn grip!"

"Well, *Lord Stone,* this ... this is *no* life!" she cried, her breath hitching. "You deign to come to your castle at midnight or the next day. Are you sure there's no cute nurse hanging around you?"

Then Nadine stomped off to the fridge while I, unable to cope with death at the hospital and marital strain at home, collapsed on the apartment sofa, nursing my bruised feelings with extra doses of self-prescribed therapy.

Rx

Jack Daniels Tennessee Whiskey   80 proof

Disp: 750 ml
Sig: 10 ml prn for agitation
Refill: prn

*   *   *

Leaving the pool for home, I trotted into Mother's kitchen, stiffening ambivalence bouncing from one side of my brain to the other, the percussions becoming the distant drumbeats of a migraine.

Mom wiped her hands on an apron and brushed a stray gray lock from her cheek. The Swedish blue of Sophie's kind eyes blinked at me. Mom, her own self living in the smoky shadows of Dad's anger and doubt, drew light and warmth into any room even so. Her gentle face always possessed a delightful quickness and life.

"Are you all right, dear?" she asked, soothing my caustic muse. "Is there a problem at the pool? Anything I can do?"

I ignored her query, my jaw hardening with an inherited taciturn stoicism, and pulled down a tall glass from the cupboard. Then I reached for the decanter of JD.

"Mom, where is the bourbon? It's not here in the cupboard."

"Father finished it yesterday. We haven't been to the liquor store yet. Can't you do without a drink tonight?"

Damn! Without answering I trotted out to my car, opened the trunk, and retrieved a half-spent container of Jack Daniels. Jittery hands unscrewed the cap and fired the bottle toward my lips. I swilled a good two ounces. The fifth in hand, I returned to the kitchen. Within minutes ice clinked in contralto. I swirled more of that whiskey, and then set myself down on a kitchen stool. The blessed JD electrified my insides. I needed it to wash away this wretched day.

"You work so hard, dear. Do you truly like doing surgery?" Mom asked, giving me a look of disapproval.

"It's in my blood, Ma. What can I say?"

"Try and find more time for your family, Ira. Work is not the be-all and end-all. It nearly destroyed your father."

"How do you do it, Mother?" My vocal chords stiffened, and I gulped down another slug, my free hand opening and closing convulsively. "Put up with Father's incessant tirades, I mean. My God, he still treats me like a small child."

"Ira, dear. He simply can't help it. Please try to understand. And … do you have to drink that awful poison?"

She bent down and removed freshly baked bread from the oven. A wonderful aroma filled the room, the image with me even now when I smell dough rising. I peeled away into my bedroom, closed the door, and stepped out of my swimming trunks into an uncertain future.

CHAPTER 8

Now I lay me down to sleep,
I pray the Lord my soul to keep...

Eighteenth-century prayer

Appleton

Often a corporation or university would send an employee for a tune-up, as it were, though frequently that stretched into treatment for prevention of a relapse. Larry was just such an individual. He was a recovering alcoholic and ... a pilot. We are never *recovered* or *cured*, I was told. I was soon to discover that we are forever addicts who must stay far away from mind-altering drugs, recovery being a life-long process of keeping Slick in hibernation.

Fletcher, our home-group leader, escorted a handsome, smartly dressed black male into the room. "Gentlemen, this is Larry. He has been sent here by his employer. I'll let him explain."

After reciting the Serenity Prayer, we all introduced ourselves. Finally, "Hi, my name is Larry, and I am an alcoholic."

"Hi, Larry," we all answered in unison.

His hair was short, eyes level, cheek bones prominent, Jamaican accent engaging. Larry spoke quietly, but one could feel his tension and anger at finding himself at Appleton.

"I am not sure why I am here, but my copilot ... I work for Continental ... reported that I was a bit under the weather. But, hell, I have been sober for ten years."

"Your supervisors worried that you might have had a relapse," noted Fletcher, rubbing an earlobe between thumb and forefinger.

"Like hell."

"What happened?"

"We were laying over in Houston, and I went to bed at our hotel. I had a bad case of the sniffles, so I took some NyQuil. I kept coughing and swallowed more of the medicine." His face worked briefly. "Finally I tossed another gulp or two down and went to dreamland. After four hours I got up and made ready to head for the airport, but first I stopped in the Marriott gift shop for a newspaper. My copilot was there and saw me, as he describes it, walking a bit unsteadily. So here I am. I had not drunk any booze."

"You guys have any ideas?"

"In fact, NyQuil has about ten percent alcohol and dextromethorphan, a synthetic narcotic," responded Bounthane, my neighbor, who had introduced himself as an alcoholic and Listerine addict, fidgeting with his hands. "If you took a lot, that could have had an unfortunate effect."

"And a small bit of alcohol in your system might send you into a relapse, even with foods cooked in alcohol, driving the brain to demand more drink," said Fletch. "If you did not follow up with any of the 'miniatures' in your hotel room, then a true relapse is unlikely. But we can all see the dangers here. Larry will be discussing this with his counselor."

The pilot rolled his eyeballs, teeth grinding.

"Okay, Alamo, how did your day go?" queried Fletcher.

We all enjoyed Larry and his subsequent discussions. His planned three-day stay turned into three weeks—perhaps a much needed tune-up before returning to work. He had not been attending AA on a regular basis, and as it turned out, the airline pilot had, indeed, treated himself to a few miniatures that same evening. In the end, even Larry was glad he had stayed. He had relapsed, but fortunately the copilot had his back.

The next day

I sighed as I read a pink slip notifying me to head for Betsy's office. Upon entering I noticed something new in the room, a red beanbag on the floor below the window. She waved me to my now-familiar chair and then reviewed her notes and glanced up. "Ira, many people use alcohol to relieve stress and even hide their problems. However, like bulls tempted by a matador, once hooked we alcoholics and drug addicts cannot stop. We do not see the sword behind the red cape. Recovery is about not just getting the poison out of our system but also learning how to find a better way to deal with hurtful issues in our lives, so that we do not use or drink.

"You don't seem to talk much about your brother, Michael." She set her clipboard down. "Fill me in."

"I'd rather not." My fingernails dug into my palms.

"You need to address this issue sometime. It might as well be now."

I stood up. I wanted to take the bronze pen holder on the desk and slam it against her mouth. It took all of my fortitude to restrain my irrational self.

"Tell me how you feel, Ira."

"Angry. Scared."

"Please sit down and relax." She followed my eyes, which were focused on the object. "No one is here to judge you. Give it a try."

I heard her voice, but my attention turned to a goldfish swimming in a miniature aquarium by Betsy's open window. Partially drawn filmy curtains billowed inward with an occasional breeze. I heard myself begin to speak slowly, feeling as if I were eavesdropping on a recalcitrant past—a past I wished to forget.

Ontario-Minnesota Boundary Waters, 1962

Michael, with his grace and strapping build, could have been mistaken for a movie star. But lately the young man seemed pale, as though the flu recently had laid him low. He reached into a bucket and chucked me a fresh Canadian minnow. It slipped out of my hand and landed on the canoe floorboard. The tiny silver and black fish squirmed on its side. Just then a great northern rose up out of the waters of Lake Namakan, flipped its tail, and splashed back into the deep. I sighed, enjoying the pristine fragrance of pine and birch.

"Ira, I've decided to change my major at Ohio State. Premed is not for me. Geology, that's what I really enjoy. Remember how Mom and Dad showed us all about the layers of the earth and rocks in the Missouri River cliffs? I'm starting my junior year this September, though the change requires that I add on special courses in a fifth year. What do you think?"

"Well ..." I paused and ran my fishhook first through the mouth of the wiggling minnow and then out a side gill. "I'd say it's great that you found your calling. Did you tell Dad?"

"Yeah. I received the standard lecture. When that didn't sway me, he tried putting me on a guilt trip. That sailed wide of the mark." Mike closed his fishing box and then stopped and listened to a moose bugling in the distance.

"So?"

"So, a funny thing happened. It just came out ... sort of. I said, 'Dad, I love you. And I want to be a geologist.' Well ... he became very quiet and walked away. I think he was almost crying. The next day Mom came up to me, gave me a hug, and whispered, 'So now we have a geologist in the family. Mike, how wonderful.'"

Something unkind took hold of me.

"And our sister? Does she know?"

"Not yet. I'll tell Jocelyn when she returns from her travels."

The sun rolled higher in the eastern sky, giving way to fat storm clouds announcing themselves in the northwest horizon. The wind picked up, rotating the canoe southeast. The boat strained at its taut anchor rope.

I reeled in my line. A burst of wind whipped around my face as I corked the fishhook. "Cripes, if I tried that, he'd have me for lunch."

"Maybe he's just isolated. He so wants to advance at Eli Lilly but seems stuck." Mike reeled in his line and tilted the rod to inspect his minnow.

"Maybe. Still, he won't let people get close to him. Least of all his family ... 'cept maybe you and sometimes Jocie."

I eyed my fishing rod. The one Dad had bought for me. The one that became the center of Father's bruising lecture on how to fish. How to cast. How to treat the Canadian Customs officials. How to wear the life vest. And then, driven by anger that boiled over, I grabbed the pole.

Michael gripped the gunnels of the boat, trying to keep it from spinning into the water as I stood halfway up. *"Ira, what are you doing? That rod cost Dad over fifty bucks!"*

Fifty bucks … fifty fucking pounds of my flesh! I launched the fishing pole as if it were a lance. The weapon struck froth near a submerged boulder.

"Ira, for crissake …!"

"Sorry, Mike. I'm running on a short fuse. Let's head back to camp." *And get a bottle of CC at the Trading Post.* Canadian Club had replaced Jack Daniels as my favorite whiskey.

"Sure, big brother. The weather looks a bit threatening anyway." As he spoke, a gust of capricious wind raked over the boat. Mike's baseball cap flew into the lake and sank under a white cap.

"Dang! Oh well." Michael scratched his ear. "Ira?"

"Yeah?"

"I love you too."

"Uh, thanks, Mike." Something felt twisted inside, alien and formless. I shuddered, dwelling on why I had such difficulty saying, "I love you too"? My little brother, ten years younger than I yet wise beyond his age, shook his head, stowed the tackle, and hauled up the anchor, while my festering mind turned back to simmering frustrations at the hospital.

CHAPTER 9

There is a tide in the affairs of men,
which, taken at the flood, leads on to fortune;
omitted, all the voyage of their life
is bound in shallows and miseries.

William Shakespeare
Julius Caesar

Appleton

I was to continue my history with the counselor the next day. I'd already had my exercise session, spiritual time-out, breakfast, and meds when I approached the main building. Outside sat two smoking urns—skinny, tall receptacles with wide bottoms, appearing for all the world like an Arabic hookah. Three colleagues were gathered around them, swirls of smoke rising, drifting.

"Hi, Sebastian. What's up?" I coasted over to his side.

"Hey, Kemo Sabe. Did you hear the news? Larry, that airline pilot, is back. He apparently relapsed again. Airport security caught him with alcohol on his breath. He was on the way to board his plane in LA." Sebastian picked a shred of tobacco from his tongue.

"So Fletcher told me. They assigned him to our home group again."

My roommate closed his eyes, inhaled deeply, and then fired smoke out nostrils and a pursed harelip. "Balls, man. There are days I think this stuff is better than my alcohol and hydrocodone put together."

"But not PCP," offered another kid on the block, a skinhead the size of a tanker, his cheroot between his teeth. Lester tucked in his shirttail. "That's why they calls it angel dust."

"How'd you get all them cuts?" Sebastian pointed to a myriad of healing pink linear scars on Lester's arms and neck, the lesions interweaving with an assortment of tattoos.

"What's it to you?" Lester grabbed Sebastian's shirt, pulling a few hairs on his chest.

"Hey! Remove your hand, brother. I'm just making small talk. Cool it."

"Fuck you, asshole!"

"Come on, dickhead. Simmer down."

"Dickhead?" Lester gave Sebastian a shove. *"Dickhead?"*

"By God, I … I'll … Crap. Sorry, man, sorry. I didn't mean nothin'."

"Okay, okay. I'm still going through some stuff." Lester took a drag on his cigar. "Got cut up in a fight couple weeks ago. Should'a seen ta other guy."

I watched him spin away, hunch his massive shoulders, and then turn back to Sebastian. "You going to that spirituality session?"

"Sure. We got two hours yet." My roommate rubbed his chest.

"By the way, Sebastian, what is that icon on the wall by your bedside?" I asked.

"Saint Bibiana, a patron saint against hangovers. So far, it's worked since I have been here."

I smiled and then trotted back toward the entrance. I scooted by the nurses' desk. A large poster caught my eye. It portrayed a burning, half-smoked cigarette overlaid with its dangers and perils: causing more death and wallet damage than drugs, alcohol, car accidents, homicide, suicide, and AIDS combined. Strangely, it appeared that the treatment center still allowed this mind-altering drug on its grounds.

I checked my watch. Time to meet with my counselor. While stirring cream into a cup of coffee, I entered her sanctuary, took in a ragged breath, and continued my story. A part of me resisted the plunge at all costs.

University of California at San Francisco, Spring 1963

At six-thirty a.m., accompanied by a flock of medical students, an intern, and two junior residents in neurosurgery at UCSF, I halted by a nursing station. The fledgling doctors-to-be were dressed out in short white coats, the residents in long whites over green surgical scrubs. One of the students, Alicia Chalmers, had been pulling the cart with a stack of patients' charts. Each metal-covered file, the edges bent and scraped, stood in a numbered slot corresponding with the room assignment.

"Dr. Stone, I have a question." The student, her stern face devoid of both makeup and warmth, kept fidgeting with the oversized eyeglasses on her nose, rapping one of the rims with a pen. She patted a racked chart.

"Yes, Chalmers?" I sighed, eyeing the woman who had been monopolizing the session on rounds with a series of never-ending questions.

I was already in ill humor after a night with no sleep. My dauntless efforts to save a small battered child with a fractured neck had failed, and the parents were shifting the blame to me. At midnight my marital helpmate had beeped me, her increasingly shrill tongue complaining about our old refrigerator not functioning, ending with, "So what are you going to do about this damn Whirlpool, *Dr. Stone!*"

The student, in an abrasive voice not unlike Nadine's, interrupted with considerable acidity. "It's about that broken neck. I myself have a two-year-old at home. Exactly how do you surmise that Christy's death was a result of physical abuse? Why couldn't she … uh … have fallen down the stairs like her … um … mother claimed?"

I pulled up short. I was in no mood for justifying my opinion to anyone, let alone a student still wet behind the ears. And the OR was paging me.

"Did you examine Christy last evening before the surgery?" I pointed my jaw at the fractious creature. "Or check her films?"

"I was studying for exams. *Sir!*" She pushed the weighty, severe-diopter spectacles up on her nose.

I'll bet. What an ass! "Bruises on her arms and legs. Old healed fractures of the long bones. Recent rib fractures. Multiple visits to area emergency rooms, a different one each time. A father with an ongoing drug history. You puzzle it out."

"*Sir!*" The tenacious black-haired creature, always boot-licking my superiors, refused to let go, her arms defiantly folded across a starched chest. "Why didn't the social workers ..."

"Sorry, guys and gals. We have to move. Dr. Kramer will assign ward duties to three students. Two of you come with me to the operating room. I hope you have reviewed the anatomy of the sylvian fissure. You're going to learn a little about a vicious brain tumor, a glioblastoma, and its excision from the temporal lobe. The OR nurses will be training you in scrub technique, and ..."

"Dr. Stone! I know you are a senior resident and all that, but I *object* to your patronizing me just because I am a woman. I asked a proper question, and I expect a proper answer."

A bitch unwilling to let go of her bone.

Chalmers, vigorous sable hair flanking her face and flying about her shoulders with aberrant bursts of energy, stood in a defiant pose with a high-decibel presence in front of the other short coats. The remaining med students all looked at each other and shrugged as if to say, *How the hell did we get stuck with her?* Because her father was California's Senator Wylie Chalmers.

With more important things plaguing my mind, I abruptly spun away toward the elevator, leaving a scarlet woman and scorched air behind.

*   *   *

The attending surgeon, Dr. Tremont Singleton, and I settled down into leather chairs in the surgeons' lounge, its cherry-wood walls buffed and waxed to a military shine. We were still garbed in green uniforms (the hospital had discarded the whites we had worn so long in the operating room), a few red decorations staining our scrubs. Mozart played in the background, adding to the smell of burnt coffee and male tension. Singleton passed a cup of java to me and then briefly shoved forefingers up under his eyeglasses, as if to rub fatigue away.

"Thank you, sir. Long case today." I sighed.

"Just so. Some tumors are like that. This one was rife with arteriovenous shunts."

"Looks like you got most of the lesion out. I thought the blood loss was going to be a real threat. Do you feel she will regain her speech?"

"If we are lucky. The most malignant of brain cancers, this tumor bed will need radiation therapy." Singleton laced his fingers behind his head. "By the way, Dr. Stone, the other neurosurgeons are quite impressed with your surgical skills. And judgment. After today I must agree with them. You were right on target with your diagnosis of disseminated intravascular coagulopathy. The DIC responded nicely to the platelet and fresh-frozen plasma infusions and stopped most of the bleeding."

He paused. "Ira, what are your plans for the future? After completing residency, I mean. You'll be finished next year."

The chairman pulled a mask from his neck and tossed it into the wastebasket. After consulting with the Patek Phillipe, he rubbed thinning white hair and focused on this third-year resident.

"I'd prefer to stay in academics. Get involved with research … here, if possible. I have a few ideas." My blue eyes held those of my chief. "I understand a position at our VA hospital may be opening up."

"Dr. Stone, please call the operator," shot from an overhead page.

Damn. What now?

"I'm heading over to my office, Ira. I'll leave you to write the orders on our patient. Let's keep her on the ventilator for a few days. I have a feeling that swelling will be a problem." Singleton stuck a fountain pen back in his shirt pocket and departed for the doctors' changing room.

I snatched up the telephone and dialed zero. "Dr. Stone here."

"Please hold for an outside call. A Mr. Michael Stone. Will you take it?"

Michael? "Sure will."

My brother came on the line. "Hi … Hope I'm not interrupting anything serious."

"For you, nothing is too important, Mike. What's up?"

"I checked at your apartment first, but Nadine suggested I page you. She … uh … seemed somewhat under the weather."

"Yeah, I know. A bit of a cold. How are things at college?"

"Okay, I guess." Michael paused. "Well, I need to ask your advice as a doctor."

"Shoot." I now had half my mind on Michael and half on Nadine.

"I have this lump, you see. And …"

"Hold on, Mike. My beeper is going off." My eyes shot down to the pager. "The ER. May I call you back?"

"Sure, I … I'll be at my dorm. You have the number." The line went dead.

I felt uncomfortable. Another *beep, beep*. The recovery room needed me stat. Suddenly, the quarrelsome medical student popped into the lounge.

"Dr. Stone, I've been going through Christy's chart. May I bring a few issues to your attention before you sign the death certificate? Do you really believe that some of your notes are appropriate? For example …"

That fucking woman again. A small brushfire grew in the pit of my very angry stomach.

*   *   *

The *ding-ding* of my radio alarm interrupted my fitful slumber. I awoke with a start and glanced at the bright aquamarine number rolling over to five-o-one. I sat up and dangled my legs over the edge of the mattress, the chenille slipping toward the floor. Nadine, breathing heavily, murmured something unintelligible and rolled over, dragging the coverlet back up.

Mike … damn! I never got back to him. It was too early to call his dorm.

I let my impatient eyes wander over Nadine's body, wondering if I should wake her before I left for rounds and surgery. I could still catch a whiff of her Diorissimo. A gentle urge played with me. *No, let her sleep.* I had made it home by eleven last night, and she was already in dream world. I had found an empty bottle of Signorello by the sink, another Chardonnay contributing to her weight gain.

I felt tension building in my naked loins, a visible erection. It had been two moons, my nocturnal comforts still denied. That long-ago evening seized my memory as I angled toward the bathroom, closed the door, and began shaving. *Shit!* I'd wanted to come in from behind. Or at least do something different. "No, Ira. That's crude. Anyway, my vagina is sore. Roll on your back, dear, and I'll help you to come ... with my fingers, sweetie. I have a towel for you." I nearly broke the electric razor as my fist tightened. A part—a very small part—of my brain had begun to rebel, feeling painfully shackled to the first "love, honor, and obey."

In the bathroom my angry digits spun on the hot water spigot.

"Jesus Christ!" I jumped back as the water suddenly burst through with a loud wet explosion, followed by spitting and hissing air. *My dear wife forgot to clear the fucking pipes after the plumber finished. Bitch.* I recovered and leaned over to wash my face as my heart resumed a normal beat. *What the hell is the matter with me?*

My beeper interrupted the wayward rumination. It was the intensive care unit.

"Dr. Stone, your tumor patient has just blown a pupil! Mr. Crane is decerebrating, and the blood pressure is rising ... a systolic of one-eighty," exclaimed an out-of-breath nurse.

"*Oh, God!* Start a bottle of hypertonic urea IV stat. Ask the on-call anesthesiologist to increase hyperventilation. And alert X-ray that we'll need an emergency cerebral angiogram. I'm on my way."

I pulled on the scrubs I wore last night, paused and blew a conciliatory kiss toward Nadine, and then dashed out the front door under the first eastern smear of a restless dawn, my dissolving anger replaced by a rising drumbeat of fear.

CHAPTER 10

I wish you well and so I take my leave.
I pray you know me when we meet again.

William Shakespeare
The Merchant of Venice

University Hospital

"Oh, thank God you're here, Dr. Stone!" Nurse Barbara Fielding greeted me, lines of extreme tension masking her normally pleasant face. "The patient's pressure just dropped to sixty."

I ran to Bradley Crane's bedside and surveyed the monitors. The electrocardiograph and pulse waves were accelerating. The BP, once too high, now continued a near-lethal descent, approaching fifty.

"Did you notify the angio lab?" I squeezed Crane's Achilles' tendons. No response.

"Yes, sir. They are ready. And the IV urea is in. Dr. Singleton called. He is stuck behind an accident on Golden Gate Bridge."

"Damn!"

"Sir?"

"Sorry. And the wife?"

"In the waiting room. She ... she knows Brad is in trouble."

"Okay, let's ..."

An alarm on the cardiac monitor peeled an emergency warning—*S-T segment biphasic, now inverting.*

"Barbara, call the resuscitation team … *stat!* We're losing him." I turned to another ICU nurse. "We need your help, Darlene. Start a Neosynephrin drip ASAP."

The hospital loudspeaker echoed a code-blue alert as the pinging EKG signal launched into an erratic pattern. The footsteps of three on-duty physicians from medicine, surgery, and anesthesiology clattered up the hall and through the doorway.

A respiratory technician announced that Bradley's pulse had just crossed over from thready to absent. The internist initiated closed chest massage as everyone struggled to snatch Bradley out of darkness, back into life.

"*Flatline!*" someone cried out. The oscillating ball on the monitor screen had suddenly spun down into the horizontal, death's signature, the grim reaper dropping the curtain. I grabbed a syringe of adrenalin off the crash cart, fixed it to a long needle, and plunged the point between ribs, deep into the heart. After long seconds of cardiac standstill, the dormant signal jumped into a rapid flutter, followed by the dreaded, coarse ventricular fibrillation.

The anesthesiologist sprung into action, snatching two paddles from the DC cardioversion unit and thrusting the electrodes against patient's bare chest.

"Clear!"

All personnel backed away. On command the technician struck the switch. Bradley convulsed, jarring the entire bed.

"Clear!"

Another incarnate-seeking shock was administered. But the lifeline tumbled flat as vital energy leaked away from Brad's heart. The scene replayed, yet beeps remained converted to a soft shrill, the Reaper determined. *Beep, beeep, beeee …*

My throat constricting, I held tight to Bradley's limp hand. I gazed at the head bandage I had wrapped less than twelve hours ago. Was there something else I could have done? Maybe I should have stayed in the hospital overnight and been closer to the patient. Perhaps I missed early signs of an impending cerebral hemorrhage. Maybe …

The veil between heaven and earth thinned, leaving only the pronouncement of death, dutifully recorded. The code-blue team departed in a gut-wrenching silence, and I no longer looked upon Bradley Crane as "the glioblastoma." He was a human being whose wife stood in the hall, weeping, her knuckle-white hands clutching a patent-leather purse.

I crossed over to her. "Bradley is dead, Mrs. Crane."

I gently held the woman as tears welled up in the far corners of her eyes and washed down her cheeks. I led Marcia Crane back to the waiting room, promising to return shortly and explain what had happened. If I could. Dear God, if I could.

While I jotted down notes in the chart labeled "Crane," Nurse Barbara, large brown eyes glistening with moisture, covered the patient and removed the life lines and ports, every defeat chipping away at her own cloak of emotional armor. The noises and distractions of the code-blue process had abated, leaving only the steady and repetitive sounds of nearby respirators and cardiac monitors.

Barbara Fielding had been Brad's nurse, his life-support, his friend and companion in a sterile, lonely world. The Lady with the Lamp. I recalled the last words I heard from Barbara before the surgery—*you'll come through surgery with flying colors, Brad. You have the best surgeons I know.*

Dr. Singleton had not arrived yet. It was up to me to talk with the wife. I did not know whom I least wished to encounter—Marcia Crane or the chief of neurosurgery at UCSF.

Same day, 6:30 a.m.

Feeling a great weight pressing down upon me, I resumed rounds with my med students—except Miss Chalmers—and with the junior resident staff.

"Two of you may join us in the OR." I faced the short coats. "Be sure to keep quiet. Dr. Stokes has a temper when it comes to any distractions at surgery. Don't even cough."

*   *   *

My beeper chirped. I grabbed the nearby telephone.

"Dr. Stone?" An irritating, brassy voice came over the wire. "This is the hospital director's administrative assistant. The director *himself* would like to meet with you and Dr. Singleton at one o'clock sharp."

"Is there a problem?"

"Yes, there most certainly is. You were the resident attending Christy Browne, the so-called battered child. One of our medical students is here making a formal complaint about the way *you* handled the case. A Miss Alicia Chalmers, the daughter of our *senator*, I hope you know! She is threatening to bring charges on behalf of the parents. This has become a very serious matter, Dr.. Do *not* fail to appear. One o'clock sharp!"

The line died as I twisted the phone cord, wishing it were someone's scrawny neck.

"Oh, Dr. Stone?" A charge nurse rushed up. "The Benhass family wishes to speak with you. When …?"

"Dr. Stone, please meet Dr. Singleton in the surgeons' lounge," came an interruption from a loudspeaker.

"This evening," I answered the RN, perhaps a bit too harshly.

I trotted toward the elevator as my beeper announced another irritation. Call the operator.

"Hold for an outside contact, sir."

"Thank you." I wiped perspiration from my forehead. I was not getting enough sleep. Agitated synapses were firing erratically, self-control weakening.

"*Ira Jefferson*, are you there?" blazed my spouse over the line. She used my baptized name when angry. "Thank you for letting me know you came home last night. I had a nice roast beef dinner planned. With Chardonnay and apple pie. You do have a family, Ira Jefferson Stone. *Me!*"

"Nadine, I …"

"Well, you won't find your wife at the nest this evening, my husband. Two can play at this game."

"Please …"

The line went dead as another shrill broadcast repaged Dr. Stone to the surgeons' lounge. My fist exploded against the elevator call button.

I waited and waited and waited. Finally the whine of the descending lift, followed by a thump, came as that ulcer grew in my belly.

On entering the lounge, a bit short of breath, I immediately caught sight of my chief, Dr. Singleton. His long, restless fingers held a capped blue fountain pen and began striking the opposite knuckles, all the while moving his lips silently as if making some calculation, his expression arctic. A quickening fear tamped down my own deep-seated fury.

"*Sit down, Dr. Stone!* Fill me in on your little catastrophe in the ICU. I spoke with Mrs. Crane. She seems to think you are God. Dammit, man, the surgery went well. *So what the hell happened?*" His forehead was a web of frowns. My boss removed his bifocals, briefly examined the lenses, and then replaced the eyewear.

I detailed the events, watching the chairman's face change color, eyebrows knitting yet closer together, the pen beating his knuckles ever faster. The operator paged me again for a long-distance call, but I could not move. Colonic jitters set in as my leather seat sucked me down.

"The man bloody well might have lived if you had simply taken him straight away to the operating room and removed that damnable clot!" rebuked the neurosurgeon in his flinty, Carolina voice, pinning me to the back of my seat with the force of his stare, his bleeding eyeballs about to burst from their sockets. "What do you mean by fiddling around with urea and Neosynephrin? The patient suffered a blood clot! *Any doctor could have seen that!*"

"Sir, there was no time. His heart …"

"His *heart?* Don't bandy words with me! Even the medical student had a better grasp of the measures you should have taken."

"Med student? There was no student there." I shook my head in confusion, rearranging myself on the confining seat, fingernails cutting into the palms of my hands. I felt certain the room was now expanding, or I shrinking.

Singleton continued his monologue, lashing out for two long agonizing moments. Then he said, "A Miss Chalmers. She observed the whole fiasco from the bedside of another ICU patient. The student informed me about your ill-advised attempts." In his anger, the chairman's Southern accent grew more pronounced. "*Ill-advised attempts*, I say!"

"But …"

"*Y'all better learn to focus, Stone*. Now, get yourself to the surgical theater and assist Dr. Stokes." Dealing me an increasingly hostile stare, he beat out his next words with his fist. "*Mark this*, my good man! We shall discuss your behavior further. Good day, Doctor."

A hard-wired raven-head had become a symbol of all that was wrong with my life. Worse yet, I had missed the long-distance call. It must have been Ohio State. I needed to phone Mike tonight. I departed, feeling the weight of Singleton's gaze pressing upon me.

"*Get with the program, young man!*" he called in a high-decibel whisper.

I dashed toward the elevator and then heard the sound of coins on the floor, quarters rolling and striking the door of the lift. An upstart hole in my pocket was having its way with me. I bit down on my tongue, strangling a scream.

8:15 p.m.

Carrying flowers, I trotted into Moravian Mansions, to our rented Spanish-style high-rise apartment near the zoo. I wondered why there were no lights on inside. Then I remembered Nadine's pronouncement—*You won't find your wife at the nest this evening, my husband. Two can play at this game.*

The dozen roses in my arms somehow seemed heavier.

Probably went to visit a friend.

On the end table, a note in Nadine's handwriting lay against a textbook: *Gray's Anatomy*. I dropped to the couch, its polyester covering wheezing, and then flicked on a table lamp and read. "Call your brother." That was it. No "I love you," no "Ira, darling."

I had hoped to come home and begin suturing the wounds of our marriage. In a fit of frustration, I fired the long-stemmed bouquet into a waste basket. I felt as if I were King Solomon having to satisfy competing demands—those of my wife and a dying patient.

The phone rang in the kitchen. I jumped up and sprinted toward the sound, tripping on a throw rug and falling against the fridge. My eyes squeezed closed as I hesitated, fearing another call from hospital administration.

"Hello!" I hollered, catching it on the last ring.

"Ira? Should I phone you tomorrow? You're a hard man to reach."

"Oh geez, Mike. I'm sorry. It's been really hectic here. I just got in."

"I can call another time if this is not convenient. It's ... uh ... about a lump I found."

"A lump. Where? You mean a bruise, a bump?"

"No, Ira. On my testicle. The left one. It doesn't hurt. The school doc says not to worry about it, that it'll go away in a couple weeks. He thought it might be a fraternity football injury. But I'm certain I would have known if I got hit there."

"How big? Is it stuck to the testis?" I found it difficult to keep my mind on Michael's lump. The image of a snarly and impudent student kept popping up, taking center stage. A senator's daughter. I was hoping that my career wasn't in the toilet—along beside my marriage.

"Aw ... it's only the size of a pea, Ira. I don't know why I'm niggling you with this. You got enough problems on your plate."

"Tell you what, Mike. Check with the college physician again in a couple weeks if it's still bothering you. And give me a call too."

"Thanks, big brother," Michael replied. "You're the best."

"So, how is school treating you?"

"I made the basketball squad. Right guard. How about that!"

I smiled at the excitement in my brother's voice. "'And your grades?' as Father would ask." The vision of Alicia Chalmers faded, leaving smoldering embers in my gut.

"Far from failing. And guess what."

"You got me."

"I think I am in love! You are the first to know. Her name is Stella. A strawberry blonde from Baltimore. Freckles. Five-foot five. And a body like ... well ... You must meet her, Ira. You should see her dance."

"Wow. Hey, little brother. The big question is can she catch walleyes?"

"We shall find out next summer. At good ol' Lake Namakan."

"Is she into geology too?"

"No. Political science. Wants to work in the State Department."

"Do Mom and Dad know?"

"I kind of hinted at it to Mom. If Nadine got Dad wrapped around an axle, we can be certain my Stella would fry his coronaries. Especially since Dad's a Republican and she is a Democrat. Let's keep mum about this, if it's all the same with you. For now … That your beeper I hear?"

"Yup. My tether to an insane life. You're smart to go into geology, Mike. Talk to you later."

I glanced at the small black box on my belt. The numerical message—*Dr. Singleton's home phone.* First—a nip of Jack Daniels. Lord, how I needed one. Or two. Thank God I was not on call. An hour later, the hammer of time, now my enemy, seemed to be stretching and contracting depending on the state of the evening's inebriation, my solace after the painful events of the day, each shedding like broken glass and leaving tiny raw cuts.

Chapter 11

If we were brought to trial for crimes we committed against ourselves,
few would escape the gallows.

Paul Eldrich

University Hospital

Ordered to appear before the chief, I had arrived at Dr. Singleton's office and levered myself into a familiar tapestry-covered chair. I focused on a picture of Professor Harvey Cushing, one of Singleton's distinguished teachers. It was hanging on the wall. Three more weeks of my residency had passed at UCSF.

The secretary, a prim gray-haired woman with a polished obsequiousness and half-glasses hanging from her neck had just ushered me into the inner sanctum of neurosurgery. Her face was unreadable, and I had no clue why the chief had summoned me. My recent days had gone well, though Singleton seemed in an irritable mood this past week. The chairman would arrive presently, she said. The med student bent on changing the world was rotating on ob-gyn, and I hopefully had seen the last of her.

I looked around. A musty smell and library shelves, filled with erudite books, some gilt-tooled, the tomes all hunched together floor to ceiling, surrounded me. Gathering dust on an end table sat an ancient Royal typewriter. Rays from ceiling lights reflected from a polished marble bust of St. Francis. On the bamboo-grass cloth wallpaper hung a tinted likeness of Singleton with his university-issue wife and two Welsh terriers. While nervously tapping a fingernail against my teeth, I thumbed through an issue of the *Journal of Neurosurgery*, where an article written by a surgeon at Johns Hopkins caught my eye.

Deep in thought, I was examining a photo. Then I jumped an inch off my seat.

"Ah, I see you are studying on hypothermia for aneurysm surgery, Dr. Stone."

Jesus!

The owner of the journal, always a man of neat and precise movements, smoothed down his suit coat, slipped into his leather chair, and swiveled to face me. Today he wore smartly cut, pin-striped blue linen attire.

"Yes, sir. Vascular surgery interests me." I laid the magazine down. A breeze from a cooling fan ruffled my hair. "Significant advances are occurring in that field, especially in aneurysm surgery."

"Thank you for coming, Dr. Stone." We regarded each other across the vast gulf of the surgeon's mahogany, lion-toed desk and its mother-of-pearl inlay. Tremont Singleton cleared his throat, his cerebral stare appearing to pass sentence on me. "I bade you stop by so that I might set the record straight regarding that battered child case."

Oh, shit. Here it comes. Cold sweat dripped from my armpits.

"Just so. I've reviewed the films and the chart and discussed the situation with the pediatricians, nurses, ambulance technicians, and social service."

"Yessir."

A long deafening pause drove up my respirations.

"I don't understand how …" A buzzer rang. "Yes, Martha?"

Singleton listened. "Tell Dr. Stokes I will call him right back." A big sigh. "Dammit, it never ends!"

"Sir?"

"Not you, Stone. The research committee is rejecting another application for the renewal of our spinal fluid shunt study."

"I'm sorry, sir. I was looking forward to helping with the project."

"Just so." The chief's fingers drummed his desk. A patch of sunlight on the desk persevered in its slow shift to the right.

"As I was saying …" He coughed. "As I was saying, I don't understand how one medical student could make this university stand on its ear, but her manipulative techniques were quite remarkable. Fortunately, Senator Chalmers stayed out of the issue. In fact, he phoned me from Washington to see if he could help to smooth things over."

Huh?

"Just so." The brain surgeon brought his hands together so the fingers embraced and then continued. "The bottom line? We now believe that you handled the entire case with skill and tact. Both the chancellor and I wish to apologize for any duress caused, as well as compliment you on your judgment and patience." The chairman picked up his fountain pen, held it in midair as if in deep concentration, and then dropped it onto a green felt desk-cover.

"Thank you, sir." *Thank you, thank you, thank you!*

"The courts are in charge of the case now. No doubt you will be subpoenaed to testify."

"Yessir." My fingers fussed with my wedding ring, twisting it back and forth.

"Life okay on the home front?" Dr. Singleton peered at me over his bifocals.

"It's been hard on Nadine, sir. We'll work it out."

"We have all been through that, Ira. See you at surgery tomorrow."

"Yes sir! I'll be there."

*   *   *

That evening I skipped up the steps of our apartment building, taking them two at a time. I arrived home early and hoped to take Nadine to a play or dinner at the Sir Francis Drake. Excitement mounted, and I wanted to tell her about my conversation with the chief.

My forefinger flipped the hall light on. "Nadine?" I recall shouting.

But only a dampened echo answered. I swung into the kitchen, an echo of Trappist silence greeting me.

"Maybe she is working late at the travel agency," I mumbled.

I lifted the phone and dialed, listening. "Hello. You have reached Golden Gate Travel. Our hours are …"

I sighed, cradled the receiver, and wandered to the dining area. My fingers poured four ounces of Jack Daniels on ice, hesitated, and then splashed in a double. Weary legs and sore feet carried me to our bedroom, where I sat down heavily on the mattress, on Nadine's side. A strange feeling swept over me. Loneliness? Confusion? Almost a sense of desperation. I wanted to cry. But something—or someone—forbade it. My eyes snapped onto a portrait of Mom and Dad. An almost lethal tightness grabbed my throat.

I hefted the bourbon to my lips and shot down another slug. My body felt like ice. My stomach remained on fire, limbs in a state of tense muscular suspension, creased forehead damp with sweat. Choking, I ran to the bathroom and leaned against the sink, gripping its edges, my knuckles white and shaking.

"No," I rasped between clenched teeth. *"No!"*

I riveted my eyes on the bathroom looking glass, my blurred image mocking me, like a future death mask. *Who is that man gazing back?* Albert—for a split second. But only for a split second. Dad wouldn't cry. Which was the lesser evil? Nadine seeing another man or Father winning again? He always said Nadine wasn't right for me. *What should I do?* The solution? Swallow another two fingers of Jack. I relaxed as the wonderful elixir anesthetized my synapses, washing my problems away—or merely washing them into another estuary.

God, I feel so much better!

A burst from the telephone jerked me into the present. I waited, hoping the ringing would stop. The persistent creature demanded to be answered. I was not on call. I veered back into the bedroom, my gait increasingly unsteady.

The phone silenced itself and then rang again. *Damn!* "Yes?" My tongue struggled to form the word.

"Ira? Is that you?"

Good Lord. Mother.

"You don't sound very well, dear. Are you ill?"

I squeezed my lids closed and took a deep breath. "Hi, Mom. I'm ... uh ... a touch of some bug ... sort of. Sorry about the way I answered."

"Oh, Ira. It's about Michael." She started to weep. "Your father and I don't know what to do. He ... my baby ... he ..."

"Mother, did Mike see the urologist? Go to Dr. Korth?"

"Yes. We visited with him today, Ira. It's cancer. My baby has cancer," she quietly sobbed. "Dr. Korth is ninety percent certain. He is going to remove the tumor tomorrow at St. Luke's. And some lymph nodes in the pelvis."

"What ...?" The moment hung in its own eternity, and I felt a terrible chill immobilizing my gut. "What did Dr. Korth tell you, Mom?"

"He didn't say much more, dear. Only that Mike would miss the rest of this semester at college. Do you think we waited too long to see the specialist?"

I didn't know what to say. *Testicular carcinoma.* What terrible force had muzzled me when Michael had first called for help? It was too fearsome to contemplate.

"Ira? Are you there?"

"When ... when is the operation, Mom?"

"At seven a.m., he said. Ira, your father is wondering if you would call Dr. Korth. We don't understand all the terminology he used."

"Of course I will. And I'll meet you at the hospital in the morning. Has Mike already been admitted?"

"Yes, dear. Room 425." She sighed, and I wondered what she was thinking. "Michael seems to be taking the whole thing in stride ... as if he were going to undergo a simple appendectomy. He asked us to send you and Jocie his love and say not to worry. He knows you are always so busy. He didn't wish to bother you."

"I ... I guess he caught me at a bad time a few weeks ago." I nearly choked on my words, breathing increasingly difficult. "I ...ahh ...well ... how is Dad taking it?"

"He doesn't say much. But I can tell he's devastated."

"Mom, is it okay if I stay with you guys tonight? Then we can go to St. Luke's together. I'll get one of the other residents to cover for me."

"Oh, Ira. You and Nadine are welcome anytime. Please ... please come on out."

I hung up, but my hand would not let go of the receiver. I knew what Father was thinking. *Dammit, Ira. You're a doctor. Didn't you learn anything in medical school? Your own brother for God's sake! Dr. Korth said that the testicle should have been excised the day Michael called. The Lord help us if it's too late now.*

All I could think about was Mike and the family at Lake Namakan and the scent of walleye pike frying on our campfire. Teaching Mike how to fish and water ski. While strong arms and broad shoulders paddled the canoe, we had talked about life and family and the future. We had cemented a bond of fierce family love. *So why did I ... how could I have missed the boat?* I kept asking myself. I had received an 'A' on my urology final in med school at Georgetown. I knew what should have been done. I knew it!

Still numb with alcohol, my marriage going awry, and Mother's dreadful news, I folded my hands and closed my eyes. I decided to take a taxi, what with bourbon whiskey on board and all. A wracking guilt now lodged like a splinter deep in my memory bank.

CHAPTER 12

…And if I die before I wake,
I pray the Lord my soul to take.

Eighteenth-century prayer

The Boundary Waters

My mother, Sophie Lindstrom Stone, grew up in Chisholm, Minnesota, close to the iron ore beds where I would play. A Swede through and through, she spoke the language when we visited with her family, a strategy which infuriated Dad and amused us kids. Mother was one of those kind people whose mind saw only good where others perceived evil intentions. The boundary waters to the north became a favorite vacation site for all of us, particularly Mom's two brothers and Dad, the walleye pike fishermen. We offspring inherited that compulsion to join up in the north woods, where we found a deeper meaning to our lives.

*   *   *

I slapped a mosquito on my thigh and then continued picking my way down the slope in front of our Canadian cabin, the family get-a-way on Lake Namakan. All of the Stones, including Michael, had taken a much-needed vacation together. I gazed across the waters toward the Minnesota shore and then cocked my head at the call of a loon riding an overhead thermal. The hot sun seemed to drift behind swirls of clouds, blunting the edges of shadows as I felt the warm glow of rich yellow birch and jack pines.

I could not think of any place on earth I would rather be. I paused as I caught sight of a pair of cheerful chipmunks chattering away on a moss-covered boulder. They stopped and eyed me.

The object of their curiosity appeared to be the green and gold swimming trunks, still wet from a morning swim. My brown hair had just been subjected to a brisk cross wind. I've been told that my stone-blue eyes reflected my Swedish heritage, the rest of me my father's Scottish ancestors. My six-foot skeleton, two inches shorter than Michael's, carried one hundred and fifty-five pounds on a thin frame.

Today I should have been in a good frame of mind, but I wasn't. I was scared, scared for my younger brother, for …

In a brief moment a couple of cheerful animals changed my mood. I chuckled briefly at the two perky chipmunks, and hiked toward the tethered Lund gently bobbing on water tainted dark by its iron content. I clattered onto the wooden dock to inspect the dated deck boat riding on its choppy inverted reflection, its fiberglass exterior gleaming in the warm sunlight. The craft rocked with the waves, and the rhythmic but muted *slap, slap* sound played on my ears. I wondered if God were sending a message in Morse code, though, if so, my intelligence centers couldn't decipher it, my thoughts crashing into each other. My lungs gave a great sigh as I pulled on the lines mooring the inboard-outboard. Two fishing poles, Mike's and mine, tilted up against the gunnels.

Michael no longer possessed the strength to paddle, let alone swim to safety. I assisted my brother into the power boat, checked the gas gauge, fooled with the steering mechanism, and uncovered the inboard motor to vent gas fumes. I needed to busy myself. Noon was approaching.

I squinted at the gaunt figure resting in the copilot's seat, swaying like a limp ragdoll with the rocking of the boat. He wore a life jacket, though it would not protect him from the inevitable. I tore my eyeballs away from the bones pushing up beneath his skin, looking anywhere else but there. Anywhere.

"Shall I fire it up, Mike? Everything all right?"

"Let's do it! I'm okay, Ira. Just need to take it slow. Man, is this air exhilarating!"

Again, I heard the waves *slap, slap* against the boat, tapping out some enigmatic message from above. Michael swiped at a mosquito above his scalp. Clumps of dry hair, now more gray than brown, flew into the air and drifted like snowflakes to the water. Most of his head was bald anyway, the hair-loss accelerating with each turn of Mother Earth.

My brother lifted a portable radio from a cubby hole and flipped the switch. Amid some static, a news report announced that the Warren Commission found no conspiracy in the assassination of President John F. Kennedy. Then "Moon River" filled the air.

"I'm worried about Mom and Dad. I truly pray they can accept what's happening." My brother coughed up a teaspoon of phlegm laced with traces of blood, waited a minute to catch his breath, and then added, "It's super to have the whole family here in Canada with us, but I feel great that just you and I are going fishing today. I won't have much time with you guys anymore."

"Shit, Mike. That smog in California will kill all of us before … uh, sorry, Mike. Just a figure of speech." *Dammit, sometimes I wonder where my head is.*

"You're right … that smog will kill all of us before old age does at the rate civilization is moving. It's okay, big brother. It's easier for me if we treat our mortality like it's front and center and not hiding in the wings. Hey, let's get a movin'!"

"We've got Canadian minnows swimming in the pail. I'll hook your bait for you. You know … the Coumadin and all."

I sighed, listening to Mike's wheezing. He had the patience and inner strength of … of our mother. Yet here he lay, like a broken bird, cancer eating at his lungs and kidneys. My brother, twenty years old, had been struck down in the prime of his life. Michael was supposed to marry his Stella and father her children. Give grandkids to Mom and Dad. He was no longer a basketball star, rather a withered, spindly specter of his former self. Still and all, the young man was a star of greater dimensions, and I was thankful to be his brother.

My fingers twisted the key. The motor roared into action, and we knifed westward, skirting a series of islands, and then over the lake toward our favorite fishing hole. The wind streamed through my hair and across my skin, the sensation invigorating.

"God, this is beyond great. Ira, remember the day it stormed so badly when we came out here? A few summers ago." Michael eyelids were closed as we savored the pinewood fragrance. A sudden burst of breeze whistled around the radio antenna, playing like a muted and mysterious base fiddle.

"Sure. The summer the water came up to the cabins. A beaver dam had burst up stream." I slowed down the cruiser as a water skier, arcing out behind a Larson, whipped by.

"It was you and Dad who took me fishing back then. And you, Ira, found the time to show me how to bait the hooks, and cast, and ... well ... everything." Michael grinned. He had lost a couple teeth. "You don't recall? About later, I mean."

"I don't understand, Mike."

"Sex. Mom and Dad seemed too embarrassed to talk about the propagation of the human race. They left books for me to find when I was thirteen. You explained everything in a way a stupid kid like me could understand. Sperm. Eggs. The ol' hard-on. What to do—and not do—with it. Jeez, Ira. Who could ask for a more terrific brother? Not me, for certain. Even Stella ... oh, well, never mind, bro."

I flinched and turned my gaze toward a phalanx of Canadian geese landing in the water.

"Uh, thanks, Mike." I sensed my ears burning, sort of like a blush, but with words sticking somewhere in a great frozen sadness.

Then came the Bubble Room.

*   *   *

When it was evident the malignancy would no longer fall to standard chemotherapy, oncologists put Michael through an experimental protocol at UCSF. The treatment involved massive doses of radiation and drugs. Unfortunately, bone marrow, where the blood elements form, also would be damaged. He lived inside a bubble shield that surrounded his bed, supported by positive air pressure. The transparent plastic sphere protected Mike from bacteria and a dreaded infection. The shield permitted advanced therapies to encourage new marrow growth and give birth to blood elements once more. At the end of every day Mom, Dad, and I—and Jocelyn, when she was in town—visited Michael at the Cancer Center. We prayed and watched Mike waste away to a shell of his former being, his body retreating within itself.

"How's it going, Mike?" I spoke into a handheld microphone as my eyes stroked the bones of his face, like a blind man trying to remember how it used to look. The barrier and rush of oxygen dampened communication.

"Ira, you wouldn't believe the RNs I've got," my brother returned with a hoarse whisper. "Every one is a beaut! I got a date with the brunette when I get sprung from Alcatraz. Don't let on to Stella, though." Michael grinned. "Marla—that's my daytime nurse—can't touch me while I'm in here. She reaches through those arms in the bubble to give me my bath." His voice gravelly, he chuckled while my fingers squeezed one of the plastic sleeves. "I told her I use condoms too, and she cracked up!"

I shook my head, unsure whether to laugh or cry. Just then Nurse Marla entered the room. She glowed with a special kind of charity, roses kindling in her cheeks. The radiant smile on her lips and cheeks, like a breath of spring, screened the sadness of treating an unconquerable cancer.

"Well, so you are the famous brain surgeon. Mike has been boasting about his sister and brother. I can see the resemblance between you and Michael." She pushed her arms through the sleeves and then wiggled her fingers into plastic mitts.

"Naw, I'm barely out of training here. Thanks for the compliment, though. How is the fisherman faring?"

I watched the nurse pick up a vial from a nearby chute in the biosphere, withdraw five milliliters of cortisone, and inject the amber drug into a rubber cap. The medication traveled through a tube dwelling in his left upper chest, lodged inside Mike's subclavian vein.

"Your brother is our favorite patient. He never complains and always has a joke for us. His hematocrit is beginning to rise, but the doctors say that his platelets and white cells remain too low to expose him to any environment outside the envelope." She looked at Michael. "I'll be back shortly to give some Compazine and help with your nighttime snack." Marla tossed me a pleasant grin, checked a dial on the oxygen outlet, patted the human envelope, and then gently closed the glass door behind her.

"Stopping by tomorrow, Ira?" rasped Mike, his crab-hollowed cheeks at a frozen angle.

"I'll be a bit late. I'm on call."

"I made my will today. Not much to give, but I want you to have my fishing rod."

I swallowed and glanced away. "Mike ..." I knew I had to be straight with him. The man was dealing with eternity better than anyone else in the family. "Am I allowed to fish with it?" I managed a smile, though it was an effort. "It's the lucky fishin' pole."

"You bet."

"I'll let you catch some shut-eye, bro. God bless. Here comes another one of your harem."

"See you, Ira." Mike half closed his tired eyes, dark smears beneath, their blueness now diluted as if a faint lamp glimmered through, illuminating a new pathway, life moving farther from tenuous moorings.

As I entered the hallway a stunning woman passed by and then turned. "Oh, are you Mike's brother? He looks very like you."

"Yes, I am. Ira Stone. Do you work here?"

"Oh, no. Mike is a ... a friend of mine." The lovely strawberry blonde smiled and extended her hand, which I grasped. "My name is Stella DeLeon." She gave a big sigh.

We chatted briefly. As the woman began to turn away I replied, "Michael thinks a lot of you. Perhaps we could meet again under better circumstances."

"Yes, the Lord willing."

*   *   *

I walked down the neon-lit hallway that harbored a trace of ozone and antisepsis in the air. I retraced my steps toward the elevator. Two doctors in white coats passed me by, pacing their rounds a step or two faster than the rest of humanity. On the first floor a chapel caught my eye, and I slipped in. No one else was present. Perhaps three dozen souls could fit comfortably into the room. It was plain and nondenominational. A single cross stood on a pedestal. Stressed and riddled with guilt, I dropped to a wooden pew and bowed my head. My heart seemed to beat so very fast as I struggled to speak with the Lord, beg His forgiveness, but all my plugged up ears could hear were whispers from the walls. Words rent with despair froze on my lips while little drops slipped through my fingers. My grief streamed out, surrounding, choking me, like ocean seaweed enveloping a swimmer. If only I could turn back the clock. Instead, it kept moving ever forward, *tick … tick …*

*   *   *

After a half bottle of Jack Daniels that night, I slid into the land of shades and unbidden dreams, spying a pair of loons, the birds sailing a rising thermal, calling out again in the boundary wilderness, their warble echoing over the waterway, our canoe rocking with the waters of Lake Namakan. Embalmed by grief, I held Michael while he slept, my brother's head feeling like an immovable weight, a weight only slightly assuaged by his final words to me: *"You got to stop beating yourself up about this. I am going to take your pain with me."* I did not know what it meant back then. I gently placed Michael, one foot in life and one foot in death, at the bottom of the vessel, Valhalla-bound.

Take my pain with him? I shook my muddled head and gazed at an ochre-orange sun slip-sliding away through a western sky rinsed with cotton and blood, my mind still swimming through a deep sleep. The loons were now silent, the only sound the gentle *slap, slap* of wavelets against the drifting boat.

I awoke to find that the earth's star was ascending, spreading its shafts of early light, palpable, warming and igniting green chlorophyll in the trees. Another morning had announced itself, and the day was good. I just did not know it.

*   *   *

Michael's death and my survival were now inextricably linked, for he
died on my watch. The Lord seemed not to have answered my prayer, and
forthwith began a future darkened by my widening disbelief in God, that
dark and heavy root of my soul lying in torment. When Michael passed
away, something also died inside of me—like a limb, leaving a phantom
pain in its wake.

CHAPTER 13

Appleton

It was evening—no, it was night, chilly and dark but moonlit. Usually I jogged around the quarter-mile track, though this time, wearing shorts and a polo shirt, I decided to run along a forbidden path that took me through a partially forested pasture. This was off the reservation, but I was getting cabin fever. I was breathing hard and slowed down to a trot. My ears picked up an occasional dog barking or owl hooting, but mostly there was only the crunch of tangled leaves and twigs underfoot. Then I stopped and listened. It seemed like the muffled sound of voices. *What on earth?*

I found myself deep among the trees and wasn't sure what I should do. I turned and pushed my way through a thicket of pines, coming closer. Strange. The incoherent sounds had ceased, but someone moaned and then cussed. I stole my way to the edge of a weeded clearing. And then I saw them.

"*Jeezus, Henry!* Try me harder, you prick-sucking wimp," came a strident whisper from a girl with her legs widely spread. "Don't give up, you dickhead. Don't ... dammit! Hey, weenie, I'll bet you can't even come. Get the fuck off me. Come on, Lance, baby, you're next. I need a hot climax. Hope you got a bigger fucking tool for my little ol' pussy. Poor baby-boy Henry can't get a goddamn hard-on."

"Hey, you got a real treat a'comin', Ellie." Lance, obese belly in the forefront, unbuckled his belt, corduroys shackling hairy thunder-thighs.

They did not see me as Henry rolled off, mumbling something undecipherable, and grabbed a cheroot from a nearby jacket. Lance, trousers now fettering his ankles, kneeled down in the moonlight, a large pulsating offering in one hand, a burning cigarette in the other.

"Wow, Lance!" The girl, red skirt pulled up, knees toward the moon, her naked butt lying in the flattened weeds, shuddered. "You may be a fucking hog, but you feel damn good! Almost better than crack!" Moonlight flashed from her left fourth finger.

As the twosome worked into a frenzy, a third guy—I recognized Crow—sat nearby, playing with his dick and drinking from a bottle. He passed the Wild Turkey to Henry, zipping up his fly after failing dismally in the rutting department. The guys were not in my home group, but I knew them. I looked more closely at the woman, that willowy twenty-something girl with a cloud of fair curls and puppy-dog eyes. *Her?* I would have never guessed! I knew her by sight only, and I now felt a mixture of intense pity and curdling anger. How could she … how could *they* have betrayed all of the rest of us? Yet, in what way was this really different from some of the things I had done in my less-than-stellar past?

I didn't know what to do. Run in, yank Lance from her, and confront them? Scream unkind words at these lecherous addicts now violating an Appleton sacred trust? Slip away and report them later? They were consenting adults, committing no unlawful offense, yet they had broken a moral commitment here at the rehab center.

"What's the matter, dog-breath?" chuckled Crow as he pulled from the bottle. He then handed it to Henry. "Can't get it up? Likely you don't even shave, you little pecker."

"Fuck you!" Cheekbones jutting out against the smooth skin of his face, Henry rounded on Crow and spit, "Go shit in your mother's face, asswipe." I could see Henry's fist opening and closing, and I knew this wasn't the end of it.

I wound my way back to an evening home group meeting. I was disgusted. The maddening question over that flagrant violation troubled my sleep.

The next day

Morning arrived with a raw, expectant quality. I did not squeal on the girl and her three sex objects. It was none of my business. Or was it? Now I had an appointment with my counselor.

Michael. The recollection of my dead brother still bothered me. I had not forgiven myself, so how could God?

Betsy sat fingering the Star of David hanging from her neck. She reviewed my file and remained quiet for the longest time. My counselor picked up her clipboard but did not write for several minutes. "I am sorry about your loss, Ira. How did Mike's death affect you in later years?"

"I'd rather not go into that right now. Please."

"I see." She checked her notes again. "Tomorrow we shall take up death and how you dealt with bereavement."

CHAPTER 14

Out, out brief candle!
Life's but a walking shadow, a poor player
that struts and frets his hour upon the stage
and then is heard no more.

William Shakespeare
Macbeth

UCSF Medical Center, December 1966

Following Alexandria's birth, I sat in a chair in Nadine's postpartum room at the University Hospital, concentrating on a metropolitan scene on the other side of her window. In the shadows of Golden Gate Park, humming traffic circled round and round, vehicles entering and exiting, rather like my life, where people came and went. I seemed to make significant acquaintances and then lose them. Why? What were the flaws in my character? My wife certainly could have detailed them for me. But damn, what did she know?

I had returned from a meeting in San Juan and learned I had passed the Board exams with flying colors, as an examiner had told me. Now, on the last day of December, our second and last daughter, Alexandria Lee, was born. Lexi was a tax deduction. Like her sister, Denni, she had her mother's good looks. Unlike Denise, Alexandra's personality would turn out to be a bit more like her mom's, except for one detail.

As my second-born grew up, she had much difficulty relating to other children, quite unlike Nadine. It was years later before we understood that she suffered from bipolar syndrome, labeled manic-depressive disorder when I was in training. I am still baffled how I could have missed another diagnosis. Of course I was absent from home during much of her growing up period, and Alexandria's trust in any safe haven within her father's arms began to topple. Another small detail crept into Lexi's existence, but back then Nadine and I were woefully ignorant of her subterranean social life, one destined to become intimately interwoven with mine.

I had been appointed assistant professor at UCSF and chief of neurosurgery at the Fort Miley VA Hospital. Medical students and residents from the university rotated through our service. Research activities were many and included laser investigations at our lab unit. The latter studies on the explosive effects of laser impacts on the intact rodent brain drew government interest and eventually required my getting top secret clearance to enter the Redstone Arsenal in Alabama. My academic career had taken off. And the US Congress was casting a curious eye in our direction.

One particular day, which I remember quite vividly, we were setting up another experiment at our lab—we being Lloyd Golden (Raytheon engineer), Stratford Sheen (PhD in physics), Stanley McIntosh (MD and PhD in biophysics) and Ira Stone (yours truly in surgical greens). Up to this point, we had found that anesthetized guinea pigs would cease breathing instantly after a brief pulse of laser radiation focused on the cranium, and our team then had only a suspicion as to the cause, a theory we needed to prove. We had arranged to aim two dozen small calories of coherent red-light energy onto one square millimeter of the intact skull and delivered it as a single two-millisecond laser pulse from a ruby crystal. We needed to see what happened at the foramen magnum, where the brain and spinal cord normally were joined.

All of us were tense, nervous about the forthcoming result. Losing our research funding versus understanding the risks of employing lasers in both medicine and warfare lay in the balance.

Today's target was another anesthetized guinea pig. He lay on our little surgical table, sporting buck teeth and whiskers. After administering an overdose of Fentanyl, I used a scalpel to separate head from body. After fixing the head within the target site, I incised through the scalp, divided the skin, and exposed the cranium. The skull appeared thin, even bluish.

Stanley struck a wall knob which triggered a visual signal outside the lab entrance:

WARNING
LASER ACTIVE

"Okay, the guinea pig is decapitated and the head clamped, guys. Let's try this experiment again," I announced. "Go ahead and direct the marker light onto the cranium, Stan."

"Liquid nitrogen circulating. Powering up." Lloyd toggled a control lever next to a bank of capacitors. An eerie humming followed as the charge accelerated.

"Protective lenses, gentlemen." Stratford handed out copper sulfate glasses, which we donned. The room turned a pine-tree green.

I went over to check the target one more time.

"Don't touch that! Get away, Ira!" thundered Golden. "My apologies, Doc, but we don't want a surgeon to lose his fingers. It's too dangerous there now."

"Sorry." Properly chastised, I jumped back to safety, my heart missing a beat.

A 3,200-frame-per-second Kodak Instex cinema camera had been programmed to film the entire head of the guinea pig as the laser struck its frontal skull. Stanley, in his US Navy whites, eyeballed alignment once more and then stood back. "Camera ready."

"Okay!" Stratford, in jeans and polo shirt, peered at the cathode ray screen. *"Fire!"*

Lloyd flipped a switch. An ear-splitting crack rendered the air, followed by a breathless stillness that filled the room.

"See anything?" someone anxiously asked. We looked more closely at the target.

"Nope," another responded. The foramen magnum did not appear unusual.

"Not jack shit," a third declared.

"Damn ..." I glanced up from the rodent's head. "Oh, well. It's the government's money. Stanley, have you ...?" I stared at his pressed whites. "Good God, Stan. You got brain all over your uniform!"

"Lord help us!" was all Stanley McIntosh could say.

We gawked in disbelief.

"Well, that answers one question," Stratford exclaimed. "Let's develop and check the film ASAP before the VA yanks our funding," he urged, tongue in cheek. Sort of.

We all waited impatiently while the engineer ran our film through its bath in the darkroom. There it was—an explosion had jammed the brain down against the virtual spinal cord. Gray matter had detonated inside the closed cranium!

Even though only one-tenth of the energy traversed the frontal bone into the intracranial cavity, a tiny bit of neural substance lying just under the skull had vaporized and, being mostly water, within milliseconds expanded into gas by a factor of twenty-two point four. The effect was obvious. Faster than the eye could see, the blast had rocketed the lower half of the brain out the foramen magnum, through the air, and against the decorated navy shirt. The implications? At the time we did not know.

A few weeks later the House Armed Services Committee of Congress showed intense interest and toured our facility. And that was the last we heard. Further monies for our research were denied, reasons unknown.

*   *   *

A few days later, I sat in my windowless cubby hole at the Veterans Administration hospital, listening to "Aquarius" while reviewing charts for the monthly morbidity and mortality conference, or M and M. We surgeons talk about our successes early on, but it is our operative complications and failures that we remember as the seasons pass by.

The secretary buzzed my office.

"Yes, Anita?" I responded. "What's up?"

"Hi, good-looking. I'm transferring a call from Mr. Kenneth Donavan, the secretary of state! Wouldn't tell me what he wanted. Sounded mysterious, though."

"Uh oh. Don't know the man personally. Switch him over. By the way, thanks to all you guys for the birthday gift. Thirty-five years. How about that?"

"Smile, Doctor. With what the government pays, we all knew you likely couldn't afford that new briefcase, so everyone chipped in. Bye."

A click was followed by an unfamiliar voice.

"Dr. Stone, your name came up as someone who might help us with a rather onerous situation. One of our Peace Corps workers, a Miss DeLeon, twenty-two years old, had a terribly bad auto accident and suffered significant head injuries. She is comatose and on a respirator in Caracas, Venezuela, at a small private clinic. Her sister, an RN by the way, is requesting an American neurosurgeon to go to Caracas and evaluate her condition. We were hoping you could fly there and provide assistance to the locals. At our expense, of course."

"Wow. Uh … okay. You've caught me by surprise, Mr. Donavan. Let me check out coverage with the surgical director here and my colleagues. Give me your phone number, and I'll get back to you back in a few hours."

"Telephone me ASAP. The president has authorized your travel as an official tour of duty. Confidentially, this will make headlines, and after all, we must make him look good, mustn't we?"

Oh.

"Doctor, I know you will take good care of her. The family is counting on you, as are we."

Caracas, Venezuela

Later the same day I found myself on a Pan American flight, sipping my favorite Jack Daniels after the hectic day. I could not in all good conscience refuse to go, could I? After all, it *was* the secretary of state, and my job might be on the line. My passport had been stamped with a visa written in Spanish at the Houston International Airport, where I had changed planes. With me I brought an assortment of packaged sterile surgical instruments. As I flew skyward I sat riveted, wondering what lay before me in this South American country. Would she need surgery?

Arrival at Caracas went smoothly—until I entered Immigration. Six gents, slouched but dressed in khaki uniforms creased into steel, were gazing up at an old black and white Motorola TV on which a soccer game was being replayed, between Venezuela and Honduras as near as I could determine. Boisterous cheering came from the riveted audience. One of those honchos opened my passport and gaped at the visa entry. He chuckled and motioned to his supervisor, followed by much discussion in rapid Spanish. Being conversant only in English and German, the meaning of their debate escaped me. Soon a mini-crowd formed.

"What is going on?" I scratched my head.

"Sorry, Doctor." A Venezuelan with a wolfish grin stretching his cheeks regarded me through the middle lens of his trifocals and shared their discovery. "But this visa is for Mexico, not our country." His face then assumed a stern demeanor, his chin jutting out at an imperial angle while he drew out a thin blue suspender strap with his left thumb. "We cannot permit admission for you, *amigo*." He glanced at the departure board. "The next flight out to … to … Miami leaves at nine tomorrow morning. You may wait in those chairs over there."

I stood there, dumbfounded, staring at a row of wrought-iron seats attached to cement. *Stupid gringo that I am, what do I do now?* After much haggling and a number of US dollars disappearing into the boss's trousers, they allowed entry provided I turned over my passport, which I did with much reluctance. The agent in charge, a man with emphatic garlic and nicotine breath, then handed me a note stating my permission to visit the state. Of course, it was in Spanish, embossed with a very official seal stamped amid a grand display of authority. The officer warned me to keep said document on my person at all times, or else.

I passed into Customs, where I had to curl my toes even further. They insisted on unpacking and checking the instruments. So much for sterility. Fifteen minutes later, drills, retractors, rongeurs, sutures, and a mess of other operating needs lay bared and scattered on their table. A huge Caribbean insect marched defiantly across a Kerrison punch and then jumped off as I gathered up the mess.

It was not quite one o'clock in the morning when I corralled my equipment and hurried with my travel bag into the lobby.

"Dr. Stone, over here!" A grinning young man in blue jeans and white polo shirt was waving. I dragged myself to the friendly greeter and set my paraphernalia on a bench. He kept brushing a mop of straw-colored hair from his forehead. My situation was looking up.

"Hi. Ira Stone here." I am sure I gave an exasperated smile. "Sorry for the delay, but a snafu occurred over there." I waved my arm toward the glass partition and explained the situation. "Here is the letter in lieu of a visa and passport."

"Welcome to Venezuela, Doctor." His enthusiastic greeting was infectious and accompanied by a firm handshake.

"Outside the hospital, please call me Ira."

"Steven Parkwater." He gripped my hand. "Everyone calls me Parky. I am one of two Peace Corps workers down here. There were three of us … until Stella's accident. Let's head out, and I'll fill you in. You might as well bunk with us if you like. We have plenty of room, and you look beat."

I gratefully accepted the offer, and we trotted out to a yellow Volkswagen that had seen better days. Parky retailed the tragic and gripping story of a courageous blonde from Wisconsin.

"This is Stella's third year of service in Caracas. We knew each other at the University of Wisconsin."

Damn, that name sounds very familiar. A long-ago image unfolded in my mind. *No, it can't be!* I took in a deep breath.

Parky swung the Volkswagen onto a street slick from a recent rain. Dim street lights washed through a fine mist. Lightning flashed in the distance, reflecting off low-lying cloud banks, followed by distant thunder. Omens and portents. The Caribbean air was heavy, sultry, a bit briny. I could hear the faint melody of some Hispanic celebration perhaps blocks away. Steven Parkwater carried on.

"We spend most of our effort here teaching basic public health and sanitation to the poor in the outlying districts, though Caracas is our base. Charley Burchleigh is senior in the Venezuelan Peace Corps station. He re-upped last year after taking some courses at Wisconsin. Charley feels particularly bad about what's happened. I think he was a bit in love with her. Well, we all are pretty tight."

Parky seemed to find it difficult to proceed, but he gathered himself together and continued as the tires hummed over concrete.

"Our beautiful Stella had been somewhat despondent over the loss of her boyfriend. Apparently it was a cancer of some sort."

My chest felt tingly and a bit tight.

"She then joined the Peace Corp. Recently Stella was working near Maracaibo, close to the lake. It's about four hundred miles west of here. She needed to return to Caracas for supplies and intended to take a flight, but the weather had turned sour. The planes were not flying then, and Charley suggested she hop on a bus back to Caracas." He cleared his throat. "Which the girl did."

A period of tearless silence followed.

"The bus route passes near Lake Maricaibo and through some rather challenging mountains. Well, the people here drive like they do in New York City, but on narrow roads, which can be fearsome even in good conditions.

"Apparently the bus driver was puffing weed while whipping down a steep incline in the mountains. Coming the other way appeared an eighteen-wheeler. Neither vehicle could stop on the slippery pavement, and … well, you can imagine what happened. Most of the passengers were killed. Stella survived but with severe head trauma. No fire, fortunately. An ambulance eventually arrived and transported her to a local hospital, Clinica Valdez, here in Caracas. Stella's on a respirator, and it just doesn't look good.

"Charley is with her now. One of us sits with her all the time. We cannot trust the nurses to suction her and look after her if the vent goes haywire. Or if the electricity goes down, a common occurrence here, even in good weather."

"Huh? Aren't the nurses RNs?" I wondered aloud.

"I can't figure out what they are. Keep in mind that in this part of the world people consider a nurse just a notch above a prostitute. The pay is terrible, education limited, and motivation just isn't there. Parents shudder when their daughter chooses to enter the nursing profession. Charley and I don't have a lot of medical knowledge, but at least we can be there and call the anesthesiologist or neurosurgeon if something goes wrong. The doctors seem rather good, but you would be able to tell that better than we can. We're on our way there now."

"Now? It's almost three o'clock in the morning, Parky."

"Hey, you're big news here. USA and all—*el* brain surgeon from *'oosa,'* as they say. This will hit the front pages tomorrow. The locals all are waiting, a bit nervous. Well … hell, so am I."

"Okay, let's do it!"

"You might get a surprise."

The Beetle bounced over a pothole and then buzzed through a residential area. We turned into a narrow avenue, stopping before the Clinica Valdez, a clinic and small hospital. A crowd of almost two hundred people were milling near the entrance.

"Parky, what's going on?"

"Your welcoming committee, Ira. They are the doctors and nurses, and all their friends and relatives. And *their* friends and relatives." He winked. "You are a very important *hombre.*"

We exited the car and approached the front entrance, where the assemblage respectfully parted, excitement electrifying the air. A short Venezuelan moved toward us, his right hand extended. A small coterie in hospital whites followed behind.

"Dr. Ramón Vargas, please meet Dr. Ira Stone, from California. As you know, he has been asked to help evaluate your patient, since the family is hoping for transfer back to the States. Dr. Stone, Dr. Vargas is the chief anesthesiologist at the clinic and is managing Stella's respiratory care."

Vargas stepped forward with a bit of hesitation and then gave me an earnest handshake. He waved his left arm toward the gathering audience. "Doctor, we have all eagerly awaited your presence. The entire clinic is at your disposal. If you would be so kind, please accompany us to the patient's bedside." He spoke perfect English.

"You are more than kind to wait so patiently." I glanced at Parky, who nodded his head. "I am honored to be here and would be pleased to follow you."

Hushed, perhaps worried, tones flowed from the crowd. The procession, led by the anesthesiologist, with Parky and me in tow, marched into the hallway. As we neared the patient's room, the obvious concerns became restless murmurs. Parky leaned to my ear. "They are a bit fearful that you will find something wrong with Stella's care." I sensed he was also apprehensive.

All of the medical personnel passed into a dimly lit room, we with them; the odor of disinfectant was unmistakable. Onlookers, the curious and concerned, remained outside. A near-holy quiet descended. I drew near the bedside of a young woman, unconscious and breathing with the aid of a ventilator, sighing at the rate of twelve per minute. She had had a tracheotomy performed. A tube now exited straight out from her wind pipe and passed to a respirator giving off its sighs.

Someone turned on overhead lights. Now I could see that her battered and swollen face was as white as Dover chalk, except for two moles on her right cheek. The anesthesiologist informed me that one week had passed since the terrible collision. He handed me a stethoscope, perhaps for want of something more constructive to do. I dutifully listened to the patient's heart and lungs and then felt her pulse. At least I appeared to be a real physician, though I was certain that he knew far more about the systemic organs than I did.

I stood up and glanced about. A young nurse, hands folded as if in prayer, hovered at attention by the foot of the bed. A man in civilian clothing stood up from his corner chair, appearing a bit dazed. Apparently he had been sleeping.

"Dr. Stone, this is Charley Burchleigh, my colleague in the Peace Corps. Charles, this is the neurosurgeon we have heard all about," Parky rushed to say. "Charley has stayed here all night with Stella, so he's still waking up, as you can see."

I took in the unsteady man standing before us. He was ungainly, tall and thin as a rail. His clothes, black jeans and yellow striped shirt, appeared to have been slept in for days, and a week-long moss-like beard had formed. He wore his brown hair long and braided down to midback.

"Hello, Mr. Burchleigh," I responded. "Parky has told me so much about you ... and Stella. I wish we could have met under better circumstances."

"It's Charley, please. Dr. Stone, it is my pleasure. Forgive me for looking like a shipwreck."

"Tonight we both fall into that category."

I turned back to the patient, a strawberry blonde. And stared. *Lord, it can't be.* Edema and contusions distorted her facial features. I pulled back her closed eyelids, which then fluttered. The pupils were dilated and failed to contract with light. Pressing on the stylomastoid bones below the ears, a painful stimulus, resulted in a minimal reaction, just an extension and inner rotation of the limbs. Stella's reflexes were hyperactive, abnormal. She had suffered a devastating injury to the brainstem, whether permanent or not I couldn't be certain, though it didn't look good. And the very real possibility of either temporal lobe or cerebellar herniation existed. I was unable to discover any signs of pressure sores—thanks to the attentive Peace Corps guys, no doubt. I stood back and took in her features more closely. *Yes, dear God. She is the same girl I met in the hallway that day.*

"Please, Dr., here is Stella's angiogram." Dr. Vargas withdrew a set of films from a manila jacket and inserted them into a view box on the wall. "If you don't mind ..."

Everyone quickly parted, leaving a pathway, as if willing me to thread my way toward the moment of truth, if there were one. My exhausted eyeballs scanned the films. *Moderate cerebral swelling. No midline shift. Ventricles appear small. Minimal signs of herniation. No hematoma.*

I asked the doctor about her vital signs and chemistries, seeing as I could not read Spanish—verified by my visa fiasco. Her blood gasses confirmed good hyperventilation.

"What do you think, Dr. Stone?" wondered Charley aloud. The room fell heavy with expectant silence, everyone seeming to hold their breath as one. The nurse's knuckles remained in a tight and prayerful position.

"She has no blood clot. Her brain edema is grave, but proper measures have been taken." I paused for a minute, rubbing my chin and staring at the comely woman on life support. Then, "I see no reason to alter her course of therapy. She certainly has received excellent medical care."

Charley gave a sigh of relief and translated for those who didn't understand English. Suddenly cheers and clapping erupted. Several hands propelled another man to center stage. He smiled, his heavy mustache and goatee stretched by the effort. He was of medium height and bald except for crowning fringes of gray hair. I sent a perplexed look toward the Peace Corps workers.

"This is Stella's neurosurgeon," responded Parky. He gestured toward the man in a long white coat. "You just made serious points with everyone here. They thought you would find something wrong, and that would be highly embarrassing. Thanks for improving American-Venezuelan relations, Doctor."

We walked away, and my long-ago exchange with Stella tumbled through my mind. *"Oh, no. Mike is a … a friend of mine … My name is Stella DeLeon."* I remember replying, "Michael thinks a lot of you. Perhaps we could meet again under better circumstances."

"Yes, the Lord willing."

*   *   *

While waiting for administrative permission to fly Stella home, the local neurosurgeons invited me to give some talks at the University of Caracas, which I thoroughly enjoyed. It was a pleasure sharing scientific ideas with the many colleagues I met in South America, followed by dinners and toasts to one's health.

During one of our visits to Stella, Parky, and I were standing in the hall outside her room when suddenly the nurse burst through the doorway, screaming in Spanish, *"Something is wrong with Stella's breathing!"*

We dashed inside. Stella was turning blue, the respirator emitting an intermittent beeping alarm. I disconnected the ventilator from her tracheostomy. Her airway was obstructed. There was no time to don gloves. I grabbed the suction tube and clicked on the wall vacuum suction.

"There's no suction! What the ... ?"

My fingers frantically disconnected the tubing and reconnected it to the inlet of a nearby suction machine on wheels. Again nothing! It was not plugged in. Parky grabbed the cord lying on the floor and pushed the prongs into a wall receptacle. I switched on the machine. It worked, thank God.

As Stella strained to draw in her next breath, I pushed the rubber suction tube down her trach and tried to grab hold of the obstruction. The attempt failed. Stella's breathing weakened and then ceased. I pounded on her chest, hoping to dislodge whatever was stuck down there. Then I suctioned her once more. The sound of the vacuum suddenly ceased when the tip of the tube latched onto the culprit. I pulled it slowly out of the trach tube. A large, dried mucus plug clung to the rubber tip.

I reconnected the ventilator and watched Stella's chest re-expand, color returning to her face. A few minutes more and the anoxia would have been fatal. I felt Stella's pulse and gripped her hand in mine, holding on to it for the longest time, giving thanks to the God in whom I no longer believed.

That evening I opened my wallet and gazed at a photo of Michael, remembering his long-ago phone call. *"I think I am in love! You are the first to know. Her name is Stella."*

*   *   *

Attending to our patient and our efforts to transfer Stella to the USA, as her sister had requested, filled the next five days. She required a military air ambulance with nurses, ICU capabilities, and, hopefully, an anesthesiologist. I obtained federal permission to bring her to my VA hospital. Charley or Parky, depending on who was caring for Stella, handled the phones, communicating with our embassy in Caracas and with either the Peace Corps Office or State Department in Washington.

After several bureaucratic snafus, the Pentagon arranged to divert a

C-133 military air transport, the "*Globemaster*," one of the MAT turbojets deployed during President Lyndon Johnson's Vietnam War, from its Tokyo-to-Andover Air Force Base run. We were on standby for the flying hospital, which would evacuate Stella to Travis Air Force Base, San Francisco.

On the final day in Caracas, all the medical personnel (and all their friends and relatives, and *their* friends and relatives) gathered together at the airport to see Stella off. Everyone had bonded so closely that there was not a dry eye as the medics and loadmaster carried Stella up the tail ramp.

*   *   *

On the flight home, my thoughts wrestled with justifying such extraordinary expenditures of money, resources, personnel, and effort. I weighed these against the life—or death—of one American citizen. Even so, I was immensely proud of America's compassion and power. Daily I held Stella's hand and prayed for her recovery. When I imagined her beneath the bandages and bruises, I saw a stunning young warrior dedicated to helping the less fortunate, selfless in her quest for peace.

She was a strawberry blonde with deep, cerulean blue eyes, a true veteran who died from a pulmonary embolism one day later at the VA hospital.

I wept that evening, quietly so no one would see, no one except my bottle of Jack Daniels and a new moon. I wept because, you see, in a way I had loved her so damn much it hurt, and I felt crushed by the leaden weight of failure, by the loss of another human being in my care. She was a true soldier, her likeness destined for the hallowed halls of Valhalla. And perhaps God needed a Peace Corps worker up there with her Michael. Perhaps.

I had to steel myself against breaching that isolating barrier of professional detachment, against getting so close to my patients ever again. I was beginning to discover how successfully bourbon Manhattans eased the transition.

I dreaded phoning her sister.

*   *   *

A ward clerk made the call to the Sir Francis Drake Hotel and then handed me the phone. I waited for someone to pick up on the other end.

"Good morning."

"Hello. Miss Starling?"

"Speaking."

"Your name is on the call list for Stella DeLeon. I believe you are her sister?"

"Yes."

"I am sorry we haven't met yet. I am Dr. Stone, the surgeon who was caring for your sister."

"Was?"

"As you know, Stella arrived safely from Caracas. I am distressed to say that today she suffered a respiratory event. We did all we could, but she passed away an hour ago. I ... I wish we could have done more. The cause was—"

"My sister? Dead? Oh my God, oh my God! You let her die?" Weeping and a dreadful silence followed. "I ... I'll phone you back. *Dear God.*"

I cradled the receiver and wondered, *Strange. She didn't wait for an explanation. Too devastated, I imagine.*

An impetuous breeze had caught the tail of my brother's ashes that joyless, windy day. A cloud of his dust, sprinkling my coat, even yet stuck to me.

Later that afternoon

"Dr. Stone?" An RN from ICU approached.

I stopped making rounds. "Yes?"

"It's about Stella."

"Uh huh?"

"Well ... you know her sister was visiting Stella an hour before all this happened. We were tied up with an emergency ruptured aortic aneurysm. We thought that her sister, a Miss Starling, being a nurse and all, would notify us of any difficulties. The monitors indicated all vital signs were okay, and ..."

"Sister? No one told me her sister was here."

"She said not to bother you and that she would call you in a day or two. Just thought you should know. Miss Starling left suddenly after five minutes and never came back."

"How strange. You'd think that ... well, never mind. Thanks, Ronnie."

I resumed checking the lab work on a patient, but an uncomfortable feeling dwelt within me. From a room next door came the lyrics to the song "Message to Michael."

Chapter 15

All I have seen
teaches me to trust the Creator
for all I have not seen.

Ralph Waldo Emerson

Appleton

During our home group sessions we heard numerous stories of lives gone awry—damaged body organs, multiple DUIs resulting in jail time, automobile accidents followed by disability or death, doctors losing their license and livelihood, attorneys disbarred, all manner of job failures, fractured necks from shallow water diving, and disastrous gunfights.

Barfly was one of these.

"Hi, my name is Bounthane, and I am an alcoholic addict. Some call me Barfly. It's easier to remember," he chuckled.

"Hi, Barfly," came the phalanx of voices.

Barfly was totally bald. He wore tinted glasses and kept rubbing his nose. He wore a Hawaiian shirt, its lower two buttons undone.

"Bounthane, today you're giving us another example how your life became unmanageable," said Fletcher.

The subject was sitting next to me, quiet but bouncing his left knee up and down, the leg resting on a nervous foot.

"Well, you see, it was like this. I was embarrassed for the wife and kids to see me drinkin' from a whiskey bottle. If Molly ... well, that's m'wife ... found one hidden away, I'd have to listen to her mouth for days on end. But I just couldn't stop it—the drinking, I mean.

"I figured she wouldn't notice a couple Listerine bottles in our medicine cabinet. I hated the taste, but in a few minutes a good slug of the stuff would make it okay. Soon I was stockin' up Listerine in the garage rafters, inside the toilet tank, and in the wheel well of my car. I even bricked some up inside of the house walls. That's how insanely desperate I was getting."

Everyone looked at each other, eyes wide, then back at Barfly. Some nodded in sympathy, having been there.

"I started to get this here stomach burning, you see, so I would take more Listerine to deaden the pain. I went to the doc, but he couldn't figure out what was wrong. 'Course I didn't tell him about my drinking. It got worse, and then tests showed real bad liver damage.

"No one could find what the problem really was. I knew, but even then I could not stop! Finally Doc Smith admitted me to that ICU place. I was turnin' yellow. I went into these here withdrawals, with seizures n' all. Molly, she discovered containers of the stuff after tearin' our place apart. My life was in the toilet, but I didn't die ... well, you know that ... and Doc sent me here. Molly's medical insurance is payin' for it, thank God."

I wish mine did. But still it's cheaper than their having to shell out for liver failure.

"Thanks, Barfly. Comments, anybody? Ira?"

"That mouthwash not only contains over twenty percent alcohol but also toxins like methanol."

Barfly, fingers tremulous, fastened the third button in the fourth hole on his shirt.

"Anyone know the experiment of the frog in hot water?" asked Fletcher. "Sebastian?"

"If a frog is put in a container of boiling water, he jumps out immediately. If the animal is immersed in warm water that is slowly brought to a boil, the frog sits there until he dies."

"A metaphor for our addicted lives, is it not? If the trauma from a lifetime of drinking all occurs in one day, we either breathe our last or jump out. But instead, the water around us is slowly brought to a boil over a number of years until we die from our affliction—unless we wake up and climb out before the grim reaper taps our shoulder."

*   *   *

Betsy motioned me into her office for our conference. After listening to Barfly, I could not get the thought of Crown Royal out of my mind. Damned if I was going to tell her that.

"According to our records, you only drank the occasional social cocktail until you were in your residency, Ira." My counselor set her pen down and eyed me. "Though you did often use the bottle as a tranquillizer, it sounds as if you were not a really heavy drinker until the last few years, with a few exceptions. Most of us start earlier in life, though there certainly are those, like you, who fit well beyond the average in the bell curve."

"It is strange. I had my first drink at the age of fifteen, but my serious alcohol intake did not begin to grow until my late twenties, during my training. I guess I justified it by saying, 'I work so hard that I deserve a cocktail when I come home.' I usually never drank except in the evenings. Until later, I guess."

"Did memories of your brother Michael have anything to do with your rush to get to that cocktail?"

"Of course not!"

"Uh huh. And then you went to Penn State."

Yes, Nadine and I went to Penn State. "It was during the midseventies. The chairman of surgery there made me an offer I couldn't refuse."

Penn State Hershey Medical Center, December 1975

"Make way! Sorry. Watch the IV pole!"

"Good God! Careful, my friend."

"She's seizing! Where do we put her?" yelled an ambulance technician.

"Over here, guys," instructed Claudia, the ER charge nurse.

The medical technicians rushed a convulsing female through doors held apart by two orderlies. The techs hastened the comatose woman to one of twelve draped enclosures in the emergency room. Pandemonium ruled tonight, accompanied by the pungent smell of life gone awry, of death patiently tarrying. A screaming teenager was in premature labor. One homeless schizophrenic suffered with pneumonia. A near-lethal gunshot wound had been inflicted during a family dispute. Two drug addicts yelled obscenities. And now a patient with grand mal seizures.

"Where did you find her, guys?" I restrained the shaking arm while our nurse inserted an intravenous line.

"On the steps in front of the Hershey movie theater," responded one of the emergency techs dressed in navy blue, a black phone with antenna jiggling on his hip with each movement. "We checked her ID. Had her insurance program with this health care unit, so here we are. Name is Winston, Charlene Winston. Thirty-eight. No medical info. Bystanders said the client just collapsed and began to shake all over. She lost bladder control." The technician held on to padded tongue blades lodged between Charlene's chattering teeth.

Blood and saliva dribbled or spouted from her mouth, depending on the state of the respiratory reflexes. I ducked as another cough shot bits of scarlet sputum into the air, onto the ceiling. Her body stiffened, her head and neck arching backward, arms and fists clenching in clonic flexion, jerking legs extending, stretching as the fiery powers of Vulcan shot through her body. The electrical storm in her inflamed brain demanded more and more oxygen, even as pulmonary spasm stifled the oxygen and carbon dioxide exchange.

An ashy gray overtook the alabaster white and crimson hues of Charlene's skin.

"Let's get her intubated ASAP. Claudia, grab the crash cart while I push IV Valium." I reset the tranquillizer drip and then strapped her right upper limb to an arm-board.

The violent quaking softened, and Charlene's lacerated lips fell slack. My rubber gloves grabbed a suction line and aspirated bloody mucus from her throat.

"What do you want me to do, sir?" My resident arrived and trotted over.

"Intubate the patient. I'll keep suctioning."

The tech handed over an endotracheal tube. Dr. Tellini edged the jaw and swollen tongue down with a lighted retractor, located the vocal chords and, rather smartly, passed the airway into her windpipe.

"Start the Pancuronium. Give four milligrams of morphine IV." Dr. Fabian Tellini, now a second-year resident in neurosurgery, connected our patient to a mechanical respirator. Life-giving oxygen returned color to her cheeks. The shaking ceased as the muscle relaxant paralyzed all motor units. Tellini snatched a stethoscope from around his neck and listened to Charlene's chest. He drew in a deep breath of relief upon hearing the sighs of good airflow through both lungs. No signs of aspiration.

"Dilantin?" Claudia Vogel looked at me as she held up a vial of the anticonvulsant.

"Eight hundred milligrams. Slowly. Let's put a hold on anymore Pancuronium and see if the seizure activity has stopped. And notify the chief resident in neurosurgery. That dilated pupil on the right looks suspicious. Put in a Foley cath. Then let's get her to X-ray for an angiogram. Ask Social Service to locate any family."

"Yes, sir. We're on it!" Claudia twisted away, her hand reaching for a telephone.

I bent over the patient and directed a penlight beam into her wandering eyes. The left pupil constricted. The right remained dilated, frozen.

"Doc, if you don't need us any longer, we'll be on our way." The burly technician snapped closed an aluminum cover to his ambulance file. "My beeper is buzzin' again. I hate this lousy cold weather. Looks like snow."

"Thanks for sticking around. By the looks of it, you guys are earning your keep today."

Fabe—that's what everyone called our resident—and I turned our attention back to the new patient. She had thick nickel-blond hair, now smeared with blood and bits of gravel. I guessed she was quite pretty under more pleasant circumstances. Her breasts fell slightly to either side, pigmented nipples indicating a history of pregnancy. No lumps palpated.

No masses in the abdomen. An appendectomy scar. Clear urine drained from the Foley catheter. Scattered bruises, probably from the seizures on cement steps.

"Claudia, while we're waiting for the cerebral angiogram, let's get some plain films of the head, C-spine, and chest. Portable ... here in Emergency."

"Will do."

I trotted to a sink and scrubbed my hands, dodging a gurney being rushed by four personnel, one squeezing a ventilator bag. Another physician was compressing a bloody high-caliber wound in the man's thigh. A scent of alcohol trailed the stretcher transporting the household warrior, who survived the battle—so far.

Dr. Tellini scratched Charlene's foot with the back of his reflex hammer. The height-challenged physician-in-training could never find a white coat to fit; the cuffs protruded a good three inches when unrolled. He had large ears and deep brown eyes, finely combed black hair and soft features. Friendly, perhaps overly impetuous, he was the maestro of the affable greeting.

My eyes tracked the readout on the EKG and blood pressure monitors. I turned toward the RN. "Claudia, how is your mother doing?"

"Her leg pain is completely gone, thanks to you. She's back to tending her garden ... a little soon, perhaps. But you know Mom. Thanks for asking." The nurse smiled as she adjusted the flow rate of the Dilantin solution.

"Sir?" Fabe Tellini looked at me. "Don't you think we should get a neurologist to evaluate her epilepsy?"

"Later perhaps. With that dilated pupil and the possibility of temporal lobe herniation, we might need to get her to the OR tonight. We'll wait for the angiogram scan to rule out a hematoma."

Charlene's eyelids fluttered and her left foot moved, almost imperceptibly.

"Looks like she's beginning to respond. Did you give any urea?"

"Not yet. Do you think we should?" The resident pocketed his reflex hammer.

"Let's hold off and see what the scan reveals." I grabbed the wall-mounted ophthalmoscope and peered through Charlene's pupils to inspect the retinae. "Well, well ... interesting. Dr. Tellini, let me borrow your stethoscope."

With the ventilator on hold for a few seconds, I listened over the pulsations of Charlene's carotid arteries, along various places of her scalp, and lastly over her closed eyelids where I detected a strange *swish, swish* synchronous with her heart beat. I concentrated.

"Dr. Stone?" Nurse Vogel peeked around the drapes. "Her husband just arrived. Shall I have him go to the waiting room?"

"Yes, please. Tell him we are sending her for an angiogram scan, and I'll meet with him shortly after I review it."

"Do you want me to type and cross-match her?" Tellini squinted at me as if his allergies were acting up.

"Not yet. After we check out her plain films." I grinned at the resident. "You might be in for a surprise."

*   *   *

An hour later, Fabian followed me to a nearby office where a set of Charlene's X-rays taken in the ER hung in a row on backlit view boxes. "See anything unusual?" I queried while readjusting the position of an image.

"The chest appears okay. There is some straightening of the cervical spine." The young doctor scratched the back of his neck, frown lines running through his forehead. "It's the ... um ... skull film. There's an odd density in her right orbit. Maybe a calcified tumor?"

"Did you examine her eye grounds?"

"No, sir. Not yet."

"Her right pupil didn't respond to light because there is no pupil. She has a glass eye, not a temporal lobe herniation." I pointed to the density on the skull film. "I doubt she'll need surgery tonight."

"A ... glass eye?" His face turned crimson as he stared at the X-ray.

"Fear not, Dr.. I made the same mistake a few years back. It's a lesson one never forgets." I handed back the stethoscope. "And have a listen to her head. I'll meet you in Radiology thirty minutes from now. We can go over the arteriogram study together."

Dr. Tellini cocked his head as an urgent announcement came over the loud speaker. He breathed a sigh of relief. "A code blue. Not for me, thanks to God."

*   *   *

Followed by the resident surgeon, I walked into the conference room where the nurse had escorted Charlene's husband. The man, slight in stature, appeared a nervous wreck, his tie hanging loose, his right foot tapping the leg of his chair. His left leg was missing, the pant leg folded and pinned. He grabbed his crutches and stood up.

"Mr. Winston, this is Dr. Tellini. I am Dr. Stone from the neurosurgery service." I grasped the husband's hand. "Please keep your seat."

"How is she, Dr.? What happened? May I see her now? How—"

"I know you're anxious about Charlene." The resident and I sat down. "She had a convulsion, but the aftereffects are clearing up. We just reviewed her cerebral angiogram, a dye test where our radiologist injected contrast media into arteries leading to her brain. It provided us with a good map of the circulation. We found the problem."

"Is it serious?" Danny Winston appeared as if he had suffered through too many crises recently. He wore a blue flannel shirt, the collar frayed.

"Charlene has what is known as an arteriovenous malformation. An AVM in the brain. She hemorrhaged from abnormal and weak blood vessels. The angiogram demonstrated a small blood clot near the speech area on the left side of the cerebrum." I tapped my left temple. "The bleeding has stopped, and the clot is not a risk at present. That is what precipitated her seizure."

"Dear God … What is the next step, Dr.?"

"We should let her rest under close monitoring in the ICU while the swelling resolves. When she is awake, perhaps in a few days, we can discuss possible surgery to remove the AVM and the clot."

Tellini and I were leaving the room when we heard, "Fuck you, Doc! Fuck all of you!" An inebriated ER patient dashed by, followed by two security officers. An IV line, minus the dextrose-and-saline container, dragged on the floor, trailing after the man as he bounced off the walls.

*　*　*

One week later I angled toward the nursing station in the neurosurgical ICU. I grabbed the chart for Room Six, reviewed the vital signs for the previous twenty-four hours, and then headed toward Charlene's bedside.

"Evening, Mrs. Winston. You're looking much better today. You must be happy to be off the respirator."

"My...my...my..." She stared at me while struggling to form her words. "My...ohhh..."

"Can you understand what I'm saying to you?" I reached for her wrist, felt her pulse, and then folded her tremulous right hand in both of mine.

The patient nodded yes, watery eyes reflecting her fear and frustration. A tangle of wires traveled from her chest to a blinking heart monitor.

"Okay if I call you Charlene?" I let her limp arm return to the mattress.

Another affirmative nod.

"As we explained to you and Dan yesterday, you have had a small stroke from a bleed. The hemorrhage occurred in your speech area. It will take a few months for you to be able to talk again. The weakness on your right side will improve much faster. You will need therapy and patience ... especially patience, but I'm quite optimistic." I smiled. "The good news is that you are young and in otherwise good health."

"When ... when ... when?"

"When is the surgery?"

She nodded again. "When ... when ... mmy ... my?"

"Don't be upset. Everyone understands that talking is a struggle for you. The operation to remove the abnormal blood vessels is in the morning. At seven o'clock." I squeezed her hand. "We will take very good care of you, Charlene."

She gave me a worried look. Upon leaving I noticed an image titled "Saint Lucy of Syracuse" dangling against the wall over her head. The virgin and martyr held a shaft of wheat in her right hand and her eyes on a golden plate in her left.

After departing the ICU, I walked down the hall with Tellini and two of the other residents, followed by an intern and student. We turned into the waiting room to visit with Charlene's family—Danny Winston, his three offspring, and Charlene's mother.

"Is there anything more I should know about tomorrow's surgery, Dr. Stone?" Danny's voice quivered on the edge of fear, as if dreading the unknown.

"Charlene will be asleep for many hours. The anesthesiologist will take excellent care of her. We went over the operation in some detail with you yesterday. If you think of any further questions, please ask the nurse to reach me."

"Look after her, Dr.. She means the world to me." Danny had already sustained enough trauma in his life. Surgery on Charlene must have been almost more than he could cope with. Then he said, "Dr. Stone, this is my mother-in-law, Mrs. Freda Lang. And these are my little ones—Wanda is six, my Mary is ten years of age, and Billy just turned fourteen."

Wanda, her big sea-blue eyes staring at me, curtseyed and skipped behind Grandmother Lang. Mary brushed a brunette lock behind her ear and gave me a nervous smile. Billy, rosy-cheeked and appearing uncomfortable in the hospital environment, accepted my handshake, and then retreated beyond the group.

Freda Lang, the spitting image of her daughter in the future, held on to my grip as if to will her strength into Charlene through me. "Dr. Stone, the nurses seem to think you walk on water. We feel so fortunate to have Charlene in your care. Though my daughter is not, I am Catholic. I will light a candle for you and Charlene."

"I thank you, Mrs. Lang. We have a good team here." After a few words of encouragement, I turned and headed back to the radiology department. "Nice-looking children," I observed half-aloud to myself.

*   *   *

That evening Jocie called, and we chatted about our parents. Then, out of the blue, she said, "Ira, I am praying for you. If you ask God for help, you will be able to stop your drinking."

"Damn it all, I'm okay, Jocelyn! I can stop any time I want." Heart-pounding silence followed. "Sorry. Really, all I have is a few cocktails at night after a hard day's work." But down deep inside I wanted to talk about our brother, Michael. And Stella. I just could not bring myself to do it. Instead I stuffed those feelings away to eat at me.

With one of Charlene's films in my right hand and a cocktail in the left, my eyes focused on the arteries of her angiogram and then on my whiskey, both harboring feeders to a deadly lesion.

CHAPTER 16

Because I could not stop for Death,
He kindly stopped for me;
The carriage held but just ourselves
And Immortality.

Emily Dickinson
Because I Could Not Stop for Death

Penn State

A week after admitting Charlene Winston, I was completing early morning rounds with three residents, one intern, and two medical students. My headache had disappeared, and a one a.m. dose of Valium had steadied my nerves. Tellini asked permission to scrub in on the AVM case. The surgery would begin at seven, an hour from now. We halted at the intensive care unit nursing station to check on Charlene and review her chart.

"Dr. Stone, I have gone over all the lab data, EKG, and chest X-ray. No problem areas, sir." Fabian Tellini handed the chart to me.

"Tellini, isn't there some way this hospital can get a white coat to fit you?" I grinned at the short man fidgeting with his sleeves.

"Don't I wish, sir. When I'm rich and famous, I'll have mine made to special order."

I leafed through the chart and then passed it off to the station clerk.

An overhead page rang out. "Dr. Stone, please call the operating room."

"Well, Tellini, they're ready for us. Let's check on our patient and then I'll meet you in Room Three."

We crossed an aisle and drew up to the patient's bedside. Danny and Wanda were leaning close by, the daughter gripping her mother's hand.

"Good morning, Charlene." I felt her steady pulse in her free wrist. "Good to see you again. Dan, Wanda. Charlene, you remember Dr. Tellini. He was one of the physicians who examined you in the emergency room. He will assist me at surgery."

"Good … good … ohhh …" She sighed and nodded at the resident.

"Dr. Lois Merriman will administer your anesthesia. You met her yesterday. She is terrific. We are on our way to the OR now and will see you there in a few minutes."

I turned my attention to the IV fluids and slowed down the patient's intake. An antibiotic, Vancomycin, dripped into an arm vein. A central venous line ran from the right jugular vein to Charlene's heart.

Then I felt a tug at my pant leg. Wanda looked up at me with misty eyes. "I am going to pray for Mommy. Grandma asked us to."

*   *   *

"Hello, Dr. Stone. Dr. Tellini, we hear that you are going to assist. Nice to see you again." The circulating nurse, Janice Blake, glanced up while connecting a set of suction tubing into wall receptacles. She seemed to be swearing under her breath.

"Janice?" Fabian turned toward the RN. "Want me to put the Foley in after she's asleep?"

"My goodness, no, Dr. Tellini. We'll take care of that." She laid the plastic tubing aside to help move the patient.

Attendants rolled Charlene into the theater and assisted in the transfer to the operating table. Gentle country rock music flowed through the air, followed by "Sylvia's Mother."

"I love that song," said someone I did not know. "Dr. Hook."

A nurse busied herself with laying out hundreds of surgical instruments over sterile green drapes on a rear table. Her backside faced me, and I wasn't certain who she was. I did see a colorful cap tightly fitting her head, a few wisps of honey-blonde hair escaping in back.

Dr. Merriman spoke softly to the patient, holding an oxygen mask close to Charlene's face as she lapsed into a deep slumber.

"Dr. Stone, we have a new scrub nurse with us." Janice nodded her head toward the multicolored surgical cap. "Tamera is out with the flu. This is Stephanie DeLeon. Everyone calls her Steffi."

"But ..." I hesitated. "But this is an AVM. We can't operate with nurses untrained in vascular neurosurgery. No one told me. Won't—"

Steffi turned toward me. "I'm so sorry, Dr. Stone. I just now found out my assignment. Perhaps ..."

"She is outstanding," countered Janice. "Knows all the microsurgical instruments. She has studied and scrubbed-in with neurosurgeons at the University of Pittsburgh. And more recently at Baylor in Dallas."

"Baylor, huh?" I stared at the svelte woman behind a mask.

"Yes, sir. With Dr. Jurgeon and his team." Her heavily lashed and enormous, fawn-colored eyes seemed to burst with a Venusian intensity.

I glanced at Janice and then back to Steffi. I found myself having difficulty pulling my gaze away, a different part of me making the decision. "Okay. Let's see how it goes." *I hope I'm not making a mistake.*

"Carry Me, Carrie," now flowed from the speaker, Steffi humming along. Then she said, "Thank you, Dr. Stone." The nurse pivoted back and resumed lining up the microscissors. Her instruments lay marshaled as if preparing for a military crusade.

Christ, another compulsive, I too quickly judged.

I crossed over to the X-ray viewing panels and pushed angiogram films into recalcitrant holding clips. For a few minutes a nervous fluorescent light flickered behind the studies.

"Dr. Tellini, you can see where a large portion of the AVM has been obliterated by our interventional neuroradiologist. He certainly is a whiz at these new catheter techniques." I aimed my index finger. "Note where acrylic emboli have occluded over half the arteries to the lesion ... especially those from the left middle cerebral artery. It's a large one, and many of the anterior cerebral and basal ganglia feeders still remain. We have a long day ahead."

"It appears as if the hematoma has stabilized," suggested Tellini.

"And the swelling has receded." I turned toward Charlene, now deeply anesthetized. "Let's get her head into the skull-clamp."

An hour later the patient lay with her cranium and shoulders rotated to the right. The resident had shaved the left side of her frontal-temporal scalp. Masked and gowned, I checked the battlefield terrain.

I stood behind Charlene's head, on my left the floor-mounted microscope with its bilaterally attached Sony TV cameras. Dr. Tellini placed himself on my right. Nurse Stephanie DeLeon, standing on a lift above Tellini and me, positioned herself to the right of the assisting resident. Her main field was a thickly draped, stainless-steel table overhanging the patient's torso. To the left of the patient and hidden behind an elevated sterile drape sat Dr. Merriman, presently drawing blood for oxygen and carbon dioxide analysis. A large screen displayed real-time electronic read-outs— Charlene's EKG pattern, blood pressure, respiratory CO_2, and anesthetic drug concentrations.

Faint pulsatile beeps intermingled with the ventilator's sighs. Spotlights illuminated the operative field as Tellini and I finished stapling drapes to Charlene's scalp.

"Okay to begin, Lois?"

"Sure thing, Ira. Shall I keep the blood pressure normal for now?"

"Yes, thanks. Scalpel." I held out my right hand. Before I had time to think, the knife handle slipped into my fingers, where it seemed to come alive.

Startled, I glanced up, holding Nurse DeLeon's rather compelling gaze longer than simple acknowledgement required. I couldn't decide if her eyes were more brown or more yellow. Maybe a dark amber. Or a light cinnamon surrounding expanded, black pupils. The orbs, flanked by her long sable eyelashes, possessed a glowing quality. The scrub nurse seemed never to blink. I did not know why, but I felt as if my mind were being excavated, as if she could read my mutinous thoughts. Perhaps even those to which not even I had access.

"Dr. Stone, are both suctions working okay?" inquired the circulator.

Quickly refocusing, I turned back to the operative field. "Yes, Janice. You might reduce the suction flow on my left."

"Yessir."

The scalpel cut into Charlene's scalp, leaving slivers of blood in a horseshoe-shaped incision above and forward of the left ear. The music had changed.

"That tune is familiar ... who's playing?"

"ABBA," Steffi replied, handing me a sponge and a furtive look.

"Oh, yes. One of my favorites," I added, memories of a microvascular fellowship in Germany crystallizing in my head, giving me an unexpectedly warm feeling. I stripped the soft tissues down over the ear, thus exposing the skull. "Skin cli—"

Before the words were out, the nurse had already placed the clip applier in my gloved hand.

"I have a fetish for their songs. ABBA is one of my collections," she added a soft voice.

There was a silky, yet bubbly, timbre to Steffi's words. I suddenly felt like a planet briefly wobbling in its orbit. A sphere frozen, codified since childhood. The sensation disturbed me.

"Press a bit tighter on the skin until I finish clipping the edges, Dr. Tellini," I prodded.

A spark of electricity seemed to flash deep inside, likely within the right side of my own brain. And then it flickered away, as if stamped out by an invisible presence on the left.

I retracted Charlene's scalp flap. "Cranial drill."

Steffi passed the air-powered instrument over to my right hand and delivered an irrigation syringe to Tellini. She gave him a smile and—I nearly missed it—a wink? I centered my attention and bored two holes in the skull, the drill-bit aborting automatically upon perforation of the inner table of bone.

"One ... two ... three ..." Janice counted the blood-tinged used sponges as she tossed them into a floor bucket. Her mask started to slip and she adjusted it. "Five ... six ... seven ..."

"Craniotome." I grabbed a smaller drill with a side-cutting bit to open a window in the skull. A piercing whine shot through the room as the drill spun between the burr holes, through bone. The resident cooled the site by irrigating with saline solution. A strange electricity permeated the air, causing me to lightly shiver. I quickly recovered.

"Easy, Tellini. This isn't your Lamborghini. You don't need to hose it down like that."

"Yes, sir."

"Ira, the pCO_2 is thirty-five. How does the brain feel?" inquired Dr. Merriman.

"Firm, but not tight. Could you open the spinal drain now and hyperventilate her carbon dioxide down to thirty?"

"Will do. Let me know when the brain is relaxed. Do you want any urea or mannitol?"

"No, let's try to avoid using osmotic agents." I turned to Steffi. "Dural hook and scissors, please."

Our eyes locked briefly, and then she pressed the instruments into my hands and glanced down. I incised the dura mater, exposing Charlene's cortex.

"Janice, we're ready for the scope now. Room lights out. Surgical chair, please."

My initial reticence at training a new scrub nurse had given way to frank admiration. I wondered how Steffi would manage the micro-instruments in the dark, under stress. Wondered ...

"The pCO_2 is thirty," reported Lois Merriman, breaking into my musings.

"Sounds good. The brain is quite soft now. You can halt the CSF drainage."

The anesthesiologist clamped the plastic tube running from Charlene's lumbar spine and measured the amount of cerebrospinal fluid in its container. I drew aside the dural membrane covering the brain.

"Wow!" exclaimed Tellini, his eyes expanding. "Uh ... sorry, sir. What a mess of vessels," he continued more quietly. "They look like clusters of pulsating worms."

"Now you can see why these are called arteriovenous malformations. Without the angiogram as a map, we would not be able to determine which are the arteries and which the veins. See the greenish-yellow tint? It's bilirubin, a red blood cell breakdown product." I pointed my bipolar forceps at a pigmented zone in the frontal lobe. "The blood clot lies under here."

I settled back into my surgical chair, steered the microscope into position, and then lowered the OR table until the surface of Charlene's cerebral cortex came into sharp focus. In a way, the undisturbed tapestry before us was quite exquisite—wet and shimmering shades of reds, blues, grays, and yellows, all masking a deadly monster. Beauty masking the Beast.

A large, wall-mounted TV monitor displayed the magnified image as seen by me in the scope. Audible gasps came from the nurses and anesthesiologist, their raised eyes tracking the blood swirling through paper-thin vessels, each pulse threatening to split the dancing stygian tubules. There was a rhythm to it. The enlarged veins, leeches rippling with every pulse, sucked oxygenated blood away from Charlene's starved vital centers, leaving despotic glial scar, now the generators of her epilepsy.

"Tellini, keep irrigating at brief intervals. Air and light from the microscope will dry out the pia-arachnoid." I lifted my hands. "Jeweler's forceps and diamond blade, please."

I felt the instruments float into my fingers as if by magic. She was a new nurse, at least new to me, and the encounter took me by surprise. Perhaps it was a fluke? I tented up the arachnoid, a spidery and translucent membrane holding cerebrospinal fluid against the brain, and then stripped open a tiny hole over the sylvian fissure, between the frontal and temporal lobes. The CSF escaping into Dr. Tellini's suction tube appeared like water, warm and crystal clear, with a hint of yellow from the previous bleed.

The cerebrum relaxed further. I could see only the tip of that deadly iceberg, the main mass of coiled vessels hidden from view, rather like mountains eclipsed by their foothills. I launched into the dissection at an edge of this living Medusa, a bloody tumor of twisting snakes that seemed to take on a life of their own. I attacked a miniature python, its three furious heads diving deep into the organ where Charlene lived.

I passed off the forceps and knife blade and held up my left hand. In silence Steffi thrust the suction tube into my fingers. It was as if we were communicating by thought waves, as if we had worked together hand-and-glove for years. It was a very strange feeling. The pace picked up while the faint and steady background beep of the cardiac monitor continued.

"Microscissors."

Somehow she already knew the proper curve and length I needed. Alternating scissors with bipolar forceps, I sliced away adhesions and thickened arachnoid, electrocoagulated small vessels between the brain tissue and the AVM, and then developed a trough around the lesion.

"Leyla retractors."

In succession, Steffi handed over three metallic, flexible ball-and-socket arms. I attached them to an extension from the OR table and tightened the internal cable of each retractor, causing the arms to become rigid. We then fixed the stainless steel retractor ribbons at the end of each arm to support the brain, drawing the gray and white matter away from the AVM. Gradually, under magnification, each abnormal artery and vein was electrocoagulated and severed along the edge of the mass, the micro-instruments docking like space ships within my palm as Steffi joined the siege to outflank Charlene's deadly nemesis.

Who is this woman, this Steffi? I marveled. *Where the hell did she come from?*

Steady surgical fingers moved millimeter by millimeter, avoiding a direct confrontation on the pulsating lesion. Instead I kept at the edge of the AVM, slowly isolating the enemy from its blood supply. To do otherwise invited disaster, an uncontrollable hemorrhage leading to paralysis or death or, worse, a permanent coma. The drumbeat persevered, a bit faster, perhaps, as the Doppler sound reflected Charlene's cardiac contractions in real time. Her blood pressure dropped slightly.

Five hours later, half of the AVM had disappeared as the distended vessels collapsed, succumbing to our dogged onslaught. I sat back and stretched my arms.

"How is she doing, Lois?"

"I've started a couple units of blood. We're keeping up with the loss, but I'm sure the worst is yet to come."

"I agree." I glanced at Steffi. "Where did you get the fancy cap? It adds a lot of color to our day."

"Yes," chipped in Lois. "She promised to make one for me. They're cool."

"Stop by my townhouse, Dr. Merriman. You can choose your own pattern. Uh … you, too, if you like, Dr. Stone."

"Sorry, honey," Janice hurried to say as she changed the suction filters. "The man's married."

Steffi didn't respond. Instead, another rebellious curl of honey-blonde hair sprung away from under the cap.

"I am going to rest a minute before we begin again." I opened and closed tired fingers.

"Perhaps I can help, Doctor." Stephanie stepped down to the floor and moved a splash-bowl full of warm water. A faint twist of perfume hovered near the woman. She gently grabbed my gloved hands, lowering them into the soothing liquid. With a firmness that took me quite by surprise, the scrub nurse kneaded my fingers, massaging out the fatigue and tension, her pressure melting stiffness. A part of me wanted to resist, but something stopped me.

Within minutes Steffi released her healing grip, yet this simple act set in motion a life force quite foreign to me. I felt weird, new. As something kindled within, I was even a bit fearful.

"May I take a five-minute potty break, Dr.?" asked Stephanie.

"Everything is under control. Go ahead. I don't want to change scrub nurses now."

While Janice recounted sponges, I pointed out anatomy to the resident. Steffi promptly returned and stopped by the anesthesiologist. "Do you need anything, Dr. Merriman?"

The anesthesiologist glanced up with a questioning look. "No, thank you." She then continued with check marks on her blood pressure chart.

The nurse proceeded to scrub, gown, and hop back up on the stand.

I sat back down and held up my hands, preparing to tackle the enemy once more. The suction and microscissors, already poised for action, were placed in my grip. Deeper and deeper I slipped around the nest of vipers, approaching the living center. And then—

The patient coughed on her endotracheal tube. And coughed again.

"Jesus! Lois, what's happening? She's waking up!"

"Oh, my God!" Steffi leaned over and pointed to the dimly lit floor. "Look!" An IV tubing had become disconnected.

"Christ! How on earth …?" cried Lois. The anesthesiologist grabbed the plastic line and reconnected the loose ends. "It's our drug port!"

She snatched up a syringe of pentothal and rapidly injected the anesthetic through a rubber stopper. Within seconds the patient's muscle tension receded, and everyone gave a huge sigh.

"Thank God," breathed the anesthesiologist. "Uh oh. Charlene's blood pressure dropped down from two hundred and ten to one-eighty but no further, and the pulse is slowing."

"Damn, damn, damn!" I whispered to myself. "Something's not right here." I readjusted the microscope. My index finger gently touched the cortical surface. "Dr. Tellini, release the retractor locks while I hold the blades. *Quickly!"*

"Yessir … oh, blessed Lord." Then I heard a soft prayer in Italian.

The brain was swelling, reacting to the abrupt blood pressure changes. I snapped the metal retractor ribbons away before they dug into the expanding brain. One of the small arteries in the AVM burst, a brisk flow of blood washing over Charlene's cerebrum.

"I've begun the nitroprusside, Ira. The blood pressure is falling back down, but I don't see any improvement in the brain." Lois pulled her eyes away from the TV monitor, her voice registering a trace of panic. A nurse anesthetist joined Lois, assisting with blood administration.

Steffi had already slid the suction tube into my left hand while my eyes remained glued to the awakening monster. With bayonet forceps, the scrub nurse held a cottonoid under the scope. I latched on to it with my bipolars and pressed the tiny muslin against the rent, sucking on the cotton patch. The hemorrhage ceased.

Janice, standing behind Dr. Tellini, let out another sigh of relief. "Dr. Stone? Shall I get more blood on reserve from the bank?"

"All units, please. Also have the fresh frozen plasma and platelets here in our cooler." I released pressure on the cottonoid. The field was dry. "I can't continue until the brain relaxes. Irrigation!"

Tellini washed body-temperature saline solution over the cortex again. Another fragile vein ruptured, inundating the surgical field with a film of blood. Then another vessel broke loose.

"Infuse more blood now, Lois. The swelling may be from a deep hemorrhage beyond the visible vessels. We're in for a difficult time." *Right in her speech area, damn it to hell!* "I have no choice now but to proceed," I exclaimed, mobilizing all the internal resources and training at my command. "Increase the hyperventilation and start mannitol." *Stephanie DeLeon, I hope to God you can stay with me.*

While Tellini irrigated and suctioned as ordered, Steffi continued to react one step ahead of me, her long and slender fingers delivering vital instruments, weapons then fired at the Medusa, clips and electrocautery aimed at arteries and veins bent on sucking life out of their host. The vessels fell to the assault, one after the other, but the bleeding would not cease.

"Lois, have the FFP and platelets gone in?" A note of desperation traveled with my query.

"All in. We're behind on the blood. The lab tests confirm disseminated intravascular coagulopathy. Can you hold up for a bit?"

"I can't. No matter what I do, the blood won't clot. The hemorrhage just won't stop! Got to get all the AVM out or she will bleed out on the table." I glanced up. Steffi was looking at me, her eyes filled with concern, or maybe something else …

The ping of the Doppler changed ominously. The rate picked up. Shock was setting in, and I felt as if I were losing control. What had I done wrong? I was a surgeon, dammit. Somewhere I had failed to dot an *i* or cross that *t*.

"The blood pressure is sixty," warned Merriman. Her assistant was squeezing the pressure pack encasing another unit of red blood cells.

Ninety percent of the AVM had been eradicated. But the remaining tentacles refused to bow to the assault. Blood, now running like water over a dam, refused to coagulate. I felt as if I were swimming upstream against a raging river.

"*Bipolar!*"

The forceps was already before me. I steadied my nerves, suctioned away to uncover one of several bleeders, and squeezed the bipolar tips across the culprit.

"*On!*" I commanded. Tellini stepped on the electric-current pedal. "*Hit it!*"

The brittle artery merely disintegrated, its walls refusing to seal, leaving a greater hemorrhage in its wake. Charlene's normal clotting mechanisms continued to fall to the dreaded DIC, her system failing to respond to fresh frozen plasma and platelet infusions.

The brain became softer, but I knew it was due to the plummeting blood pressure.

"*Clip!*"

Steffi handed a loaded applier. I tried to close off another artery, but the viper cracked, becoming two. The pulse beeps suddenly slowed, skipped, and then chattered.

"Oh, Lord," whispered Lois to herself, though everyone could hear. And then, "She's in ventricular fib! Pull the overhead table from the patient. Janice, call for the crash cart. *Stat!*"

"The bleeding has stopped—*because there is no blood flow through her brain!*" I raged. *Please, God. She has three children. Please, please, please …*

With dispatch Steffi cleared away the overhead trays, and I disconnected the skull pins and then covered the cerebrum with cottonoids. Another anesthesiologist rushed in and pressed his palm on Charlene's chest, pumping blood toward the cerebral hemispheres.

"*She needs cardioversion … now!*" Lois lifted paddles from the crash cart.

The minutes slipped by while Lois shocked the heart, but an anoxic death now strangled Charlene's higher centers. I knew it was too late. The brain was dying, one compartment succumbing after another, color flying from her lips and cheeks. I was stunned, my emotions battered and exhausted. The clamor in the OR seemed somehow distant to me, time slowing down. I went through the motions like a robot. Then I heard a voice. It sounded far away, echoing.

"She's dead, Ira. We did all we could." Lois, her own grim face drained of color, stood at Charlene's side, feeling for the pulse that wasn't there.

I stripped off my gloves and leaned back against the wall while the nurses covered the nude corpse, now a wax figure melting away. Dazed, my back to the wall, I slid to the floor, resting on my haunches. Tightness skewered my throat. *Naked we came and naked we leave*, the minister had said at Michael's funeral. *Naked we came and naked we leave.*

"Dr. Stone … Dr.?"

I looked up. A blurry, angelic vision seemed to waver before me. Then she spun into focus.

"Sorry, nurse." I pushed myself back up. "What do you need?"

"Here is the chart, sir. The orderlies are ready to take the body away. Do you wish to write your op note now?" While handing over the patient's record, Stephanie gazed at me with glistening eyes. She appeared to be as disturbed as I in this unkind hour.

"Yes. Thanks, Steffi. By the way, I appreciate all your help today … yours and Janice's. You both were outstanding. I … well, I … I'm sorry that we had to meet under these circumstances. I mean …"

She touched my arm. It was like a wisp of warm wind. I felt a tenderness that told more than words could express. Tenderness meant for me? Or …?

I needed to speak with Charlene's family. *God help me.*

*   *   *

An hour later, slipping through an overwhelming sense of defeat, I walked down the hall to my office, carrying with me the smell and stress of the OR. Of death. Everyone had gone home. In the glow of an evening street lamp outside my frosty window, I sat behind my desk. Strife and vertigo clutched at me. My eyes fought back tears; my frustrated hands clenched, pounding the ink blotter. I turned and stared at unfocused images of my parents, brother, sister and me, a portrait of life on the credenza, with Dad's hand on Michael's shoulder. *I am going to take your pain with me ...* Then I glanced back at a depiction of my father, but it was me. I had never noticed the scowl on my face before. There was only one kinsman that would relieve that feeling of failure, and he waited for me at home: my ever faithful Jack.

Soon there would be a morbidity and mortality conference, and I would have to explain what went wrong. But I could not explain it. How could IV tubing become dislodged, its open end laying on the floor like that? *How*, for Christ's sake? The M and M loomed ahead, and the chairman will demand answers from Merriman and me.

I left my office. Outside of our hospital complex, I crossed the parking lot. Even without looking I sensed she was there. A nurse was walking toward a red Firebird about fifty feet away. *Steffi*. My chest suddenly drew in a large quantity of air. *Should I go to her and say ... say what?*

Oh God, she's looking at me. What an angelic smile. I waved, and then with some reluctance my feet steered me away, in the direction of unstable sanity. A strange and curious presence had surrounded her, that indelible afterimage now floating in my consciousness. I almost turned back. Almost.

*   *   *

Four days passed after Charlene's surgery. I had finished with the last clinic patient of the day. A bit hyper, I stood at the office doorway, and my eyes wandered around the room, observing some wall photos from the past—an old Indian guide in Ontario, Jocelyn in her Allegheny Airlines attendant uniform, Michael water skiing. And there, above the credenza, Mike's stuffed walleye pike. I gripped the pendant hanging from my neck, feeling as if my little brother were in the room with me.

The noon hour arrived. I had planned on organizing slides for my lecture next week—"Correlative Neuroanatomy for Medical Students." Instead I sat down, snatched up a newspaper, and thumbed through it. An announcement hooked my eye. An obituary notice.

*Charlene Winston died on ... she is survived by her husband,
Daniel, and her three children, Wanda, Mary, and William
of Hershey. Remembrances may be sent to the Susquehanna
Funeral Home ... where the viewing will be held Saturday
from one to three p.m. A brief service and burial at the
Church of St. James will follow.*

My hand pushed the paper away, and my moist eyes stared out the
window, through the trees and beyond, the surgeon seeking a glimpse of
the hereafter. What would I, could I, say to Charlene when we met in time?
Looking back, I know my warped disbelief in God's divine oath came
from my very fear of the Almighty. That fear and whiskey had become
enshrined in the same coin.

*   *   *

The next day at home I sipped freshly brewed coffee while perusing the
Saturday news. My early morning headache rapidly disappeared.

"Daddy, please come with us to the Planetarium. We promise to be
quiet," begged Lexi.

"Yes, please, please, Daddy!" Denni, blond hair bouncing on her shoulders,
pulled on my hand and chipped in with, "We never get to see you."

"I have too much to do, girls. Mommy will take you to Pittsburgh,
and I will see you when you return," I hedged.

Their faces turned from childish glee to ... to something else.

After they departed, a part of me continued to agonize over Charlene's
passing and burial. Another side struggled to run away, to build up
protective escarpments, pretending it all never happened. I donned my
suit coat and walked toward my robin's-egg blue Thunderbird. A dry wind
whipped through the air, skimming around my head and neck, its fingers
pulling at my scarf. Inexorably drawn by some unseen force, I drove toward
the other side of town. An inner voice whispered, *Don't do it! Turn around.*
But it seemed as if I hadn't learned and, rendered powerless, remained a
pawn of persistent destiny. *The Church of St. James.*

*   *   *

I was no stranger to this tiger of death, a winter specter riding high on my shoulder. Long ago it had been terribly personal with my brother. But for a day, this surgical disaster under my own hands seemed somehow remote—as if someone else's fingers had held the scalpel.

The church occupied an address on an elm-lined side street. I hesitated, hearing a faint "Ave Maria," then slipped into the Southern colonial-style building. I sat down on a rear oak pew. There must have been a hundred friends and relatives in front of me. I strained to peer through the dim illumination, my eyes barely making out the frocked minister reciting passages from the Bible.

> *Simon Peter said unto him, "Lord*
> *whither goest thou?" Jesus answered him,*
> *"Whither I go, though canst not follow me now;*
> *but thou shalt follow me afterwards ... "*

As several disorienting minutes slid by, my eyes focused on the ecclesiastic surroundings, on the casket above a draped catafalque. *How long does the soul hover near the body?* was all my agnostic brain could think. Fanged shadows of past and future surrounded me, transporting memories back into that faraway day and the casket of my dead brother. My chest tingled, then tightened. My breathing was stifled, for I felt that I was now joined to Charlene inside that box, my insides screaming. Little voices floated up—the far away sobbing of her children.

I remained riveted to my seat, never more desperate to flee anywhere on this earth. Before me lay the image of my patient trapped motionless atop her bier, to join with the bones of ancestors forevermore, ghosts of those snakes, writhing, staring at me through that window in her cranium. I felt a searing pain, and I knew I *never* should have come. My hands shook so, the hands that ... that ...

Charlene and her family had entrusted me with her life. Now she was ... gone. In her death I felt terribly, frightfully alone, my soul damaged, exposed. A spasm of mortal agony passed over me. I sensed the stings of a flayed conscience, as if God—or someone—had thrust a thousand scalpels into my very core. Reverend Michelson's affirmation of the Lord's words swelled through the nave—

"Verily, verily, I say unto thee, The
cock shall not crow, till thou has denied
me thrice ... "

But his words would not stick to me. Summoning superhuman effort, I rose up, unsteady. Wary of catastrophic emotional consequences if I stayed for the burial, I knew I could not face the family this way. I retraced my steps out into the blinding winter afternoon, absolution and songs of solace trailing behind.

My eyes tightly closed and lungs grappling for air, I leaned against a Scots pine, my stomach tied in knots. Bright sunbeams triggered purple images, dazzling then rapidly resolving. A gentle breeze flowed, and then I felt a soft tugging at my coat. I opened my eyes and looked down. Next to me stood an innocent six-year-old, draped in sunlight and smiling up at me.

"You're Mommy's doctor, aren't you?" Kind blue eyes, with a trace of sorrow and trails of dried tears, gazed upward. Wanda grabbed my hand, and we began to walk together. "She really likes you 'cause you're so nice. Aren't you going to come in and wave bye-bye to Mommy?"

"I ... I already said bye-bye, Wanda." The lump in my throat constricted without mercy as I sat down on a gravestone.

"Nanny says she is in a happy place, and we will see her again." The child wrapped her arms around my neck, giving me a hug from a higher power. "I have to go back into the church now or Daddy will worry. Please come and see us again sometime. *Please.*"

I watched the angel fly back through a wilderness of mirrors and re-enter the chapel. I turned, kicking pine cones as I walked back to my car, listening to scarlet cardinals calling from elm branches. I breathed more easily now, little Wanda having released the thousand scalpels pressing against my ribs.

I drove over the pike toward Grovenor Road. Swirling images of myth and reality cascaded before me, Father standing by me like the Rock of Gibraltar. I was strong. Men don't cry ... especially doctors. We were trained to accept death. But the child in me was not, and I felt myself collapsing inside like a castle of sand.

I was relearning a dreadful lesson about the limits of my profession, and I did not want to be a surgeon anymore.

Please, please, Daddy! We never get to see you ...

I brought my car to a screeching halt, bouncing over a rocky berm, my chest constricting again, anginal fear gripping at a heart pitching in the sea of moral uncertainty. I pulled into the leaf-covered side road where clusters of elm trees stretched skyward. I grabbed my briefcase, clutching, hugging my teddy bear from a bygone era. I was forty-two. All those years without Daddy saying, *I love you, Ira.* Then the inexorable will, with which the inner child holds life to ransom, moved into play. Tears, starving for affection, broke loose, flooding a young boy's cheeks. Great drops of pain fell through my fists and onto the floorboards.

Chapter 17

The time has come the walrus said,
to talk of many things,
of shoes and ships and sealing wax,
of cabbages and kings.

Lewis Carroll
Through the Looking Glass

Appleton, Step One meeting

In our home group we had formed ourselves into the usual circle, facing each other. My turn to present Step One had arrived. *I do not want to do this. Can't we leave well enough alone? Okay, I won't drink again. I promise.* Then I saw Fletcher's white board.

THE TIME HAS COME THE WALRUS SAID ...

Our leader warned, "Many of you newer guys are thinking just what I thought many seasons ago as I faced my own virtual mirror. 'Enough is enough. Let me out of here, and I will never touch the stuff again!' Well, it doesn't work that way. This is a festering disease we have, an unrelenting cancer spreading its tendrils. This scourge will always recur should we fail to follow the message set down by Bill W. seventy years back. Step

One is the onset of a lifelong commitment that we ignore at our peril, the consequences of which are a recurrence—a *relapse* in AA and NA terminology. Such a lapse in our resolve may be lethal, to which many of us can attest. Here we are, carrying out a premortem autopsy on those of you who return to using and drinking. Witness the destruction of some of our own addicted friends and relatives."

Uncle Barley. My foot nervously tapped the tile.

"Ira, now it is your turn. Take those memories out of your vest pocket and lay them on the table. Give us the first of ten examples in your history showing how you were powerless over drugs and alcohol, how you found your life to be unmanageable," instructed Fletcher, fingering his left earlobe. "No one is to interrupt, but take mental notes for questions and comments after he is finished."

I fidgeted with the assigned paperwork I had prepared, like a reading of *Cliff Notes* summarizing a dark and menacing drama. I was more comfortable with speaking before a thousand doctors than dredging up submerged canker sores from my long-ago past, let alone doing it in front of a dozen men. Especially men, as opposed to the fairer sex—though my experiences seemed to belie the word *fair*.

Mines on a road, waiting to detonate. That was how I felt, so engulfing was this plunge years backward. The men in my home group leaned forward.

> "**December 1975.** I intended to drink one shot of Jack Daniels. Instead I had three. Well, maybe six. Nearly five ounces of whiskey used that night. **Event**—I took a Christmas gift to my scrub nurse. **Effect on others** ..."

Even then I could hear the ice cubes bouncing, tinkling, heralding the amber waterfall to come, my mouth watering this day of my baptism into a different kind of spirit. And so it began. *Come on Ira. What's the big deal? Just get through this and go home. You've done your bit.* But I couldn't stop there. They would not let me.

Penn State, Christmastime

The same evening, after I had finished rounding on my patients at the medical center I strolled aimlessly through a field of grass and trees, my feet aimed toward the parking lot, heading for my Thunderbird. My family was still in Pittsburgh, now enjoying a play, *The Sound of Music*. I was desperate to distract myself from encroaching funereal thoughts. And that beast of curiosity had awakened, Steffi's faint twist of perfume still lingering in my brain's amygdala.

It was nearly Christmas. *Christmas! All the doctors gave gifts to their nurses on this holiday. So why not me?* Then and there, while foraging about for some justification and failing to judge any consequences, I decided to get her a small holiday present. I do not even remember what it was. But I recall where she lived, in a townhouse near Lebanon, a few miles east of Hershey. With her son, she had said. Close to a golf course. I obtained the address from a phone book in my automobile trunk and headed out.

On the way I stopped at my home, picked up our cocker spaniel, and changed clothes, fumbling with everything I touched as if my motor skills had become deranged. Two shots of Jack Daniels solved that problem … no, three, as the tranquillizer began to get a stronger grip on me. My skin crawled with increasing apprehension, for I was peering down another hazardous black diamond ski run.

I studied my motives for cheating on Nadine. Well, at the moment I did not think I was really doing that. Why in God's name had I even considered going to the nurse's home? What was I thinking? The scuttlebutt was she'd been divorced and had become Fabian Tellini's girlfriend. I was a married man with two wonderful children, one in grade school and the other in junior high. Yet Nadine had become a very angry and obese lady, wracked by a heavy depression that a psychiatrist could not seem to break. The more she depended on me for her self-esteem, the greater my difficulty in relating to her, even after a multitude of marital counseling sessions. But, hey, that wasn't my fucking fault! What the hell did she expect of me? Besides, a lovely svelte nurse, highly intelligent and demure, had entered my life. A stick and a carrot. I had no clue what the blow-back might be, but at that point, that evil bedfellow Slick insisted I needn't have a care in the world.

Driving through central Pennsylvania that night was an experience, as if tunneling through the tides of time. Long tongues of hills reared up, purple in the recessional twilight, and seemed to breathe and sigh ever so slowly, reaching out to lick the byway. Insects swirled in the beams like stars cut loose from their orbits. Small wood-frame houses, dimly lit and often huddled together as if for warmth and company, leaned out of the forests while I rolled onward.

With nervous anticipation awakening, I wheeled my car into an empty spot on crushed limestone near her home and killed the motor. I sat in my car, petting Buffy while we watched a symphony of fireflies, trying to come to grips with the day's events.

Dammit, Ira, you got shit for brains. Turn this car around!

I dithered and then, with reluctance, my fingers twisted the key. The Thunderbird roared back to life, and I headed home, common sense struggling to take charge.

I got as far as a filling station a block away before I took a swig from the flask in my glove compartment. *Ira, you big chicken. She won't bite you. Go on back. Now! Nadine isn't around.* I spun the wheel and returned, coasting to a stop on gravel and stepped out of the car.

"I need another drink, dammit." An insidious burning gnawed at my insides. I caught sight of Steffi and a little boy bouncing a ball together. My heart skipped a beat. With the gift-wrapped box in my hand, sucking in a quick breath, I walked up to them. My crocodilian brain *wanted* that woman. Indeed, it could smell it, feel it, taste it.

And then there was that boy.

"Mommy?" The child, gripping a softball, stamped his feet on hard clay.

I smiled at the lad. "I loved to play ball when I was your age." Turning toward Steffi I stammered, "Hello Steff ... uh ... Miss ... Miss ..."

"DeLeon. My, what a surprise." She hesitated for a breathy second, perhaps two. "Hi, Dr. Stone. Meet my son, Mikey."

"Mikey?"

"Well, it's Michael, but he prefers Mike. Or Mikey." She bent down. "Honey, say hello to the doctor."

"'Lo." The lad glanced at his mother and drew back, standing eye level with the cobalt bad-girl pedal pushers, the nylon barely covering her pelvic bones and shrink-wrapped so tightly it announced every curve and valley of that whippet body. Yet there was a contradictory aristocratic bearing.

Mikey pointed at Buffy. "Oggy."

"Doggy," repeated Steffi. "Isn't he cute." She stood up. "What is his name?"

"Buffy. It's a she." I stroked the puppy's neck and waved at Mikey. "Want to pet her? She really likes little boys."

He glimpsed up at Mom and inched toward the puppy, her tail beating the air.

"It's okay, Buddy." While Mikey patted Buffy's head, Steffi explained, "Buddy is his nickname. His … uh … father … started calling him that. We divorced two years ago. He's … gone. Mike is living somewhere in North Dakota, I think. Drilling oil wells, or some such."

"Oil? His skills must have been in great demand."

"I guess." She became somewhat evasive, as if carefully threading her way back from the past while scuffing gravel with her running shoes. Then Steffi watched Mikey play with Buffy. "His last name was Starling. I took my maiden name back."

"Sorry. Didn't mean to pry. Say, are you thirsty or anything? Maybe Buddy would like a milkshake? There is a Baskin-Robbins not too far from here."

"Thanks, but it's his bedtime." This woman of Celtic delight took in a deep breath, stretching her blouse. "You're more than welcome to come in, if you like. For coffee … or whatever. If you don't mind the mess. Maybe you could treat Mikey to his storybook while I straighten things up?"

"What do you say, Michael? Want to hear a good story?"

Mikey was more interested in Buffy, fascinated by the wagging tail. "Oggy!" He tried to hug Buffy's neck.

"Buddy, be careful. That is just a puppy dog." Steffi pushed Mikey toward the front door. "It's time to go in, my love."

"I'll take you up on your offer." Remaining trapped in the beam of her charm, I fell to her suggestion. "Is it okay if I leave my car here?"

"Of course, Doctor." Steffi threw me an amused look and brushed a tangle of hair from her forehead. She tossed back her head, revealing the soft white of her throat. I had the strangest notion the nurse was taking my measure.

And I hers. My eyes captured the fair woman's figure with greater care. About five-six, lithe and long-legged, sloe-eyed, a demure smile. Her right cheek had a mole, the beauty spot holding my attention for few seconds. Big gold hoop earrings dangled from her ears. Her pelvis swayed in a remotely provocative fashion as she walked ... or was I merely reading suggestion into the image? A series of contradictory shudders sluiced their way through me, the haunting distraction not altogether unpleasant.

"By the way, Steffi, I appreciate all your help at surgery. You have been outstanding. Here is a small Christmas gift in appreciation." Now I remember—a box of Swiss chocolates.

* * *

"... '*different* tiddely pom,' said Pooh, feeling rather muddled now. 'I'll sing it to you properly and then you'll see.' What do you think of that, Mikey?" I gave the boy's shoulders a squeeze.

"Read more." Mikey fidgeted on the couch, quite excited, perhaps because a man was telling the story.

"Bedtime, my little one," Steffi chipped in.

"No bed, Mommy! I want Pooh!" the boy cried, kicking his feet up and down.

"Now, now, Buddy. Let's be nice, if you want the nice doctor to read to you again." She latched on to Mikey's bare feet, tickling the bottoms, and the lad let out a high-pitched giggle. Mikey's toes attracted my eye.

"He has webbed skin between the outer three toes of his feet," I noted. "Wow, you have mallard blood, Michael."

Mikey looked at Mom, a quizzical expression on his face.

"He means you have wonderful feet and can swim like a duck," she laughed. Steffi glanced at me. "He was born with some webbing of his toes, but it's not enough for any corrective surgery. It just makes him more special."

Michael grew a half an inch in ten seconds.

I nodded and lifted Mikey up, noting his proud, smiling amber eyes. Like Steffi's. I was taken aback when the boy planted a kiss on my cheek. How strange, the feeling inside me. For some reason the image of Wanda came to mind—*Daddy says she is in a happy place and we will see her again.*

The scent of perfume drifted by—Panthere de Cartier—as Steffi leaned over to pick up her son. And I, in free fall, found myself breathing her in once again. She had changed her blouse. No, just the top buttons had been unfastened, revealing a gold locket on a chain. But it was the cleavage that gripped my attention. I struggled to look away. If I didn't, I would be undone on the spot.

"Mikey, say good night to Uncle Ira," she prodded. "And to Buffy."

"Read Pooh ... read Pooh," Mikey whimpered.

"I apologize, Dr. ... uh ... Okay to call you Ira? I mean, when we're not working together?" Looking down at the carpet, she permitted herself a smile.

"Please do," my tongue replied, taking its next step toward that fecund tree bearing forbidden fruit.

"He usually minds quite well. It's not often we're graced by such a super storyteller."

She whisked Michael into her arms, nuzzled him with her nose, and marched toward the steps leading up to his bedroom, all the while singing in a military cadence, "Bud-a-rum, bud-a-rum, bud-a-rum ... bum ... bum. Bud-a-rum, bud-a-rum, bud-a-rum ..." And I heard the boy laugh as they disappeared.

I stood up to stretch. Giving me new energy, wayward thoughts popped again into my head—the anticipation of a pleasured evening, perhaps. I did not know what I expected. I gazed around the small living room. It felt cozy—two solid-blue armchairs, a tiger-striped gold and emerald divan flanked by mahogany end tables, and a multicolored Tabriz rug through the center of the room. I wondered if Steffi and her former husband had purchased the carpet in the Mideast, seeing that he was an engineer for oil companies.

The Good News Bible lay on one of the end tables flanking the couch, George Bernard Shaw's *The Miraculous Revenge* on the other. Buffy had fallen asleep next to a heating vent. I felt as if I had driven the Thunderbird from one country into another, as if something new and strange were about to happen—a life beyond my understanding—and I needed to learn a new language, study a very strange culture.

I began leafing through Shaw's short story when a distraction caused my gaze to rest on one wall. A photograph of a woman, likely in her mid-thirties, hung slightly askew. In the image she seemed surprised, with an air of being caught off guard by the photographer. Her hair, streaked brunette, hung in pageboy fashion, with the ends curled inward. The lady held the hands of two rail-thin girls, each with almond-shaped eyes. I approached the portrait. I was certain one was Steffi, perhaps twelve, with her honey-blond hair braided, a black Labrador puppy in her arms; the younger girl's strawberry-blond hair was styled like her mother's. They were standing on a dock at water's edge. Perhaps her father was behind the camera, the origin of a gauzy shadow thrown toward the captured pair. I felt a strange spectral force emanating from the grainy snapshot of an earlier time. My eyes jerked back to the strawberry blonde once more.

A sudden headache, accompanied by blurry visions of a deathly white girl, spun past me and then died away. I shook my head and took in a deep breath, shaking, not knowing why. As my erratic pulse stabilized, came another voice.

"Recognize her? Can you believe Stephanie DeLeon once wore her hair in pigtails?" chuckled the girl behind me.

Her voice startled me. It seemed throaty, sexy. I was almost afraid to turn around. I could feel her closeness, and a thousand overlapping thoughts raced through my mind. Thoughts of …

"I … uh … which one?"

"The pretty one with the *pigtails*, silly. On the left, of course."

"Uh huh." My reasoning processes were in serious trouble.

"My sister there died after a head injury."

"I'm sorry. You must miss her." I turned slowly, only able to concentrate on the warmth behind me. "And I … uh … notice you've … ah … grown up a lot."

I slowly pivoted, finding myself face to face with glistening golden-browns, the two of us breathing each other's oxygen, my polo shirt millimeters from provocative breasts behind soft velour, her scent a magnet. "Take a Chance on Me" played in the background. The spark within, once dampened, ignited, and now the fuse was lit and burning—and almost out of control.

"Dance?" she asked, scrunching her shoulders and placing her hands around my neck, her bedazzling eyes never leaving mine. "Those cramps in your hands, are they all gone?"

"Yes, thanks." I tried to come up with a sagacious or witty comment, but I remained tongue-tied. Her hair had slipped its mooring, now falling free beside comely cheeks, the appearance more than a bit seductive.

"Merry Christmas," she breathed. "You've certainly brightened a boy's holiday."

As a fetching smile made its way to lips of peach red, the space between us melted and disappeared. I found my arms embracing her narrow waist. The melody slid into "Does Your Mother Know?" as we glided across the Tabriz. She moved up against my body, her pelvis brushing the growing tightness in my crotch. Her warm breath flowed across my face, and a mysterious passion infected me. Like food filling a hungry stomach, the mere presence of Steffi seemed to sate a long dormant desire, and logic could not defeat that feeling.

Our lips moved dangerously close. I noticed a lone tear sliding down her left cheek. It caught on a fine scar running sharply toward her mouth, hesitated, and tracked along the nearly invisible white line. I slowed to a standstill and wiped the droplet away with my thumb. It was nigh unto impossible not to touch the scar. Indeed, it was now a trial not to caress every part of her body.

"Steffi, you're crying. What is the matter?"

"I feel so terrible about what happened on Monday. I've been thinking about it every day. I don't even sleep at night … just dream. Nightmares. How on earth do you keep your sanity?" The nurse peered into my eyes and sighed.

"Steff. You can't imagine the troubled feelings I've had. I'm sort of overwhelmed. I … I've really had no one to talk with."

"But your wife …?" She scratched her left forearm and then jerked her right hand away. "Surely she understands?"

"Nadine? She has her own issues, I suppose. I think that discussions of death and dying are too threatening for her. Lord knows, I found out how much Charlene's passing just about drove *me* off the deep end."

"Oh, Ira, if only I could help." Steffi pulled me even closer to her, and I sensed a rising passion of need flowing between us. At least that is what I thought at the time. She pulled her arms from around my neck and grabbed my hand. "As your nurse, I prescribe Jack Daniels and soda this very instant."

How did she know what I drink?

Stephanie inched away, space and light reappearing between us once more.

Eyes glinting, she drew me back to the couch, removed a nursing journal from on top of a cushion, and patted the couch, insisting I sit down.

"Steffi, I don't want to cause you any difficulty. You have been more than …"

But she disappeared around the corner, into her kitchen. I heard the tinkling sound of ice rattling in glasses, once and then again, as the music changed.

"Buffy," I whispered. "What am I doing here? It's your job to keep me out of mischief."

"Ira, are you talking to yourself?" Steffi glided in and, with a flourish, handed me a cold tumbler of my favorite potion, hair cascading over her face as she leaned forward.

"To Buffy. She's my conscience." I accepted the cocktail, studied the bubbles clinging to ice cubes, and took a measured sip. And then another.

"Yes, here is to Buffy, our conscience." Steffi sat down to my right and raised her glass lightly against mine, the clinking sound awaking the cocker spaniel.

"Our" conscience?

Buffy jumped up and crawled between Steffi and me, settling her snout on her master's thigh. I smiled and stroked the sable coat along her spine.

"Well, I can see who rates here," Steffi bantered after swallowing a dollop of her drink.

She laid her left hand on top of mine, slowing my motion. "I ... I had a puppy dog once."

I felt her shudder. It was strange, as if a warm Caribbean wave were suddenly breaking over a submerged coral reef, her fingers like dancing sea anemone.

"The one in the picture?" I wondered aloud. "He or she looks like a black Lab."

"Her name was Missie," Steffi permitted, her tone whispery, perhaps confiding a filigreed secret. "She died from ... from ... she just died. I buried her in our garden ... close to where that photo was taken." Steffi, still holding on to my hand, her response vague, paused as if distilling formless memories. "She ... and my sister ... were my world. Maybe that is why Charlene's death disturbs me so much."

I failed to understand the connection. I decided this was not the time to peek into the past of a woman I'd so recently met.

"Steffi, I ... uh ..." I swirled the ice and quaffed another sip. "I went to Charlene's funeral today. I suppose I was wrong to even consider doing so. I've never experienced that before. I mean attending the last rites of a patient. I ... I mean who died during surgery ... my surgery."

"Yes," was all she whispered.

I felt uncomfortable and hesitated. Baring my feelings was a new trial for me. But within minutes my agony had slipped loose, that anguish radiating from a hidden place that now only she was allowed to see. A stranger. And that surprised me.

The nurse pivoted her head way from me, hiding her face. "Oh, Ira. I can't imagine. I know that I could not have stood the hurt." I sensed the pressure of her tremulous fingers, now wrapped around mine, fingers that delivered a brief but suddenly painful squeeze as she turned back.

Black Hills gold. That's what came to mind as I stared into her eyes, seeing flecks of canary yellow patterned among the chestnut brown in each iris, her pupils widely dilated, their powerful void drawing me inside, beyond the dewdrops on her lashes.

"Thanks for understanding, Steffi." I tore my gaze from hers, struggling to find a safe place to look, settling for a tiny glacier bobbing up and down in my bourbon. "I had to leave … watching the body … her children …" I felt my chin stiffen. "It's … nearly impossible for me to explain."

Buffy slid back to the carpet and curled by a chair.

"Don't even try. I saw what you did at the operation. You were *so* masterful, and I was very proud to work with you." She set her crystal down, grasped my face with both hands, and turned me toward her.

Steffi paused, and I felt a bonding, like the longing souls of two bodies being welded together. She drew me closer, her hair falling in feathered patterns on either side of flushed cheeks. Our lips were poised on the brink of hazardous commitment, at the dawn of a new destiny. I knew it was too late. I knew not who made the first move.

Her warm hands slid from my cheeks and reached to the back of my neck. At the same time, I placed my drink on the floor and pulled her against me, our wanting lips within a hairbreadth of each other and then suddenly pressing, melting. Warm. Soft. Then hard, the strength and intensity stunning. Her mouth opened widely to receive my tongue, a sensual moan traveling from deep within her throat. She started to pant through her nose, a fiery breath, as she lightly massaged my neck, electrostatic energy flying from her fingertips to the very nerve endings of my skin. I entered a long, soaring moment as alcohol and the promise of sex severed the tendons of any will to resist.

Brittle chains snapped loose, and a cold jacket of Yellowstone ice melted from my heart. I felt as if I were sinking into comfortable amniotic fluid, too frightened to move for fear the dream would end. Her hands slipped over my shoulders and down my back, her fingers crawling under my sweater, caressing, slowly moving around to my stomach and up to my chest.

"Hmmm ... nice and furry," Steffi purred as she laid her head on my shoulder. "I don't suppose you'd consider staying with me tonight? I have plenty of Jack Daniels."

Her index finger touched my nipple, ever so softly. A spark gap. That message sent an electromagnetic field reverberating through my gut. My crotch tensed even more as I fell headlong into her persistent entreaty, handcuffs snapping shut.

"You're not leaving me a whole lot of choice," came my reply in a whisper. "You've got my complete attention." My wayward hand tossed down another gulp of spirits to smooth the pathway.

She smiled a coy grin, the ends of her lips turning downward, then untangled her fingers from under my sweater and brushed back a lock of hair with her left hand. The right descended, resting on my thigh, nearly, but not quite, touching the tumescence straining against the threads of my trousers and driving deeper the innate urge to couple, to plunder her heavenly body.

The nurse lightly pressed her face next to mine and softly bit my earlobe, whispering, "Well, then, my good doctor, I must attend to my bedroom. It's on this floor, in the back. Fix us both another drink, if you like, and make yourself comfortable."

"Uh, is Buddy okay? I mean ..."

"He's out like a light. You may go up and check on him. At the end of the hall, beyond the spare room."

I heard the soft click of her door closing.

*   *   *

Stephanie caught me just as I finished tiptoeing back down.

"What a handsome young man your son is, Steffi. And you ... uh ... just took my breath away. I have your drink ready."

We met halfway down the corridor. In a misty fragrance she held out her arms, and I grasped her hands with mine.

"Is Buddy asleep?" Steffi rubbed my wrists between her thumb and forefinger.

"Totally out. I couldn't help noticing earlier that he has eyes the exact color of yours." I pulled her a bit closer, noticing then she seemed to chew on her right cheek in a weird undulating fashion, though I paid little attention to the habit.

"My mother's were the same. Little Michael inherited most of his other physical characteristics from his father. Even his personality—Michael has a calm and even disposition. I'm a bit more excitable, I guess." She rose up on her tiptoes and pressed her breasts against my polo shirt.

"You mean exciting, Nurse DeLeon. I have never met anyone quite like you." I wrapped my arms around her, drawing her in hard against me in a tight embrace.

"Ira!" Steffi suddenly screamed, breaking away from my clasp. *"Ira, stop! You're hurting me!"*

"Steff? What ...?" I tripped backward against the wall, still holding onto her hand.

"I was suffocating, Ira. *Damn you!* Didn't you know you were hurting me?" She appeared dizzy, frightened, her eyes volcanic and fearsome, her sudden rage rifling through me like a blast of hot air. *"Am I next?"*

"Next? What? Good God! I'm sorry, Steffi. How ... where?"

But she turned her head from me so I could no longer see her face. Ignoring my query, Steffi jerked her hands from mine and darted for the kitchen, myself in stunned pursuit. She looked at the tumbler of whiskey and folded both of her hands around it. Seemingly oblivious to all else, the woman put the glass to her lips and emptied its contents. Still shaking, she yanked open a drawer, nearly dislodging it from the cabinet, rattling the cutlery. Tremulous fingers untwisted a bottle cap, shook two pills into her palm, and tossed them into her mouth. Then she filled her empty crystal with tap water and swallowed the medication. It was a wonder that she did not shatter the vessel.

Stephanie, sinking into an emotional tar pit, slid to the floor, her eyelids closed, mascara bleeding, arms wrapped around herself, fingernails digging into her quaking shoulders.

Recovering from a state of near psychic concussion myself, I gaped at the crumpled figure on the kitchen floor. Her hair hung like a golden waterfall, covering her face. Steffi's sapphirine gown, adhering to the wallpaper, now failed to cover her bared legs and pelvis. Her bent knees were pulled together, falling to her left. I saw a faint ectoplasmic glow about her, and that frightened me.

My eyes swept over the helpless woman, her nubile beauty staggering, my blood still boiling after the invitation to a night of heated passion. At least I'd thought it was an invitation. Finally, I swallowed and willed some semblance of calm to gain a foothold.

"Steffi ...?" I hesitated, tiptoeing through strange landscape, unsure what had just transpired. "May I help you up, Steff?"

"Nnn ... no," she stuttered.

With agonizing slowness, her head wobbled side to side. The glass of water dropped away and rolled with a clatter over the linoleum. Her fingers jerked, claw-like, the woman neither asleep nor totally awake.

Not wishing to precipitate another outburst, I backed away, forcing my gaze from the curly honey-brown hairs of womanhood carpeting her mons veneris, her mountain of love. Still, I had an overwhelming desire to pull her back into my arms, to tell her I ... *My God, am I in love with her?*

I felt as if my heart were beating at the base of my throat, the idea thrilling, scary, even terrifying. Love, honor, and cherish—my wedding vows to Nadine, the three sacred dimensions of marriage. *How did I get mixed up in this new and crazy affair?* I asked myself. *With my scrub nurse! I'm a grown man. A surgeon. I should know better, for crissake!* I grabbed the half-empty bottle of Jack Daniels by its neck and fired two desperate swallows down my throat, smoothing neural pathways for delayed carnal desire.

I stepped past Steffi and picked up the container of pills. No label, yet the shape and color of the tablet, round and pink, were unmistakable. Quaalude—enough to sedate a large man. And Steffi weighed one hundred and twenty pounds, if that. I glanced back at my fallen nightingale. Eyelids half shut, slow breaths. She remained sitting upright in her eerie repose. Again I thought I saw a blue halo shimmering around her damp skin, as if a field of unstable electrons were collapsing. Then it disappeared. I must have imagined it. What form of creature truly lived inside Nurse Stephanie DeLeon?

I couldn't just leave her there on the floor. I leaned down and parted her hair so I might see her face. The eyes were blank and canceled, retreating to some point in the great beyond, both pupils widely dilated—so wide that I once more nearly tumbled headlong into them.

Strange, I reasoned. *Neither this tranquilizer nor alcohol does that to the eyes.*

"Steffi, let me help you to bed."

"Sss … sorry, Dr. Stone. Sometimes I get these terrible migraine headaches. I know you did your best."

Did my best? What is she talking about?

Steffi leaned forward and pulled down her negligee. Her hands kept overshooting their mark. Suddenly she shot me a brief hateful, almost malignant look, as if eyes and mouth were mounting an attack, but then she fell back into a hypnotic trance.

I latched onto both of her moist wrists and raised her up, Stephanie's legs teetering. She appeared drawn, as if a plague had worked its vengeance on her. With mixed feelings, I placed an arm around her slender waist, held tight, and led her into the bedroom. I could feel her now-steady breathing and smell her perfume, the taste of her kisses lingering. She leaned into the bed, finally rolling onto her side. Her lids closed as she surrendered herself to a deep sleep. In the background the music gave way to UB40 playing "Red, Red Wine." I pulled up her coverlet and clicked off the table lamp, feeling myself pulled into the complicated current of a bizarre woman's life, a perilous something hemmed in and restrained, a carrot hiding a barbed hook. I shivered and then turned toward the door.

Before departing, I peeked in on little Mike. The boy's arms were clutching a book with a picture of Pooh and Piglet on the front cover, Pooh's fist trapped inside a honey jar.

In the living room, I picked up Buffy and aimed toward the foyer. The photo of Steffi, her sister, their mother, and Missie snagged my attention again. Sometime between then and now the scar on Stephanie's cheek and soul had been inflicted. The frame was slightly tilted, and I took my fingertip and realigned the portrait. Who had been holding the camera? The father? A white-noise chill washed through me, and I didn't know why.

But it was the strawberry blonde with cerulean blue eyes who again grabbed me most. *DeLeon ... DeLeon. Stella? Stella! Oh my God oh my God oh my God!* My world tilted as memories, roosting like bats, suddenly fluttered from their caves. My brain, smothered by alcohol and the promise of sex, had been ridiculously naïve, failing to peer around that death mask. I had been in denial. Trembling, I lingered for a moment and then departed, letting the front portal snap shut behind me, "Red, Red Wine" disappearing. I dreaded the nightmares my sleep would endure.

The anguish of the evening and the pleasure of the drink seemed to be merging at an unsettling velocity, denying me my options as some form of evil became a new perversion of that very pleasure. God help me, I could not stop myself. I was trapped in the valley of Steffi's bosom, her cleavage singing to me. A Siren's quicksand.

Stephanie DeLeon Starling was a terrific nurse. Indeed.

And lovely. More than lovely. Plus something indefinable, disturbing.

And I wanted her.

But now a Peace Corps worker reappeared, and I needed to relieve the suffocation. My earlobe, once stinging pleasantly from my nurse's bite, now felt cold and wet from her saliva.

*   *   *

Upon returning home, I watched Buffy. She panted and lifted her forepaw. I tossed two biscuits onto Buffy's rug and then poured myself another JD. While the grateful dog chewed away, I walked into the living room and sat at the piano. My nervous digits danced across the keyboard, searching for a solution to the DeLeon puzzle that threatened to destabilize my carefully planned future.

Twists and turns of liquid thoughts kept surfacing. First, Charlene.

And then Steffi. One dead, the other alive. Guilt, and then obsession. Snakes suffused with blood, hemorrhaging. Erotic fingers crawling under my sweater, caressing. An EKG warning—*beep, beep, beee ...* A scream— *Ira, stop! You're hurting me!* Dilated, frozen pupils from a dead Charlene. Expanded, hypnotizing pupils of a living Stephanie. Both women with twin black pools still excavating my mind.

Finally, sleep overtook me, but two more women now slept in my bed, dislocating my sense of time. I should have run away as fast as I could.

Chapter 18

Swirl, swirl!
How the ripples curl
in many a dangerous pool awhirl!

E. Pauline Johnson
The Song My Paddle Sings

Appleton, Step One Meeting continued

At each meeting three or four patients gave examples of their powerlessness over alcohol or drugs. This morning James, a hard-core addict, began his story. I was to follow. James, a local boy of thirty-five, had close-set eyes sunk deep in their sockets, propped up by dark rings. The man, six-five in stature, had heavy black hair. He started with the usual introduction. James then launched into his description, his voice raw and shaky. He had already attended two treatment centers, yet he'd relapsed within a few weeks. The man was trained as an engineer but had not worked for over three years. He just couldn't let go of that cunning, baffling, and powerful drink.

"And I was receiving disability income after my back fracture, so Christie, my wife, had to go back to waitressing. Besides, the judge took my driver's license after my last DWI. Christie left me home to take care of the two girls. Junie is two years and Leslie only six months. I kept sneaking out to this corner I know to get some OxyContins for my back pain. So

Christie hid the keys ... but I had copies. Then she put a Club lock on the steering wheel. Well, I got a towing company to remove that thing. Later, I totaled that Ford. Fuck it all.

"I sold the children's toys and clothes to buy alcohol 'n drugs. I couldn't get to her bank account or purse. When she gave me grocery money, I lied about the bill so's I could get cash back.

"One afternoon last month I put the kids into their little wagon and hauled them down the street to the State Store. Got my Ancient Age and made a stop at the park. Drank the whole damn bottle and passed out. When the wife got home and found no one there, she got in her old Chevy Malibu and drove around. She must have been truly hysterical."

James started crying, grief choking down into his guts, his back heaving, shoulders shuddering. We all shifted in our chairs. I wasn't sure he was going to finish the story. Another new patient began to hand him a box of Kleenex but was waved away by Fletcher.

"Some woman found little Junie standing on the main street and bawling her eyes out. It was raining. And cold. And ... and ... Junie was taken to the police station, and they called Christie. The wife had put a wrist bracelet with Junie's name and phone number on her tiny wrist."

James fidgeted with a pencil, silent, working his mouth.

"Are you finished?" inquired Fletcher. "What about the infant?"

"They never found Leslie." The pencil snapped in two, pieces dropping into his lap, the patient reduced to a despairing, breathless whimper. "Never found her ... never found her."

"How do you feel now, James?"

"How the fuck do you think I feel?" cried the man, his pain exploding from beneath a thin and shaky veneer of human skin.

"Anything more you want to relate?"

After a few deep breaths, "I ... I took up with this here lady ... well, I guess she weren't no lady ... after waking up in her bed. I swear I don't know how I got there. I caught herpes and gave it to my wife. Then Christie up and went to live with her mother and took Junie. The judge sent me here. Again."

"Comments, anyone? Derrick?"

That afternoon—life unmanageable

"Quiet down, everyone. Let Ira continue his first step." Fletcher nodded in my direction. "Ira?"

"Hi, my name is Ira, and I am an alcoholic."

"Hey, Ira!"

"So, of course, Ira, you walked away as any sane man would do, did you not?" Fletch asked, tongue-in-cheek.

"Not exactly." With pregnant yet unsettling thoughts, I wondered how I had allowed myself to be sucked even deeper into her clutches. But, God help me, I liked it.

"Please note, gentlemen, how the daily intake of alcohol, even when there is no detectable blood level in our body, has a sustaining and corrupting effect on our thinking, days, weeks, even months after we stop drinking. Our sick brain even yet might harbor the delusion that a lady's flattery will never compromise." Fletcher nodded at me. "And then?"

I felt as if I were paddling through a swamp, my home group now fifteen pairs of red eyes hovering just above the water level among the twisted cypress roots, alligators all hoping I would fall from my skiff. Paranoia still infected my alcoholic brain.

How the fuck do you think I feel?

Christmas time, Hershey, Pennsylvania

My working hours had returned to at least eighty or ninety per week as I approached the height of my career. Before the present days of resident training management by our sterling PhD educators who replaced the doctors working in the trenches, physicians were quite accustomed to such rigor. Our spouses, in large part, were not. I often arrived at my castle just off Church Road at nine o'clock or later. Nadine, bless her, had dinner ready. Before eating, it was my habit to jog over the nearby hills, followed by cocktails—Jack Daniels or Canadian Club to deaden the turmoil within. Soon, other matters affected my late arrival home, affairs driving my behavior in ways I never would have thought possible.

* * *

We leaned over stainless steel basins and completing the ritual of cleansing forearms prior to surgery. Soapy water dripped from our elbows. We wore green scrub suits, our lower faces covered with masks.

"Dr. Tellini, how many times must I tell you? In this country the mask must cover the nose as well as the mouth," I sighed, irritated. *One of these days ...* "I'll have the nurse fix it for you. Again."

"Yes, sir. Sorry, sir. Thank you, sir."

"Tellini, is this your first meningioma case?"

"First one. I studied up on ... mff ... thank you, Miss ... the tumor last night after stitching a scalp laceration in the ER." Fabe Tellini squirted more Hibiclens soap on his hands. "This patient's mass seems rather large on the cerebral angiogram. I'm surprised she doesn't have more symptoms. Just headaches and a clumsy left hand."

I kneed the metal plate, releasing more water. My nose twitched at the strong scent of cologne drifting from my resident.

"Unlike glioblastomas, these benign tumors are slow-growing," I explained to the trainee. "The cerebrum is seventy percent water, and local pressure squeezes out the water as if the brain were a sponge. The neurons, though displaced by the mass, can function for months or years until reactive swelling or seizures occur." I kicked off the knee-high water switch and backed my way into the operating theater, where the lyrics of "Please Mr. Postman" welcomed me.

"Good morning, Dr. Stone." Steffi beamed a smile, one at the same time disturbing and becalming.

She winked and handed me a sterile towel to dry my arms and then turned around to her instrument table. After my heart resolved into a stable thump-thump, I returned her greeting. My eyes latched onto her colorful cap, and I remembered her invitation to stop by her home and choose one for myself. Somehow, I had forgotten to pick up the prize.

"Hi, Ira." Dr. Merriman glanced up from our patient's chart. "Her blood pressure is one-hundred thirty over eighty-five. I've dropped the

pCO_2 to twenty-eight. The spinal drain is off now. For a seventy-year-old lady, she is in excellent health … apart from her tumor."

"Lois, you might continue her Decadron."

"The steroid is in. Ten milligrams."

Steffi returned from the back table. Standing before me, she held out a sterile gown, and I ran my arms through the sleeves while the circulating nurse, Janice Blake, tied the backside of the gown. The heat of the moment was almost unbearable. I watched Steffi lift a pair of sterile rubber gloves off the table and shuttle back.

"Size nine, correct?" She stretched the left glove open to receive my hand, cocking her head. She gave a big sigh. "Larger than most surgeons use."

"Uhh … huh." I slipped in one hand, and then she stretched open the other glove. "Perfect fit, Steffi … thanks." I looked up and met her gaze, drowning in the twin indigos.

A cough followed by a clearing of the throat came from the other nurse behind me.

"Will you be using ultrasound, Dr.?" Stephanie inquired. "We have it in the room ready to go." Her eyes would not release mine.

"Most likely." *Break away, Ira.* I pivoted toward the resident, my ego searching for a life preserver.

"Prep her now, Fabian." *Steffi's playmate,* I nearly added. "We haven't got all day." *I'd give a fortune to know what each of them is thinking.*

After draping the patient, I prepared to incise the scalp. "Lois, okay to begin?"

"Anytime." Dr. Merriman snatched up her clipboard and penned check marks to map the pulse and BP.

I looked to my right. Steffi reached in front of the resident and handed over the scalpel. A sliver of crimson rose as I pressed the blade into the patient's skin above the right ear. Tellini used the suction tube to aspirate away the trail of blood. The young man was, in fact, becoming a very good surgeon.

We hardly spoke a word as the surgery progressed. Like the magical sword Excalibur, the proper instrument appeared. Always on time, or, perhaps, a second before, even in the dark, after the microscope had been ferried into position. I picked up the pace, and Steffi stayed with me, teammates working hand-and-glove again. The tumor did not stand a chance. I wondered if I did.

* * *

The resident was placing a final staple into the scalp wound as I pulled off my gown and slammed it into a hamper. The galea had kept tearing when sutures were tightened, annoying me.

"Nice work, Dr. Stone. I sent the tumor to pathology," commented Janice, the circulator. "Tamera will be back on duty tomorrow. Steffi has been assigned to another service. Cardiocascular is short of help, so …"

Jesus. I'd forgotten. A twinge of panic rapidly converted to unfocused anger. My face felt suddenly tight-skinned, my chest wall tingling. I glanced at Steffi but saw only her backside as she cleared instruments off a Mayo tray. Of course. She had been pinch-hitting while Tamera was ill. And Tamera Vintner was an excellent scrub nurse. So why did I have this unwashed and curdling sensation, as if I were losing control. I maintained an iron silence, but my hands, governed by an obscure center, fisted into knots of tamped-down fury, a collage of stifled emotions hammering at reason, a Nordic firestorm of blind rage taking charge.

Suddenly the dam broke loose, irrational behavior spilling over. I lifted a nearby glass IV-fluid bottle from its stand and hurled it against a side wall, the deafening crash resounding throughout the theater as ruptured glass exploded.

"Damn it to hell!" I spun around and aimed toward the side exit, four stunned people staring at me. "You can't do that! Switching scrub nurses back and forth on me! *No, goddamn it! Why … are … you … messing … with … me!"*

As I neared a side exit, the main double doors burst open.

"Sweet Mary and Joseph! What is going on in here!" The OR supervisor swiveled her capped head this way and that. "We heard an explosion! *And* some *very* unpleasant language."

The female commandant surveyed the room, her constipated cheeks and rimless bifocals targeting the thousand little glass pieces reflecting from the floor. She then regarded me with a poisoned stare. The hefty matron stood still, fisted hands digging into generous hips.

"Just an unfortunate accident. Dr. Stone bumped into the pole supporting the IV bottle, and it hit the wall," explained Lois. The anesthesiologist looked at the two nurses. "No harm done. Our patient is fine."

"Hummph. *If* you say so." She glared at Steffi, who happened to fall in her line of sight. "Well, don't just stand there. You have another case to follow."

The supervisor, her countenance still harboring an advancing pinch, wheeled about and stomped out of the room, one hand still on her hip, the other fluttering to her generous bosom.

"Jees-us H Christ! What's with her?" wondered Steffi a bit too loudly. "It's a miracle her lips don't disappear completely into her face … uh, sorry."

"Welcome to Penn State, Steffi," snickered Janice, shoulders shaking with stifled mirth. "This is one of Hester's better days. What she really needs is a good fu …"

"Now, now, Janice," chided Lois. "Even the walrus has ears. The patient is waking up. Let's get her to Recovery." Dr. Merriman, a miniscule smile playing on her lips, glanced at Steffi and then me, finally slipping a stethoscope into her ears.

I resumed my departure for the doctors' lounge, the fractured glass imprinted on my mind, the splinters of my life. Humpty Dumpty was all I could think. I knew I would be called to account in the chairman's office. What I couldn't address was the reason for my unseemly behavior as my life became more and more unmanageable. What was that all about?

Walking down the hallway, I tried to organize a student lecture in my mind, but the reason for my outburst kept intruding. I stopped by the office to check on the mail before heading out to see patients. My secretary looked up from an insurance form as I walked in through a side entrance. The fifty-two-year-old woman had a frown on her face, her ruby lips tightly gripping each other. Gray streaked her neck-length raven-black hair. She was chewing and cracking bubble gum and then quickly slipped the Bazooka from her mouth with tissue paper.

"Dr. Stone, I wish you wouldn't sneak in like that. I thought you were in surgery all day." With a frustrated sigh, Evelyn Fillmore tossed the recalcitrant document into a pile of similar papers. "More trees cut down to produce this sh ... uh ... mess."

"Hi, Evelyn. We finished early. So what's new on the home front? Is Clifford's leg healing okay?" I loosened my tie.

"Oh, sure. I think he is using the fracture as an excuse to avoid returning to work. I informed my hubby that I was going to break another limb if he sits around watching TV much longer," kidded Evelyn. "He says he's planning on seeing you for a second opinion. Hah! I explained to him that you operated on brains and that maybe you could do a transplant."

I chuckled. "Well, tell him I said hello. Any calls?"

"Just those eight-hundred-number guys wanting you to justify why you need to do a disc operation on ... I can't remember which patient it was now. I reminded them that you have spent enough hours spinning your wheels, returning their calls, and playing tag with their voice mails. I don't think I am on their favorite people list."

"It's the times we live in, Evelyn. Think I'll go next door and do a bit of freshening up. Maybe shave and put on a clean shirt." I bit my lower lip.

"Another fight with the missus, huh? Anything I can do, Ira?" Evelyn unwrapped a second stick of bubble gum.

"No ... but thanks. Think I'll sneak out and take in a movie tonight. *Godfather 2* is playing."

"I didn't think that you were a DeNiro fan?" She was poised to pop the gum into her mouth.

"I'm not." *A DeLeon fan, it would seem.*

I waved at her and then angled toward the hall leading to my office. Upon entering, my eyes grabbed hold of the gold and magenta barometric clock on the credenza. It revealed the time—half past the hour of four. Flanking the chronometer were two photographs. On the left was Nadine with her blonde hair in a fetching twist. In the picture, she stood, looking straight at me with her emerald-greens as I entered the room. She wore a huge grin. The camera flash had caught her reaction to a surprise birthday party, as I recall.

"Nadine, if only …" I was stuck for words, now trapped between two persuasive truths. Or lies.

To the right of the timepiece perched a photograph of my family. Nadine had shot this image. Everyone except Sophie, my mom, was in a bathing suit. In the center, my father, Albert, sported his swimming trunks in patriotic colors. Dad's arms clasped the shoulders of Michael and me. In front of them, sitting on lounge chairs, were Mom in a dress of floral print, her hands folded on her colorful apron, and my sister Jocelyn in striped shorts, gazing wistfully into the great beyond. My parents and Jocie still lived two thousand miles away in Napa, near San Francisco. I picked up the portrait and inspected it more closely. Until now, I hadn't fully appreciated how lovely my sister was.

The large hand of the clock had moved a full two minutes. I replaced the picture, scooted around my desk, and signed letters Evelyn had left for me. Communications to patients, insurance corporations, attorneys, medical boards, hospitals, employers, workman's compensation companies, referring doctors, social security—I sighed and fired the final paper into my out-box. I checked for more minutiae to distract me, to keep me from listening to my hair grow. But my desk was clean, almost too clean. Like Dad would want. I gazed out the window of my prison. Somehow I had to escape. Without realizing it I reached out, opened the bottom drawer, and retrieved a bottle of JD. Our lips joined, and I swallowed. I dwelt inside another prison—my head. *Steffi and Stella.* I simply could not weave them together into anything coherent.

Nadine and Stephanie were like magnets—one repelling me, the other attracting, with about equal force. It had been a month since I had sex with Nadine. And then it seemed like a duty. A marital function. Certainly not to beget another child. Alcohol, not desire, had catalyzed the event. I dwelt on that for a minute … or less, mindful that sensuous thoughts of Steffi were squeezing out remembrances of my high school sweetheart.

"The hell with it." Casting caution aside, I grabbed my razor and a fresh polo shirt and headed for the bathroom. Before departing I tossed down two more grenades from my pint of hidden Jack.

That evening, an ochre-yellow sun slid westward below the treetops. At the park, my car purred to a stop behind Steffi's red Pontiac Firebird. My pulse rate had picked up when I first spied her auto. I hadn't been one-hundred percent certain she would show up as planned. I crossed to Stephanie's car. No one was there, but heat was still rising through the hood. I took a gravel trail down to the pond, tiny stones scrunching underfoot.

"Steffi! Mikey!" I hollered, waving at the distant figures throwing chunks of bread into the water.

I ducked under a spruce branch, knocking off pine cones. A wayward branch smote my chin as if to warn me away. I detected a wild smell, an earthiness that reminded me of the Boundary Waters up north. The woman enthralled me, and renewed thoughts of her were driving me forward with reckless abandon, the event of the previous night fleeing from conscious concern.

Then I was jogging, restraining myself from racing as fast as I could. She stood only a stone's throw away, laughing, her voice playing like musical bells. My heart pounded as if minesweepers were dropping depth-charges into my chest.

I forced myself back down into a slow walk as the slanting dusk light depicted her more clearly now, a damsel formed with exquisite composition, long dangling hoop earrings reflecting tiny sparkles. She was slender, her womanhood undeniable, giving shape to tight-fitting jeans—designers, priced well above her pay grade. Her bare midriff was tan, contrasting against the whiteness of her shirt, its tails tied together in front. No bra. I ached to rush into her arms and kiss her long and full. I was out of breath, but it was the electric field I had entered. The phenomenon had entrapped me, choice no longer mine. Our gazes, hers and mine, connected, creating an expectant intimacy, the insanity rapidly deepening.

"Uncle Ira, watch me throw food to the duckies!" Mikey wound up his right arm and hurled a missile toward the pond.

"Hey, Buddy. Your aim is improving." I looked at Steffi. "And so is his pronunciation. What happened to 'uckies'?"

"Well, we've been working on that," she chuckled. Steffi bent down and gave Michael a shoulder hug. "Haven't we, honeybun? We wanted to impress Uncle Ira, I think." She stood up and winked at me. "He ... uh ... thinks quite a bit of you. Well, so do I, Doctor."

Steffi reached out with both hands, and I grasped them. Her fingers seemed to be squeezing mine, pulling me closer, or was I merely wishing that? I wasn't certain. Yet our bodies closed the distance. I sensed tremendous pressure returning to my loins, an autonomic response I just could not govern, a contradiction in my Stone upbringing. Self-control, not unbridled lust, had been the proud banner inculcated by Father.

Though we were touching, the invisible field strengthening by the second, I stiffened and almost moved away. The life force of Grandma Stone's legacy was doing battle with my other self, with the wild man under the waters of another pond. A desperate confusion roiled inside me. But then I found myself once more peering into the abyss of those powerfully dilated pupils, concentrated blackness so deep it frightened me, yet held me fast—like an exotic cobra hypnotizing its prey.

"I think I am falling in love with you," she whispered. Somehow that made everything okay, and I felt a surge of wild affection pass between us. At least that was what I chose to believe.

Steffi's hands wiggled under my polo shirt and massaged the small of my back, each movement pressing me closer to her. Then she broke off eye contact and laid her head against my chest.

"It seems so safe here in your arms," she whispered.

"I believe I have come under the spell of the Good Witch of the North. I've fallen for you too. Head over heels, actually." Something dangerously feral was taking control.

Then, my gaze fell on Michael. The boy appeared oblivious to us. He had wandered to the shore's edge and was talking to clutches of white feathers, the ducks quacking and bobbing with the waves. *Michael.*

"I need you, Ira. God, I've been so lonely ... until you came into my life." She nuzzled my chest with her nose. "Besides, you have added some excitement to an otherwise dull operating room ... what with throwing IV bottles and all."

I felt her body shake with a stifled chuckle, and I too broke into laughter as the tension inside me leaked away.

"Jeez, you make me feel good." Ignoring the fleeting memory of her outburst the previous night, I pressed hard against Steffi's pelvis, my hands holding, massaging, her buttocks. "I don't suppose … ah … Junior here would like another Pooh chapter read to him?"

"Perhaps a very short chapter." Her long, dark lashes rested briefly on her cheek and then swept up, eyes meeting mine.

Nothing was said about Stella. It was as if she never existed.

* * *

Walking with a subtle hip thrust, Steffi snuck off to her bedroom while I finished explaining about bears and bees to Mikey. Soon I heard the soft tread of her slippers returning, and I looked up from *Pooh Corner*. Wonderfully cleavaged, she swept in, trailing a celestial scent. I blinked.

"Hey, you guys." Steffi sidled up to the sofa where I was discussing the merits and risks of Pooh sticking his paw into a bees' private honeycomb.

"Mommy, Uncle Ira is so funny. He pretended to be a bee." Mikey turned to me with … was it a look of love? "Show Mommy. Show her!"

I stood up, and wrapped myself in a fake tiger skin, a throw-cover over one of the blue chairs. Then my elbows folded into wings and I rushed about the room, all the while making a buzzing sound. I dashed behind Steffi and nipped her buttocks between thumb and forefinger. *"Zzzzzt!"*

"Ira!" she squealed, jerking her bottom around.

The boy doubled over with laughter. "Do it again, do it again!"

"I think we made our point, Buddy."

"Uncle Ira, where is Buffy?"

"Well, Mikey, he's at home. Probably sound asleep already. And that's what you should be doing."

I hefted the child and whirled him around and around through the air, Michael's arms flapping in the breeze. Screams of joy echoed through the room, and Steffi held her hand to her lips, likely praying he would land safely. I lowered the human honey bee to the carpet, and the boy and I rolled over together in an uproar.

"Wow! Okay, Buddy, bedtime," announced his mother, briefly picking at her forearm.

"You must value this dear child every moment," I said quietly as I sat on the floor and pulled Mikey into my arms, cupping him to my heart.

Steffi threw me an inquisitive look. "Give Uncle Ira a big hug and thank him for reading to you."

"Thank you, Uncle Ira. Will you be here in the morning?" He hesitated and wrapped his arms around my neck. "Are you my daddy now?"

I coughed and glanced at Steffi. "He sure is talking a lot today."

"Remember, Buddy?" She grabbed Mikey by the hand and led him toward the stairs. "We decided you could call him Uncle Ira, okay?"

"Aw, okay. Can he come over tomorrow?"

"He is a very busy doctor. Maybe soon." She winked at me and mouthed, "Really soon!" His mother marched the boy away. "Bud-a-rum ... bum ... bum ..."

I gazed after mother and son. *They certainly seem happy. Wonder what happened to make her break up with ... what's his name ... Michael ... Michael Starling?* I sensed a hidden, uncharted darkness.

"Okay if I fix myself a bourbon and soda?" I called out after her.

"Oh, sure. Mm ... my house is your house. You know wh ... where everything is. I'll take the ss ... same."

"Thanks," I returned, noting her slight stutter.

I hauled the half-empty bottle from her kitchen cupboard and ran streams of Jack Daniels into two short glasses, adding ice and a splash of soda water. I took a swallow while wandering about the warm domicile. I passed by an Indian dream catcher and stopped short at the photo of the two sisters, their mother, and the dog.

"My mom's name was Trudy." Steffi came up behind me and slipped an arm around my waist. "Trudy Ross before she married and became Mrs. DeLeon. We used to live just outside of Annapolis, Maryland, on the Severn River. My father died from a lung tumor when I was a kid. He smoked a lot. And Mom ...uh ...fell down the stairs when I was seventeen.

A blood clot on her brain killed her. That's when my Aunt Melonie … she lives in Baltimore … took me in until I went to the University of Maryland."

I nodded, noting she had not mentioned Stella. "It must have been tough growing up with no parents. So your dad was deceased at the time of this picture. Who shot the photo?"

"A neighbor man." She did not elaborate. "Why all the questions? Don't you believe me?"

I felt her arm go rigid. An awkward silence ensued, the stillness tremulous, like the surface of a pool—a very deep pool. I wasn't sure which way to tack.

"You're upset, Steff. What happened back then? You act as though the photo haunts you."

"Stop trying to pry into something that does not concern you, damn it! Please *leave* if you feel the need to act like a fucking investigator!" Her words came rapidly, in dark and twisted shapes. "Haven't you done enough damage already?"

"Oh, my God, I apologize. I am way out of bounds here." And then, in a playful manner, I rushed to say, "Hey, you volunteered the family history. I truly don't mean to sound as if I'm meddling in your past." I stroked her hair. "Steffi, you're *really* angry. I said I'm sorry."

"It's just that … that I've been under a bit of a ss … strain." She twisted around to face me. "I'll tell you some day. Not now. Don't leave. Please ho … hold me."

She stared, unblinking, into my eyes, pleading, fearful, haunting. I set my glass aside and folded her into my arms. Our lips joined, and I felt her tongue burrowing in, searching. I knew that something was amiss, but the ardor of her embrace set caution and common sense adrift.

"Honey, come." She gave a loose forward flip of her hand. "Bring our drinks into my … uh … boudoir," she murmured in my ear, her emotions snapping into a hundred-and-eighty-degree turn. "I have two candles burning." I caught a whiff of night-blooming jasmine. While unbuttoning her blouse, Stephanie's flushed cheeks flanked a rapidly rising, beatific smile.

The floral scent seemed like déjà vu. I inhaled deeply, picked up our bourbon and sodas, and followed her down the hall to Pleasure Island. Her blouse fell to the floor as we turned into the bedroom. The flickering glow of the tapers dancing in wax drove shadowy omens to flutter about her face. By the wall stood a brass bedstead, the duvet rolled down. Steffi challenged me, letting me take full measure of her firm breasts, rising and falling with each breath. I toed off my oxblood brogues. She kicked away sandals, unzipped her jeans, and drew them off, revealing black lace panties.

"God, you're beautiful. If only ..." *I were single*, came to my mind. I was stunned by this vision of pulchritude—slim, curvaceous, soft white skin reflecting undulating lights and shadows. Perhaps I had been reading too much into her come-hither stare, but any hesitant thoughts, like our clothes, fell away.

"Well, Dr. Stone, are you just going to ss ... stand there?" She took a long swallow of her drink and patted my cheek. "Here, allow the nurse her ministrations. Trust me, my pet."

Steffi twirled, arms over her head like a ballerina, stopped in front of me, and pulled away her panties. My fevered lungs expanded deeply, and I found myself completely under her spell as "Strangers in Paradise" soared through the air, a dark and taunting heat spilling, spreading, from this beguiling princess. My heart now beat out of control, my ribs shaky. She dropped to her knees and pressed her cheek against the fabric expanding in my crotch. Her hands crawled over my pant legs, unfastened the zipper, and stripped loose both my vigilance and leather belt. The trousers fell to the floor as I quickly drained my glass, tossing it on the bed.

Suddenly and with an animal directness, warm lips attacked me down under. "Steffi ..."

"Hmmm?" In the vanguard of highly skilled foreplay she became the ends of my nerves, soft fingers slowly moving rhythmically to and fro, electrostatic energy building and recharging seminal condensers, the drumming of hoof beats rising to a visceral and near-religious thunder.

I tore off my polo shirt and swayed on my knees until she levered me onto my back. "Steffi ... Steffi! Christ, you're driving me crazy," I heaved. "Damn, that feels so good. Beyond good!"

Her hair tumbled onto my abdomen. Panting through her nose, she then swung her bottom toward my head and then straddled my torso with her legs, her calves tight against my sides, like a jockey clinging to a Thoroughbred. Her long fingers remained coiled around me, at first each movement now synchronous with the beat, beat, beat of the background "Marrakesh Express." Her pulsatile energy accelerated the divine grip harder, faster, her lips urging.

Breathing inside her fiery passion, a delicious vertigo engulfed me. It was new and exciting and wonderful. I glued my hands to her buttocks, pulling her down, my tongue targeting that swelling bud of pleasure and pain, caressing. I heard a guttural moan.

"Hmmmm ... hmmmm!" Short rapid breaths fired through her spastic vocal cords, her nostrils. She arched her back, shoving her belly against mine, her entire body trembling.

I felt myself tighten, visceral, painful shocks belting my groin. Sudden thunderclaps from the heavens rolled through me, into my hands, precipitating a grasp reflex, my fingers clamping Steffi's bottom with such a whirlwind force it caused her to cry out.

"Ira! *Ira, Ohhh* ..."

"*Steffi!*"

At that instant air shot from my lungs, and blood, now hot and thick, roared into my head as I erupted below, time stopping still. A bolt of lightning had smote, a spasm of joy charging through me, ebbing away in bountiful throbs.

"*Ira!*" she cried out once again as I found the target once more. "No more, you wonderful man. Let me catch my breath." Her buttocks rose up, and she rolled over, collapsing to the floor, resting beside me. "No one has ever done that to me before. No one. Jesus, I saw stars. Just when you came. Then I ... Ira?"

I sat up and spun around to lie face to face. "What, baby doll?"

"I think that is the first time I've truly had a climax. I mean a real one." She ran a finger across my brow. "Your treatment is awesome. Will you be my doctor?"

"I'll be more than that." I kissed her cheek. "I think I'm falling in love with you."

"Don't move, handsome." Steffi jumped up, padded to the bathroom, and returned. "And I shall be your nurse." She toweled off my thighs and then chuckled and tickled my feet.

"Hey, Miss DeLeon. That's not fair." I scrabbled away from her. "You just found my Achilles' heel."

After freshening the two cocktails, we sat together against the headboard, the adulterous duvet covering us to mid-abdomen. I took a hesitant sip and then sensed something was not quite right.

Steffi covered her face with her hands, trying to hide her recurring agitation. "Ira, I've had some bad times with sex. I'm sorry I am so nervous. I owe you a little explanation. Mm … Mike and I, we …"

"Steff, you needn't drag out the past," I rushed to say, squeezing her left hand.

"I'm afraid that I am toting a lot of bb … baggage. Tonight … on the floor … you … ah … made me feel like a ff … female again." Steffi paused. "A cat in heat." She chuckled briefly and then bit the fingernails on her right hand. "My ex and I … he … I had to sneak my Buddy away and start a new life. Michael was the perfect gentleman when we mm … met. Swept me off my feet. Flowers. Treated mm … me like a queen. Then we married. In Houston, Texas."

Her words tumbled in short, clipped sentences, the music gone, almost as if a different Stephanie were speaking. Her face was drawn, eyes narrowed and focused on something only she could see. Steffi swished the ice cubes around in her drink and dispatched half the contents. I spotted a pink tablet preceding the Jack Daniels.

She shivered, as if chilled. Her left hand felt limp and clammy, now devoid of warmth.

"Are you ill, Steffi?" Worried, I pulled the covers over her.

"Why, Dr. Stone, I'm absolutely fine," she whispered in a monotone, her voice ethereal, perhaps half an octave lower. "Did you know that

Mikey's father nearly killed us? One day he left me for dead. I don't really remember, but I think he used the butt of his rifle. In Fargo, North Dakota."

The stutter had vanished again, though her syllables were running together. I tried to cipher what she was telling me. *That drug—another Quaalude? But why? This is weird. Her first husband must have been a monster. No wonder she is so uptight. But how come all of a sudden? What the hell is going on?*

"Did you call the police, Steff? Did he hurt Mikey?" I asked, becoming caught up in a field of anger.

"Uh huh. The sheriff ordered him to stay away from us. We packed and hauled ass before that ... that bastard knew what was happening. You cannot imagine what life had become living with Mike. Buddy doesn't recall any of this. He's ... okay."

Simple sentences, I thought, but what a deep and hidden weight they seemed to carry.

"Damn! Is little Mikey's last name still Starling? It was Michael Starling, wasn't it?" I twisted over on my side to see Steffi more clearly.

"Yes, and yes. The paperwork and legal notices to change Buddy's family name are somewhat daunting. But someday ..."

"Steffi, I need to ask a serious question, seeing as we seem to enjoy one another's company."

"Shoot, Doc." I saw a hint of a grin cracking her porcelain features. Then her little habit took hold again. She began to chew on her right cheek and grind her teeth.

"Is there a chance Starling Senior might show up on your doorstep? You know, gun in hand and all that. Does he have any custody rights in the eyes of the law?"

"He has no idea where we are. Believe me, he wouldn't come within a hundred miles even if he knew my address. No way, honey," she managed to say. "Anyway, Ira, baby, in for a penny, in for a pound. I need you to fuck me now. I need you inside me. I'm so cold. Please make me warm again. Fuck me hard. Fuck me ..."

With a lazy motion, Steffi kicked off her covers. Her middle finger searched through the hair on my chest and found the target. I kissed her neck and rolled on top. The pressure intensified inside me. Unanswered queries submerged themselves. She flattened her back and spread her legs, inviting.

"Please, dear doctor. Please," she entreated, her voice sounding detached. Her eyelids were closed, her chest heaved, breasts rising.

I felt as if some strange power were delivering me toward Steffi's womb as I slipped into her birth canal. I began to move my pelvis against hers, thrusting back and forth inside magnetic coils, passionate energy building.

"Fuck me, my darling. Don't stop." For a split second, I thought she was crying out to someone else. "Harder, make it hurt. One big pony. Biggest one ever. Baby, you do make me feel *good!*"

I had entered a foreign land, a world not of my making. But the sexual heat was so intense, all I wanted now was the volcanic release, flesh and blood unable to bear it any longer. There was nothing else. Nothing. Violent chasms and pressure ridges formed, hammering at the door, but the final temblor kept me waiting.

"Give me a baby, Dr.. Wonderful, beautiful sperm. Come to me." She flexed her thighs and wrapped her legs tightly around my buttocks, pulling me closer.

"*Baby?* Steffi, don't you …"

She pulled my mouth to hers, trapping me with her tongue. Then her long arms shot to the cheeks of my sit bones, hands holding me against her as I slowed, another side of me suddenly wary and confused. With a primal fluidity she arranged her own pelvis into a reverse thrust, impelling herself against me.

"Steffi!" Every fiber in my body contracted. "Steffi!" I cried out again, my voice ragged. My muscles seized, loins swelling to a frenzied pitch, my flesh throbbing, erupting.

I collapsed upon her. Her legs slid flat to the mattress, me still inside. Her breasts pressed into my chest. Steffi's head was turned to the side, tears like diamonds caught in the candlelight, streaming to the pillow, her breathing deep and regular. I rested, feeling both becalmed and disturbed, sweat soaking my body. If she were off birth control, it was beyond too late to repair that problem. I found myself too exhausted to wrap my mind around it. Yet, the room seemed peaceful. My body was numb, relaxed. Gently, I withdrew from Steffi, and her hand dropped away.

"Steffi?"

I levered myself off her body. She was ... was dead asleep.

"Steffi?" I brushed her chin, but she merely turned over on her side, respirations heavy. I checked her pulse. Slow and regular.

She mumbled indecipherable messages, a sister mixed somewhere within, anesthetized words, demons from the past.

The windowsill candle guttered and then died. I sat on the edge of the mattress, waiting, staring at her. Finally, "Steffi, I better head for home." *If I have a home.*

I shook her shoulders. "Are you okay?" But this woman born of wind and sea failed to respond. I kissed her forehead and then aimed for the shower. Upon returning, I dressed and drew the cover over Stephanie. Something had crawled into my periphery, picking at the edges of a scab. A warning? Or maybe the shadow of a foreign ecstasy, rash and cunning? God, how I felt the madness in her head, spilling over like a ruptured oil line, snuffing out life as I had known it.

"Did you fuck with Stella too?" came a whisper as she turned over, an anesthetic rapidly overtaking the woman.

"Steffi! Your sister was in the hospital, for God sake! *What do you mean? Jesus!*"

My body shuddered. A shot of fear rifled through me and then disappeared. I was washed out by the emotional tension, the perilous extramarital sex. Outrageous. A crazy, wonderful, convoluted experience, hiking at the foot of a tamped volcano. *"Give me a baby, Doctor."* *Dear God, please let that be wishful thinking, the alcohol talking.* I stared at the slumbering beauty, her tresses masking half of her face. She made my heart trip, and I knew that I still was thunderously in love. And I wanted a son, but that required a new and vulnerable conjunction of the human body.

Did you fuck with Stella too? My fingers curled into a fist as I stared at her. "Why did you say, *'Did I fuck with Stella too?'* What in hell ...?"

I was about to leave when a book on the floor caught my eye. It appeared as if it had been thrown against the wall, the pages in disarray. I picked it up and glanced at a bookmarked leaf penned with today's date, then read—

> *I can't help it, Stella. I love him so! What should I do? I know what you want me to do, but—Oh God, he has put such a spell over me! And he is good to Mikey. What would Mommy want? I miss Mommy. I have to go back down now. He is waiting. I bet I can fuck him better than you did! Ha! Then we'll see. Then we'll see.*

I looked up. *What the hell is that all about? Good God, she seems crazier than a loon! What should she do? Lord, what should I do! I damn well knew what I should do.* But a part of me—that reptilian, besotted, decision-making part—just could not let her go. Another drink. Maybe that would clear my head.

I replaced the diary, feeling as if it were burning my fingers. I eased the bedroom door open and tiptoed upstairs toward Mikey's room and peeked in. The boy was fast asleep. A Jungle Jim blanket, loose from its moorings, lay crumpled at his feet. I stood there for the longest time.

CHAPTER 19

Is love a tender thing?
It's too rough, too rude, too boist'rous,
and it pricks like a thorn.

William Shakespeare
Romeo and Juliet

After publishing numerous scientific papers and a two-volume text, *Malignant Tumors of the Brain*, many invitations to teach in workshops and give lectures as a visiting professor in cities throughout the world arrived. My professional career accelerated while my family life plummeted. How could I have allowed this to happen? Because I wore alcoholic blinders. "The family be damned and full speed ahead!" was my unspoken mantra.

I remained a stranger to my wife and children while I kept chasing a different rainbow, for I was in love in that parallel universe. High-testosterone love.

*　　*　　*

"Hello, Dr. Stone. Ready for another busy day?" Janice wheeled the first surgical case into the OR. "Foley catheter?"

"Yes, thanks." I surveyed the anesthetized man. He had a ruptured disc, and his two-hundred-fifty-pound torso would make the surgery run longer than usual.

"Okay, Dr. Merriman?" Janice cracked open the urinary catheter kit. "He's quite deep now. Go ahead." Lois nodded at the circulator.

Janice prepped the groin and penis. Then she stretched and fixed the sleeping phallus with her left hand, dipped the catheter tip into KY jelly, and inserted the tube through a recalcitrant urethra into the bladder. She pressed on the patient's lower abdomen until bright amber fluid issued forth, draining into a plastic bag.

"Nice technique, Janice." The compliment came from a nurse just entering the room. Steffi, with soapy water dripping from her elbows, strolled past me and picked up a sterile towel. "Good day, Dr. Stone, Dr. Merriman."

Steffi gowned herself, assisted by Janice from behind, and then arranged her face into a smile. "I checked the myelogram, Dr.. A large L-4,5 herniation?"

"Uh … yes. Severe back and left leg pain," was all I could say. I bunched my eyebrows and looked back, thinking, *Damn, I thought she would be in la-la land for two days.* I glanced at the candy-striped cap covering her hair. "I see you have a different hat on today."

"Like it? I stitched it together late last night. Couldn't sleep, and sewing soothes my nerves." She busied herself, readying the sterile field for battle with the disc fragment.

I scratched my forehead. "Oh?" was all I could manage.

Steffi's backside now faced me. I watched her buttocks and then tore my eyes away, my line of sight shooting upward to her side table. Her hands were steady as a rock as she marshaled the instruments. *Wonder what she is doing tonight?* I shook my head. *I'm on call. Better stay home and bond with Buffy.*

Nadine was far from my mind. My heart carried another torch, its perilous blaze fanned by remembrances of a nurse's caressing fingers. No longer would I wrestle with danger signals flashing like neon signs hidden in a fog. My loins, trapped between high levels of male hormones and the merciless Stone mandate for self-control, ached to distraction.

*   *   *

As dusk slipped quietly over the town, I headed toward Church Road. I pulled in the drive, hesitated, and then strolled up the walkway to my warm abode. Well, mine at least for now. Under a nearby streetlamp, children were jump-roping on the street and singing,

"Don't call the doctor, don't call the nurse.
Call for the lady with the alligator purse ..."

The closer I got, hands in pockets and shoulders hunched up to my neck, the more I wanted to turn around. A part of me hoped that Nadine would be in a nasty temper and give me an excuse to broach the subject of a separation. But Nadine was rarely in a brackish mood those days. Instead she pacified her stifled anger by eating, her passive-aggressive weight gain now driving me over the edge. I jumped when a bat flew toward my face and then darted away.

Divorce. The idea had lain dormant, occasionally peeking out from its dusty closet. Still, it was just a word, its true meaning masked, the emotion chilled and truncated. Divorce, never really an option before, now weighed heavily on my mind. *Do I truly want to leave my little girls? Do I ...?*

"Anyone home?" I hollered. I doffed my suit coat and draped it over the back of a cane-bottom chair.

I heard the patter of feet and then broke into a broad grin as Buffy tore around the corner, skidding on a throw rug. The black cocker spaniel barked a joyous greeting and leaped up against my legs, pawing my knees.

"Hey, tiger! Gosh, it's good to see you." I bent over and scratched Buffy's ears while the puppy's tail thrashed the air.

"How about a cookie?"

Her forepaw answered, rising up.

"Hello, love," greeted Nadine, slipping in from the kitchen. "The girls were waiting up for you. They are so proud of their grades this month and wanted to show you the report cards, but it got to be too late, as ..." Her lip curled sarcastically. "May I fix you a drink before dinner? Well ...

of course, *what* was I thinking?" she added, the acerbic ambush soon compelling my hand to pour a double.

"I …"

"Ira? I've been meaning to ask you. Do you know a Stella?"

"Ss … Stella? Why do you ask?"

"You were talking in your sleep last night. The words were jumbled, but it sounded like 'Not with Stella! No!' That was it."

"She … she was Michael's girlfriend, remember? The Peace Corps worker. I told you the story. It must have been on my mind. Was that all I said?" My heart pounded against my ribs.

"Yes, dear. I'll go fix your dinner now."

Later that evening I stood alone before the bedroom window, gazing through my reflection toward another. *I know I love you, Nadine, but …*

The cold glass pane before me misted over, its edges icing. From another room I heard a child's voice, my Lexi, crying, softly singing,

Jesus loves me! This I know,
For the Bible tells me so.
Little ones to Him belong.
We are weak, but He is strong …

The following late afternoon I walked into my office and dictated a letter to one of my referring colleagues. The intercom buzzed. It was Evelyn.

"Dr. Stone, it's five-thirty. I need to bring Clifford to the airport. He's going to Chicago to visit his sister. Okay if I take off?"

"Certainly. It's crappy weather outside. Drive carefully. I will be in the OR all day tomorrow. I'll check in between cases."

"Thanks. Bye." She clicked off.

It was seven by the time I completed a pyramid of those goddamn insurance forms. Dr. Tellini beeped to inform me that he had rounded on all my patients and saw no need for me to come by. My eyes glanced at the ceiling, discovering cracks I had not noticed before. Beyond my windowpane, sunlight filtered through fast-moving clouds, dimming as the wavering fireball hung lower in the sky. I thought about taking Buffy for an evening jog. Maybe finish reading *War and Peace*. I had to busy myself or become unhinged.

From my Chesapeake sailing days a familiar message within me cautioned—*the storm signals are warning you to come about*. But another voice had already won me over—*I need you to fuck me now. I need you inside me. I'm so cold. Please make me warm again. Fuck me hard. Fuck me.* I felt pressure against my fly as my hand, obeying testicular demands, picked up the telephone. She answered on the first ring.

"Hi, Steffi. I ... uh ... wasn't sure if it was okay to call you. Am I interrupting anything?"

"Ira! God, I'm glad you called. Now my day is complete. How *are* you? I miss you *so* much. Mikey wants to see Buffy again. Oh, dear, I'm just prattling on. See what you do to me. Ira? Are you there?"

Each syllable of undisguised pleasure nipped and plucked at my heartstrings. So thoroughly did I enjoy listening to her melody that I forgot to respond. "I wasn't sure you were going to show up for work today. But you were a master of the back table, as usual."

I could hear a saccharine smile travel over the wire. "Why, thank you, Dr.. You still are my doctor, aren't you?"

"That's why I called, Miss DeLeon. Perhaps you and Michael could hop into your Firebird and stop by my office ... for a checkup. You've never seen the inside."

"And afterwards let's go to my place, and I'll fix you a delicious dinner. See you in twenty minutes."

The phone went dead before I could answer. I held my breath, exhaling slowly, waiting for the adrenalin to dissipate. *Ira! Are you insane? Stop this while you can!* But I could not.

My nerves of steel, serving me well in the operating room, now failed as the sun dropped lower in the west. It wasn't just the idea of another night with Steffi. She was coming *here*—to *my* part of earth, bringing us both closer to the edge of discovery.

At the time I could not fathom that extramarital sex was like a snake turning to consume itself from the tail, cannibalizing its own body. The thought of sex beyond marriage, once so alien to me when I was a med student, now seemed without option, the idea exciting, unfamiliar, and perilous—as if I were crossing borders into a dangerous foreign land. But all of that, and three shots of bourbon, was what had driven me to pick up the phone and call my *femme fatale*.

That evening I stood outside the doorway near the library, adjacent to my office. Bright fluorescent lights shimmered in the empty hallway. I heard the elevator to the fourth floor ping and then slide open. Steffi, with her son in tow, trotted toward me while I held my door for them. We entered the library, Mikey bouncing ahead in his OshKosh B'Gosh overalls.

The boy, eyes wide open, spun around and hopped up to me. "Where is Buffy?" Mikey turned back and wandered around the room, peeking under chairs and tables. "Is she hiding?"

"She's at my home, probably curled up on her blanket." I chuckled as I watched Buddy search for his four-footed friend.

"Home? Can we go there?" Michael checked this out with Mom.

Stephanie and I glanced at each other, and then she responded, "Buffy lives in a nice house. It's too far away."

The lad thought for a minute and looked at me. "I wish you and Buffy lived with us." Then the bright cover of a magazine caught his eye, and Michael skipped over to the bookrack.

"You certainly are lovely tonight, Steffi." I grabbed both of her hands in mine and squeezed.

"Hi, my pet. No hello kisses?"

The door closed behind us with a confident snap. I drew the beauty to me, hesitated as our eyes—mine granite blue and hers golden brown—met, and then pressed my lips onto hers. Her mouth was warm, her tongue wanting. Her hands found the back of my neck, her finger tips resting, connecting. Her chest leaned into mine.

"Hmmm, this is where I belong," sighed Steffi. "Doctor, I'd let you perform an examination, but I wouldn't want to compromise your principles ... You do have principles, don't you?" she murmured in my ear.

"Your force-field is destroying my foundation of common sense, Nurse Steffi. Would you like to inspect the facilities?"

"Uh ... huh. What about Mikey?" She glanced at her son.

"It appears he's enthralled with those journals. My tour won't take very long ... barring any complications," I grinned, checking my watch. "We better move before the cleaning personnel come."

"Buddy, Uncle Ira is going to show me his ... uh ..." Steffi turned and smiled at me. "Office. We'll be back in a minute ... or two."

Little Mike flipped a page, more interested in the pictures than a surgeon's suite.

I took Steffi by the hand and led her next door.

"This is my inner sanctum. Not much to look at, but it is away from all the commotion."

"Mikey and I seem to be seeing less and less of you, Ira. Committees, patients, research, publications, meetings—where will it all end? I hope this isn't a hint about our future, my sweet."

"You are number one. Don't worry. I shall be at your beck and call."

"Hmm." Steffi's eyes wandered over the furniture, coming to rest on the photo of Nadine. "Your wife?" I detected a slight edge to the words, a sudden below-zero frost.

"Soon to be former wife," I nodded. "Taken nearly five years ago. In Munich, Germany."

"She's very pretty." Steffi picked up the likeness. "Do you still love her, Ira?"

This was not the path along which I wanted the conversation to go. "We've been hitched for nearly twenty years. She's not the same person I married. We seem to be drifting apart." I sat on a corner of my desk, tapping my foot on the carpet.

"But do you still *love* her?" Steffi replaced the photo on top of the credenza. Her liquid voice hardened, coy teasing draining from her eye sockets.

I suddenly found myself struggling to find safer ground, a place where rusty, ironclad commitments did not intrude. I swallowed. Of course, I still loved Nadine. Or did I? Why was Steffi forcing a rapid breach? My thought processes wobbled, like a top spinning off center.

"One's feelings for a spouse of so many years don't vanish overnight.

I ... I suppose I would be lying if I said I felt no love at all for Nadine." My tongue stiffened. "It's just that we have little in common anymore." My granite blues pleaded with Steffi to abort this line of brittle questioning.

"*Really*, Ira. Are you *lecturing* me? About love? I remember your exact words two days ago—and I quote, *'I think I'm falling in love with you!'*" A cold and caustic fury had crept into her tone, the nurse's widely dilated pupils now strafing my body. The scar on her left cheek turned angry, painful, standing firm like a mooring around which her loathing rippled. "I'm *so* sorry I misread your ... your declaration of love for me. For *me*, Ira-boy."

"Steffi, please ..." I stood up and grasped her hands. "Don't do this. I adore you. I just need some breathing space."

"*Breathing space!* While you had sex with *me* instead of your wife? So all I am is a surgeon's slave? Your personal concubine to ... to pillow and plunder at will?" Her eyes, darting quickly about, blackened with venom and a hatred more blinding than the sun. "This was all a setup, wasn't it?" She picked and scratched fiercely at her arm. "From the very beginning! *First my sister, and now me!*"

"Wha ..."

My nurse ripped her fingers away, her countenance scarlet, eyes filled with loathing, words now dripping white-hot in full-throated savagery.

"You know that's not true, Steffi. Please lower your voice. One of the staff might hear." I edged away from a woman I suddenly did not know.

"*And now I'm a liar, is that it?*" Stephanie spun around, aiming for an onyx paperweight on my desk. She hesitated. Then she spied the portrait of my family, raised it up, and slammed it against the wall. The glass frame splintered and shattered to the floor. "*That's* what I think of the name *Stone!*"

"*Jesus*, Steffi!" I felt cornered, not knowing which way the hellfire would blow. I had to get her away from here. My own disordered sanity was suddenly garroted, in rapid free fall.

"Well, Dr., did you enjoy fucking a defenseless woman in her low-class tenement?" She slowly pivoted, a twisted smile retracting into her face like cat's claws, and then she looked me up and down. "Obviously my sister and I are not the first to fall to your charade, you … you *cunt-sucking piece of shit!*"

Rounding on me, she drew back a fist and fired it at my cheek. But my left hand intercepted the missile in midflight. I held fast to her right wrist. I wanted to hold her, pull her body against mine, dispel her wrath. I really wanted to *fuck* her. There. On the carpet. In that crazed moment, I drew her heated torso to me, but her left arm lashed out, the palm of her hand exploding against my cheek. I was too stunned to feel the sting.

"*Steffi!* Please, I do want … need you." My right arm wrapped around her waist, trapping the shaking woman, hauling her tight against my chest.

She struggled to disengage herself. I wanted to bed her, not fight her. My penis swelled, and I thought it was the friction of her body. I kissed the side of her neck, hoping to calm her. But Steffi was like a she-lion whose cub was under attack.

"Ss … stop it!" she shrieked, shaking her head violently from side to side, pupils shimmering like scorched motor oil. *"You're hurting me again!"*

"God, I'm truly sorry, Steffi." I found myself rapidly pulling in air, struggling to regain mastery of my own emotions as I released my grip. For a split second, something from the past stumbled by and then disappeared, leaving me chained and powerless, the Stone dominion subjugated.

We stared at each other, our passions whipsawing, both backing away.

Finally I said, "Steffi, may I walk you to your car? Please forgive me if I have pained you. Let's …"

"Mommy, I'm ss … scared." A little boy dressed in OshKosh B'Gosh overalls stood at the doorway, a ripped cover slipping from his fist.

Is this a scene Mikey has lived through before? Stillness filled the battlefield. My feelings still churning like an anchored canoe in a thunderstorm, I took a step toward Michael. But Steffi darted in front and grabbed her son by the hand. She spun on her heel and bolted for the exit, Michael tripping over his feet in an effort to keep up. I watched in shocked silence as the two disappeared down the hall.

I sat down at my desk, elbows on the ink blotter. I felt myself tremble, shaky breaths and a profound melancholy flowing through me. Someone had shoved a lid over the rabbit hole, blocking all escape. My chest began to tingle as my anxiety soared. I picked up the splintered photo of my family and laid the broken frame on the credenza. Then my hand grabbed a role of adhesive tape from a nearby examination room and used it to pick up the remaining slivers of glass from the credenza and floor. I gazed at the fractured picture, feeling Father's flinty eyes fixed on me.

An hour later my beeper vibrated, the abruptness of it startling. I noted the call-back number. The beeper fired off again. *Emergency.*

"Dr. Stone here."

"This is Dr. Tellini, sir. A gunshot wound to the head just rolled in. Self-inflicted. Looks terrible. We have the man on a vent. His name is Joe Cooper. Getting an angiogram now. I've alerted the OR."

"Thanks, Tellini. I'm on my way." Jack Daniels and Nurse Stephanie would have to wait. My pager buzzed once more, and I dialed her number, my toes curling. "Steffi?"

"Hello, Dr. Stone. Ss ... sorry to bother you. Please come over. As soon as possible. Mm ... Mikey is crying. He wants you to read him a story." I cringed, listening to her slurred entreaties. "And ... I need you. Please come ... hold me ... let me explain ... I'm nothing without you ... don't leave ... I know you love me ... I understand about the twenty years ... I ..."

Another barbed hook, the target anesthetized as my ambushed psyche continued weaving its own misery.

"Steffi, I uh ... I'll shoot on over as soon as I can. But it may not be until two or three in the morning. There's a gunshot wound in the ER, and I am on call."

"Sweetheart, do you want me to scrub in? The night-call nurse won't mm ... mind."

"Just tuck Mikey in for the evening and tell him ... tell him Uncle Ira misses him. Okay if I come by later?"

"Is Fabe ... Dr. Tellini operating with you?"

"Don't know. Why do you ask?"

"Just curious, that's all. We'll be here waiting for you. And Ira?"

"Yes?" The heat of her recent anger still bit away the words *yes, my love.* Dammit, even so, a part of me wanted to say them, but at that moment my tongue could not.

"I need to mm ... make it up to you ... my outburst, I mean. *I love you so much it hurts!* I know you don't believe me, but I will prove it to you. Please stay with me, oh, please."

"I'll come as soon as we get out of surgery. Good-bye, Steffi." I had another home, a wife, two wonderful children, but I was throwing all that away. By then I had entombed Denni and Alexandria, leaving them without a daddy, tossing my two girls to the fucking curb. I pined for a drink—*even more than I wanted them!* My sick and endangered brain should have been in intensive care.

> *"Hope for the best, prepare for the worst,*
> *So said the lady with the alligator purse."*

CHAPTER 20

There is always some madness in love.

Friedrich Nietzsche
On Reading and Writing

Appleton, evening

Tonight would be filled with a community AA meeting at our assembly hall, followed with new work assignments. Each of us had to take responsibility for one of several jobs—men's snack-kitchen cleanup, vacuuming the hallway carpets, emptying trash buckets, straightening up library books. I had noticed that Lance, Henry, and Crow were missing, and I suspected that they had left the treatment center for good after their little sex orgy. I never returned to that copse of woods. It was off limits anyway. Barbed wire fences and locked gates did not exist here. Nothing prevented voluntary departure, though persons ordered here by the courts risked a future peering through iron bars after unauthorized leaving.

One day I was sitting with several men enjoying dinner. The women, separated from us by glass windows, ate in the same building. I had just swallowed a mouthful of Sprite when a distant, violent scream came from outside. In three minutes Nurse Amelia Levinstone rushed inside, up to Appleton's director, Dr. Gus Hendricksen, as he moved his chair back from the table next to us.

"Oh God, Dr.. They're all dead! *Dead! There's blood all over!*"

"Amy, what are you talking about? Who? Where?" Hendricksen jumped up and wiped his hands on a napkin.

"Ellie, Crow, and ... and ... I think the other one is Lance! I thought I heard a strange noise from the wooded area, you know, where the path is. I went over there, and there they were ..." She turned away, catching her breath, gagging as if to keep from vomiting. "I had to chase the dogs and rats away. And the smell. Dear Lord, stab wounds everywhere, necks slashed open, a knife in Crow's back. Crow was lying on top of Ellie, you know, like they were ... uh ... having sex ... like ... oh God! Lance was mutilated, his penis stuffed into ..."

"Okay, okay, Amy. You needn't go any further. Call 911 *stat!* Then hit the gong in front and send everyone to assembly. And check with personnel and ask them to call any of the counselors not on site and tell them to come into the assembly room immediately. Don't do anything else until the police get here."

"Yes, sir." The RN and the director dashed away, leaving the rest of us stunned and speechless. Then most of us ran toward the assembly hall.

I remained glued to my seat. *Jesus, Jesus, Jesus! I could have saved them. If only I had owned the guts to report what I had seen! What are you going to do now, Ira?* I had made another wrong turn. I wanted a drink. Shit, I *needed* a drink. I *deserved* a drink!

AA, group meetings, and counseling sessions were cancelled for that evening and the next day. I arrived at the assembly hall late. Marin County investigators were swarming all over the complex. I knew it was only a matter of time before they questioned me.

Two days later, it was time to continue Step One. All of the group members, buzzing among themselves, were turned toward me as I resumed the story of my unfaithful behavior.

"Okay, guys, quiet down. Your opportunity will come. None of us have a lily-white past. So, Ira, did you get back to Nadine?"

Penn State

"What a frightful mess. Joe Cooper's whole left hemisphere wiped out by a 45-caliber bullet." I cut a suture held up by the resident as he closed the skin.

Tellini shook his head. "Do you want to keep him on the respirator?"

"Yes. Ask the pulmonologist to consult. No Decadron," I recommended. "I gather the police say it was suicide?"

"Yeah. The lab is doing a tox run. Cooper's girlfriend found some crank under his bed."

"The district attorney won't be able to question the patient, I'm afraid. His speech center is gone ... permanent-like."

"Any hope for recovery of his right limbs or vision?"

"Doubt it. Maybe the leg, a bit. He might walk again after long-term rehab." I hesitated. "By the way, are you going out with any nurses here?"

"Nurses?"

"Yeah. The female variety. You certainly have been away from the old country long enough to understand the word *nurse*." I bit my tongue. It was not fair to bring him into this. Or was he already in it ... or her.

"Nothing in a serious way."

I let the issue drop. I liked the man. He was very talented. But I did not want to be part of any woman's harem, the reverse notwithstanding.

After the surgery I was tired and should have gone home that early morning. Instead, I sought the excitement and promise of Stephanie DeLeon and her whiskey libations. And the boy. *The boy*. I was a trapped man, invisible coils tightening.

I went to the townhouse complex but kept circling the block as the weather deteriorated, rain changing into sleet. The more I circled, the more flummoxed I became. Finally I turned the wheel in her direction. The sleet was nearly horizontal, slamming into my auto, pushing me away. But nothing could delay me now. Nothing. After heading over the weedy gravel drive leading to her abode, I caught sight of the red Firebird and jerked to a stop behind it. I stepped from my vehicle, ice crystals stabbing against my face, and glanced at her windows. The lamp in Steffi's bedroom backlit her drapes. Then, for an instant, the curtain jiggled, as if someone were peering outside.

Overhead the sky was ominous, the sleet turning into freezing rain. Denuded, shimmering limbs of skittish oak trees reached skywards, disappearing into the raven firmament.

I darted around a hobbyhorse on steel springs, continued up the steps, and depressed the buzzer. I rang a second time. No response, though a distant dog bayed in the night. I returned to the front walkway. Now her window was black. Agitated, I opened my car door and drove away, but not before my eyes caught sight of a GMC wagon. Fabian's. My resident appeared to be well bedded. Perhaps even embedded.

The following afternoon I finished clinic and trotted toward my Thunderbird. Four o'clock chimes rang out the hour.

"Good afternoon, Doctor."

I halted in my tracks. There she was, Stephanie DeLeon, perched on a bench, sucking on a lock of hair. She wore faded Levis, snug around her long thighs, with a slight flare at the bottom. Her turquoise-green blouse was tailored, leaving no doubt about the womanly figure beneath. A satin ribbon gathered up her shoulder-length ponytail.

"I wouldn't blame you if you don't wish to speak to me." Her eyes dropped toward the ground, coming to rest on her penny loafers. "Just got off work. The OR isn't the same when you're not there. I mean, all the nurses say that." She paused, subdued, as if searching for words, biting her lower lip. "How did your gunshot case go? I heard that the patient was pretty devastated."

"Yeah. Devastated." I felt my stomach clench. "May I sit down?"

"Please. I hoped you would."

"Steffi, about Stella. No one is more saddened at what happened than me. If only ..."

Stephanie looked away. "That is all in the past, Ira. I'd rather forget it."

"But ..." I sighed, not knowing what more to say. Stella would have to wait for another day.

We plunged into an awkward silence, punctuated only by the chirping of blue jays. I wanted to touch her, somehow connect with her true emotions, find a gentler path to the real Steffi. But the force of her violence yesterday stayed my hand.

"How is Mikey?" I managed to ask. "Is he at daycare?"

"Uh ... huh. They stay open until seven." Her eyes welled up. "Oh, Ira, what is to become of us? I'm falling apart, and the medicine only makes things worse. You ... ah ... knew that, I suppose."

"I've seen the Quaaludes, Steffi," I admitted, wondering who provided the drug.

"It's a prescription."

"Hmm."

"And I keep having dreams about a ... a shark on top of me. Oh, God ..." A shiver appeared to roll through her body. "The tranquillizer helps me sleep better."

A shark? "By the way, I came by your place a little after three last night, but you didn't answer the buzzer. I was worried about you."

"Oh, I had taken my medicine. Guess I didn't hear you. And I was so distraught ... I needed someone ... I needed you to hold me ... close." Steffi reached into her purse. "Here, now you have the key to my heart, if you will take it. You are welcome anytime. You ... you have my oath on that. It unlatches the front door ... it opens ..."

I sighed, hesitated, and then accepted the key, sticking it into my sport coat pocket. I wished I possessed another key, the key to her query: *Ira, what is to become of us?*

"I have to take care of some business at home this evening," I lied. "Pay bills and stuff. Will you be okay?"

"Oh, sure." Steffi, a wistful smile on her lips, touched my hand. "You're still upset with me, aren't you? I do love you, Dr. Stone ... so much so that my mind goes crazy. I'll try to keep a leash on my ... uh ... tempestuous behavior. Call me when you're in the mood for ... for reading to Mikey."

The warmth of her fingers melted away my anger, anesthetizing the sting of yesterday's storm.

"You're messing up my mind, Steff, though I do miss you. What else can I say? You've turned me inside out." I had the urge to kiss her on the cheek. I really didn't want to leave. "I love you too. I'll give you a ring tomorrow."

"A ring!"

Oh, Lord. "I meant that I'll phone you."

Steffi laughed. "I know what you meant … this time." She lifted her left fourth finger. "But I can always dream, can't I? *Ciao*, good doctor."

"By the way," I mentioned over my shoulder as I was leaving. "I saw Dr. Tellini's car near your home last night. At three a.m. He must know someone in the same complex." A drop of rain struck my shoulder as I headed out, my inner self drowning in an upwelling of slippery confusion and resentment. Or was it something else—jealousy hiding the truth that I had two women? *What's good for the goose …*

I did not look at her as I departed. I rubbed the spot on my hand where she had touched me, as if to preserve it and push it into my veins. I felt as if our two souls had embraced at that point, the union greater than the sum of its parts. Or perhaps it was the joining of matter and antimatter, with the annihilation of both.

A few days later my mistress and I were sitting together on the divan at her place. Children's books lay heaped on the floor. A mantel clock chimed the evening hour of ten. Two empty tumblers of whiskey and soda made wet rings on end-table doilies. My increasingly vitriolic wife had been trying to reach me, but alcohol continued pushing unanswered wedding promises farther and farther away.

"You're meningioma surgery went really well the other day, Dr. Stone." Steffi leaned her head against my shoulder.

"And it looks as if they're going to let us keep you in neurosurgery, Nurse DeLeon. After my outburst, I've kept a low profile in the supervisor's office. I hope they didn't take it out on you."

"I … uh … sweet-talked Horrible Hester. Told her how great the Penn State operating room was and complimented her on her new hairdo. I did omit that her face looked as if it were caught in a vise. Sorry, that's unkind. But what a creep."

She hesitated, biting her lip, her mood changing. "And … oh, Ira, about Fabe Tellini. Yes, we dated … and slept with each other. But that is finished.

Anyway, he has a new girlfriend now. Some blond nurse in Obstetrics. Maybe you know her. Except for Mikey, you are now my one and only."

But my paranoid mind wondered if the strain in her voice suggested something perhaps quite the opposite, mixing truth and doubt in equal measure.

"Besides, Mikey needs a daddy. And a brother," she whispered, stroking the linen cloth of my white shirt and then dropping her hand to my thigh, driving out lingering doubts.

I felt Steffi's body heating up, like butter on a hot plate. But I was not ready to provide anyone with brothers or sisters.

"Can you imagine what my body feels like next to you, Ira? Bubbly warmth and dampness ... down here." She pushed my hand over the contours of her pelvis. "You truly want me, don't you," she seemed compelled to continue. "Me! And when we get married, I'll show you what a great wife really is. In bed. Every night!"

Her fingers wandered, flipping loose one of my shirt buttons. She toyed with the hairs on my chest.

"I adore you, Ira. Even if I seem to act like a willful child at times. If you can't talk to me, then ... well ... I'll always be here for you anyway, my handsome lover."

"I think it's your eyes, Steffi."

"My eyes?"

"That's what snagged me. In the OR when I first saw you. You were a beautiful Arabian princess secreted behind her veil, permitting only her captivating eyes to be seen." I unfastened one of four snaps on the back of her green silk blouse.

"Captivating?" she asked. Her tongue played in the twilight between parted lips.

A second snap came away.

"Uh ... huh. Like, I was captured."

Then the third, the quiet tick masked by the ruffle of silk. At the same moment, her wayward index finger found the nape of my neck.

"Kiss me, Ira." I felt her heart hammering almost out of control. "Kiss me before I die!"

We both ignited, white hot, our whole beings galvanized toward one thing. I never heard the fourth snap, her bodice dropping away as our lips embraced.

Her hand tugged on my shirt. In a fit of impatience, she yanked loose the buttons, tearing them from their moorings, her fingers running over the skin of my chest. "Come with me to the bedroom?"

"I'll follow you to the ends of the earth."

We stood up and Steffi wavered, her knees seemingly weak from the promise of passion, like a cat in heat. She drew her body close against mine and bore into my hard flesh, pressing, throbbing against her belly as I held onto her shoulders. Then she backed away, and her hands unzipped my fly.

"God, what a beauty. Bring him with you, my sweet," Stephanie urged as she reached down and draped her fingers around my penis. "Hey, what is this? You snuck on a condom, you tricky man. You aren't carrying some frightful disease, are you?"

"Well, no, Steff, but ..."

"Good. My lips are allergic to rubber." Her fingernail hooked the prophylactic and stripped it away. "Now, doesn't this feel better?" she asked, gripping my prick.

"We better get to your bedroom, or I'll mess up the couch."

Steffi put an ear to my chest. She scrunched up her face, giggling. "Uh oh. I detect a cardiac arrhythmia."

"Sex overload syndrome. You better stop ... like right now." My pulse accelerated, exceeding a hundred and ten by a wide margin.

"Okay, but you'd best behave and honor my every wish." She let go. "Fear not, my good doctor. I am on birth-control pills. I can show you the bottle."

"That's not necessary, Steff. Really."

"Oh, Ira. I want you so bad." The nurse reached about my back. "If you can't marry me, at least carry me across the threshold into the bedroom."

I swept the damsel up into my arms, as if she were but a feather. I kissed the side of her neck while we sailed down the hall, into her boudoir. I set her on the edge of the mattress and stood before her, between her legs.

Her knees closed fiercely against my thighs. She lunged forward and kissed me on my nipple, rubbing with the tip of her tongue.

"Ira ... Oh, Ira. Kiss me down there. Like you did before. You do like my pleasure node, don't you? Please ..."

Steffi, sans panties, separated her thighs and lay back, her forelegs hanging over the mattress.

"Make me come again. God, that was heaven! I am yours! Don't you understand that? I am your eternal concubine, no matter what the future brings, your lips possess me."

"Close your eyes and dream of us forever, Steffi," a voice within me answered as I kissed her thigh.

While "Ebb Tide" floated through the air, my wickedly naked nurse spread her long legs. She flexed her knees and hips, her heels pressing on my back, muffling screams of ecstasy with her forearm, biting into the flesh as my tongue found its target, pressing, pulsing, electrifying, the intensity growing. Suddenly came forth an enraptured cry, almost blood-curdling in its fervor, one even now ringing in my ears.

I released her and laid my head against her tummy, over her pelvis. Bubbling and tinkling sounds arose from her gut, the music heralding one of many climaxes, like miniature thunderclaps in slow motion, the tremors of her body focusing in the pit of her belly.

*   *   *

An hour later, I crawled beside her on the duvet. She appeared numb. Dewdrops welled up in her eyes. I guessed they were tears of joy. Yet I wasn't sure. She rapidly recovered, which was more than I could say for me.

"Ira, let me dash into the bathroom for a minute. I'll be right back.

"Honey, are you all right?"

"Hmmm ... am I ever!" She jumped up, brushed her lips against my cheek, and danced away on tiptoes, returning in seconds.

"Now! Just lie on your back, big boy. Let me do the labor. You need a rest." She chewed on her cheek, stared, and sighed. "A challenge, but mountains were meant to be climbed."

Stephanie straddled my pelvis with her knees while kneading my rigid penis and then lowered herself onto me. Tingles billowed into tiny detonations inside my body as I felt myself slip deeper and deeper inside her. She paused a moment, as if to savor a sensation, and then launched into slow thrusts against me, and then faster as the tide within her rose up, each movement catalyzing the next, driving both of us into wave after wave of animate bliss.

"Steffi … Angel, you make me feel so damn *good!*" I clutched her feral breasts and taut nipples.

Purring and then strange guttural sounds came from her throat, followed by a bizarre ululation as she ramped up a sensory firestorm so powerful that every nerve in my body was singing. For a heartbeat she seemed to waver but then recovered. Minute by minute, Steffi labored her pelvic thrusts into a primitive frenzy, perspiration now a sheen on her forehead, her hair matted in sweat. Faster and faster she fucked, bringing me into a state of galactic rapture, my loins about to explode.

The woman now appeared oblivious to me or her surroundings, as if hurtling toward some ill-defined destiny. She squeezed her eyelids closed, peering, perhaps, at a vision, a daytime dream of an ancient past. She must have been under the command of another master from long ago, a puppeteer battling her love for me. Torrents of tears now rushed over her cheeks, dropping to my chest.

I let out a gasp, tiny creatures of life feeding into Steffi by the thousands. She knew it was happening. Her body collapsed on top of me. Aftershocks.

My ears were ringing, and the pitch of her respirations started to change, but then—

"Watch out! Watch out, Stella! The sh … shark! Dear God, help!" came a scream from above me.

Suddenly, Steffi's mouth formed a rictus of pain, yet no immediate sound came forth. The woman broke out into a keening, shattering, high-pitched wail so terrible it froze my heart and sent bubbles of fear chasing along my spine. She raised her head, her hands beating some invisible creature. The beast within her rose up, cymbals crashing, fists lashing out with a terrible ferocity, thrashing me without mercy, scratching at my face, trying to tear my eyes from their sockets.

"*Steffi! Stop! Steffi!*"

"*Daddy! Did Stella fuck really better than me? Did she!*"

"Wha …" Blood fountained up from my cheek as her rabid fingernails clawed, flaying my skin.

"*Did she!*"

Besotted by sex and intoxicated with Steffi, I lay beyond any comprehension of the sudden change in my mistress, throwing up my arms to defend myself, latching onto her slippery wrists. Then, just as abruptly, she ceased her attack, dropping on top of me, falling into a dead faint, the only movement two final thrusts of her pelvis. Then silence, except for her breathing. And the violent pounding of two hearts as I pulled her away.

"*My God!*" Horrified, I gaped at her. "What kind of a witch are you! Where the fuck do you hide your demons?"

I shivered and pressed the pillow to my left cheek, which had taken the brunt of her assault. I looked at Steffi again and shook my head in disbelief. She was two persons living within one skin. Her cry still ringing in the air, the woman lay coiled up in a fetal posture, lids shut, in a trance. I turned on the lights and broke away toward the bathroom, stared at the mirror which gave back my blotched face, and surveyed the damage. *She almost got my eyes. Scratches and cuts, some on the right, the worst on the left cheek—good Lord. That one is nearly a twin to Stephanie's scar.*

I returned to the bedchamber and fixed my gaze on the woman. For some strange reason the brunette mole on her right cheek drew my brief attention. Her moaning breaths were slow and shallow. I didn't know if I would stir up a hornets' nest should I touch her. She seemed to be in a deep sleep. Finally, I stroked strands of damp hair from her forehead and wiped tears from her cheek.

"Steffi … Steffi, what in the name of Satan has possessed you?" I jiggled her shoulder, but she did not move.

This nurse was a living magnet, drawing me toward her, even as I nursed my bruises. Stephanie wasn't evil. Or was she? This Steffi DeLeon sailed through seas of extraordinary passion, her passage punctured by bursts of irrational anger, leaving me bobbing in her wake. She certainly wasn't dull. The woman had turned my life upside down and, *God help me, a part of me liked it!* She was the antithesis of everything my previous self had stood for. This nurse extraordinaire made me feel alive, wanted, free. John Barleycorn and Peter, Peter, Pumpkin Eater had cast the deciding votes for this creature who instilled such carnal desire.

I pressed two fingers on her radial artery. The pulse was one hundred and strong. I retracted Steffi's eyelids. The pupils were so dilated that jets of a red light reflex would fire from each retina. She did not react to any stimulus. Stephanie must have ingested a large dose of Quaalude and something else, I thought. I drew the duvet over her naked body and dressed myself.

"Uncle Ira?" The words jolted me, and I sharply inhaled. It was little Michael, standing in the doorway, staring hard at … at me, and whimpering. "Did you hurt Mommy?" His tiny voice raised the hairs on the nape of my neck.

I saw the brown-haired tyke standing with the corner of a small blanket in his fist, his thumb in his mouth. He wore pajamas with Donald Ducks printed all over. His eyes were wet, frightened.

"Oh, Mikey, Mikey." I swathed a bath towel around my lower body, scooped Buddy up into my lap, and sat on a chair, holding a damp washcloth over my cheek. "Mommy is sleeping. I think she might have taken some medicine." I gave Michael a squeeze.

"Mommy sleeping." Mikey seemed to think everything was all right now—Mommy was sleeping and Uncle Ira was holding him. "Tell me a story?"

Now? "Uh … You bet I will."

Regaining control of my breathing, I carried Michael into his bedroom and set him on the mattress. It was a junior bed, no longer a crib. I leafed through another of the lad's favorite collection and began to read, the effort arduous.

Mikey, his eyes glowing and fixed on me, laid his head on a Jungle Book pillow. "Did you fall down?"

"Yes, Mikey, I fell down." I started to describe Pooh Bear.

"You aren't mean like Daddy."

I stopped reading. "Do you remember Daddy?" I asked.

Little Mike shook his head side to side.

"How was he mean, Buddy?"

"Mommy said so. He hurt Mommy."

Realizing that the child was caught in a tragedy not of his making, I wondered if this three-and-a-half-year-old had lost more than just a father. "Do you want to see Daddy some day?"

A long pause. "Daddy did bad things."

But do you want to see Daddy some day? I rubbed my chin and decided not to pursue the query. A tiny seed of an idea germinated in my remote consciousness.

"Have you ever tasted truffula fruit?"

CHAPTER 21

Before God we are equally wise
—and equally foolish.

Albert Einstein

Steffi and I continued to see each other. She never recalled the event where she lashed out at my face. At first it was with trepidation that I had sex with the woman, but it seemed that she had gained control over her emotions—at least the violent ones. So the adultery continued. I gained more confidence in our secret meetings, and Nadine became more and more suspicious. Eventually I told my wife about Steffi and that I was contemplating divorce. Yet neither Nadine nor I could bring ourselves to take the final step. Now we had separate bedrooms.

Summer arrived, and it seemed to me like just yesterday when the era of Steffi DeLeon had ruled my life. It began in Caracas. Sitting at my office desk early in the evening, I slammed a raft of insurance forms down onto the blotter. I laid aside my pen and kept glancing at an unopened envelope, the words PERSONAL & CONFIDENTIAL scripted in flowing letters across the front and below my name—a missive addressed in Steffi's handwriting. Evelyn had discovered the letter on my carpet next to the door early that morning. I finally snatched up the fragrant, canary yellow envelope. While tripping over images of her, my tongue trapped between my teeth, I used a thumbnail to strip open the sealed flap and read:

191

Darling,

I didn't know where to send this letter. So I mailed it to Janice and asked her to bring it to your office and slip it under the door. By the time you read this, I shall be living in Le Mars, Iowa. I am sure you remember Dr. Calvin Washok, that physiatrist I told you about. I met him at that conference in Chicago.

He has been begging me to marry him. Seeing no future in Hershey, dearest, I finally agreed. Please don't think ill of me. Working for a rehab doc will be a new experience.

Mikey sends hugs and kisses to Uncle Ira. He is talking a blue streak now. He won't let anyone else read about Pooh Bear to him. Not even me! He is growing up so fast I had to fit him with the next size of OshKosh B'Gosh pants. I found some at Penney's last week.

I have a job in Emergency at the local hospital. I tried to get an OR position, but no slots were open. Nothing else to say about that, I guess.

Mikey and I miss you!

Love,
Steffi

PS. They tell me that Le Mars is the ice cream capitol of the world!

My vision blurred. I knew this was going to happen after she took off like a butterfly in July. Even so, the letter took me by surprise, changing the shapes of things a part of me had begun to know and desire, twisting them out of recognition. Still, it was for the best. I felt as if a storm cloud had passed overhead, going on to drench another town. *Le Mars.* I stared at the walls and heard someone weeping; then I felt self-conscious, as the Stone armor renewed itself.

I stuck the note between pages of *Physiology in Medicine* and murmured, "But she still loves me." My sick mind, attempting to read between the spaces of her words, simply could not give it up. *If drinking doesn't kill me, her memories certainly will.*

Nadine, of course, was relieved that Stephanie had the good sense to settle a long way from Hershey. I agreed ... sort of. "Why should you rearrange your entire life for that ... that trollop?" she had demanded.

Yet the issues between my wife and me continued to percolate. In the evenings Jack Daniels or Canadian Club provided me heaven-sent consolation, permitting me to avoid any soul-searching. While keeping my cards close to the vest, six ounces every night was just about right.

Sometimes eight. Ten on a bad day. You see, I could not give up *both* mistresses, whiskey *and* Steffi. That evening, I double-dosed myself and then nursed and stroked the bottle, peeling off the label, wishing I were peeling away Steffi's clothes instead. Booze and tits.

A few weeks later I visited our Episcopalian pastor—Nadine had switched from her family's Presbyterian Church. During the past several years church attendance had instilled considerable anxiety in me. Now, I felt guilty about seeking help only in a crisis.

"As I live and breathe! Dr. Ira Jefferson Stone! So good to see you, Ira." Peter Shaddox extended his hand, offering a firm double-grip handshake. "We see your wife every Sunday. Everyone misses you. Nadine says your work is going well. And I want to thank you for the attention you gave Joe Cooper and his family in June. Please be comfortable." He waved his hand toward a seat, a captain's chair near the corner of his walnut-veneered desk.

Between thick wool carpeting and rich mahogany ceiling beams, I settled myself before a man framed by polished bookshelves and their learned volumes. On my right hung a Marrakech landscape with snow-capped mountains ascending behind.

I'd always liked the clergyman, a stalwart man with twinkling eyes and thick black hair, flags of gray at the temples. I felt slightly uncomfortable in Shaddox's presence but content that I did not need to fortify myself against any pious criticism. I found him to be a good listener, a healer of the troubled psyche and soul, when Nadine and I sought marital counseling. Perhaps it was because Peter Shaddox had endured his own slings and arrows, refusing now to judge his fellow man.

"Thanks for seeing me, Father. I heard that Joe Cooper had passed away. He suffered a pulmonary embolism at the rehab center. Those drugs wrought havoc on him and his family. He never did regain any speech after shooting himself."

"Yes, he was buried in our cemetery."

With three flicks of his lighter, Shaddox summoned a flame, lit a cigarette, and brandished the smoke. His puffing seemed to go with the Carolina settlement paintings gracing the other wall. "One of my vices. And how is life on your front?"

"What does God think about a man who no longer can find it in his heart to love his wife?" I paused, struggling to grasp hold of some word, some phrase, that might render coherent meaning to the jumble of thoughts that plagued me. But words kept getting tangled on my tongue. "I ... uh ... found another woman," was all that spilled out.

"What does God think? I suspect He thinks you have been blessed with knowing two women," said the minister without missing a beat. The cigarette ash was an inch long and burning.

That was not the answer I expected. It caught me off guard. "Blessed? *Jesus* ... oh ... sorry, Reverend, but my life has been pure hell."

"*Sturm und Drang.* A place you and I most often create for ourselves. With Satan's help, of course. A firestorm of self-recrimination. Those fires of hell are found within ourselves. Unfortunately, we too often distract our mind from old wounds by opening up new ones, one relationship for another." Peter Shaddox focused on the embers smoldering in his fingers. "Rather like this cigarette, wouldn't you say? When I inhale, I get immense pleasure, cushioning my stress over a recent argument with my daughter. But here's the rub—an hour later, I feel guilty. It causes cancer, heart disease, osteoporosis, and a host of other ailments. To lower my anxiety,

I light up another one. I just can't seem to give it up. Simply put—our feelings don't have a brain. Storm and stress."

"I don't see …"

"But the Lord, in His infinite tapestry and wisdom, has blessed us with choices. I can keep on burning cigarettes in my mouth or I can find an alternative. Like chewing Wrigley's Spearmint instead. Or even my favorite, Double Bubble. So far I have failed miserably. Yet, I warrant He has not damned us to Dante's Inferno. We condemn *ourselves* to the ravages of such self-imposed guilt. One of these days I shall cease supporting the cigarette companies. Until then, the struggle goes on." He waved a hand through the coils of blue smoke as the ash bent to gravity. "The struggle goes on."

Feeling a sort of kinship with the man in vestments, I tried to restrain a smile.

"Her name is Steffi." The words, unintended, tumbled out.

"Pretty name. Much like Lucky."

"Lucky?" I furrowed my eyebrows as I focused on the trembling but defiant ash.

"My lady's name is Miss Lucky." He reached to the side table and caressed the soft pack with graceful fancy. "Lucky Strike.

"Ira, you are only human. Like Joseph and his robe of many colors, that long white coat you wear does not confer immunity to the ills and frailties suffered by the rest of us. And neither does your MD degree. *Medicinae Dr..* We've put you on a pedestal, well beyond our reach. That is a very lonely place to be. Not only can we not comfort you in your hour of need, we don't even realize that you require any succor. And then your Steffi comes along with no warning label." Shaddox inhaled and released double jets of smoke. "You would have to be made out of more than stone to resist such a temptation. No pun intended, Ira."

"Yes, sir." I hesitated. "I wish I still loved Nadine. I don't feel much of anything, except sorrow."

"Sorrow?"

"Uh huh." I tilted my head back and stared at the ceiling. A cobweb, looking like a silken parachute, snagged my attention. "I … wish … If only she tried to understand me, where I was coming from. Now it's too late."

"Too late?"

"Our life, Nadine's and mine, is finished. Kaput." I shivered. "And Steffi is about to marry another man," I added.

"Ahh ... I see. You had two women, and now there are none. It takes a strong man to weather that storm, especially when sick patients add weight to a vessel already plowing through choppy seas." With consummate skill the pastor tapped his smoke over a cut-glass ashtray, releasing the dying cinders. He glanced out his window and then carried on.

"Let me offer a modicum of advice, Ira. In your mind, lay Steffi aside in a safe place. Don't try to stop thinking about her. Just whisper to her that you love her and you are tucking her away. Then help Nadine through this crisis. Nadine needs you, and I believe you need her. Dwell no longer on the past, and don't burden yourself with the future. The alpha and the omega are merely the stuff of unkind dreams, as they say. Stay in the present. The world, even your world, is too large to tackle all the problems at once. We men, feeling hemmed in by the past, are prone to wander from the fold, and you are struggling with the rights and wrongs in your marriage. That is more than enough on anyone's plate. The rest, God willing, will wait for another day. In the meantime, surrender your load to Him."

"Thanks for listening to me. I need to digest your thoughts, Reverend." I began to rise from my chair.

"If I may, there is a bit more I should add." With a perpetual look of intense concern, his great blue eyes fell on me once again, and I retook possession of my seat. "Perhaps I can help the three of you look at your lives through, shall we say, polarized glasses. To deflect the glare of self-recrimination, as it were.

"As difficult as this may seem, try to view Nadine as a terribly frightened human being. She finds herself quite isolated in the world and, perhaps, made a wrong turn. She was trapped, even blinded by the excitement of being a surgeon's wife. When the two of you ignored the warning signs ..."

I fidgeted and then felt myself button and unbutton my sport coat as Shaddox continued. "Nadine resorted to the enticements of overspending and overeating and …" The minister searched for a noncommittal phrase. Finding none, he said, "Even suicide."

"Jesus," was all that I could say. The map of our marriage had been clearly there, but I had refused to acknowledge its existence, let alone trace with some intelligence the twin paths as they diverged.

"Nadine has asked me for help. I can't do it without you."

"I didn't think she cared for me anymore." I felt my eyes begin to sting. "I suppose for the sake of the children …"

"Yes, yes, perhaps … Ira, as a medical scientist, do you believe in God, that He exists? And forgives us our sins?" Shaddox snapped open a cigarette lighter, firing another Lucky Strike.

"It's … uh … hard, Reverend. Sometimes I …"

"Here is the way I see it. Just a theory, of course. The certainty of our Creator lies in our genes, our DNA, to be more specific."

"Desoxyribonucleic acid."

"That's the one. Primordial man believed a higher power ruled because the earthlings back then possessed the uncanny talent to recall distant memories of a god-like spirit, a dwelling inherited and passed on down through thousands, perhaps millions, of years—very likely by way of selected and species-specific DNA patterns. Some might even call this the presence of 'the Holy Ghost.' That information, locked up by God in a DNA software package, became masked and secreted away in our primitive brain when we learned to think for ourselves. Mankind then lost the ability to remember divine events and commandments occurring centuries before … though the memories are still hidden in there—hidden and disguised, occasionally released in dreams or revelations as allegory, perhaps. Thus with the power to think began the origin of emotional conflict."

Peter Shaddox tapped his cigarette. "It is much like the swarms of salmon knowing how, when, and where to spawn. Without emotional conflict, by the way. They cannot think, yet they know. We've labeled that phenomenon *instinct*. Spawning is shackled inside their DNA, and that memory is carried on from generation to generation. If they had a *choice*, imagine the internal struggle that fish then would endure. Interesting, don't you think, Ira?

"Free will in life was given to us, beginning with Adam and Eve, the Lord's grand experiment. I often wonder if He should have stuck with the salmon and such. Instead we went from apples to atom bombs. Choices. Not unlike the ones you have now—Nadine or Stephanie."

I was too stressed to think it through. I stood up and gave Peter my hand. "Thanks, Rev. You have provided me much to chew on." But deep down inside such acceptance was blocked for me by that sucking bog of sweet addiction, a dark sickness for which my brain had refused treatment. I tried standing on tiptoe to see the horizon, but the future remained as dark as a celestial black hole.

"Living life is a struggle, Ira. Only dead men don't struggle." Then he thought for a moment. "Or maybe they do—*'to sleep: perchance to dream,'* as Hamlet once said." The man of the cloth raised a benedictory hand. "Come back and see me, my son. May the peace of Jesus Christ be with you." But all my troubled ears could hear were the hoof beats of those Horsemen in the far distance.

Nadine and I resumed marital counseling, and that seemed to put a governor on my out-of-control thinking. That December our family flew to Tucson, Arizona, to spend the Christmas holidays with my parents. Denni and Alexandria were excited to visit Grandma and Grandpa again. Indeed, thrilled to have Daddy in their life once more.

I was having my fourth drink on Christmas evening. We had just sat down for dinner when the telephone rang in my parent's home. Mother, with a curious look, informed me as she handed me the telephone that the caller was some woman. Yes, it was Stephanie. Everyone looked at one another, mystified. That is, everyone except my wife, whose jaw muscles clenched (in harmony with Father's). She muttered the word, *"Tart."* Dad cleared his throat and glared at his plate.

I had no idea how Steffi tracked me down. I believed she and Mikey had been doing well, but now Steffi cried uncontrollably. Calvin Washok had beaten her without mercy. No, she did not provoke it. Little Mike and she had fled while the good doctor was carousing at a local tavern. Would I come and help her? She did not know where to turn.

Steffi was hiding out at a motel called the Rattlesnake Inn in Cherokee, Iowa. Between sobs came her question, begging for an answer—what should she and Mikey do?

Cooler heads would have suggested other alternatives than my warped decision. But I had been drinking. My entire family was stunned when I knocked down three fingers of my irreverent whiskey and then left. Father called after me, "*Ira, you can't do this!* Think of your children, your wife! Stop!"

He did not say what I expected (and deserved): Grow up, Ira, or you will never amount to anything!

That very night I flew to Sioux City, adding high-altitude dementia to my state of insanity. The past and present had merged once again, subjugating thought and reason as I renewed my shuttle between Nadine and Stephanie.

Down deep inside I knew I was crossing another dangerous reef. My Avis rental brought me to Cherokee. Patches of snow covered the ground, edging twigs and tree branches in white as I stepped from my car onto the frosty gravel at the Rattlesnake Inn.

A chilly burst of wind came up, pushing a wooden sign hanging from squeaking rusty chains. The lone word ICE scrolled across its chilled face. I hefted my bag and nervously headed for cabin seventeen, a refuge huddled with its siblings against bad weather. Like all the others, Number Seventeen had a green plastic gingerbread garland running up each side of the structure, joining its partner at the peak of the roof. I thought back to the last Christmas season when I first met Steffi, carrying a box of Swiss chocolates.

I stopped in front of the door. The resonance of coins striking a cement stoop unnerved me. Another damn hole in my pocket. What the hell was I doing here? Insanity. Even so, my unsteady hand reached through a synthetic Christmas wreath and struck the knocker, its icy brass suddenly reflecting a dead man's image ... *stroked the bones of his face* ... then fading while the figure shook his head as if in alarm. Shuddering, I averted my gaze. It was nigh unto midnight. A fine cold mist pelted my cheeks.

"Who's there?" It was Steffi's voice. She sounded muffled, shaky.

"Ira. It's Ira."

"Dear God!"

Stephanie peered out and then threw open the door.

"Darling! I thought you were *never* coming!" She teetered backward and shut the door after I walked in.

Reapplying the locks, Steffi then spun around, a bit unbalanced, and faced me. She stood quietly with one hand on the wall, as if unsure of what should come next. Then my former nurse removed her Ray-Bans.

I quivered at the sight. Blood and edema fluids had forced her left eyelid shut. Strange hues of blue and violet discolored both cheeks, stained further with dried trails of tears. Her lower lip lay split apart, traces of dried blood caking the rent. A silver clip gathered Stephanie's lovely honey-blonde hair behind her neck. She wore Levis and an open-neck sweater, dark red stains scattered atop the shoulders.

"*Good Lord*, Steffi!" I reached out and touched her cheek. "*Calvin did this to you?*"

"I was fortunate to get away with my life. Michael and I loaded my car with our few possessions and ran from there before he returned from his favorite bar." She winced, stared at the floor, then dabbed her right eye with a Kleenex. "I am so scared, Ira. The man is a maniac when he's been drinking."

"Did you contact the police?" I hauled off my new Bordeaux jacket, a Christmas gift from Nadine, and hung it on a wall peg.

"No. His family has powerful connections in Iowa. I wouldn't stand a chance." She sat on a faded leather settee. "I think he was a bit jealous of Mikey."

I glanced around the room.

"I rented two rooms. He is in that adjoining one." She pointed to an open door.

"How is he? I sure have missed your son." We went next door, and I pulled the cover snug over the boy's shoulders, quieting Michael. "Must have been a bad scene for him."

"He was frightened but not hurt—physically. Ira, might we leave early in the morning? The farther away we are from Calvin, the better I will feel."

We returned to Steffi's room. She twisted a platinum ring from her finger and tossed it on the dresser. It bounced against the mirror with a sharp crack.

"Sure thing. Is there space for me in the car?"

"There is room in the back seat for Buddy and some boxes. You and I will commandeer the front." A miniature smile flickered across her cheeks.

"I might as well unpack a few items. First, let me take a peek at your lip." I settled on a couch, gently pulled Steffi near to me, and examined her face. "It looks worse than it is. The lip could use a suture or two."

"No sutures!" She grabbed my hand and spoke in a delicate whisper. "Ira, thank you for coming. Mikey and I didn't know where to turn."

She began to grind her teeth and then chew on her cheek in that strange undulating fashion, the movement rapidly passing, a nervous habit I continued to ignore.

An uneasy strain had accompanied me the entire trip, but now I felt a warm flow settle over me from her touch, from the fingers that had passed me surgical instrument with consummate skill. Fingers that had caressed me, loved me. Nadine faded as Steffi once more gained supremacy. Reverend Shaddox slid far into the distant background. I wanted to kiss the injured woman sitting next to me.

"Where shall I spend the night?" I wondered aloud, snapping open the tan suitcase lying on a baggage rack.

"You take the empty bed. I will sleep with Michael. While you're unpacking, I'll have a shower." Steffi stood up and sauntered toward the bathroom. My eyes gained traction on her still-fascinating buttocks. I had once more inhaled the body odors of Nurse Stephanie, and they would not wash off. Of course, they never had. Slick, unto whom I had declared my fealty, would not let me walk away.

I was enraged and wanted to kill the guy who did this to her. I promised myself that someday there would be a reckoning! Someday.

I undressed and pulled on my pajamas. The heat from Steffi's touch had lit a small fire inside of me. I could feel the pressure as I listened to water dancing against tile, and I sighed, recalling the excitement of our extramarital showers together. A radio sat on the nightstand between the two beds. I turned it to easy listening music from ten years back— "Guantanamera." My tired eyes spotted a minibar, and I drew out two miniatures of Canadian Club and a bottle of soda. The cover of the ice bucket was tilted, cubes overfilling it. I figured she had already had a cocktail. I certainly would have. I poured a pair of drinks, staring at the captivating stream of alcohol as the splash of Steffi's shower ceased.

She padded back into the room while the Sandpipers launched into "Kumbaya." I thought my eyes were playing tricks on me again. For a brief moment a sparkle of pale blue surrounded Steffi, like a spirit blessing the room with a mysterious penumbra of pulsing energy, an electronic benediction. My eyes riveted on her body draped in a pink see-through nightgown. The sheer fabric rippled from her taut breasts, nipples in the vanguard, and then descended over her hips, but no further. The injured sex goddess was not wearing any panties. Her look of desire mixed with apprehension, honey glints reflecting from her pupils. I knew then that she wanted the same damn thing that I did—industrial sex to make up for all the time lost, like an addict in relapse. I handed her the Canadian whiskey and soda, swirling the cubes against the glass.

As she accepted the offering, I sniffed the air and greeted her with, "Panthene de Cartier, I presume?"

"I wondered if you would notice. Thank you for the drink, sweetie."

"You smell so sexy." I caressed her unfettered hair, falling like a glistening waterfall down to her shoulders. A wave partially covered her left eye. "Do you have any other bruises?" I stepped back and swallowed, my eyeballs wandering over the contours of her body. "Guess not. None that I can see. You can be sure that your Calvin will come to regret what he did to you, that I promise."

She folded her arms and attempted to smile, but pain restricted the motion of her lips. "Cute jammies. Daffy Ducks? I'm impressed, Dr. Stone." Stephanie's giggling caused her navel ringlet to dance.

"Cute jewelry," I returned, pointing at her midsection. Laughing, I patted my pajamas. "Mom gave these to me on my last birthday." I drew in a long swallow of my Canadian. "When we were kids, we wore PJs with Daffy Ducks all over. Mike inherited mine and ..."

"Mike?" She glanced at her son. "I don't understand."

I hesitated. "My little brother ... his name was also Michael. He was ten years younger than me."

"I guess I never knew much about your family. Well, I suppose we both have dark secrets. You mentioned Jocelyn and your parents but never a Michael. Where does he live?"

"He died from cancer. In '65. He was twenty-one." I had reverted to my professional façade and spoke in clipped sentences. I finished my drink, and my agitated hands quickly poured another.

"I'm sorry, Ira. I simply didn't know," replied Steffi, covering her lips with her left index and middle fingers.

"I have found it difficult to talk about my brother. We were very close, and his passing bothered me quite a bit. I know ... it seems silly after all these years. But Mike went through hell and back." I wanted to stop this conversation, but it was as if I were driven by Steffi's presence to continue. Like after Charlene. I compromised with, "Christ, I shouldn't be talking to you about this after all you had been through."

"You must tell me more tomorrow." Steffi let out a big sigh. "Hold me, Ira. You may not believe this, but I am terribly horny this evening." She stretched out her arms toward me, erotic passion once again smoldering in those dark amber-gold eyes, eyes that said *yes* in big capital letters.

I stepped into her talismanic field, feeling that memorable hot rush. A familiar pain and appetite crescendoed from the pressure building down under. I wanted to kiss her lips. I could not. "My love, do you think Mikey will be okay by himself tonight?" The words trailed off, the unspoken implication hanging in the air like curling trails of candle smoke.

"I thought you were never going to ask." She licked the cut on her lip. Steffi slowly undulated her pelvis in rhythm with the lyrics of "Come Saturday Morning." Then the intoxicating damsel stepped back and unbuttoned my pajama shirt.

"Jesus, Steff, have I missed you!" My fingers crawled under her negligee and caressed her bottom.

"Hmm, that feels *so* good. Ira, honey?"

"Uh huh?"

"You're the only man who has made me have a climax. A real one, I mean." I gently drew the nightie over her head. "Do you remember what you did?"

"Uh huh." I lifted the naked nurse into my arms and gently swept her onto the bed. "I carried you across the threshold of your boudoir."

"No, silly. After that." She swatted my behind. "Oh, you know what I mean."

"No, what do you mean," I hedged.

"Ooh! I can't kiss you." She fondled my penis, her good eye sparkling. "It hurts me too much. But you can kiss my … me. Or maybe you have grown tired of Nurse DeLeon?"

"Absence makes the heart grow fonder, Steffi."

"Or more lustful."

She placed a cushion under her hips. Set in relief by the lunar corona of her hair, another pillow framed her head. My heart hammered through my chest, and I levered myself on top of her, my knees between her legs.

In full relapse, it was heaven having Steffi next to me again.

*   *   *

"Do I make you that nervous?" I asked, returning from the bathroom.

"I just took one half of a Quaalude. My heart was going to jump out of my chest if I didn't." She forced an impish smile onto her face and pointed to my erection. "Baby, he does want to fuck me, doesn't he?"

"Is that an invitation?" I grinned.

"More like a command." She gave a slow wink with her good eye. "With the pillow under my butt."

I knocked down a long draw from her Canadian and climbed aboard, sliding next to her.

"If this is a sample of your commands, I am your faithful slave," I quipped, nuzzling her neck

"Am I to take that as a pr ... proposal, dear doctor?" She rubbed my chest, her fingers running in delicate patterns through tangled hairs.

"At least it is a basis for discussion, sweetie. First, we have to resolve your present marital status. And mine. I don't think you are into bigamy."

"Okay. You're right. Let's forget such weighty problems tonight. I need you inside me."

Steffi separated her legs and guided me into her willing birth canal. I lay quietly on top of her, feeling the distant thump, thump of her rapid heartbeat against my chest. My eyes took in the battered woman lying under me. She now seemed withdrawn, even distant. I wondered if I should just let her sleep, an idea rapidly discarded.

"Steffi, are you all right?"

"Fu ... Fuck me," she whispered, as if speaking to someone else.

She grabbed my buttocks, pulling and locking me against her. I moved, slowly at first, then faster, a rising tide of passion and uncertainty sweeping over me.

"*Fuck me ...*" The royal decree rose from deep within her throat, traveling over steamy waters from faraway.

I trembled, muscles knotting up, not knowing where this climax was leading, the memories of others now carrying ever-sharper edges. I blinked and now saw a strawberry blonde staring up at me. I slammed my eyelids shut and reopened them—*Stella on a respirator!* My world spun counterclockwise, time running backward.

"*No, no, no!*" I screamed.

But the machine kept recycling, expanding her lungs at twelve per minute. *I love you, Stella!* I was trapped in a black and white movie, devotion and horror compounded together. *I love you, Stella!* Her spastic arms moved, wrapping around me, holding me tight, her pupils still dilated and nonreactive.

"*Fuck me ...*" once more came from far away.

I remained locked in a time warp—*I think I am in love! You are the first to know. Her name is Stella. A strawberry blond ... What do you think,*

Dr. Stone … what do you think, Dr. Stone … My sister? Dead? Oh my God, oh my God! You let her die?

"Fuck me, Daddy!" A distorted laugh erupted. *"You can't screw Stella anymore. I saw to that!"*

My brain could not fathom her hypnotic tongue. I dared not to look anymore, though my body could not cease following her command. Perspiration ran off my back as the drum roll of sexual combustion pounded in my ears. Suddenly the river crested with an explosion, starting deep in my pelvis and radiating to all corners of my body. In an ecstatic transport I joined tightly to this female form, holding her in a frightening embrace until the pressure in my loins abated. I collapsed on top of her. Though the sounds of the ventilator had disappeared, I feared opening my eyes, yet did so.

"St … Steffi, I …" I paused.

That long-ago patient was replaced by a honey-blond nurse, looking like a limp rag doll beneath me. Except for fine slits, both her eyes remained closed. Her respirations were now quiet, slow, her heated skin now cold and clammy. With ambivalent reluctance I pulled away and lifted her right eyelid. The dilated black pupil contracted sluggishly in the overhead light. I shuddered, feeling as if I had just copulated with two dead women.

"See, Frank. *I* do it better than Stella," came a whisper from far away. "See …" Silence.

"Steffi?" *Where are you? How much Quaalude did you really take?*

I shook her now undefended body, trying to get some reaction. She mumbled and turned over. I knew she had taken the drug. But why? *What the hell is going on?* I pondered that while I lay down next to her. *She is terrified of carrying it to consummation with me,* was all that I could conclude. But now that terror, being contagious, infected my very being.

It would seem that I was riding a banshee's broomstick, Stella behind me and Steffi in front, destination unknown. Both had become the rabid ends of my nearly severed nerves.

My wobbly legs took me back to the minibar, where I uncapped another Canadian Club and tossed it down. *"Steffi!"* And then another. I had to. My body demanded it. I needed the treacherous serenity that came from sucking on my devoted whiskey, again and again and again. I just wished it did not leave me with such headaches and nervous hands, the side effects now more frequent. The idea never occurred to me that alcohol—or now the lack of it—might be the witless cause of my hallucinations. A fleeting thought occurred—had she put something in my drink? I returned to the sofa, my body falling through liquid space, eyes swimming in their sockets. I dreamt of a sensuous mouth covering mine, drawing the very breath of life from me. I felt ... I felt loved and abandoned at the same time. This nurse and her sister, working by wit and witchcraft, had ensnared my body and soul. I sucked yet again until all the miniatures were gone. Every one.

Sweet and sour. Steffi and Stella. Canadian and Quaalude. And something else.

*   *   *

"Uncle Ira, Uncle Ira!" shouted little Michael the next morning. He had run into our room and spotted me scrunched up on the sagging couch. "Mommy, look who's here!"

The boy danced and jumped toward me as I fought to open my throbbing eyes. I glanced at my watch—six o'clock the next morning. I felt a gigantic grin stretch my unshaven face, the evening's worries replaced by the joy of seeing Mikey once more.

"Hey, Buddy! Boy, have I missed you." Shaking cobwebs and pain out of my head, I rousted my body. "And look how you have grown!"

"I'm four years old now. See, I have Donald Duck pajamas." He hauled up his shirt, baring his belly button, and then stared at my PJs. "What's your duck's name?"

"Daffy. Daffy Duck," I chuckled. "Looks as if Mommy is still sleeping."

"Mommy hurt. I was scared." Mikey ran over to his mother's bed and then back to the couch. "I'm glad you're here. Will you read to me about Pooh?"

"You bet." I wrapped the child in my arms and gave him a tender squeeze. "Tonight before bedtime."

Little Mike giggled as my whiskers tickled his cheeks. Suddenly the boy chirped, "See my feet?" as he pointed toward his toes.

"Wow! That is so you can swim like a duck. You are really special." I gave him a friendly punch on the shoulder. "Let's go brush our teeth and surprise Mommy when she wakes up, okay?"

"Okay." Mikey grasped my hand, and we ambled toward the sink as if we had never been separated. I had never felt so close to Mikey as now, as if he were my own son.

But rational thinking remained drowned in the bottle—I had abandoned my wife, my girls, and my parents at the Christmas dinner table, the certainty of unintended consequences blinded by that internal committee governing my head.

Steffi, Mikey, and I drove back to Hershey. A few weeks later she found a job at the University of Maryland Medical Center in Baltimore. It was difficult for me to determine how capably she performed there. And my mind went crazy wondering if she slept in another man's arms. Even so, I kept groping for that elusive treasure as I edged toward the next incautious step.

CHAPTER 22

Leave her to heaven
and to those thorns that in her bosom lodge
to prick and sting her.

William Shakespeare
Hamlet

Appleton, Step One Meeting, continued

It took me an hour to tell the story of my flight back into Stephanie's arms that Christmas. When I finished, no one said a word. Perhaps each was recalling his own travesties based on ill-advised, drug-filtered decisions. The old institutional clock on the wall ticked doggedly away.

Fletch started to touch his left earlobe, but his hand fell away mid-flight. He responded in his typically erudite English. "Ira, you can see how applejack becomes a creditor bleeding us of all self-sufficiency, independent thinking, and any will to resist. It certainly happened in your case, especially the *will to resist* part, once you bit into the forbidden fruit. It is like going to bed with a beautiful girl and waking up with one uglier than sin. Whiskey and your Stephanie DeLeon were a deadly combination for your thirsty 'opiate receptors,' as it were. You were pouring gasoline on a campfire."

He nodded for me to proceed, and I once again stepped out of a broken cistern into the past.

"**April 1978**. Intended to drink two glasses of CC. Actually had five. Used ten ounces of whiskey. **Event**—divorced Nadine. **Effect on others**—"

Daddy, Daddy! We're going to play "Duck, Duck, Goose." Come and watch us! Please!
Daddy, Daddy! Will you come to my ballet recital?
Are you going to show movies at our slumber party, like you said?
Daddy, please don't leave us. Please, please! We'll be good. We promise!

"Dear God," I whispered. "I died and they buried me." Their hurt was too much. The massive tombstone bought and paid for by my girls weighed heavily atop my pine box. *How can I ever come back?*

The room turned so quiet you could have heard a pin drop. My voice quivered, the pages of my history now blurry as again I sailed into those uncharted waters, plowing on, cold sweat dripping from my armpits.

*   *   *

By December of 1977, I had published one-hundred scientific journal articles and given fifty professional presentations. I was working hard on another textbook and delivering frequent lectures. At the Atlanta Congress of Neurological Surgeons meeting in October, three months after Nadine and I had separated, I put on an exhibit illustrating numerous cases of astrocytoma surgeries.

Steffi and I were in constant communication. I had drunk too much of her. My brain was irrevocably addicted. Friends and colleagues around me kept warning me about the dangerous path ahead. But I was in denial, and any attempt on my part to cease this perilous endeavor resulted in painful withdrawal symptoms. Our love had turned into a runaway train. To my way of thinking, there was no problem, only excitement and joy, the chains of Stone ancestry ripped apart—and that made me ecstatic. No problem, said Slick, the armed dragoon in my brain who soaked up ever increasing quantities of whiskey, the sponge ever growing.

Steffi, new gold double-hoop earrings dangling from her ears, joined me in the big city to assist in my exhibit. The display went off better than I had expected, and Steff was a terrific helpmate. We discreetly shared the same hotel room, and around then we began making plans for matrimony.

One afternoon we took a break together in our Hilton bedroom. I recall her wearing a vibrant blue print dress of whispering silk with a tucked bodice that arrived at a point below her waist, the fabric taut across belly and breasts, seams strained. My brain was bursting with thoughts of a quick roll in the bed. Instead we fell into a slight disagreement that escalated into a violent war of words. Steffi spun into a bedeviled shrew, screaming out of control, and then, with an inglorious swish of her skirt, she tore out of the room, her purse looped over her arm. Like a Texas tornado—all sound and fury—she had this insane way of twisting a simple dispute into a verbal donnybrook, but it seemed that something deeper gnawed at her. I was stunned, not understanding the meaning or the reason for her thermonuclear response. I suspected, in retrospect, that Stephanie had been sending me a subliminal warning. Of course, looking back, there was nothing subliminal about it. And my tendency toward demanding to have things *my way* did not help, instead blinding me.

In July 1977, Nadine and I separated. I tucked Lexi and Denni into a lagoon at the back of my mind, pretending they would eventually understand. The formal divorce from Nadine followed in the spring of '78, and then I rode off into the sunset with my spurs a'jingling.

In a fever, Steffi and I wed outside Baltimore, Maryland. Mikey was thrilled, and so were his mom and I. Somehow, I felt myself now complete. The Stone *rigor mortis* finally crumbled, replaced by freedom of spirit and unbridled sex. The fact that the most precious things in my life, my two girls, were taken from me by my own hand seemed of little consequence back then.

How could I have done that?

CHAPTER 23

Be careful when you fight monsters,
lest you become one.

Friedrich Nietzsche

Appleton, in the morning

"Mr. Stone, how is it that it took you nearly a whole goddamn ten days to report what you had seen? California did give up smoke signals in favor of Edison's telephone." Sheriff Strickton, a tall, angular man, eyed me, an angry vein pulsating in his temple.

The director, my counselor, the police officer, our home group leader, and I sat in in straight-back cane chairs in Hendricksen's office. The window was closed. Sun reflected off a granite pen holder into my eyes.

"I ... I didn't think it was any of my business." I glanced at Betsy and then inspected my shoes. "You know, like ... like I needed to stay on my side of the street ... kind of."

"*Ira Stone*, common sense would dictate a more critical viewpoint," she countered with a tart demeanor. "At Appleton, what affects one can affect everyone! We had made it clear early on that each of us is to report any violation of the rules of conduct. This is to protect patients and caregivers. And now three people are dead. For God's sake, you *know* what these drugs do to you."

"I ... I realize all that. It's just that ... I don't know what to say. I ... uh ..." I felt my innards squirm under the heat of her gaze.

"You can see that there is a reason why we keep the sexes apart. Addicts and alcoholics in our diseased state lose all sense of maturity, and in some cases we have never risen beyond of our hormonal-driven adolescence," added Betsy. "In previous years we tried mixing men and women within the same unit, but some were always missing the natural boundaries of society and wanted to push the limits. Until we have gained more tools with which to work, Ira, throwing a bunch of us together without restrictions is like pouring kerosene on smoldering ashes."

"Stone, we will need you to come down to headquarters and make a statement later today," instructed the sheriff, clearing his throat so loudly it jarred his scalp-rug. "I would like your director to also be present. Please call my office for scheduling, Dr. Hendricksen. Of course, you may bring the institution's attorney, if you like, though it shouldn't be necessary."

Later that day I found myself shuffling along, aiming toward the administration building. My eyes were fastened on my feet as I kicked a pine cone. I heard a woman's voice crying softly. She sat on a bench under an oak tree.

I stopped and beheld a frail lady holding a handkerchief, dabbing her cheeks. Her hair was blonde and curly, with traces of silver, her eyes large and sad. She wore a blue-on-white polka-dot dress.

I reached down and tossed the pine cone onto the grass. "Hello. May I help you? You seem a bit lost."

"Oh, thank you. You are very kind. It's just that I came from ... from ... Oh, dear."

I was at a loss how to help but hated to just leave her alone.

"I don't suppose you knew a patient. She ..." A long pause followed.

"Men don't associate with the fairer sex. It's not allowed."

"It's about my daughter, Eleanor. She was just starting to get better. I prayed and prayed until my knees hurt that this time she would come home to me and not fall prey again to that ugly stuff."

"Did she leave Appleton? Have you seen her?"

"Ellie? She's dead. My dear sweet Ellie is dead."

Oh, dear God. I sat closer to the woman and folded her hands in mine, willing into her the strength I no longer had.

"She'd almost finished high school. Ellie was a cheerleader and at the top of her class. Until she met that terrible man. The police claimed he was selling her cocaine and meth-something."

Cocaine and meth. "Yeah, really bad drugs." I was at a loss for appropriate words.

"Maybe her death is a blessing. Maybe the Lord needed her."

"A blessing?"

"Maybe. I don't know. She was taking medication for AIDS. The doctor said she got it from her drug use or from unsafe sex. I know she never had … you know … intercourse with men. She must have injected something with unsterilized needles."

"Uh huh. Yes … I suppose." I glanced at the lady, then away. "Are you staying long?"

"I rented a week at a bed and breakfast. They say that the coroner needs to examine Eleanor's body. Then I will have her taken home to Seattle for burial. I told the sheriff about her disease." Her red eyes were dry now. Perhaps talking had helped.

I released her grip.

"She is with Jesus now," smiled the woman.

"God bless you, Ellie's mother." My throat constricted. My own eyes welled up. A greater authority must have been listening, healing. I took in a deep breath.

"Oh. I *am* sorry. I did not mean to cause you any grief. You seem like such a nice man."

"It's just that … that I had heard about her. I liked her a lot. I better go. I am late for a meeting."

"Thank you for stopping by."

"You're very welcome, ma'am."

I arrived at the Step One meeting. We sat around in our usual circle. Everyone was abuzz over the recent events. Everyone except me.

Our group leader entered the room. "Let's quiet down, guys. My name is Fletcher, and I am an alcoholic."

"Hi, Fletch."

"Ira, give us the next example of your being powerless over alcohol, of your life being unmanageable."

I couldn't help wondering what our group leader was thinking after this morning. My eyes scanned the notes in my hand.

> "**October 1978.** Intended to drink two shots of CC. Actually drank eighteen ounces of that whiskey. **Event ...**"

Another ill-advised chapter in my life played out, and my fellow addicts nodded with a kind of empathy. They had all been there. I should have seen it coming—one shot between me and damnation.

Hershey, Pennsylvania

Steffi obtained a position as a triage nurse in a nearby private hospital ER. I barreled forward in academia, and several university deans were reviewing my credentials for a chairmanship—a chance to walk in the Elysium with other demigods. Mikey approached the age of seven years and was building his own little career toward an academic future. I adopted him as my own son after Steffi's half-hearted attempts at locating his father bore no fruit. Adoption seemed the right thing to do, for Mikey's dad had been a despicable brute. Indeed, I loved the boy as my own, and that hole in my gut began to fill.

In the meantime, Nadine, Denise, and Alexandria moved to Durham, North Carolina. They also took Buffy, my conscience.

At that point, Steffi's medications—Quaalude for her spiky anxiety and amphetamines for dietary weight-loss—were in fact legal and available by prescription. I know. I often wrote those for her, in spite of the fact she already possessed an eye-stopping figure, quite thin and well proportioned.

Her narcoleptic behavior during copulation continued to befall her. I had become rather accustomed to such and was no longer much concerned, since the foreplay more than made up for her schizoid climax. I knew, of course, that her drugs played a role, but I remained in denial, in a trance, building my reality from only a part of the truth. Canadian Club, my drug of choice now, had increased a bit to eight ounces in the evenings, double on weekends. Steffi was now my wife, and CC remained my mistress, both giving me that heady rush. I *deserved* both. After all, I was a damn hard worker and a good provider, wasn't I?

I spent a Saturday deer hunting with one of my colleagues. The next day at nightfall, after Stephanie and I had enjoyed a few cocktails together, I fell into an uneven nap on the couch. Steffi kissed me on the cheek and informed me that she was going shopping for a while. I detected the scent of Panthere de Cartier, her weapon of choice, trailing as she closed the front door. I briefly dozed off, only to be awakened by children singing a *Mother Goose* verse near our window.

> *"Ring around the rosy,*
> *A pocket full of posies,*
> *Ashes, ashes,*
> *We all fall down!"*

My mind, like developing Polaroid film, suddenly sharpened, deciphering. *She wears that perfume only on special occasions.* I sat straight up, unfocused jealousy driving up my heart rate, panic setting in. *Where is she going?* Then I reconsidered. *Why am I being so paranoid?* But I belted down a large gulp of straight CC and launched into action, following quickly after her. I caught sight of Steffi jumping into her Firebird. Leaving little Mike asleep and alone at our apartment, I leapt into my own car as the falling sun, now blood-red, pulled a blanket of deep purple through the sky, the night settling around me like a slow blindness. The fact that I not only left a child by himself but also drove above the speed limit while intoxicated failed to concern me.

Stephanie tore out of the parking lot, smoking her Firestones, exhaust pipe ablaze. She sped across town, darted into another apartment complex, and skidded to a halt, tires sledding on gravel. I tracked her with nervous stealth as I slipped, backlit, into the perilous shadow of my elongated form. My wife quickly looked around and then knocked at number 158. A silhouette with huge shoulders opened the door, closing it after she entered. I thought about my old 30/06 rifle in the trunk. The firearm was locked and loaded, the safety on—the gun, not my frenzied behavior.

A dog howled nearby. I retrieved the firearm from my Thunderbird, rationality cast aside, daggers slicing reason in the ghostly indigo. I waited, hard on the grotesque heels of tremulous silence, the feral glare of a malignant, high-octane resentment setting in, gnawing, growing by the minute, my temples throbbing. I waited—and waited and waited. My body shivered as my brain took in the tortured trees sticking their claws up into the dead sky.

Two a.m. passed, my sorely castrated and tipsy heart thumping. Two-thirty saw the bitch steal out and walk toward her car, the man with his left arm enfolding hers, the right attached to a glowing brightly cigarette. Under a hint of buttery light from an overhead pole they kissed in the shadow, and a white-hot fireball of anger burned through my stomach, my innards now hit full force by the extent of her deceit. My hands felt the muzzle rising up, and I heard myself call out, the two in my gun sights. My chest suddenly expanded, pulling in vast quantities of hot air as both turned toward me. Oh, how I wanted to put her in the ground that moment.

"*Oh, my God!*" Steffi screamed. "Don't shoot, Ira! It is not what you think! Dear Lord! Put the rifle down! *Please!*"

The stranger stood frozen on the spot, voiceless, dropping his burning smoke.

With delirious intent my whiskeyed finger jerked the trigger. A sharp crack echoed. The slug whistled by his head, though not by much.

"Come on, you little shit. Drag your sorry ass back to our fucking nest."

She broke loose from her partner's grip and careened toward me, stumbling on the gravel. My wife came to a stop, breathless, her eyes full of pain and dread as I lowered my weapon, the faint smell of gunpowder hanging in the air.

"If you ever come back here again, Steff, I won't be responsible for what might occur."

"I was just ... we're just friends. I won't see him again. I promise!" An assurance, I feared, that might not be a certainty. Her face was rigid with terror. Thinking back on it, I wasn't sure if it was because of him or me. There was something else going on, but I could not lay my finger upon it.

"You mean like you promised to not see Fabian Tellini. Is that what you mean, Steffi?"

"Ira, please ... please."

"Leave your damn wheels here. We'll pick it up tomorrow."

The stranger lit up again and then crept away, a wayward shade joining the heavy blackness.

My intoxicated foot punched the accelerator, a bit too fast as we took off into the curdling night. I wondered how close I was to pulling the trigger again. Another swallow of CC and I might have done the deed. I knew she had been screwing him. I just *knew* it. I simply could not follow that thought to a rational conclusion.

A fabric of treachery was taking shape, and I could feel her love peeling away like a thin layer of cheap varnish, my own false heart facing circumcision. Over the succeeding days, a ghostly calm descended.

We moved into a new apartment near the med center. Denni and Lexi, trapped between two worlds, would visit us on occasion, but it was so terribly painful for them and for me when they returned to North Carolina. They balked at spending holidays in Hershey, soon refusing to come at all. Later they confided in me. Standing before my girls one evening, Stephanie devolved into a witch, threatening to *kill* them if they ever appeared on our doorstep. A terrible sadness swept over me when I heard this, and I knew there would be no end to the reckoning. The fear and anguish my children must have endured ...

Steffi's bizarre behavior devolved even further, and I suspected she still was seeing her male friend and that he might be the source of surreptitious drugs. I just could not prove it. I needed to mount some sort of surveillance. I tapped our telephone with wire, safety pins, earphones, and a recording apparatus. It lay in the bushes next to the line coming down the brick wall, and the audiotape ran only when the call circuit was activated. Every day I played back the cartridge. Steffi's faithlessness was rampant. I waited, an obsessive paranoia—justified or not—ruling my behavior. I could feel the skin of an internal storm bubbling, swelling like a balloon ready to burst.

One evening in 1980, I was departing from the office, brooding about my secretary. Evelyn had been wearing sunglasses, hiding an obvious bruise to the left eye. She and her husband had argued earlier, and I wondered if he had been battering her. I planned on taking her out for a drink the next day, seeing if she would vent her emotions.

The clouded sky swept into an undertaker-black. I had become more and more worried that Stephanie's paramour would show up, the gent who likely had taken over my drug-dealing job—by prescription in my case, of course. I had to tear myself away from this unholy nest, distance myself from an impending catastrophe. This tardy realization, marinating in high anxiety, rode on my shoulders like the head of the Headless Horseman.

Upon arriving home, my ears commenced a deep and painful ringing. My hand reached for the brass doorknob. The image of a shaking head reflected off the polished metal and quickly dissolved. My heart tripped … it couldn't be! I squeezed my eyes shut, pushed the door open, and stumbled into an eerie stillness, my skin shrinking.

"Steffi? Hello?" Amid the prickling malignancy came a strange sucking sound, like somebody draining a drink with a straw, a huge invisible vacuum drawing out every ounce of oxygen. "Anybody home?" A floorboard squeaked while I crept with stealth toward the kitchen. A stiletto of light stabbed in from the cracked-open door. My feet inched forward against a faint and familiar rusty smell. I entered the chamber, my cerebral liquids congealing. *"Jesus, help us!"* I stood there, recoiling, petrified, hearing a dry shriek within me. I finally gathered myself against the icy chill running down my spine.

"Steffi, Steffi! How …?"

There she was, my wife, lying dazed, semiconscious on the floor. Stephanie's cheeks were swollen, black and blue from hemorrhage. Her naked form was writhing, convulsing, snaking hard along the wall. Opaque liquid and small gouts of blood dripped from a scalp laceration and then pooled onto the floor beneath Steffi's head. Her swollen lips were silent, emitting only ratchety respirations. I remained frozen on the spot. Then I mobilized my wits and quickly looked around for signs of an assailant. Not another soul was lurking that I could see, at least not now. Nobody, except those god-awful, frightening shadows.

As she quieted, I leaned over and listened to her heart. Her pulse was fast but regular. Air filled her lungs, though some secretions bubbled in the bronchi. Familiar arms then reached up and waved in the air. An eyelid rose, revealing her pupil, a deep well of toxic water reflecting darkly at the bottom, the other lid too swollen to open. Steffi coughed, whimpered, and turned over on her side. I grabbed her body and held her tightly to me as I kissed her bloody cheek. My throat clenched, and I knew then that the taste of her blood would never leave me.

As I lifted her, I saw it, something shiny. A kitchen knife lay there, stained with blood. Her blood? I did not touch the blade. A sultry evil hung deeper in the air. A drop of sweat rolled down my back.

I glanced up and spied a boy standing in the kitchen doorway, forlorn, thumb in his mouth, a thin sound of panic coming from his lungs, his wet eyes filled with the invisible color of worry and dread. *Did Mikey witness this dreadful trauma?* I hugged the child to my breast and tightly held him as I brought the boy back to his room.

Then I carried his mother to the couch, grabbed a wet handtowel, and cleaned her face and neck. I wrapped her head with a bath towel until I could get some dressings. The scalp laceration needed suturing, but the hemorrhaging had ceased, leaving just minimal oozing. It was rather jagged, unlikely caused by a knife. By then she was breathing okay, struggling to sit up. She stared at me but would not—or could not—tell me what happened. A newfound lover? Leaving her resting with an ice pack on her cheek, I rushed outside, retrieved my recording cartridge from behind the apartment, and dashed over to the office to gather up some antiseptics and bandage material.

While in my library I stopped to quickly play the tape, looking for a clue to her attacker. I listened, transfixed, frozen, like a pillar of salt. The final message played.

"Please help me. *Oh God, he tried to kill me!*"

"Who is that, ma'am?"

My ... my husband. He went to his office. I think he is coming back. Please send an officer!"

"Give me your address and that of his office."

"Mine is ...

Steffi had just called the sheriff, accusing *me* of battery, and the troopers were on the way! *Jesus! What the hell is going on?*

"*Steffi!*" I screamed. I felt a surge of unfocused fear, a sense of menace swelling up as my hand grabbed a bottle of JD by its throat, hauling it from within the credenza. If there were ever a time for a stiff drink, it was now. *Dear Lord, it was now.*

In short order the police arrived. A knock came on my door. I opened up, and there stood two patrolmen to greet me. The smaller one with eyewear kept fingering a ready nightstick, his spectacles reflecting my desk lamp. The larger officer kept pulling at his mustache.

"We need to speak with you, Dr. Stone." The short man, eyelids perpetually widened with an air of one suffering from thyroid disease, fixed me with his gaze. "Sergeant Loomis and I are here to place you under arrest."

"*Arrest?* My lord, what for? Did I forget to pay a parking ticket or something?" was the best I could reply. I rubbed my forehead and grimaced. "I guess you guys aren't joking. What on earth is the charge?"

"I am Lieutenant Strapton. A Stephanie DeLeon Stone ..." He checked his clipboard. "Your missus, has claimed you assaulted her. You are her fuckin' husband, are you not?" The cop postured himself into a Napoleonic stance, contracting his eye muscles in a fit of impatience.

I swallowed, unable to find the proper response. Finally, "Yes ... yes, I am, but I never touched her. I'm not that kind of man. There's been some terrible mistake."

"Sure, Doc, sure. You have the right to remain silent ... anything you say can ... assault and battery ..." The lieutenant's Miranda warning sounded disconnected, distant. Unreal. "Please accompany us down to the station. You may phone your fuckin' attorney from there. I'm sure we won't require these." Strapton tapped the metal handcuffs hanging at his belt.

"And there is some mystery over the wife's name," added Loomis. "Is it *Stephanie* or *Stella*? She's still confused, it seems. It states Stephanie DeLeon Stone on her driver's license, but she insists her name is Stella. That a nickname?"

"No, sir. I don't know what to say. Stella was her sister. She's dead."

The two officers looked at each other.

Christ, I must be dreaming a damn nightmare! What is Steffi up to? My heart and mind in a turmoil and flanked by two of Hershey's finest, we departed the Medical Center and stepped into the waiting cruiser. *What am I going to do about my surgery in a few hours? And early morning rounds? My job, my license! I am going to I lose them! What is going on? Steff! What have you done! Who did this to you?*

I was desperate for Jack Daniels or CC or anything! I felt as if my body had been impaled upon a rapier's point. The other shoe had dropped. But even *still* I was in love with the woman! *I could not help it,* reason long since AWOL. The thought, *My God, am I sick!* crossed my mind but only for a nanosecond.

*   *   *

I fidgeted while sitting in front of Lieutenant Strapton's desk, a wobbly oak affair under a slowly revolving ceiling fan. A squeak accompanied each rotation of the blades. Sergeant Loomis, a man with the lobster-red jowls of a heavy drinker, leaned his sizeable butt against a windowsill, and observed his partner take information from me. This sergeant, in a nervous twitch, kept looking at his watch and cracking his knuckles. And yours truly? I stared at an incongruous print of King Louis XIV pinned to a side wall.

I turned toward the official scribe. "What am I supposed to have done to my wife, Lieutenant?" But I knew. Of course I knew. Yet I had to overcome my bad-guy image, the unhealthy portrayal rapidly escalating in the eyes of the men in blue. No one would really believe me—not the police, not the judge, not the attorneys, nor my colleagues. Beside myself, only two people in the Keystone State would believe me—her assailant and Stephanie DeLeon Stone, though I was not even sure about that assumption, given her state of mind.

Strapton, appearing as hard as cobblestone, slammed down his pen. "No one deserves the kind of beating she...what's her name?...Stephanie got. She's in a fuckin' terrible condition and presently under treatment at your fuckin' emergency room. What the shit is it with you fuckin' types? And that kid..."

"Mikey! Is Michael all right? Where is he?" I tried to stand up, but the other cop's hand pushed me back down. "I've got to get to my boy! He needs ..."

"Listen, you worthless bag of chickenshit, you ain't goin' nowhere near that kid or his ma. They need to be kept safe from the likes of you."

"Okay, okay! What's going to happen? May I go home or am I sleeping here tonight?"

"When we're through with the fuckin' paperwork, you can leave, but do not approach within a mile of your fuckin' apartment if ya don't want jail time. You got it, asshole? The judge will deliver a restrainin' order against ya when the fuckin' sun comes up. Don't make matters worse for yourself." Strapton adjusted his glasses, overhead lights bouncing off their surfaces. "Where ya stay is up to you. Fuckin' hotel. Friend. Relative. Just not home. Check with yer mouthpiece after you've had some breakfast." He whispered, "Fuckin' cocksucker."

He never mentioned the knife. Maybe it had been meant for me.

An hour later, I turned the key to my fuckin' office, slipped by my desk, and slumped on the couch. With elbows on my knees, I dropped my head into my hands. *What should I do, where to go?* I didn't have the heart to tell anyone what was going on. Hell, I didn't *know* what was going on. A Venus flytrap. That was all I could think.

After a night on the office davenport, I completed early rounds and canceled my surgery and appointments. Jack Daniels stood on his head in the trash basket. The desk clock chimed eleven times. I was desperate to call Steffi, fool that I was. I mulled over the vexing thought. Neither the police nor my attorney said anything about phoning, warning me only against a physical presence near my family.

I hemmed and hawed, dithering and drawing aimlessly on a sheet of letterhead. The cradled telephone laid next to the desk blotter, daring me to dial home, a mere mile and a half away. Home? That's *my* home ... I paid the rent! Damn, I could stand it no longer. *She must have been released by now.* My fingers hefted the receiver and dialed the numbers. One ring. Two. Three. I slammed the handpiece down. My gut burned. Steffi was manipulating me. Or *was* it Steffi? I needed a drink. I reached for the drawer, forgetting that I had emptied the bottle. I clutched the phone again and dialed ... and waited. But the voice I wanted and dreaded to hear did not answer.

Suddenly I heard a faint sound of crying. Evelyn was at lunch. I was in no mood to see anyone. I stood up and peered down the hall. Then I noticed a head bobbing around the corner. *What on earth ... Some kid from peds?*

I sighed and took a step toward the hallway intersection. "Hey, sonny, are you lost? Where ..."

The brown hair disappeared, and I darted after the child. "Oh, my God! Mikey! How did you ... Where is Mommy?"

Michael turned, remaining silent as he sat on the floor. His eyes appeared to focus on the linoleum. I picked the lad up, held him in my arms, and gave him a loving squeeze. "Mikey, please ... where is Mommy? Is she downstairs in the car?"

"Mommy's sleeping in bed."

"Is ... is she ok, Buddy?"

"Her face doesn't look very good, 'n she is talking funny."

"How did you get here? Who brought you?"

"Nobody, Daddy. I walked."

"Walked ... You walked!" *I don't believe this. The kid traveled over a mile?* "How did you know the way?"

"You showed me. Remember? We went together once after school." Mikey hesitated. "I stopped at all the red lights. Honest."

Good God.

"I almost got lost once. Some lady helped me. She thought I was running away, but I wasn't."

"Let's go sit down in my office, on the couch." I released little Mike and took him by the hand. We entered my library. I loosened my tie and sank into the leather with a *whoosh*. The boy tapped his shoes against one another and wiped his cheeks.

It was then that I saw it. Or them—bruises over his legs and arms in the shape of a belt. *Jesus!*

"Mikey, what are these marks from? Did someone hit you?"

The lad was quiet at first. "It was my fault. I was being bad. I won't be bad again. I promised Mommy."

I did not know what to do. But I was going to do something, and soon.

"Daddy?"

"Yes, Buddy." My hands tousled the boy's hair.

"I'm scared." Again the boy bumped his heels against each other, the clicking speeding up. Tiny tears formed on his eyelids. "Are you coming home tonight?"

"I want to, but I can't." I fought the urge to make a six-year-old understand a court order, but Mikey would never comprehend. Damn it, neither did I. "Maybe in a few days."

"Mommy isn't going to take me away like you and she did before, is she?"

What? I pulled Michael's chin toward me. "In Iowa? What do you mean, *'like you and she did before?'* Wasn't Calvin being mean to you? Didn't you *want* to leave him?"

Mikey was silent, and then he mumbled, "I don't know. But ... but I was glad to see you anyway."

What in heaven's name lay beneath those words? I studied the lad. Something in the back of my mind ignited, like another part of an algebraic equation unfurling, one with so many unknowns. I was not about to be the cause of Michael losing another father. I had some research to do.

"Let's get you back, Buddy, before Mommy calls the police to find you. I promise you won't lose another daddy if I have anything to say about it."

I dried Mikey's eyes with a tissue, and we strolled, hand in hand, toward the elevator.

"Daddy? ... Aw, never mind."

"What is it, Buddy?"

"Nothin'."

I hunkered down to Mikey, eye to eye. "Try me."

"Sometimes I pretend that I am Piglet and that Pooh Bear loves me ... Daddy Michael doesn't love me," he sniffed. "Daddy Ira, do you love me?"

"Oh, Buddy. I've loved you since the day we first read *The House at Pooh Corner* together. And I always will." I pressed the child against me. I could feel his beating heart. *And I always will.*

With some trepidation I drove Mikey to within a half block of his home. I watched as he walked away and then through the front door.

Two week later His Honor finally gave consent for me to drive to our townhouse and retrieve my personal effects. Two different but nervous cops accompanied me. They did not want to be there. Shit, neither did the accused. My mind was scorched by her fickle passions—the voice of an angel, the eyes once more those of a cobra. As I gathered my courage, some neighbors stopped by, assembling on the sidewalk to see what was going on. I knocked on the door, waited, then rapped again. The portal suddenly opened. Steffi and a scowling nurse friend stood there, defiant, arms locked and folded over their chests. A few bandages adhered to her scalp.

"Hello, Steff. I'm here to pick up my things." My eyes searched for Mikey.

"Michael is with a sitter for the day, if you are looking for him. Seeing you here would be *way* too stressful for him." The corners of her lips curved into a smile that settled at half-mast, her look of savage sweetness no longer foreign to me. Fatigue shadowed her eyes, her incandescent mood twisting.

"I see. Well, may I come in?" I felt like a duck out of water, even though this was my home. Or used to be.

The small crowd increased to about twenty curious and whispering onlookers.

"Be my guest. I have no idea what you expect to find," she replied in a loud and scornful voice that could have cut glass. "You took everything with you the day before you … you came back to beat me. An attempt to kill me, no doubt."

"Why are you saying that, Stephanie? *Why?*"

"Did you come here to *verbally* abuse me also? Please finish with your search and just leave!" My former scrub-nurse glared at me like a tigress with flattened ears.

"I hope they put you away for good!" came a strident whisper from Steffi's friend.

I gritted my teeth. While the apprehensive men-in-blue stood by the front door, I wandered around the townhouse. My clothes had disappeared, along with my treasured briefcase, a birthday gift from the VA hospital nurses. My closet and dresser drawers stood empty. All my fishing gear and sporting equipment vanished. I could not find any mementos or photos of my childhood, my daughters, Mom and Dad, or my brother and sister. Nothing remained except a multicolored cap on my dresser, the prize I forgot to pick up once upon a time. I did not yet see my likeness hung in effigy. Without thinking, I grabbed the walleye-pike icon hanging from my neck chain. *At least she didn't get this.*

Steffi sauntered alone into the bedroom as I was about to leave and quietly hissed words I shall never forget. "*Satisfied*, Dr.? Oh, by the way, remember when you let that patient die? What was her name? Charlotte, wasn't it? My goodness, Ira, I wonder how the IV line got disconnected? About the time I took a potty break, wasn't it? That poor anesthesiologist wasn't happy when I passed by her and inquired if I could do anything for her. Dear me. You should have been more observant, *Doctor.*"

Oh, dear Jesus! "What's going on, Steffi? Why did you do this? Revenge? At me? What have I done to deserve this?" My innards trembled, and fine moisture gathered over my forehead as I faced my estranged wife. I then sat down on the bed and lay my head in my hands. "Tell me, for Christ sake."

"*Do you really want to know?*" A glare of pure hatred spilled from her eyes. "Before we met I obtained a nursing job at that VA hospital in California." She glanced at her nurse friend, who had just walked in. "I got hold of Stella's records, and it was obvious you let her suffocate! It was too late to bring a malpractice suit against you—the statute of limitations had passed. Instead I found out where you moved to and worked. And here I came, to be your OR nurse. *To find out what type of devil you were!* And then … But your terrible charms trapped me, just like they did Stella. I believed you truly loved me in return … *Until you raped and beat me! Just like you did Stella!*"

I was speechless and nearly staggered back into the living room.

"Come on, Doc." My escort laid a hand on my shoulder. "We better leave. Check with your lawyer." The sergeant waved me toward the door.

Outside, we were heading for the cruiser when suddenly the woman I *even yet* dearly loved devolved into a banshee in tights, shrieking after me as the small crowd of bystanders edged forward. Feet planted on the front stoop, her electric eyes ran me up and down with a scathing look, the scar on her cheek turning scarlet.

I watched, my mouth agape.

Somewhat unsteadily Stephanie leaned forward on the steps, mumbling. Her arms flapped at her sides, while she foamed with head extended. Shivering inside, I wondered if Steffi were entering an epileptic state. Then her lids opened, eyes flashing bright like coals in a dying fire, thighs spread, feet glued to the concrete. Her left hand began to strike forward, but then she slapped her own ear, as if trying to kill a buzzing insect burrowing within.

A wry half-smile crept across her face, her countenance rearranging itself. She blinked and then delivered a series of staggering punches.

"*Dr.* Stone, tell the officers and all these good citizens how you murdered a patient on the operating table!"

The crowd inhaled as one.

"And Sergeant, did you know that this stellar surgeon here *inflicted a horrible death on his very own brother? And my darling sister suffocated under his hand!* Murdered, in fact! Dear God, his last wife was fortunate to get rid of him. How *evil* can one man be!"

Everyone's eyes shot open. This Good Witch of the North had devolved into the Wicked Witch of the East. Surrounded by a brief penumbra of blue, she balled up her fist and shook it at me. *"On you, Ira Stone, and all your descendents, I place the curse of Satan!"*

Stephanie faced heavenward, hands clasped together in prayer. "Thank you, Lord. Mikey and I are lucky to still be alive." She curled toward me and the police. "Officers, keep him *away from us!"* Steffi's lips twisted even further. "If anyone sees him near here," she pleaded with the spectators while aiming a quaking forefinger at my chest, "call the police immediately! *My life and that of a small boy depend on all of you!"*

Steffi and friend bolted back into the townhouse and slammed the door. Astonished, my own shoes now cemented to the pavement, I looked hard after her. I was in shock, my heart filleted by a master illusionist. And I did not understand why. *This is the woman I married?* She was a western diamondback whose long-ago rattle I had refused to hear.

Checkmate.

No one moved or spoke for minutes. Soon, the whispers evolved into mutters as angry eyes turned toward me. The constable cleared his throat and led me past the murmuring throng and into the cruiser. I would have to wait for the trial. I wondered where Mikey was. Hell, I even questioned where the fuck *I* was.

Our love had flowered into a terrible madness, and I now felt as if my mind had been brutally raped, its most intimate trust and affections excoriated.

The cruiser dropped me off in front of the hospital. Shaking inside, I walked into my office. *Maybe I am that evil.* I tried to sneak past Evelyn, but my secretary could always catch me, as if she had internal radar.

"Dr. Stone, a patient called and … you don't look so well."

"I'm … okay." But I could not hide the tremor in my voice or the moisture on my cheeks.

She stood up, a quizzical demeanor on her face. "No, you are not! We have been together a long time. You look torn up inside."

"Steffi had me arrested." I told her the rest of the story and, fearing some moral analysis, struggled to maintain composure.

Instead, Evelyn reached out and pulled me against her. That was when I broke down and cried like a baby.

"Oh, Ira. It will all turn out as the Lord wishes. And you have all of us here for you."

And I did, even though my pride and self-respect had been eviscerated.

Chapter 24

It is as hard to see one's self
as to look backwards without turning around.

Henry David Thoreau

Appleton, another day

I had finished another segment of my story. A minute of near-sacramental silence followed. I gathered myself up, feeling somewhat stronger. My past had become an open book, a new experience for me.

Then Fletcher surveyed the group. "Anyone have questions for Ira?"

"I do!" Nolan's hand shot up.

This eager fellow patient was a lawyer from Kalispell, Montana, who wore short cargo pants. Riotous brown hair sprung in wavelets from the top of his scalp. From his neck dangled a heavy bronze chain with a medallion, a circle surrounding a triangle at its center. He leaned into my personal space.

"You gave a good account, Ira. All we heard about was the chemical, alcohol. But what about you, the person? Are you an alcoholic?"

"Sure. Okay." A terse reply. I still could not come to grips with the true nature of my condition.

"I did not hear anything about other drugs. Most of us have had poly-drug use. What about you?"

"Nothing else."

"Your history mentioned Valium," reminded Fletcher, breaking in, his clear brown eyes settling on me.

"That's just a tranquillizer. You know, to help me sleep," I hedged.

"Valium is a benzodiazepine. When you were weaned from ethanol and Valium, the benzo actually inflicted more agony than did the alcohol. Think about it. Are you not also a drug addict?"

"Oh," was all I could muster. *Benzo-bait? A junky? Dope fiend? Not this guy!*

"However, let us keep in mind that alcohol is in fact a drug akin to a class-two narcotic, though legally dispensed without a medical prescription and without a doctor of pharmacy degree."

"You did not mention blackout spells." Nolan leaned forward again. "Do you recall any?"

Someone rapped on the side entrance from the kitchen ... My hand managed to open the door. No one was there! Not a damn soul ... "Ira Stone! Garth stood right in front of you! He said that you just shuffled your feet and stared at him. What is going on with you?"

I closed my eyes. "One, I think." But I had the feeling that others had occurred. My first wife reminded me of many such events while I was drinking.

"Comments?" Our leader looked about the gathering.

"I'll start." Sebastian wore another Harley-Davidson tee shirt, white with charcoal lettering this time. "Three broken marriages and a fourth a gnat's eyelash from a coroner's inquest." His ponytail bounced as he talked, pounding his right fist into the opposite palm. "You admit your marital life was unmanageable, what with your romping through woman after woman. What character defect contributed to your failure to love, honor, and cherish till death do you part?"

"Huh? I didn't do anything. I provided for their kids, for crissake! Those women were the ones to cause the separations. I explained all that." My finger ran around the inside of my frayed collar. "I worked hard. Damn hard."

"*Arbeit macht frei*, Kemo Sabe," returned Sebastian. "'Work makes us free' was Satan's inducement at Auschwitz. It becomes impossible for guys like us to see our role in a divorce. Work? Is it possible that you were so full of your working self that the wives failed to receive any affection and understanding from you, as you sacrificed them on the altar of your ambition? Even your children, perhaps? Work? Ira, I see a lot of me in you. I always criticized my women but could never keep my side of the street clean. We are like intensely focused bird dogs, losing sight of the *cherish* part of *love, honor, and cherish*. It's worth thinking about."

"Thank you." I was too numb to even consider this, yet I sensed something eerily familiar in those clanking chains.

Fletcher's thumb and forefinger squeezed his earlobe as he checked his Seiko. Lunchtime was approaching. "Derrick?" Another patient, a Texas wrangler.

The tall, wiry man with a hooded sweatshirt displaying the words DALLAS COWBOYS nodded toward me. Pale yellow hair with an untamed cowlick and in desperate need of scissors fell below his jug ears, ending in sickle-shaped sideburns. Bushy eyebrows arched their backs like two angry cats. Flashing two gold teeth, he spoke in a raspy, cigarette-tortured drawl, his vocal chords molded by years of Marlboros.

"Y'all seem to gloss over your feelings about Denni and Alexandria. Tell us a bit more about your daughters?" Intense wolf-gray eyes seemed to shimmer like stainless steel above his flat, rawboned face.

I stared at my fingers, knuckles now white and locked in prayer. *Can't we do this later?* I just could not come to grips with the facts. The facts. What were the facts? Images of Denise and Alexandria slipped in front of me once again. *Daddy, where are you? Daddy, please don't leave us. Daddy, what will happen to us?* As they disappeared, my ears heard the triple ringing of the bells of doom. I had lost my kids, my wife, my grandchildren, and my God. It's a wonder I still had a job. I did not deserve to be forgiven.

I looked up. "Denni struggled through college, wandered from job to job and then pulled herself together. She spent a summer teaching English and helping at a Bombay leprosy hospital, and … and I'm sorry. This really hurts. I didn't mean to …" I fought to check the tears from breaking loose, but they had a mind of their own. *Denise, I simply wasn't there when you grew up. How can I make it up to you? Christ, how can I even make it up to me?*

A moment of unsettling quiet followed.

"None of us here meant to, but we damn well did!" Nolan stabbed the air with his pencil, jumping in again. He leaned toward me and bore in as if he were a prosecutor grilling, flaying one of his fucking defendants. "And Alexandria?"

"She became a drug addict. Like me," I managed to whisper. *Forgive me, Lexi. Dear God, I am so sorry.*

"So you admit you are a damn drug addict?" My interrogator fired another broadside.

"That's enough, Nolan," cautioned Fletcher. "Ira will have an opportunity to be confronted by his daughters."

And my son, I wish, wherever he might be.

"We all can see the power of these drugs, what they have done to our ungoverned lives—even in the face of imminent death and destruction of self and family." Fletch stood up. "Okay, let's close and head for lunch."

We formed up the circle.

"Who keeps us sober?"

"Our Father who art in Heaven ..."

That same evening I found myself in the library once more, chewing on pretzels. Was Steffi out of my life? Not quite. Maybe not ever, without surgical excision. The Step One meetings had been traumatic, but strangely enough the urge to drink was not there. It felt good.

I grabbed the local newspaper and reread the bulletin—

> *Murder suspect apprehended. Henry Stamen, known meth addict, was taken into custody by City police and turned over to the County. The young man had been hiding out at a local San Francisco flophouse. Authorities are not giving out any more information at present, though an anonymous source says that one of the Appleton patients had been a witness. This follows ...*

My stomach clenched. I dropped the paper and headed for supper.

After our meal I sat down on a bench by a pine tree. *Might you tell us a bit more about your daughters?* Denni seemed to keep her head on straight. But, sadly, Lexi had inherited my defective gene.

The next morning it was Derrick's turn to continue his story about the unmanageability of his life. I did not learn about the affects of methamphetamine until Alamo told us that he saw real-life images of armed men coming after him with sabers drawn, certain death imminent. He emptied his .357 carbine at the imagined attackers, nearly killing innocent bystanders. The Texan wept bitterly, his head in his hands, as he tormented himself with his story of what he called *tweaking.*

"Yeah, I stood there aiming at the front walkway when a black came toward me, his knife drawn.

"'Stop right there, you ass fucker!' I hollered.

"But he just kept coming. My headache returned, blinding me in a white-hot hatred. I felt as if sweat was leaking from every pore, my body kind of like pulsing. He was the bastard causing my hideous sores, and I had to kill him before he got me. I raised my piece, took aim, and fired. And fired again, emptying my weapon.

"Somewhere out there I heard a voice crying. I turned and ran into my house, needing a fix to take away the sting. I peered into a mirror. There he was again, like a photographic negative! I believed I had slain the shit. My fist smashed the looking glass. Hot blood drenched my clothes as I fell into a coma. Apparently an epileptic seizure occurred. I remember waking up in solitary. I had shot a neighbor in his arm and paralyzed my sister with a bullet to her spine. She ain't never going to walk again. Oh Lord oh Lord oh Lord ..."

A long silence followed as we all regrouped our own memories before another spoke. *Jesus, is that what happened to Steffi?*

"Tomorrow you will continue with Step One, Ira," Fletcher reminded me.

Chapter 25

I've grown certain that the root of all fear
is that we've been forced to deny who we are.

Frances Moore Lappe

Hershey, Pennsylvania

I discovered Ira Stone, a man I did not know, sitting in his office, shaking. The whole staff knew what had occurred with my wife, Stephanie—residents, secretaries, doctors, nurses. They all had heard. In subtle and not-so-subtle ways, many of them had warned me against a relationship with Steffi, but I had pickled suet for brains. They had witnessed Nero fiddling while Rome burned. Still and all, they were my friends and now only wanted to help. Anthony Brookhaven, one of the older trainees (Fabian Tellini, now married to the obgyn nurse, had gone into private practice in New Hampshire), and Evelyn Fillmore arranged for me to fly to St. Paul, Minnesota. They even deposited me at the Harrisburg airport, making sure I at least got that far. They had to do my thinking now.

I spent the next week attempting to recuperate at my good sister's new home in a suburb of St. Paul. My parents, still residing in Tucson, happened to be visiting Jocie. I could not look Father in the eye. I knew what was running through his mind. I just *knew* it. And the nightmares, gone since that first evening with Steffi, resumed with a vengeance, those oh-so-familiar dreams of my two arms surrounding, grasping, holding a naked lady under water. I could not breathe.

I returned to Hershey. Our junior resident, Preston Jones, invited me to rent a low-dollar room in his high-dollar bungalow near the med center, and I gratefully accepted. I was now a displaced citizen bunking in a nice ranch house on Cocoa Avenue. Preston, a stalwart man of roguish charm, and I each shared two galaxies—the hospital and the rest of the world. I grew attached to the talented young man, who wowed his friends and me with his keyboard skills at parties.

Preston was working one night. I remained alone in ash-gray isolation, eyes bloodshot, my hair in disarray, buckets of tears rolling down my cheeks. My guts were riven inside out. Deliverance interruptus. With calculated viciousness Steffi had taken me to my weakest point, where desire met unshackled chains. My hand threw down another slug of snake medicine. I waited for the burn in my stomach, for the promised tranquility that refused to materialize. No longer could I drink my pain away. I hadn't been able to for many moons.

Oh God, I hurt … why am I here? The room wobbled. *Why? Steffi, I love you! … Why?* My white knuckles gripped the seat, trying to fracture the wood, like my life, busted into so many shards … "*Why?*" I screamed aloud. Ten thousand *whys,* and I could still not wrap my brain around this one. After ten thousand tears, the King's horses just stood and watched, shaking their heads. I knocked down another shot. *At least Jack loves me.* I peered through the bottom of the tumbler looking for hints, but all I saw was a distorted Steinway.

Why? Of course I knew why. I just could not face the truth.

I stood up, weaving a bit, my derelict mind falling back on itself. "Damn it, damn this piano, damn the judge, damn …" I gazed out the window overlooking Cocoa Avenue. I saw my ulcerous reflection in the glass. *Who is that guy?* "I don't know you. *Do you hear me? I do not know you!*"

This brain surgeon, going through bizarre withdrawal of a different kind, could not answer his own question, having made his error by choice. The physician could not heal himself. Not yet. Likely not ever. Nemesis, that psychopathic goddess of retribution, had won. Now I had to live with everyone's, "We told you so, Ira!" At least I had the presence of mind not to slam a brick through Preston's window—but only because there were no bricks, and the bottle of Jack Daniels was too precious. For now I had to bury my dueling emotions at sea if I wished to resign from this game, a game I was playing while blindfolded.

I switched the radio on. Patsy Cline was singing "I Love You So Much It Hurts." Soon her words were drowned out by the bathroom shower, where I tried to wash away my graveyard of memories and shame. My taste of freedom away from Father Stone was short lived—Stephanie giveth and Stephanie taketh away. And I wanted to drive a very sharp stake through her fucking heart.

My life was a contradiction. On the one hand, I had become a weeping and blithering sop, a jellyfish cast ashore. On the other hand, my intellect and hidden strengths had led me up the ladders of international academia and down the black-rated ski slopes of the Rockies.

Steffi dropped the battery charges. I do not know why. By the end of May 1980, Steffi and I legally separated. By the end of the summer of '81, we divorced. It was of interest that she refused to request alimony. Why? I don't know, though I admit to a begrudging admiration there. However, the court did award her child support.

I was supposed to have visiting rights with Mikey on weekends. But the woman I had loved and hated in equal portions always found some excuse to prevent that. The more I thought about it, the more my brain generated feedback loops of anger, resentment building with manic intensity.

"Damn you. This is enough of your shit." I cradled the phone after pleading with the woman. The fact was I *did* care for Mikey. I truly loved him. He was also *my* son now, regardless of the original reasons for adopting him. A lock clicked open in some remote island of my mind, leading to a plan that nibbled away at the edge, fermenting, then taking hold. *I must make a few phone calls and then get my attorney to put some pressure on Steffi to let me see our son.*

I searched through my records and found a letter from Steffi, written when she and Mikey lived in Iowa. I located the telephone number for a Dr. Calvin Washok, rehabilitation and physical medicine specialist.

As the line rang in Le Mars, my eyes narrowed. *Two Stephanie DeLeons—one sweet and loving, the other, like a female Hyde, rising up from under soft skin and lashing out with deadly intent. Was it possible to marry someone without a clue about what lay beneath?* I did not need to answer that one.

"Thanks for your time, Dr. Washok. My name is Dr. Ira Stone. You may not know me but ..."

"Actually, you and I once met at one of your neurosurgery meetings, though I first learned you were a coauthor of a fascinating article involving spinal stimulation. A nice piece of clinical research, though I don't suppose that is why you phoned me," replied Washok. "Steffi DeLeon sang your praises when she came to work for us in Le Mars. Haven't heard from her since she left, though. As I am sure you know, we became an item, so to speak."

"Haven't heard from ... But I thought she ... and you filed for divorce," I returned. *Good God, don't tell me ...* "I may sound like a blithering idiot, but she and I were wed in June of '78, in Baltimore, Maryland. You are not saying we were never legally married, are you?"

"What is it you want from me, Dr.?"

"Were you once her husband? That was my understanding. Please, you can understand my dilemma," I hurried to say, fearing I would be cut off.

"Stephanie and I lived together. With her son, Michael. Great kid. We never benefited from the bonds of matrimony."

"Not married? You ... But she said ... Steffi wore a wedding ring." *What the hell ...?*

"If so, it was not mine. Looking back, I consider myself very fortunate in that regard. One day about four years ago, Mikey and Steff simply evaporated. I neither saw nor heard from them again. Your call today is the first communication I have ever received concerning Steffi. She had her mail forwarded to a PO Box in Baltimore.

"Strangely though," added the physiatrist, "one day before she left, I was busy at my clinic when I received a visit from the sheriff. Steffi had accused me of battery. I attempted to get the police to investigate other possible assailants, but they refused. I was not allowed into my house, and then I discovered the two had disappeared a few days later. After I returned, friends informed me that someone had beaten her half to death. Some mysterious guy was allegedly seen by an acquaintance, but no culprit was ever found. Apparently the neighbors saw her face while they were helping her load up her Pontiac Firebird. Never left a note." Washok hesitated and coughed. "Seeing as she took off, the judge dismissed the case."

After he seemed to regain direction, the silence telling, Calvin Washok continued, as if relieved to be divulging what happened to someone. "Over the next few weeks, there were hints from friends and colleagues that I had abused Steffi and even Michael. Nothing is further from the truth. I loved her. We were planning on marriage. And then something happened. That beautiful woman became accusatory, moody, a bit bizarre, disappearing at times. Then ... gone like a puff of smoke. I gather she went back to you in Hershey."

"Calvin, I am truly sorry. I had no idea." I then summarized my past with Steffi and Mikey, hoping for clues.

"What will you do now? Best to forget her, my friend."

"Perhaps so. But I must speak with one other person. The senior Michael Starling. Her first, or at least a previous, husband and the natural father of little Mike." Allegedly, I now suspected.

"Ira, if there is anything I can do to help, let me know. I feel somehow responsible for some of what occurred."

"Thanks for hearing me out."

I need to discover where else the lies and fantasies lead. A boy's heart is bleeding. Why did Mike give up his son? I adopted him, love him, and will not let the lad go down the tubes. I can't have the Stephanie I married back, but I do have a legal and moral obligation to Mikey.

I hired a private detective and after a week of searching, the phone number for Mikey's natural father was found. I remember that call as if it were just yesterday. Steeling my resolve, I dialed the Florida coast.

"Hello? Starling residence," a woman answered.

"Good evening. I ... I'm looking for Michael Starling. My name is Dr. Ira Stone."

"You have made history as the first person to call us in Fort Lauderdale since we returned from Bahrain. A doctor no less. Nothing serious, I hope." She laughed. "I apologize. Don't mean to seem impolite. Mike and I are still jet-lagged, Dr. ... Dr. ...?"

"Stone. In Hershey, Pennsylvania. I don't wish to inconvenience you. I can call back later. I'm simply trying to locate the father of Master Mikey Starling. Is Mike around?"

"Lordy! Hold on a minute." The phone was muffled, but I could hear, "Michael! Good Lord! It's about your son Mikey!"

A breathless voice came on, traces of stress permeating the questions at the end of the wire. "This is Michael Starling. You have some information about Mikey? Gosh what is he, about six years old? And you're a doctor? Is Mike okay?"

"Mr. Starling, we have not spoken before, and much of that is my fault. I ... I'll try to be brief. Steffi, your former wife, and I were married and are now divorced. I adopted Mikey, yet I always felt that I had never been given quite the full picture. I'm calling because, after recent incidents, I suspect little Mike harbors some terrifying beliefs regarding his daddy, you. Now I have reason to think that much of what Mikey and I have heard from Steffi has been a fabrication."

"Hold on, Doc. Let me find a stool somewhere. We just moved back in, and I better be sitting when you tell me what's going on. Perhaps you should have a chair under you also for what I have to tell you."

"Thanks. I'll wait."

"Honey, pick up the other line and listen to this," suggested Michael.

"Dear, maybe I should check on something to eat," I heard in the background.

"No, Angela. This is too important. Dr. ..."

"Stone. But please call me Ira. This is hardly a medical call. And I have the feeling that, in some way, we are family."

"Okay, Ira. I'm Mike, and the wife goes by Angela, or Angie."

"Hi, Ira. I'm on the other line," piped up Angela.

"Wow. I am overwhelmed," I exclaimed. "You seem like really nice people, and I was frightened to death to make this call." I corralled my thoughts. "Sorry, I am struggling with how much to tell you. It is quite bizarre, and ..."

"Ira, let me paint a scenario and see how close I come to your situation. You may first ask why I never contested your adoption of Mikey. I had prayed that Stephanie and Michael might discover themselves part of a wonderful family in which Buddy could grow up. Any interference by me would have only hurt Mikey. Not because we couldn't provide a safe and secure life for m' boy, but because Steffi would pull every trick in the book to make my life and Mikey's future nothing but misery. Pure misery.

"Let me hazard a guess what happened to you. By the way, Angie knows all about this, though she doesn't quite believe it." Mike hesitated, perhaps reaching into a dark past, not wishing to get burned again.

"You, the good doctor, were going about your business one day, providing for your family, stressed out concerning issues in your profession and patient care. Suddenly, the police arrived at your hospital or office or local restaurant and arrested you. You could not fathom what was occurring. You then were handcuffed ..."

"No handcuffs," I blurted out.

"Ahh. Well, I see I am not far off the mark. You professed innocence, and indeed you were not guilty. Yet the police had seen your wife. She appeared brutalized. She cried out, *'Why did you do this to me, Ira?'* And, Lord God, you think she truly believed you had. Certainly the police and her attorney, and even *your* attorney, did. And I do not believe *reasonable doubt* was in the judge's vocabulary, once he made up his packaged mind. Divorce was granted, along with child support. No alimony, interestingly enough.

"Soon the court permitted you to retrieve your belongings from home, the dwelling to which you had been denied access, brute that you were. You went, escorted by men in blue so no harm would come to Stephanie and Mikey. What did you find?"

"Nothing," I cut in. "Everything I owned, all my family photos, my cherished briefcase ... all gone."

"And you can't prove she destroyed it all. To society, the courts, and your neighbors you are a wife beater. Or worse. No one will believe the husband. That just never happens. And believe it or not, the exact same thing happened to her first husband."

"You mean ..."

"That's right. I'm not *número uno*. And I don't even know if Terry, the one before me, was her first."

"Oh, my God! Mike, your description is eerily on the mark. My personal and professional lives both lie in jeopardy. And I seem unable to put it right."

"Do you have access to Mikey?" interjected Angie.

"Legally, yes. Practically, no.

"Won't your lawyer help?" she returned.

"I intend to follow through with my visitation rights every other weekend. I have an appointment with the attorney."

"And then?" wondered Michael aloud.

"Say ... while he is with me, how would you like me to bring Mikey for a visit with you over a long weekend? He has confused feelings about his father, his true father, his own blood. The worst Steffi could do is get the judge to withdraw my visitation rights after we return to Pennsylvania. But little Mike will have already met his daddy again. Just think of ..."

"You would do that?" jumped in Michael. "That would be a bit risky, I should think."

"Truly, I don't want to do this in revenge," I allowed, not quite sure of that conclusion. "I just want Mikey to understand that he really has a family who cares for him. And perhaps he can see for himself where the truth lies. I do not want to take him from his mother, only to prove to him that he always had a daddy who loved him and loves him now. What could be more important in the life of a child?"

"Angie, did you hear that!" Mike exclaimed. "Mikey's coming to Fort Lauderdale! Dr. ... uh ... Ira, are you one o' them angels in disguise?"

"Hardly. I'll fill you and Angie in on the particulars in a few days. If all fails, you might visit me in jail. Any angel wings will be clipped, I'm sure."

"God bless you, Ira," responded Angie.

"If you need anything, anything at all, Ira, you have our number."
Mike nearly broke down. "Call when you have a flight schedule. Until we
meet in Florida ..."

After hanging up, I leaned back in my chair and searched for some
meaning in the commitment I just made. The story was incredible. Yet,
now pieces of the puzzle began to fit. A small part of Humpty's broken
shell slipped into place. Anxiety, excitement, and determination all crested
at once as I sketched a plan. And I needed a drink. *Real bad!*

I realized that my sweaty hand still held on to the receiver. I believed
that I had been going bonkers, even leaping off the deep end, after the judge
had lashed out at me. But Mike had just affirmed a terrible certainty.

*God, I wish I had called Michael sooner ... even in Bahrain. Mikey? Hell,
he's just another kid. Why don't I simply forget him, turn to neurosurgery, and
build up my retirement fund?*

I knew there was more to it than that. Mikey was like a son to me.
*Dammit, he is my son. What should I do? Avoid inflaming Steffi and the
judge? Or do right by a small boy who believes daddies are evil at worst or
uncaring at best.*

*Stephanie truly did not think Michael Senior would hurt her son, did
she? Or did she? Maybe there is more to the story than meets the eye. If she
lied to me regarding her relationship with both Michael and Calvin, then
she very likely skewed the truth about her own parents—especially her
father ...*

I came to a decision. I would inform no one of my plan to abduct—
well, not really abduct—only temporarily *transfer* Mikey across state lines.
I had to live with my conscience. I felt as if I could never look myself in
the mirror again if I failed to follow through. I smiled. And then laughed
at the release of pent-up anger and energy. "*Damn it!* I am going to do
it!" I howled and danced and fired a generous measure of Jack down my
throat. I had never felt so focused and blissful in my life. Well, excepting
sex with Steffi, maybe. But this was different. Now I sensed a purpose. As
if it would make amends for all the wrongs I had done.

Mikey would see his daddy, come hell or high water, as my own father
was wont to say. The next step was for me to grab my attorney again, to

allow me to see my son as per court order. The order said nothing about my taking little Mike on a plane ride.

After arriving at the decision to bring Mikey to visit his real father, I kept having second thoughts. Sleep was difficult, concentration arduous. Should I? *No!* my sensible left brain demanded. *Yes!* urged the other. *If I take him to Florida, I suspect it will be the last time I will be allowed to see the boy again. If I don't, I will break a promise both to his dad and myself. If I were Mikey, what would I want?* At the last minute, the yeas won out over the nays, and I dialed United Airlines.

CHAPTER 26

There is always one moment in childhood
when the door opens and lets the future in.

Deepak Chopra

The Appleton morning was fresh, astringent even. Scattered cirrus clouds and the contrails from a long-gone jet were moving eastward miles above me. I sat on a wood-and-iron bench under an ancient pine tree, deep in thought, my mind drifting , with *Alcoholics Anonymous* open to Chapter Five: "How It Works."

Sebastian trotted by and then turned back and plopped down next to me. "So I hear they found methamphetamine in Henry and his three dead sidekicks. *Crap!* Fletcher mentioned that the bodies of Ellie, Crow, and Lance have been released. The memorial service at Good Samaritan is on for two o'clock, Ira. Everyone is invited, but we have to keep together in our home groups. You're coming, aren't you?"

"No, but thanks for asking."

"Hey, good buddy, no one is blaming you for what happened. I'd consider it a favor if you and I sat together at the Baptist church."

"It's not just what happened here. I've got other reasons. I just can't do it, Sebastian."

My roommate rose from the bench and continued on, leaving me with long-ago memories that would not wash away. Another jet disappeared over the horizon.

*   *   *

On our United Airlines flight out of Pittsburgh, Mikey settled next to the window and gazed with fascination at the receding earth. He watched me peruse the map of Florida, though he did not know why. Then I picked up a magazine. The aircraft suddenly dropped, shivered along its metal spine, and bounced back up. Mikey latched onto my sleeve.

"Daddy!"

"It's all right, Buddy. Quite normal. Pretend it's a roller coaster. You love those."

"Oh, okay." He seemed to be thinking and then announced, "I want to be an airline pilot. Or maybe a soldier in Afgha … Af …"

"Afghanistan?"

"Uh huh." He was peeking at the battle photo in my *Newsweek*. "Do you think I could?"

"I think you would make a terrific soldier!"

Michael beamed and scrunched down in his seat.

I smiled and read a bit of the magazine. My gaze soon focused afar and then returned to the lad. "Mikey, what would you most wish for in your life? Have you ever asked Santa Claus for a special Christmas gift?"

"Aw, nothing." The boy stared at his knees, as if images were flashing through his mind.

"Never, ever?"

"Nuh uh."

I returned to my reading. An hour passed while Mikey dozed. He suddenly sat up.

"Daddy, did you ever know my real dad? I mean, before I met you?"

"No. What do you remember about him?"

Silence followed, except for the roar of four jet engines.

"Mommy says he is mean. He beat her up 'n' stuff. I don't like him very much."

"Have you ever seen her being hurt, being hit?" I knew I was treading on thin ice.

Little Mike hid his face. "I saw it."

"You saw your real daddy punch Mommy?"

"I watched."

"Daddy hitting Mommy?"

"Nuh uh."

"Mikey," I whispered, as the lady in the aisle seat gawked at us. "What did you see? No one is here to punish you."

"Daddy didn't."

"Never? How do you know, son? You mean that Daddy Michael did not beat you or Mommy?" I wasn't sure he would even recall at that age.

Mikey nodded his head yes, and buried his face in my arm.

I was perplexed, not sure of the boy's true meaning. Yes, he did not hit her, or yes he did?

"Mikey, do you trust me?"

"Yeah."

"How would you like to visit your real daddy?"

"You are my real daddy. Now, I mean."

"I'm saying the one who was your first father. Michael Starling."

"He doesn't love me. Mommy says he hates me."

By this time streamlets of tears were rolling down the Mikey's cheeks ... and those of the lady in the adjacent seat, who remained religiously quiet.

"So does that mean I cannot take you to visit Michael, your daddy?"

Silence. "He doesn't want to see me," sniffed little Mike.

"That is not what he told me, Buddy. He is excited over seeing you and holding you and taking you swimming in the ocean. He cried when I told him about you. He believed he had lost you."

"He did? But he is far away. I can't go there. Mommy said so."

"Actually, he is meeting us at the airport near Fort Lauderdale."

"Oh, my Lord!" exclaimed the lady, jerking upright in the aisle seat. "Bless you, kind sir. May the Almighty bless you!"

I felt myself blushing, and Mikey's eyes expanded in disbelief, perhaps fearing some joke was afoot. He pleaded in a whisper, "No more tricks."

I promised as I hugged my son. "No tricks is right." *You've had enough tricks played on you.* "You have a wonderful family waiting. They love you. And I'll bet you look just like your first dad!"

"Really?"

"Really." In truth, I did not know what awaited us, and I was as nervous as that cat on a hot tin roof.

The pilot announced Fort Lauderdale coming up within twenty-five minutes. "Check your seat belts. Stewardesses, prepare for landing."

Mikey pulled his restraint tight and then beheld something in the great beyond, far away. Perhaps he was searching for memories of his daddy. Searching, yet frightened. He certainly could not believe it. *This must seem like a dream to him.*

Fort Lauderdale loomed larger and larger as little Michael nervously clicked his heels together. Somewhere down there was the answer to a Christmas wish, a silent fantasy about to become real. Where was this all leading? I did not have a clue. I just prayed that the boy would have a chance to grow into a strong and kind man. *We shall see*, I judged.

Mikey and I disembarked and aimed across the tarmac toward the main concourse. I drew in the faint smell of the sea at low tide, the Atlantic coast marked with warm and gentle breezes that Friday. A crowd of people gathered around passengers collecting their baggage, the carousel our agreed-upon meeting site.

"Daddy, do you see him?" Mikey's head swiveled in all directions.

"Not yet, Buddy. But the plane arrived a bit early. We can ..."

My eyes caught sight of a man in faded jeans and a T-shirt with the logo DRILLING OIL FOR MANKIND imprinted on the back, a baseball cap pushed back from his bronzed face—a face almost an adult replica of Mikey's. *There he is!* He was talking to a pert-looking redhead and checking out the passengers at the same time.

I waved, my excitement building. The couple saw us and rushed forward. I felt as if this must be the strangest and most magical moment in my life as I grabbed little Michael's hand. I didn't care if His Honor put me in jail. I just did not care.

Mikey hid behind me, squeezing my fingers. Then he poked his head around as if to check whether he were imagining it all. Buddy did not know what else to do, so he inched forward and stuck his right hand out. "Hello, sir. My name is Mikey."

With that, three adults burst out in happy faces, wiping our cheeks, everyone talking at once.

"Ira, okay if I give your son a hug?" Mike bent down as I nodded, my tongue unable to form an answer.

"Remember me, Mikey?" Mike Starling winked at Buddy and held out his arms. "I'm the one who bounced you on my knee and sang "Riggy-jig-jig."

With that little Mike jumped into his father's arms, the tiny worry lines spinning into a big grin. Angela and I laughed at the sight and turned to each other.

Extending my hand, "You must be Angie. I'm Ira Stone."

"Hi, Ira. Where are your wings?" She was a skinny thing with a humongous grin. She grabbed my hand with both of hers. Bright green eyes above carelessly freckled cheeks checked me over.

"Aw, heck. I couldn't get past the boarding agent with them."

"Any luggage to pick up, Ira?" Big Mike hefted his son on his shoulders.

"No, only our carry-on. Didn't think we'd need much for these few days, and … I, uh … couldn't exactly go home and pack for the boy."

"Come on, you guys." Angela grabbed my arm. "Time is short, so we had better get moving. Should Junior here need anything, it will be on us. In fact, on the way to our house, we have to pick up a bathing suit for him. Tomorrow we hit the Atlantic beaches." She nodded toward Buddy. "What a fancy pair of OshKosh B'Gosh pants, Mikey!"

We strode toward the airport entrance. Mikey fell fast asleep with his arms around his father's neck. Angie and I looked at each other and smiled. All seemed right with the world, even if only for two and a half days.

That evening Angela, Mike and I sat around the patio, reclining on folded chairs. "Luckenbach, Texas" played in the background.

"Sorry for the inadequate amenities, Ira," said Angie. "We are still unpacking."

"Angie, I am presently in seventh heaven. If you saw my digs, you would know what I mean." I turned toward her husband. "Who was or is your employer, Mike? I gather you are an engineer in the oil industry, though that info came from Steffi."

"Not just any engineer, Ira," boasted Angela. "One of the best. He's hired and sought after by all of the oil corporations."

"Angie, please," begged Mike. "I last worked with Aramco in Saudi Arabia. I am sort of a wildcat, an independent contractor. I fly out wherever I am needed. Mostly to put out fires."

"So I gather life insurance companies are not delighted to have you as a client," I responded.

"You got that right."

"I'm going to check on Mikey, guys." Angie turned toward me. "Ira, another Jack Daniels?"

"I shouldn't, but I will. I need something to help me digest what is happening here."

"Me too, honey," her husband interjected. "Ira may be the legal daddy, but it was my sperm that made him."

"Michael! You already have had too much to drink. Mind your manners. Ira is a guest."

"Hell, no. He is family! He and I have suffered the slings and arrows of Stephanie DeLeon. And may God help him. He is welcome in this home anytime. Anytime, dammit."

I saw Mike shudder. I wondered what he had been through. And where did Angela fit in? She obviously loved him and would do anything for Mikey and his natural father. I knew that bringing little Mike here could have severe consequences, especially from Steffi and the judge. But I refused to fret over the future. Today was all that mattered. I had resigned myself to the loss of Mikey after our return. Buddy most likely would remain with Steffi until he was eighteen, and likely I'd never see him again. Yet something drove me to do right by the boy before … before something happened to him. Before it was too late.

Many kinds of cancer can eat away at body and spirit. Cancer of the brain, I understood. The cancer of Steffi's soul was beyond my comprehension. Holding on to Stephanie DeLeon was like grasping the string of a kite flying high in a thunderstorm. You never knew when lightning would strike.

Saturday at the beach, Angie and I finished eating our ham and cheese sandwiches under the beach umbrella. The two Michaels were dashing through foaming breakers, laughing, running, and digging up crabs from the sand. I could not recall when Mikey had been so happy.

"So it seems," I said, "as if Buddy and I went through the same experience with Steffi and the cops. Even Calvin Washok in Iowa did. And maybe others. It is as if that woman were a she-dog, a bitch gone bad."

"And the sad thing is that little Michael witnessed so much of it," added Angie.

"Mikey saw his mother repeat the horrible events again, in Iowa and recently in our home," I reasoned. "The poor kid will turn out delusional himself at this rate. One part Mommy and one part Daddy-One, Daddy-Two, Daddy-Three. Oh, here they come."

With that, Mike and Mike, carrying beach pails, scampered over the sand until, exhausted, they flopped down on the blanket before Angie and me.

"Daddy … I mean Daddy Ira! Look at these crabs! Daddy Mike showed me how to dig them out through their air." Mikey, ruddy cheeked, looked at his father.

"Air holes, son."

"Air holes in the sand. Have you ever seen so many crabs?" The boy shoved the pail full of wiggling arms and shells in front of Angie and me.

"Buddy, you are astounding. Someday you must teach me how to find them. I am very proud of you!" I exclaimed.

"And check my feet out. Mallard feet, right?"

"Sure, Buddy. I'm surprised you remembered."

"So, Dr., what do you think?" smiled Mike Senior. Mikey wiggled his toes next to his dad's. "Do we both require some sort of reparative surgery?"

I was silent, stunned. I choked up, at a loss for words. I now realized it had all come together. Of course. Mike *was* the real father. I somehow felt left out of the family reunion. My eyes watered, and I turned away.

"Ira, as God is my witness, you have been more of a father to this boy than have I," Mike seemed compelled to say.

"Amen," agreed Angie. "Hey, guys. I cook up a mean squid, and we have the best species of the seven seas in our freezer. How about it?"

"All right!" exclaimed Mike. "Let's do it! And then a marshmallow roast. Mikey will love that."

At home, Angela extracted a frozen packet of squid and tossed it in boiling water. Then she headed for the refrigerator and pulled out a collage of vegetables, slicing them for one of the best meals I had ever tasted.

Following dinner, I phoned my apartment to check on any recorded messages. There were two. First—"This is Steffi. Where is Michael? *Call me ASAP!*" She sounded other-worldly. The second was from my resident. "Dr. Stone, I discharged Terramon today. He is doing really great. He has an appointment to see you in three weeks." I repeated the first message for Michael and Angie. Little Mike slept soundly in the guest room, "Luckenbach, Texas" in the background again.

"Ira, would you join me in a brandy Alexander? Perhaps you should know what I learned and what happened when Steffi underwent psychiatric care while we were married. Come in the library, and I can show you a copy of her diary. Did you know she had another child before Mikey? Another boy. Died a year after birth under mysterious circumstances. Hard to believe ..."

*   *   *

Upon my return I brought Mikey, safe and sound, back to Steffi. She, as one might imagine, responded with anger and spite. Perhaps she had some justification, but to this day I have never regretted our trip to Florida. As predicted, Steffi took me to court, where the magistrate entered an order that I could not take my son out of the state of Pennsylvania. "And I mean *not ever!*" The gavel slammed into oak.

His Honor was a bit prejudiced, for he also had been the attorney representing Nadine at our divorce. What the heck. I had more important things on my mind. Like getting the hell out of Dodge. For now Mikey would be carried in my wallet and in my heart. Stephanie's last words to me were, "And you will *never, ever* see Michael again!"

I won't forget that day in court. My son wore his OshKosh B'Gosh pants and sat on the bench next to his mother, staring down at the floor. My heart was bleeding, and it took every ounce of fortitude for me to keep an outwardly calm demeanor while justice was being dispensed. Inside I shook with resentment and sadness, assuaged by a few nips of Jack Daniels. But just as the judge signaled the session was at an end, Mikey looked up, scrunched his shoulders, and grinned at me with … was it a wink?

CHAPTER 27

There are more things in heaven and earth, Horatio,
than are dreamt of in your philosophy.

William Shakespeare
Hamlet

Our home group was eating lunch when one of the women patients came running into the dining hall, yelling in a loud voice, "Come quick, everyone! You *won't* believe it!"

"What on earth?" exclaimed Fletch. "What's going on?" He got up and trotted after Madeleine, one of the women's counselors. The entire cafeteria emptied out, and I was close on Fletcher's heels.

Everyone, men and women, patients and staff, all dashed down the steps toward the main building. In front of the entryway was a clutch of people surrounding a woman holding a baby. She was sitting on a bench and dressed in slacks and blouse, the infant in a colorful pink outfit. Next to her knelt James, sobbing, his little finger grasped by the child's fist.

We all knew who the infant had to be. James's story was common knowledge, and many of us had prayed for the family. There was not a dry eye in the crowd, and a catch was lodged in my own throat.

As the gathering thinned, I approached the couple and their newfound child.

"Hi, James. I am so happy for you. What a blessing!"

"Thanks, Ira. This here is my wife. Christie, meet one of my buddies."

"I am so pleased to meet a friend of James." After wiping her cheeks, she extended her free hand. "I think I saw you during family week."

"Yes, in the cafeteria, I believe. And this is Leslie? Such a beautiful little girl."

"Thank you. Someone left her at Childrens Hospital yesterday. No one knows who," replied Christie. "I know it is against the rules, but I just had to show James. He's been through so much."

"Believe me, you made everyone's day here." I stared at the cooing infant, thinking of my own kids. "I'll leave you guys to get reacquainted with Leslie. James, let me know if there is anything I can do for you. Anything at all." And there wasn't much any one of us wouldn't do for the others in Appleton. I couldn't believe the change in my own attitude.

"I appreciate that, Ira."

As I departed, I heard, "Little Leslie misses her daddy so much. Oh, honey, I am truly glad I came for family week."

Lexi and Denise, how can I ever make it up to you?

Later in the day I sat down in front of Betsy, who was laughing at a photo in her hand. "A picture of my grandson. He works for the state department and just got stationed in Pakistan."

"You must be very proud of him."

"Am I ever! I just hope he keeps safe there, being a Jew. So, now that you have finished Step One, Ira, how do you feel?"

"Great! No more booze, and I've got the world by the tail."

"Well, that world will come back at you, sometimes in mean ways. We addicts must be prepared to deflect the bad and embrace the good—without resorting to mind-altering drugs."

"I'm getting the picture. Finally."

"Did you ever see Mikey again?" Betsy asked.

"No, ma'am." I felt a great sadness well up inside me, wondering if I ever would ... *And you will never, ever see Michael again!*

"God works in mysterious ways, Ira."

Hershey, Pennsylvania

In the autumn of 1981, the divorce from Steffi had been finalized, and I had just returned from lecturing in Japan. My private and professional lives remained disconnected. I was not sure how long that could continue. I slowly disentangled myself from the swirl of costly emotional, legal, and financial disasters. Did I learn my lesson? No, not yet, apparently, for I was a drunk, my illness well hidden from others. I seemed driven to jump from one woman to another without any breathing space. After all, I did not need to waste time putting my life in order, for I had the perfect tranquillizer.

I met Judi Falmouth near Indian Echo Caverns west of Hershey. I'll never forget the vision of loveliness sitting on a huge stone. She was sparkling, dangerously attractive, her form illuminated by the falling sunlight, its bolt of gold shooting down between treetops close to the caverns. I was awestruck, for it appeared as if she were literally drawing the glow of day into her body. Dressed in a stylish skirt and blouse of turquoise, she had a poised yet compelling presence about her. A pleasant, somewhat guarded smile crossed her face. My attention was pulled in her direction by the noise of children's laughing. On that Sunday, the last I would likely ever see little Mike again, I had brought him to the park, where we explored caves and climbed rocks together. In a nearby wood he had ventured off to frolic with a newfound playmate, Judi's boy, Nelson. The grade-school lads chased about, and I was happy that Mikey was having fun, something so rare in his life.

Judi at first glance appeared as a prim and proper lady, tall and willowy, blonde hair down to her waist. A ravishing beauty, she was. Soon I learned that Judi preferred a New York ensemble, not expensive but stylish, unlike Steffi, who wore jeans and flats. Judi managed accounts for a Harrisburg law firm, while Steffi saved lives in the operating room. Judi had gone to a community college, whereas Steffi had earned her BSN diploma. Judi attended church, Steffi, rarely. Judi was silent with her emotions, and Steffi wore hers close to the surface. Alcohol on social occasions satisfied Judi, stronger drugs worked for Steffi. Judi loved to ski, Steffi loved to ...

After Stephanie, I needed someone quite the opposite. Like Toulouse-Lautrec in *Moulin Rouge*, I had had enough excitement in my life. I wanted an alchemist to turn gold back into lead—or better yet, silver, someone or something to give me the happiness Jack Daniels and I deserved. After all, who were more deserving?

Judi and I dated and found that we desired each other in some strange way—perhaps love, perhaps not. After the trauma of my relationship with Steffi, an iron jacket had sealed my heart, while the drawbridge to sanity remained raised. I could no longer confide my innermost thoughts and fears to another person. Earnest love at a distance, yes, but high-voltage sex with gay abandon, rarely, if ever. The sad thing was that Judi was bound by a similar moat, so we became two fortresses drifting about, never truly touching, only seeking to somehow repair the wounds of DNA and early childhood.

I was actually stunned when Judi said yes to my offer of marriage.

What was it that made me keep dashing headlong into matrimony so soon? Her affirmation came at me with such hasty ease, I was caught off guard. Without any family present, we tied the knot in Harrisburg, Judi's hometown. My elderly parents were living their retirement in Tucson and most likely fed up with my marital failures. They sent their regrets. Denni, then eighteen, and Alexandria, fifteen, refused to show up. Their hurt was palpable. I suppose they held on to a kindle of hope that Nadine and I would get back together. Once again their father was not considering his daughters' feelings, only his own. I remained the center of my universe. When guilt would surface, I took my liquid pacifier, and Judi joined me more and more frequently.

But something else drove me toward the bottle—I had lost another Michael, and that was almost more than my brittle self could withstand.

In the years that followed I worked hard in neurosurgery while Judi continued as an administrative assistant in a legal office. Both of us drank whiskey to excess, I more than she, of course. I never saw Mikey or Steffi during that time.

1985

In the meantime, I became recognized in the international courts of neurological neurosurgery and was sought after as a speaker and visiting professor. I decided to leave the good state of Pennsylvania, where bitter memories and child-support costs sans child were too intrusive. I took a private practice position in Kansas City, Missouri. During our time there Judi tried to get me to attend church and to socialize. Yet all I wanted was work during the days and booze at nights. She was being well supported, so what the hell else did she need? For crying out loud, I was making her and me boatloads of cash.

Her son, Nelson, lived with his father, who had full custody. He was a terrific lad, and I enjoyed his visits with us every other weekend.

*   *   *

"It's Sunday, Ira. Are you going to church with me?"

"Naw, I'm planning on mowing the lawn today. 'Sides, I'm not into this God thing."

"Please. You hardly ever come with me except on Christmas and Easter." Judy adjusted her pantyhose. "Ira, what *do* you believe in?"

She had no bra on yet, and wild thoughts were hijacking my brain. I came up behind, pressing my ardent pubis tight against her backside and grabbing luscious breasts. "*This* is what I believe in. Let's go to bed instead, honey."

"Not now, dear. Worship starts in one hour, and I don't want to be late." But I could feel her heart picking up a few beats.

"I want to ravish your body," I whispered in her ear. "I want to fuck you. Now." My rising willy was demanding to have its way with her.

"*Pu ... leeze, Ira.*" Judy jerked herself away and reached for a skirt of royal purple. "You have a hell of a way of making a girl feel wanted. How about something you've apparently forgotten—the language of love, with flowers and kisses? You know, like you did when we first dated? Now, come to the service with me, and then we can frolic afterwards. Okay? Come on, dearest."

"All they do is take our cash money. And for what?" The last thing I wished to do was attend a religious service.

"Pagan dollars you would prefer to spend on Canadian Club, no doubt." She pulled a matching shirt over herself. "Well? Are you coming? I'll make a nice roast for dinner for you tonight."

Bribery. I gave in, and we went together to the nearby Wesley Methodist Church. The two of us sat down near the front, where I fidgeted and fought against the smell of purification. Prayer made me tense, aggravated. I felt myself receiving internal messages: *You don't need to be here, Ira. Maybe you are an atheist, have you ever considered that? What a fool. You could be home nursing a whiskey and working on your taxes. Shit.*

"In the name of the Father and of the Son and of the Holy Ghost."

"Amen."

My distilled agitation accelerated. I did *not* want to be here. I felt treacherous fear and uncertainty roll through me. What was that all about? *This is the last time I am coming! Damn it to hell!* Again Satan won me over.

We strolled toward the Chrysler.

"I'm not doing this again, Judi! I do *not* believe in your God. I will no longer be a party to your superstitious rituals, dammit!"

I remember my wife standing on the sidewalk, her eyes wet, the mouth wide agape, as if to reply, but she changed her mind.

"Come on. Get into the damn car," I raked. I did have enough Stone courtesy to hold the door open for her.

"You ... you arrogant son of a bitch, *Dr.* Stone! You may get your own dinner tonight." I thought she was crying, but I was not sure. And I did not care. My personality continued its downward mutation as the bonds of love grew increasingly frayed.

Sadly our relationship slowly deteriorated, peppered with alcohol and occasional verbal fights against a distant and chilly background. Looking back, most of that time became a blurred memory.

Chapel Hill, North Carolina

In 1996 my partners and I had a falling out. One evening we decided to have an office meeting at the country club. One of the partners and I were drinking heavily, and the session degenerated into an alcoholic donneybrook. That mamafucker and I came to verbal jousts, and I was voted out of the club. *The renowned and eminent Ira Stone? Voted out!* Anger ruled that night, my brain deep in accelerating paranoia. *This is not my fault. That's for sure. What the hell, I don't like the asshole anyway. Who does he think he is?* But I felt a tinge of fetid anxiety leak into my whiskey-bleached bones. The more fearful I got, the angrier I became, the two soon in equal measure. Good old CC remained faithful, calming me down. But unbeknownst to me, rational belief and bragging rights were slipping further and further into jeopardy.

A long-term professional friend, Dr. Eli Chambers, professor and chairman of the Department of Neurosurgery at the University of North Carolina in Chapel Hill, convinced me to join their teaching staff. I was immensely grateful, especially since I would be near my girls. Judi and I moved to Chapel Hill where I continued in medicine. And then the sky fell in. The truth be told, the storm began long before.

Four more years passed, and nothing changed between Judi and me. Of course it was *her* fault. She simply failed to behave as the wife of a brain surgeon should! Everything would have been fine if she had paid more attention to my suggestions. I had not recognized that my "suggestions" were viewed as demands.

The turn of the century witnessed the passing of Charles Schulz, the creator of Peanuts and Charlie Brown. The movie *Traffic* gained critical acclaim for its portrayal of burgeoning drug problems in our country. And it was the year I received an unforgettable call from my third wife.

"Hello."

"Ira, this is Judi."

"Hi, sugar. How is it going with the American Cancer Society?"

"Ira, I have filed for divorce."

"Wha ... what?" A deafening stillness followed.

Checkmate. Again.

"My dear ex-husband-to-be, you still don't have a clue how you have ruined our marriage, do you? *Not a fucking clue!*" I heard a hitch in her voice, a slight slurring of words. "My attorney will serve the papers this week."

Fucking? I had never heard her use that word before. My whole world, resting on a fault line, collapsed years after our wedding vows. Anger, shock, and sadness tore my heart apart. *What on earth did I do to deserve this?* Did she have a boyfriend? If so, she hid it quite well. All I knew was that locusts had invaded the Promised Land.

At the trial of Ira Stone v. Judi Stone, the judge, a man with a generous stomach and aging pockets around nystagmoid globes, declared that half my parental inheritance should go to *her*. It reminded me of the destruction Steffi visited upon my family photos and mementos. My world tilted once again, and I was falling off. Rapidly. Yet I suppose no one cries louder than a thief whose purse has been stolen.

I struggled to understand my role in the breakup. I guess the more committed we were to each other, the harder it was to live with each other's imperfections—in my case, a surgeon's character defects were glaring to her eyes yet hidden from my own. I had given Judi everything money could buy, everything she requested. But I had missed the boat somewhere. Three wives and three divorces—I not only missed the boat, I had fallen off the dock.

With my separation from Judi, the financial hit was considerable, yet I did not endure the pain and emotional crippling I had encountered after the loss of Steffi. Why was that? Even so, I died just a little, down deep inside where no one could see. Post-Stephanie, my heart remained bricked in and jacketed by Kevlar, and Judi became the recipient of the fallout. There was something else, something dark, yet I could not lay my finger upon it. In my tiny new living room I set down my accordion and slowly spun the crystal glass of Crown Royal (I had divorced CC as well as Jack), listening to the clinks of tiny icebergs, listening for answers I still could not decode—even though the key was staring right up at me. The ice-hot heady rush of rye whisky spreading out from my gullet felt oh-so darn good, and I soon forgot what I had come to forget.

In the meantime I threw myself back into my work—teaching the residents and caring for the uninsured patient clinic. But my morning headaches were accompanied by a slight tremor in my hands—surgeon's hands. That did not bother me; I steadied them with more Valium, a benzo illegally obtained by conning a friend to purchase them with my prescription. I had crossed the line. That was a Drug Enforcement Administration no-no. I was thus risking loss of my license—or worse. Even so, I was in denial that there was a problem, my sister's warnings to the contrary. The pills rendered a kind of calm I no longer found at the bottom of a bottle. But, hell, I was a doctor, and *I* knew what I was doing.

Chapter 28

When we see a man of contrary character,
we should turn inwards and examine ourselves.

Confucius

Some type of activity filled every evening in Appleton, including on weekends. Tonight, following our AA meeting, we faced the infamous Appleton *feedback* session. I had arrived late, preferring to not arrive at all. Everyone was laughing. I sat down and asked my neighbor what was so funny. Grinning, he replied, "Derrick complained that 'Caressing a bottle of whiskey is like making love to a five-hundred-pound gorilla—once it starts, the gorilla just won't stop fucking.'"

I wasn't in the mood for gorilla and fucking jokes. We patients and the group leader were sitting in the usual circle, and I began fidgeting, crossing and uncrossing my legs.

"For all you wits and twits who are new to this exercise, let me explain," thumped Fletcher suddenly. We newcomers jerked to attention. The others smirked, remaining in various stages of a slouch. "We are all deadbeats, drunks, and addicts."

Fuck you, asshole.

"However, some of us harbor grandiose ideas of self-importance and holier-than-thou persona, such as, 'God made me the center of the universe.' Such concepts hide our soft underbellies, concealing significant fears and character flaws. The brain has become a house divided against

264

itself, good against bad. We addicts have discovered that mind-altering drugs sooth our tender bodies when these traits, obvious to others, are under attack. Though our feelings have balls for brains, here we can no longer hide behind crack, meth, or whiskey. Nolan, describe the drill to our young neophytes here."

"Each of us has kept a mental or written list of behaviors seen in one or two others in our group, conduct that polite society finds irksome or downright distressing." Cargo-Britches seemed to relish his role, and he sent us his fierce judicial look. "Taking turns, each of us will name another suck … I mean another patient now under the gun, so to speak, and mention one of his behaviors or misdemeanors that the accuser feels needs correction. The defendant may not answer, except to say thank you. He may respond after twenty-four hours of soul-searching, should he so choose." Nolan's cheeks lifted in a tight grin as he turned to Fletch for confirmation.

"That is correct. However, keep in mind that this is not a court room, Nolan. The words *accuser* and *defendant* are a bit strong. Why do I say that, Alamo?" Fletcher nodded at the lanky Texan across from me, who searched with his good right eye, worrying and scratching his left wrist, continually plucking, like a monkey. Off and on he appeared to be grinding his teeth and chewing on his cheek, jaw muscles undulating.

The rail-thin truck driver cleared his throat. Scars of meth addiction covered his face and arms. Spectral circles hovered around oyster eyes. The man appeared to shrivel up inside military fatigues. He sat as if he were Ichabod Crane, every bone in his body busted and reapplied the wrong way.

He kept jerking, darting, and blinking, and then he answered, "We ain't here to criticize nobody, rather to p … p … point out some traits or activities that earth people might reject." Alamo stopped to fuss over a chin eruption, and then, speaking in part with his shoulders and arms, he continued in his twangy dialect. "And … uh … society's disapproval may lead to resentment or sh … sh … shame, then drinking or using … which may lead to dying. So's really, we are trying to save that f … f … fucker's life."

"Exactly!" came Fletcher's swift follow-up. "The mortality rate of man remains one per person, but we addicts seem bent on advancing the time table, racing for that pine box on a slow train back to Georgia. I put the case to you—we die not from that familiar binge, but rather from a thousand little cuts. All of us are here to save the lives of every one of us crazy bastards. And why do I say *crazy?*"

Sebastian, his left foot hooked casually over his right knee, lifted a forefinger. "Because no polecat in his right mind would take these fucking drugs, these feel-good killers, inviting torture and death. We are all insane cocksuckers, each doing the same dog-and-pony show over and over again."

"You got it, brother. Crazier than road lizards, we are. Destination—the middle of nowhere. So pay attention! Each of us must step outside the maze and look at ourselves as *others* see us ... an epiphany few, in the beginning, can stomach. Our addicted brain is a bad neighborhood ... you and I must endeavor *not* go there. If we do, those persistent and corrupted thoughts will keep growing and growing, never letting us sleep. In this workshop our colleagues will point out traits that not only have screwed up our terrain on the wrong side of the tracks but also keep sucking us back."

It was as if we had become a firing squad made up of misfits in a circle. As the session rolled onward, I began to understand why "feedback" was an unpleasant experience for many of us "young neophytes." Soon I was the recipient of several charges.

"Ira, you always arrive late to our work-assignment meetings. Perhaps you find this beneath you," one asserted.

"Thank you." *Shit-face.* I started to tremble inside like an angry yet terrified puppy dog. I felt as if the core of my ego were under attack.

Another rose to the occasion. "I agree. And Ira, you tend to spend too much time away from our informal activities, aloof ... uh ... condescending, perhaps. That doctor job has gone to your head."

"Thank you." Anxiety spiked and then abated a tad, my piano-wire emotions accommodating.

A third took up the cudgel. "Yes, you appear very distant. One tight-assed son of a bitch. I wonder if your wives and kids saw you that way."

"Thank you."

That hurt. It was too close to the mark. I desperately needed a drink! I did *not* like this at all. I did not like their words pushing things around inside of me, making me feel too darn vulnerable, expanding cracks in the Stone armor.

Fletcher stepped in. "Ira, you received three hits. This suggests you might need to look at this character trait. Now, you may select someone and help save his life."

Oh, God. "Okay." I swallowed. *How do I critique one of my buddies without making him angry at me?* "I'm new at this. Can I do this at another session?"

"Sorry. One of the benefits is developing assertiveness without provoking, testing your mettle, so to speak. Please proceed."

"Well ... Nolan, I find your continual assuming-a-directorship attitude offensive," I replied, warming a bit to the task and jumping into the fray.

"Thank you, Ira." Nolan blinked several times, as if the comment had poked him in the eye.

Derrick leaped into the fray. "I agree, Nolan. I believe it would be helpful to you if y'all ceased being a prosecuting attorney in court and came down to our level." Derrick sounded as if he felt relieved now that the new kid on the block joined his side.

"Yes, Nolan ..." Sebastian, the ponytail, joined in.

And so it went. I began to feel as if some deep-seated pressure were melting away. My desire to drink left me. At least for that day. I was learning to take it one day at a time. And I finally understood what my counselor had said. "If I kicked the butt of every person responsible for my misery, I would not be able to sit for a week."

The next morning I was seated with my home group at a glass-covered table. Numerous shelves full of worn library books surrounded the assembly. Fletcher entered with a new patient, one whose appearance of waxwork perfection was immediately both fascinating and repellent.

"Gentlemen, this is Frystann."—F Deleware Short, BS, MBA, PhD, Frystann proudly announced to us later. "He is joining our bunch today. Frystann, please take a chair." The stranger, vibrating with indignation—

or drug withdrawal—approached with a hint of VIP swagger. Mr. Short displayed the expression of a man forced to endure the heroic stench of an outhouse.

The new gent, a worldly illusionist born of tanning salons, was dressed to the nines. This pillar of the yacht club sat across from me, the man taking exquisite care not to ruffle the designer pinstripes of his blue Armani suit with knife-edge creases, accessorized with sharkskin belt, tailored Charvet shirt, gold Gucci cufflinks, and spiffy high-dollar shoes. His brown hair was lacquered into a contradictory pompadour. He wore an unnerving fluorescent-red bow tie with a button-down collar, one side unfastened and sticking forward. Already I detested the guy.

With a flourish, smelling suspiciously like Biagiotti, Herr Short, a pear-shaped, height-challenged man refusing to be short, swept into his seat, his back stiff and chins held high. Each of us introduced himself, giving his home town, sobriety date, and drug of choice. Frystann, narrow-eyed and lock-jawed, refused to acknowledge our presence, except for a brief snort of derision. Fletcher invited all of us to state what we expected to get out of therapy at Appleton. The answers each of us gave had changed as we progressed week to week. "Frystann?"

Short, fingering a Phi Beta Kappa key, cast a glance over everyone in the room. His shoulders went back, as if readying for combat.

"Would someone explain in concise terms how this will help my so-called problem, were I possessed by the target of one of your fickle accusations?" he sniffed. The bowtie wiggled with each bob of his Adam's apple.

We all gaped, wondering from which planet this clown had fallen.

Finally, Sebastian, struggling to keep a serious demeanor, addressed the question after introducing himself. "We each came here for a common reason—we found ourselves sick with a disease, unable to manage both our drinking and our own lives. This program offers us an opportunity to rejoin society without the need to drink or use."

"Such twaddle. *Perhaps* you did not understand my query." Heads jerked around the table, targeting Short and his condescending pronouncements. "To reiterate—I desire a concise and proper argument illustrating how this cockamamie AA crap will benefit me. *Anyone?*" The newcomer brushed imaginary lint from his suit coat sleeve and adjusted very starched French cuffs.

Another took up the challenge. "My name is Derrick, and I am a drug addict."

"Hi, Derrick," came from all except Frystann.

"Our counselors, recovering addicts and alcoholics themselves, have been through it all. They have been at the bottom, attended recovery programs, and now help the rest of us become clean and sober. Many possess masters and doctorates in numerous fields, and I count myself lucky to benefit from what they have to offer."

"Give me a break, gentlemen." Herr Short, now even more tightly wound with disdain, stared down a veined nose. "I remain unconvinced. Give me a paradigm, some proof that the program really works." A few wrinkles now tarnished his haberdashery.

What a demanding prick. I felt the bile of raw anger rise within me, as if my own cheek had had been stung by his gauntlet.

"Why are you here, Frystann?" I asked a bit too loudly, forgetting to introduce myself. I wiped a bit of spittle from my lip and drew my chair closer to the table. "Would you rather be right or be happy?" *Asshole.* To my surprise, that voice was mine.

Like a turtle registering its distaste, the center of attention twisted his neck toward me in slow motion. Bulging eyes under wrinkled lids eyed me, regarding my person as if I were a pork-eating Semite. Then he shot back, "You seem incapable of addressing the issue. Give me facts, *my good sir.*"

"Facts! How about the fact that since the time of Bill Wilson and Dr. Bob, the Twelve Step program is the only consistently successful regimen that has kept drunks and addicts like you and me from the grave. Would that fit into your fucking paradigm? All of us are here to help each other, and that would include you!" I was mad, deep-down-in-the-gut mad. Indeed, I was surprised at my … my own self-assertiveness without alcohol on board.

Short fired back, "I dare say you have the problem, Mister What's-Your-Name-and-I-Am-An-Alcoholic. Not I." His counterattack was followed by a theatrical, yet precise, pause. "Now, how about staying on track?"

"If you wish to kill yourself, then have at it!" I scraped back my chair to distance myself, cantilevering it at a dangerous angle. I could feel indignation spike within me. My white-knuckled fists yearned to grab the fucking prig's throat and strangle him until those repellent eyes bulged even further and the other collar button snapped. I wanted to release all my pent-up hatred on that one convenient target.

"*Kill* myself?" He mustered a starched smile while fingering that obnoxious tie. "Oh, my *good* sir. I thought you all were here to *help* me. I believe those were your very words, were they not?" The grand potentate then spread his hands upon the expanse of his chest.

By now everyone must have wondered if this Rottweiler and I came from different planets, certainly not Earth. I closed my lids and drew a deep breath. I wanted a drink. *The Big Guy in the sky is testing me! He sent this bozo over to show me how my anger gets out of control. Thank you, Lord. I will do better next time.* I had just spoken to the God in whom I had not believed. Clamping down hard on simmering agitation, I focused my eyes and resentment on a wall picture—a Roman coliseum—and fell silent, refusing to be drawn any farther into a fruitless debate. My mind once again restructured itself as my brain reexamined the texture of emotions with a polygraph, steam escaping, anger converting to irritation.

That evening some of us guys—yes, I was joining in with my buddies by then—got together and made bets on how long Frystann and his materialistic trappings would last at Appleton. Sebastian won. In three days the spiffy shoes dropped out of sight. His lawyer had convinced the judge to release him from this "hellhole"—Frystann's description. All of us were truly sorry for the man. Many of us had traveled in his boots, and we knew what awaited the poor soul and his family down the line. A few days later we heard that he had been driving under the influence when he wiped out two roadside joggers. The upstanding citizen had added manslaughter to his wife-battery repertoire.

Bad tidings occurred the day after Frystann left, sending all of us into lousy moods. At our home-group meeting Fletcher gave us the news— Barfly of Listerine fame had been taken by ambulance from Appleton to the Marin County Hospital emergency room. He had vomited blood from ruptured esophageal varices due to liver failure. Our good buddy went into shock, bled out, and died before anything could be done. I had lost a good friend, and I knew that could have been yours truly if Jocie hadn't intervened.

That same morning I read in the local newspaper:

> *Henry Stamen was found guilty of voluntary manslaughter. His common-law wife and their son were present as the sentence was read. The defense lawyer claimed that the fault lay not with Stamen but with drugs causing insanity...The judge will pronounce sentence next week.*

> *In spite of his testimony, the role of one of the witnesses, Ira Stone of Chapel Hill, North Carolina, a patient at Appleton, has never been fully clarified, in this reporter's opinion. Apparently ...*

All I wanted to do was crawl under a log. With my bottle of Crown Royal. Another of my comrades in recovery had just passed away from the evils of alcohol, and *even so* my addicted brain was again demanding the same poison that killed them.

That afternoon I returned for a visit with Betsy. "Ira, I heard about your flash of anger toward Frystann the other day. How do you feel now?"

"I'm okay. I know I need to improve on that."

"Did you have some expectation that he would behave as you wished?" Her questions remained short, efficient, methodically posed.

"No. He just pissed me off. I'm over it."

"Ira, 'Expectations are premeditated resentments,' as the saying goes. When our self-centered ego feels insulted or denied, there is a derangement of the senses, with deep-seated anger bubbling up, dominating the mind. That's a common trait among us alcoholics—indeed, among many others. The Steps and a good spiritual seawall help dampen our tides of rage and unseemly passion."

"Hmm."

"Do you see now that you have had issues with anger and ego? You certainly were not a wellspring of empathy and sentiment with your early wives. You allowed no one, especially family, to get in the way of your ambition, whether professional or sexual, wouldn't you say?" Betsy paused and flipped her notes. "Which brings up another subject. Ira, you seem to attract addicted ladies like moths to a flame."

"I suppose."

"Actually, that is rather common, in my experience. Is that true of your fourth wife also?"

"You needn't rub it in."

"I'm not … I can't. I have been there myself—six husbands until I went through recovery." Betsy folded her hands on top of her desk blotter.

"Her name was … is … Monica."

CHAPTER 29

He has not learned the lesson of life
who does not every day surmount a fear.

Ralph Waldo Emerson

Chapel Hill, June 2000

"Hello. Is Mr. Evanlink ready to go home?" I had just entered the University Short Stay Unit.

"Dr. Stone! Good lord, you startled me." Monica Belmont, RN, glanced up from her book. "Sorry, I don't read novels on the job, but I was just waiting for your resident before I headed out."

Before me sat the nurse, her jet-black hair framing a smile, a wide-eyed, beautiful smile. That was all I saw. It was neither a sexy smile nor a grandiose grin, just a healthy face beaming in stereophonic sound and Technicolor. I did not know then that three months previously she had buried her husband, the father of her five children.

"What's that book you are reading?" I tried not to stare at her facial features. Or her breasts. But what the heck, I am a man, and she seemed incapable of hiding those admirable, gravity-defying attributes short of wearing a flak vest. Besides, I wanted to read her name tag.

"Oh, just some trashy fiction." She hid the cover and stood. "Your patient is chomping at the bit to go home."

"Probably needs a smoke. Or a drink." I set my briefcase on the tile floor. "Do you like novels?" *Stupid question.* "I can loan you a good one if you are interested."

Nurse Monica picked up the chart and handed it to me. "Oh, sure. But I don't get much time for that, what with my five daughters and their kids, plus working both here and in the emergency room on occasion. What is it about ... your book, I mean?"

She did not mention a husband, yet she wore a wedding ring. I busied myself with writing discharge orders and then looked up. "International intrigue, sex, and mayhem, called *The Tortuga Connection*," I laughed.

"Oh Lord. I don't suppose you have any copies lying about?" Monica took back Evanlink's chart and racked it.

"Actually, I have one in my car. I'll get it for you after I see the patient."

Heading for my auto a few minutes later, I met her in the parking lot.

"My car is just over here." I still had the Chrysler. The lawyers let me keep that. "Are you off duty now?"

"In five minutes. I need to get home and start packing for Canada. A friend has a cabin on a lake there." She had wonderfully white, even teeth, tanned, athletic arms, and mysterious, dark brown eyes in a slight squint.

"My family has a place on the Boundary Waters by Namakan Lake ... on the Canadian side. I get there when I can." I grabbed the novel from the trunk and handed it to her.

"Sounds really nice. I'll read ..." She glanced at the book. "*Tortuga Connection* while I am away. Thanks!"

My eyes trailed after the woman as she retraced her steps. *Forget it, Ira. The girl is married, and so are you.* My divorce hadn't yet been finalized, not that I gave a rat's ass. Hostility still bubbled under the surface. I sighed, opened the car door, and slammed it shut.

Upon returning home, I received an interesting call from none other than the senior Michael Starling in Florida. We caught up on our lives, and then he asked, "Ira, have you heard anything from Mikey? Do you know where he is? I have tried to locate our son, but without success. He seems to have disappeared off the face of the earth. I know he isn't in Hershey anymore. So many years have gone by."

"After leaving Steffi, I feared some consequences if I called her. He never wrote me. No, I don't know where he might be living. He's a young man now."

"Let's keep in touch, Ira. Let me know if you ever learn his where-abouts."

"Sure will."

Three months passed by. I had not heard from Monica, nor seen her at work. *Should I call her?* I had learned from the Short Stay staff that her husband died last spring. Beyond that, I knew very little about the forty-eight-year-old nightingale. Yet I felt a strong affinity toward her. What the hell was that all about? The work of pheromones? Some magnetic attraction centuries in the making? Her stupendous, infectious smile? *Crap! That was what did me in with Steffi. Fuck it all. What to do?*

Instead, I elected to write Monica a brief letter, inquiring if she'd enjoyed her vacation. Then I waited. And waited. Finally, a note arrived from Sudbury Lane. Yes, Monica loved her holiday in Canada. Her flowery handwriting revealed she was recovering from surgery on her foot. No mention of *The Tortuga Connection*. But at the bottom of the page, her phone number!

Is this really a hint? Am I being foolish? Again? Oh well, the worse that can happen is I sound stupid. Shit, I hate sounding stupid.

Monica's line rang. And rang. My nervous eyes bore into the phone, willing it to answer. I started to hang up when I heard a clacking noise at the other end, followed by "Hello?" She sounded out of breath. That was the beginning of my fourth courtship, with a Catholic woman, no less, recently a widow with five girls. And my divorce yet to be finalized. I had not yet learned.

My first date with Nurse Belmont was an unforgettable experience. When the front doorbell chimed, the door opened, and my heart skidded, then dropped to my feet as I walked in. I found myself and my ancestors under intense scrutiny, being interviewed, as it were, by her five adult children, three grandchildren, one brother, and one neighbor. I should have undergone such a composite investigation before my previous marriages. Cocktails and dinner at Bin 54 followed, the onset of a strange relationship. Would this end like all the others? Of course, for to do otherwise *I* would have to change, something I avoided at all costs, with dug-in heels.

One autumn sundown I approached Monica's entryway to escort her on our third or fourth date. The house was a modest white clapboard wood-frame building over red-brick building with a driveway giving out onto Sudbury Lane. Large oak trees, centurions guarding her front yard, had shed most of their leaves. Behind the building stood a trio of massive pines, which had been planted years ago. Pine cones and needles carpeted zoysia grass flanked by well-tended flowerbeds.

I was still a bit anxious about my newfound girlfriend. But as she opened her front door I sensed a new wave of intoxicating energy. For the life of me, I cannot recall what she wore. All I remember are the beaming cheeks, her openly contagious laugh, and the silver necklace hanging across her visually palpable breasts, a terminal crucifix hanging in space.

Later, when I peered back into my memories of that evening, I found it difficult to pursue a train of thought for one moment without it collapsing into the surreal. I could not visualize where we went or what was said … until she requested to see the much-discussed Western paintings on the walls of my apartment. We had been heading back along Hillsborough Road toward her home.

"You would?" I dared to ask. *For real?*

"My grandparents came from Big Fork, Montana, and I have some Kootenai Indian blood in me. I would love to see them."

My male brain, flooded by a sudden resurgence of testosterone, was still hardwired into an ancient drive to propagate the human race. Or something like that.

"What will your kids say? It's already ten o'clock." My heart rate accelerated as I spun the steering wheel and aimed my chariot southward down Old Fayetteville Road.

Her eyes lit up like twin candles. "Kids? What kids?"

That sealed a relationship destined to change me in ways I would never have believed. *God, you are answering my prayers.* Sex, I believed. God? In truth, the Lord and I had separated years ago, in spite of my sister's frequent attempts to save this sinner's soul. Now we entered my apartment with gay abandon.

"Monica, make yourself comfortable while I fix us something to drink. CC and soda okay?" Ice cubes were already dropping into a short glass, their music a familiar echo.

"That would be nice. Not too strong, please. I think the art is wonderful, especially the Indian. What does this say?" She had turned over the painting. "'*Red Cloud. July 1964.*' Did you know the artist?" She sat back down on the couch and brushed her skirt. Monica shifted, and I was exquisitely conscious of the pressure of her body next to mine.

"Joseph Larkspur was a close friend of my granddad. He repaid a loan to Grandma and Grandpa by giving them a few pieces of his artwork. I eventually inherited them. Some I turned over to my daughter, Denise. Cheers!"

"Cheers, Ira." We clinked tumblers. "Where is Denise now?"

"In London. She married a Welshman. They have two children. Denni's sister, Alexandria is her name, lives in Durham."

"That's not far. Is Alexandria married?"

"No. She is thirty-six and has odd jobs." I wanted to get away from the subject of Lexi. A part of me was quite ashamed to let anyone know she was a cocaine addict—ashamed and hurt beyond calculation.

I knocked down a swallow of Canadian Club. A big swallow. It felt good. Real good, burning as the lava settled in to singe my stomach, then spreading out, once more baptizing every fiber of my being. Alexandria faded away.

A table lamp reflected off Monica's eyeglasses. I stared at her dark chestnut eyes as we conversed, and I noticed freckles scattered across her cheeks. Her coal-black hair curled like tight wavelets over a waterfall, descending to midneck. Whereas my cheeks wore a serious frown, hers carried perpetual happiness and joy ... or so it seemed. I wanted to kiss those lips that made me feel so good inside. And I did.

I don't know who was more shocked, she or I. But the sparks spun into blue thunderbolts. At first I felt queasy inside, like when I first lit altar candles as an acolyte. I mean that it had been so long since ... since the last time. But the cocktail, or some other power, was working its magic, and I felt as if two were becoming one. I don't remember who made the first move after that, but lungs expanded, fingers fumbled, and excitement ascended as we threw caution to the winds.

"Monica, are you sure?" But I had already tossed all but my briefs to the floor.

"It's a bit late now." Her eyes flew wide open now, and she snapped away her bra, with my help.

"You certainly are blessed!" I managed to say.

Hearts in full gallop, we flung ourselves onto the coverlet, laughing, giggling, cooing, firing down another drink, then entering a state of frenzy as heat and incendiary passion overcame any lingering doubts.

One day following the New York City Twin Towers disaster, the judge entered the divorce decree of *Judi Stone v Ira Stone*. I hated attorneys. Belly-crawling pieces of horse manure. That was how I felt back then. But I could not admit that I was becoming paranoid—*I hated everybody at the time, Monica excepted.*

Two months later I presented Monica with an engagement ring. We celebrated by spending the Thanksgiving holiday that year in London, England, visiting my daughter, Denni, and her Welsh husband.

"Denni, where is your liquor cabinet. Got any Canadian whiskey?" I wandered about her kitchen, needing something to settle my nerves, my fourth new-wife-to-be having been introduced to my firstborn's family. It was nearing five o'clock. Well, at least it was five o'clock somewhere.

"We have gin above the fridge. Have you slowed down on your drinking, Daddy?" Her blue eyes regarded me, blonde hair curving nicely against her neck. She was a thin, lovely woman now and in terrific physical shape from exercise and biking.

"Hardly," the to-be had to say as she joined us. "But I wouldn't mind a spot of Tanqueray myself."

Denise eyed my hand as it grabbed a bottle and rushed a stream into one of her handsome crystals. I followed it with a bit of tonic water. A very small bit, of course.

"I wish you would spend more time with your grandchildren. They will be back from school shortly," my daughter sighed. "Have you forgotten that nursery rhyme you sang with us when we were young?

'This old man, he played one,
He played knick-knack on my thumb ...'"

"I'm rather under the weather, Denni. Bad cold from your wet London chill." I truly did have a distressing case of the sniffles, and a toddy always helped. After all, alcohol turned lead into gold, soothed my anxiety, lengthened life, and cured all ills. I paused, and then I added, "So, how are Elliott and Cameron doing in school?"

Denni fired a dish towel into the sink, with a bit too much force. "*Fine.* And stop avoiding the subject. I just worry that you are overdoing it."

"Fear not. I never drink on the job. Nurse Belmont will testify to that." I winked at Monica, who was stirring her own cocktail.

With a knick-knack paddy-whack, give the dog a bone,
This old man came rolling home.

Another year had gone by. Afghanistan continued to heat up, and the hunt for Osama bin Laden was on. And that was the year that Monica and I were married. We flew back to London for our honeymoon during the Christmas holidays. I was laid up with an abysmal cold. Again. I undertook the same treatment.

We settled into a happy and comfortable existence. Lots of travel and lots of sex. Then lots of arguments and less sex. Then ripening anger and resentments, usually settled by drugs and alcohol. I had to take Valium, my tranquillizer, to placate my nerves at night. I needed to avoid Crown Royal after ten o'clock. Over the next three years our sex life soon was annihilated by petty disagreements and mind-altering medicaments. Half drunk, I sought peace and quiet on the couch. I found myself unable to engage in intimacy with my partner, just sharp rebuttals. Well, hell, she had turned into a shrew—*just like all my other wives!*

Me? I still counted the days by the clock and the bottle.

Autumn 2004

I was settled in my office—I called the den my home office—writing checks and torturing a series of paperclips out of shape. The phone rang. Boston calling.

"Hi, Ira. What is the best thing that happened today?" Jocelyn always put me into a good mood.

"Hello, Jocie. Not much. Oh, okay ... you called. *That* is the best thing."

"Again you get a gold star. And you're always whining that I never come to see you. How about next week?"

"We'd love to have you. Let me know your schedule. Any special reason?"

"Do you need a reason? How about because I care for you."

Sister came for a week, though she seemed to devote most of her days to shopping with Monica. Jocelyn, like everyone else, failed in her attempt to persuade me to cease grabbing the whiskey bottle. I thought they were being overly worried and a bit interfering. I was a grown man, for crissake. I knew perfectly well what was and was not good for me! After all, I was a brain surgeon. *Dammit, leave me alone! Why is everyone butting into my business?* The truth be told, deep down inside I desperately wanted help, as my nightmares worsened by the week, and I secretly prayed to the God whom I did not believe existed—*Help me, Lord. I am dying ... dying ... dying.* Not hearing an answer, my solution was ...? More whiskey, of course.

A part of me knew the cards were stacked against Ira Jefferson Stone. Everyone's preaching, analyzing, cursing, and counseling was just not working, for I was simply unable to stop worshipping my mute, beguiling idol.

That God whom I had discarded certainly had a strange way of salvaging humankind. Back then, only hatred, resentment, and self-deification percolated through me. And rightfully so. Look at the way I had been treated. *Fuck you. Fuck everyone!* Jocie never visited Chapel Hill to join our family gatherings. She came to stick her nose in where it did not belong. Sister-dear had colluded with my wife, of all people, to enjoin me from drinking my elixir, from savoring my Crown Royal, the only friend

I had. When Jocelyn returned to her home, I did not yet know what had transpired. I was soon to find out.

A week after Jocie left, my office phone rang. "Hello, Dr. Stone. My name is Sandman House. I'm a physician in private practice, a family doc not far from your institution. May I come over and discuss a problem with you?"

"Now?" I replied. It was late in the afternoon, and I was looking at my wrist watch, the hands of time rolling toward half past four.

"If you don't mind. It won't take but a few minutes."

I listened to the concluding click at the other end and then cradled the receiver. *Shit.*

My agitated fingers, desperately ... well, at least anxiously ... wanted to wrap themselves around a glass. I tapped the desk, tarrying, eyes glancing at my timepiece again. Then a knock. "Come in," I scowled, the invitation certainly a sour one.

"Sorry to intrude, Dr. Stone. May I sit?" Dr. House stretched out his hand to grasp mine.

"Ira. Certainly." I waved him to an armchair, and I retook my throne.

"Everything go well today?" he inquired.

"Went great." *What brings you here?* I needed to get home. My heart skipped a beat.

"You have quite an excellent reputation. I hear the residents particularly appreciate your teaching efforts."

"Thanks." *Just get on with it.*

"A few years ago I was appointed to the University Health Committee, and it is in this capacity that I come here. Someone has notified me that you might have an issue with alcohol."

Say wha ... at? My heart double-tripped.

"And a physician mentioned to me that one weekend he smelled ethanol on your breath. I am not here to make any judgments but only to facilitate or provide any assistance you may need."

"A long-winded way of saying that you are offering to save me from myself. Really, I am quite okay. I just have a few cocktails at night, that's all. What's the big deal? Who reported me?"

"That is confidential, as is this meeting. Neither your university officials nor the state medical board will hear about this."

"Well, I appreciate your concern. And that of your nameless source." *Who the hell ...?*

"Please think about it. I am only here to help. You might consider going to an AA meeting or two."

"Huh? *AA?* You have *got* to be kidding!"

"Just a suggestion, that's all. There is a caduceus meeting next Wednesday."

He departed, and I thought that was the end of it. It wasn't, and that discussion remained indelibly printed in my mind.

It was my goddamn sister. I later discovered that it was Jocie who, through Nurse Monica Belmont Stone, had squealed on me. Now I hated her with a passion. Both of them.

My mind lurched into overdrive. *My medical license is at risk. Lord, how could Jocelyn do that to me? Her own brother! Alcoholics Anonymous? This cannot be true. Once the so-called Health Committee makes their report, my goose is cooked!*

*   *   *

"Monica! Do you know what happened today? One of the fucking health committee docs came into my office, *right into my goddamn office*, and accused me of being a drunk! Who ratted on me? *Who?*"

I ranted and raved on and off for an hour, shooting Crown Royal across my gums, later lapsing into a twilight state. Monica, of course, was distressed—not at the uncalled-for session in my office but rather at my unseemly behavior. I could not understand her. *How could she take the other side?* Eventually, I dragged it out of her. An unnamed someone had referred Jocelyn and Monica to that ... that academic court. They were in cahoots, as my grandfather, Ira Jefferson the First, would say. Even my dear loved ones had now set themselves against me. *Everyone* was out to get me.

I'll show them. I can and will master my drinking. I tried experiment after desperate experiment, changing from Tennessee whiskey to Leyden gin to Stolichnaya vodka, searching for the Holy Grail in liquid form. *Perhaps a different concentration, or maybe a mix with grapefruit juice.* Yet I could not for long forego my true Canadian passion—Crown Royal Manhattans. The pure iridescence of dancing light beams reflecting off the inverted cone of a cocktail glass, a crystal standing seductively on her long slender leg, clear deep amber spirits chilled to perfection, an impeccable red cherry coasting in the depths—the answer to an immense desire ready to be slaked! The mere idea consumed me, and I would keep a grip on the chalice as if it would vanish should I blink.

One would think that by then I would have comprehended my condition, but all that I learned was how to make the same mistake over and over again, like that old gramophone stuck on a single note—*your Spanish eyes ... your Spanish eyes ... your Spanish eyes ...*

On the weekends, when I threw caution to the winds, I would wake up with nausea and a terrible hammering at my temples, something that had rarely occurred in years past. Though I denied it, blackouts were becoming more frequent. Often I could not recall what I did or said the previous night while under the influence, and *even so* I believed no issue existed. Anger and paranoia were accelerating with G-force steepness. Curled up in the eye of a raging storm, I simply could not stop drinking. I had become a moth beating itself against a porch light, as if determined to kill myself. I entered a state of severe depression and crossed that delicate threshold where dying felt easier than living. My liver and kidney chemistries were ominous. I had become a train out of control.

One day something happened. I cannot explain it, but there appeared a dim lamp in the stygian darkness, as if strings of bubbles were slowly rising to the surface of a very deep pond. Looking back on it, a power higher than me must have intervened. Someone or something was answering the prayers of my many loved ones.

I remember that a formless state of curiosity grabbed a hold of me, and standing before the bathroom mirror, I heard myself mumble, "Well, it can't hurt, I suppose." *Yes, yes, of course it can! Everyone will think you are an alcoholic.* "Coward," I said to myself. "Just try it." *Don't do this! You are strong enough, Ira. Just moderate your drinking. Everyone else does.* "Sorry, but my life is spinning over the edge. Sorry."

I would never have believed it could happen. Two weeks after the good doctor showed up in my office, my arms and legs overcame my unhinged brain and mysteriously drove the Chrysler to an Alcoholics Anonymous caduceus meeting, a gathering of about two dozen alcoholics and drug addicts practicing in the various medical fields—physicians, RNs, LPNs, pharmacists, med students, social workers, lab technicians—men and women just like me! I was astounded at the many respected doctors present.

Even so, I knew with certainty that *I* did not belong there. *I am not an alcoholic like these guys. I am not a fucking souse!* However, by the end of the second meeting, even Ira Stone was introducing himself as, "Hello, my name is Ira, and I am an alcoholic." *Not really one, but I'll just say the words anyway.*

At the third meeting appeared a physician. "Hello, my name is Sandman, and I am an alcoholic." I stared at the guy, who smiled kindly at me. *The Dr. House who came to my office! Jesus. A kindred spirit.* A rather odd feeling washed over me. One cannot fathom the release which I felt, as if a link in a heavy chain had cracked. A tiny fracture, but a fracture nevertheless.

Yet my paranoia persisted. *No, he is checking up on me!*

God knows I struggled to prove I was not a weakling. *Dammit! I can do this! I can! I can!*

But I couldn't. I was still trapped between the cork and the bottle. Even so, I faithfully attended two meetings a week. By the second month, I actually enjoyed the gatherings, even looked forward to them. I began to realize I was not alone.

The Twelve Steps? *I can handle my drinking without such schoolboy activities.* Ah, the elasticity of truth. Nope, I couldn't control it, for my life had become too unmanageable ... if it were ever otherwise.

A sponsor, a kind of rigorous mentor and big brother? *I do not need anyone butting into my personal affairs. I fail to see any reason why this is necessary.* But I still could not see much beyond the top of that cork. Then one day after a meeting—when I say "meeting," I mean an AA gathering—Tonia, a recovering alcoholic, came up to me and said, "Ira, some of us have noticed alcohol on your breath and you're very irritable. How can we help you? Have you considered going to rehab?" She seemed genuine and dead serious. "I had to go there before I got free from wine and those Tylenol-threes."

"Rehab? You mean one of those jitter joints. An asylum? Come on. I'm doing better every day," I lied.

"Well, keep coming back. You aren't alone in this fight, and we need you as much as you need us."

Say what? At the time I was woefully ignorant of Step Twelve.

I simply could not admit to being timid when it came to facing my character defects, those dark shadows hanging around me like giant bats suspended upside down in the trees. Timid? Shit, I was a fucking chicken. I had arrived at the point where two roads diverged in a dark wood, and I simply could not take the pain promised by the one less traveled—not yet. Maybe not ever. It was easier to take my friendly drugs, my Crown Royal and Valium. Yet, deep down inside I knew where the trail was leading—a very high cliff. It would be Uncle Barley all over again. *Dear God, I am not like Barley. I'm a doctor, not a skid row derelict! My uncle was different, an embarrassment. I'm a … a surgeon, dammit!*

I had been using my AA meetings as a crutch, a social club. I was in a disconnected state of mind, ancient synapses in lockdown inside a living asylum. A part of me despised alcoholics and AA meetings. Another part had found camaraderie there, even fellowship, with guys like me. *Like me?* One evening my wife and I found ourselves in the kitchen.

"Monica, you seem out of sorts today. What gives?" I continued assisting her with the dishes.

"Nothing has changed, Ira," she sighed. "It is as if we are two people living in different cities. You ignore my kids, even your own. Your job, our checkbook, and the den are your life. Maybe we both need some help."

"Both?"

"I never quite got over Sam's death." She laid her towel down. A depressed countenance had replaced her super-smile. "And my arthritic knee is killing me. My doctor has me on OxyContin now."

"*OxyContin!* Jeez, Monica. You know how addicting that is." I shot her a withering look while picking up the next dish from the sink, my favorite short glass.

I could not cope with another addict in my family. One was enough—Alexandria. I did not count me among the accursed. I frowned, suddenly not recalling what we were talking about. *Oxy-something. Whatever ...*

"Ira, thanks for helping with the ..." Monica's leaden words trailed after me and fell away. I had already peeled off for the den.

I did not want to hear about her problems. I could not even cope with my own. I glanced at my drink. *God, I cannot stop.* I sat there staring off into the middle distance. Uncomfortable judgments kept pacing back and forth. *"Have you considered going to rehab?" My family, my siblings, my girls—they must all be so ashamed of me. I'm glad Mom and Dad are not around to see this.*

I spun the ice chips. Someone at AA said that Appleton was a good place to go. A small fortune for the first month, though. *I wonder if it is worth the price tag.* The price tag? It likely paled before the cost of my affliction, though that idea quickly evaporated. Still and all, this surgeon's fucked-up brain-case was housing his fucked-up beliefs along with a hardwired consortium of fucked-up consultants, all attempting to treat his fucked-up thinking—and it was not working. Alone, I was simply incapable of unlocking the cryptogram, the key eluding me as it crossed my lips once more—another ounce of whiskey.

And then, from a submerged soundtrack, a message from long ago surfaced. The Namakan—*The craft rocked with the waves, and the rhythmic but muted slap, slap sound played on my ears.* Again I wondered if a higher power had been sending a message in Morse code.

I poured more and more royal lubricant into my chalice and drank, the very earth stopping its motion, all sounds ceasing. *I can't go on like this. Monica now alludes to a divorce. My children won't talk to me. My health is slipping. I may lose my job and medical license. The guys at AA strongly hint at a recovery program.* I heard Monica weeping on the other side of my closed door. A massive lump settled in my throat, and my hands were shaking. How could I live without my Crown Royal? How could I live *with* it in this decaying lotus field, losing all honor and discipline?

I gazed at a black and white photo of my parents. *Mom and Dad, I have to do this. Please do not be angry at me, Dad. I'm so sorry.* I saw wetness on my fingers. It had come from my cheeks. I felt I was less than. My deteriorating psyche was now on dialysis.

If I go, what will my colleagues at work think? Will they point me toward the exit? What will everyone say behind my back? Still, I realized what I had to do. Even if it killed me. Or the alternative surely would. I made my decision.

CHAPTER 30

When old words die out on the tongue,
New melodies break forth from the heart;
And where the old tracks are lost,
New country is revealed with its wonders.

Rabindranath Tagore
Gitanjali

It is fascinating what detox and recovery will do. I not only discovered the difference between religion and spirituality but also realized that AA meetings were not what they had been painted to be. They were affairs of fellowship and not finely tuned religious experiences. They were like cancer survivor groups who met to share their stories and help victims through bad times. If one did not believe in God, he or she could believe in some other higher power (rather than drugs and alcohol). Just so the individual had someone—it could be the AA group, even—to whom he could surrender and turn over his problems, the addict himself no longer his own higher power. It was that surrender that gave me troubles. Still does. After all, I had been raised as a Stone, wherein relinquishing my own supremacy was a misguided sign of weakness rather than strength, but I was making progress. I was discovering that the more I permitted myself to be dependent on the Lord, the more independent and free I became.

The disease of alcoholism and addiction is one of the very few lethal infirmities that the patient can *choose* to successfully treat. Or not. I now

288

saw that the majority of addicts were not those sad derelicts only a day's journey from the gutter. Here my buddies and I, each of us, carried that monster on our shoulders. We came from all walks of life.

After leaving the cafeteria one morning, deep in my musings, I ambled along a cobbled sidewalk flanked by huge conifers talking to themselves, their trunks reminiscent of a cathedral's columns. Beaded with dew, a quilt of rich and twinkling green grass under a host of butterflies was still damp from the night chill. My ears detected the faint murmur of a distant power mower.

There was a slight tang of brine in the cool air, the result of a westerly zephyr chasing in off the Japanese Current, and the sweet murmur of birdsong and sugarplum wind in the uppermost pine branches. A pristine essence surrounded me. Yes, I had actually grown to *like* this place, this campus of addicts healing addicts amidst buildings of eggshell white.

"Hey, Hoss. It's the hour for our spirituality session in the loft," hollered Alamo in his Texan drawl as he jogged toward me. "Pascal Perez is the speaker. You will like him." He grabbed me by the arm and got his breath back. Alamo sported his usual belted camouflage attire, no longer hanging so loose. A corduroy flat cap sat at a jaunty angle on his head.

"Slow down. We have time," I said, spinning around and feinting with a punch to the left, then the right.

He ducked, bounced on the balls of his feet, and chuckled. "Been lifting weights at the gym. I feel great." In fact, his limbs had firmed up a bit, his spindly arms and chicken-like shanks now filling out. Military fatigues covered much of his artwork.

What a remarkable change. He's not scratching, is no longer stuttering, and has put on some weight. I grinned as we climbed the steps together and joined the crew sitting to face a diminutive yet steel-jawed man in jeans and a T-shirt, attire black as the ace of spades. With a colorful bandana about his head and a scorched face, the guy looked like a gypsy. He was about fifty-five and in trim, muscular shape, brawny arms wrapped in tattoos, the envy of any artist. He wrote on the white board,

An Attitude of Gratitude!

He turned back toward us, smiled, and announced, "Hello, my name is Pascal, and I am a drug addict."

"Hi, Pascal," we answered in unison.

"Today's message." On the board he added,

> *Let us be grateful for what we have rather*
> *than obsessed over what we want.*

The lawnmower fell silent.

"As some of you know, I am a preacher at a local Anglican Church and a lecturer on spirituality. My flock calls me Father Pascal. Many of you will meet yours truly during your second and third step drills."

Preacher?

"He earned his PhD at Oxford in England," Alamo whispered to me.

"Nolan, what is the Second Step?" asked Pascal.

"*Came to believe that a Power greater than ourselves could restore us to sanity.*"

Nolan and I had actually become good friends since "feedback."

"And the Third Step, Alamo?"

The angular truck driver boomed out, "*Made a decision to turn our will and our lives over to the care of God as we understood him.*"

"Wow! Okay, Alamo. And now we are going to learn some techniques to allow the spirit, and I do not mean alcoholic spirits, into our bodies and minds. I am referring to the release of material needs, frustration, and anger so that we might find the path out of back alleys toward inner tranquility and peace. A spiritual peace. Until now, our spiritual eyes have been blind, and we kept bumping into obstacles from our past. Some of us got bumped down to our very bottom, seeking help only after we had lost everything."

"Obstacles?" I felt a bit uncomfortable.

"Often they are cravings and wishes previously demanded by our self-serving egos," answered the preacher. "Here is an example." And he wrote on the white board,

If I get tomorrow what I want today,
then tomorrow I will rage over why I did not get it yesterday.

"That's what did me in. When I did not get it, I fumed and then drank." Pascal surveyed his audience. "Most people find agony in hatred and ecstasy in love. The addict's lizard-brain, on the other hand, finds ecstasy in hatred, agony in love."

"Bullshit," came a loud whisper from the back of the room. *Lester.*

The preacher gave a knowing smile. "If we bullshitters cannot get rid of our pent-up anger and depression, we will relapse into drinking and using as our 'medicinal' solution. I guarantee it."

That can't possibly happen to me.

Pascal stabbed the air with his right forefinger in my direction, and I flinched. "That is why spirituality is so important, the block and tackle of our recovery, as it were. We must look inward in order to solve our problems, not outward. We need to commit a form of suicide—extinguish that selfish self within."

I had found a brittle and ephemeral freedom somewhere out there with Steffi and alcohol, both corrupting my thinking, preventing me from finding that desperate happiness within. I had just kept roping up those angry cliffs of despair.

Derrick raised his hand. "Ain't spirituality and religion the same thing? Like goin' tuh church?"

"Religion has certain boundaries and rituals defined by one's particular denomination," responded the preacher, thumbs jammed into his Western belt. "Spirituality has no such boundaries, but it might lead us back to the God of our childhood or to any higher power we choose, the goal being a clean and sober serenity. Our brains are but one of the Lord's holy reliquaries, wherein we will find peace if we look. Or the forges of hell if we allow Slick, that depraved reveler, to hijack our moral convictions, declaring eminent domain." Slick, a mocking conquistador wallowing in my bejeweled lizard-brain, I was learning, had been "my very best friend." With friends like that I did not need any enemies.

We met with Father Pascal twice more that week, and by the third time

I sensed that I might actually survive the spiritual surgery within my soul. I was making a dramatic change in my internal attitude toward God whom I had left, the same God who keeps one jump ahead of me. As the toxins leaked from my body, the pungent anxiety I had felt during church services also disappeared. It was as though the Prince of Darkness, if not cast away forever, had been neutralized and rendered impotent—a snake shedding its skin—but the evil body and soul of the incarcerated reptile remained, waiting for me to slip, waiting to break through the shield-wall and then, should I take that first drink, plunder and rape. And I was now praying to surrender my problems over to my Higher Power, rather than petitioning for release from the pain my head had caused. Praying on my knees.

Another tumbler had fallen into place. The revelation was quite dramatic, and I knew I had to keep it that way.

I realized what my family had been trying to tell me all those years. Now, the sister whom I had hated and shunned was finding a grateful presence in my heart. Second only to my career, *I* had been the higher power in my life, and that self-imposed deity had driven out any charity for all my loved ones, including the Lord. Back then, I not only denied I was an alcoholic but had also denied the very existence of God.

One evening Dr. Simon ThunderHawk presented the most recent medical findings on addiction, society's greatest pestilence, a disease condemned by mankind even as we all headed for the nearest tavern. Blue highlights reflected from his shoulder-length sable hair. Richly endowed eyebrows rose and fell as he imparted his message. The projected PowerPoint presentation fascinated me, a physician.

"And here is the site where physiologic MRI and PET scans pinpoint abnormalities in the heads of addicts. The *Nucleus Accumbens* in the deep of the primitive brain is one of them. Statistics and family genetic studies show us that addiction—in all its mind-altering forms—has a prominent inheritance pattern, regardless of one's drug of choice. Certainly environmental factors will play a role, albeit a relatively small one." ThunderHawk looked about. "Yes, Derrick?"

"So does that mean we have a disease? My father was a deadbeat drunk. Couldn't I have *learned* my habit from him?"

"Certainly. But true drug addicts, ten percent of the population, *cannot* cease drinking or using without help, whereas nonaddicts can stop at any time they choose. Of course, they must choose to do so."

"What about these new experimental drugs, Simon? It would be great if a pill could replace Appleton ... Well, you know what I mean ..."

"I doubt that researchers will discover the silver bullet in my lifetime, so I will still have a job, Derrick. However, there will still be the need for detox, character rebuilding, and stress management. I wouldn't give up the Twelve Steps just yet. Now here is the ..."

My attention was distracted by uncomfortable memories, memories of Uncle Barley. I sighed. Dear God, if I had only known back then. If only we could have shown kindness and sent him to a rehab center. *If only ...*

"The *Nucleus Accumbens*, and herein rests a 'parasite' I call Slick, for want of a better word. It's the name I give for the crux of the pathophysiology in this nucleus. Slick, our Dracula who has merely gone to ground, is immensely patient. He lays in suspended animation, embalmed within his sarcophagus, sending out unctuous emissaries, just waiting quietly for you and me to slip. The bastard is like a troop of maggots retreating deep inside a corpse, huddling to keep warm until we deliver that fiery dose of alcohol."

Hungry, angry, lonely, tired—a cocktail of emotions that will loosen the walls of Slick's coffin, I learned. That will be the time he attempts to rise up and nudge us back on to that slippery slope, to just take that one little drink. *But only a little,* we promise ourselves. And then, we are again on that runaway train, blood dripping from our necks. We allow Slick, a fanged and brutal sovereign, once more to become the exchequer for our brain.

The Sioux Indian puckered his brow, eyes as wide as chestnuts. *"Listen to me, dammit! We are sick. We will never be cured!"* With one sonic punch, ThunderHawk slammed his pointer stick against the canvas. *"I know,* my friends. One prick of anger and one jigger of whiskey was all it took for Slick to release his snake venom in me, and I found myself in jail for vehicular manslaughter. As a paroled felon, I can never vote, and I am excluded from most jobs." His voice was deep and tight. "If we cannot control our sacred fears and resentments, relapse *will* occur. It happened to me, and it *will happen to you*. We drink and we use, leaving scorched earth in our wake, disease and destruction mushrooming as we feed the beast.

"Like Brer Rabbit stuck on Tar Baby—the more we punch it, the more stuck we get, and then one half of us in this room will return to our using or drinking, risking death from medical complications, auto accidents, suicide, gun battles, and just plain rot. Slick awakens, slipping out of hibernation, the newly resurrected dead taking over—and we just keep on punching the Tar Baby. For those unfortunates, the bell will toll, and the maw of Hades is just around the corner. A long, lonely highway it is." And then Simon ThunderHawk wrote on the white board,

> *My name is Slick. I lie here quietly. You do not see me.*
> *I wish you death and suffering. I am cunning, baffling, and*
> *powerful. I relish pretending I am your friend and lover, but*
> *in truth I loathe you. I despise you, and you will die! I am the*
> *proud excrement of Satan, and my name is Slick.*

Of interest was the finding that even the odor of alcohol at a party or the sight of a drug dealer's street corner elicited abnormal release of dopamine in the Nucleus Accumbens and environs, hijacking the pathway of desire and its obscure geometry, driving the addict toward a relapse if he or she did not have the tools to resist that first drink, that first hit. Those very primitive centers in addicts raged against the light, as it were, fighting to maintain supremacy while stifled by recovery programs. It was the corruption of those reptilian nuclei that had become that crown of thorns inherited by Uncle Barley and me, for we had received that unfortunate cluster of family genes.

As Fletcher had said at a recent home-group meeting, "You are trapped in a spider web. Every time you move toward the whiskey bottle, the entire cerebral web and its synapses vibrate. The black widow always knows where you are. Slick is not in a hurry, for dinner will always be there. You are here to learn how to disable that deadly arachnid, using both sword and mace.

"Anyone know what appeasement is?" he then inquired.

I raised my hand. "To give concessions so as to keep the peace, like what England and America did to keep Hitler off our backs."

"And what happened?"

"The Nazis kept invading more and more countries, taking over nearly all of Europe and killing millions in the process."

"Think of Slick as Hitler, the warlord of your mind."

The next morning as the dawn delivered a faint gray promise in the east, we again woke, dressed, exercised in the gym, practiced our spiritual "time out" with group meditation and soft music—perhaps the sounds of sea waves or a bubbling brook—and then attended home-group meetings. I was enjoying myself with the camaraderie, truly a new experience for me. Later that Tuesday we joined together in the loft for another spirituality discussion, our fourth session with Pascal.

Pascal Perez had invited us to "talk" with someone very important in our lives, someone loving or threatening but now remote, perhaps deceased. This turned out to be an intense experience for all, even the listeners. The dead weight of the past lay across each man like a toppled monument, and we had to crawl out from under in order to see the light, a torch often viewed, however, through a very narrow spectrum. Indeed, it was a frightening travail as I suffered my brother's blood on my hands. But I had to pull up the shade to that window, for I had yet to bury all of him and move on.

"Okay, Ira. Your counseling and workups suggest that your brother, Michael, played a significant role in your life. I have set two chairs in the middle of our circle facing each other. You sit on one, and Mike will be sitting on the other. Okay?"

Dear God. "Uh, sure." Twelve colleagues quietly regarded me as I steeled myself. My heart rate picked up five beats a minute when I took possession of one metal folding chair and faced the empty one seating Mike. A pencil dropped, sounding like a hammer. The second hand on the wall clock lurched forward, striking me a blow with each resounding tick, and the skin of my palms pricked with perspiration. *Tick, tick, tick ...*

My right hand, wanting a short glass, touched the medallion attached to the chain around my neck, a bronze walleye pike, that Namakan gift from Michael.

Then, "Hi, Mike. Gosh, I don't know what to say. I hope all is well."
I felt a cold breath of air, as if I had just lifted a gravestone, and then I
quickly recovered.

This is so lame. He is certainly better off now than he had been. I pulled
vast quantities of oxygen into my lungs and then blurted out a memory to
fill the desperate silence.

"I was just thinking about … about when you and I went fishing
together. You, Dad, and I. Remember when we all got caught in that big
storm on Lake Namakan? We wound up on the dock at an Indian home.
Rain came down in sheets, pounding like … like elephant feet, and the
Chippewa let us wait out the storm in their cottage—actually, more of a
shack. There were three of them, a father and two little girls. Never were
we so glad to see a human being. And Dad, in spite of his intolerance of
the aborigine, was truly grateful. I don't recall being treated with such
kindness."

I waited a dozen heart beats, as if expecting an answer. I focused my
inner eye only on my dead brother, and the small crowd around me truly
no longer existed. I felt as if I were talking with a disembodied sibling who
was actually sitting there.

"Why did you come?"

"Oh, Michael. You have no idea how I miss you. I …"

My chest tightened. I bent my eye toward a young man no longer
devoid of hair, with tubes in every orifice and IV lines running, but instead
wearing a tranquil smile.

"I guess you now know that I dropped the ball that year you were
sick. I was just … God, I have no excuse." I squeezed my eyelids together.
*Sergeant, did you know that this stellar surgeon here inflicted death on his
very own brother?*

"I would give anything to bring you back. Anything …" *Anything,
Mike.* My eyes were tearing up. I could not help it. It was too, too painful,
and I wanted a drink. *Lord, I hurt.* Down deep inside I was agonizing.

"Please forgive me, Mike. I know that you called me, and I just blew
it off. No, I did not. Oh, I don't know what I did." *I let you die, Michael
Jacob.*

"I … I let you go, and I could have prevented it. We were so close. Remember how we played catch, and I took you on an airplane ride to Fort Lauderdale? I was so happy to see you and Dad get together once more. Where are you now? Where …" *What? Oh, Christ.*

"You were gone from my life, Mike. Gone …"

I held my head in my hands, elbows on my knees. I wept, rubbed my cheeks, and glanced up. Little Mike had left and brother Mike was back, just resting there, smiling again, the caducean tethers to life gone. Once more he seemed like the guy before cancer had laid him low.

"You got to stop beating yourself up about this, Ira. I never truly died. Besides, I am taking your pain with me like I promised," I heard him say.

Huh? Good Lord. I actually heard him! My agony faded as I waited for the voice to explain itself.

"Our Father asked me to send Jocelyn to you," Michael replied, as if he read my thoughts.

Our Jocelyn, whom I despised? "Dear God, maybe you do exist. Maybe …"

It was just Mike and I. My eyes remained glued on the specter before me. I could actually hear Michael speaking.

"You see, brother, I am an addict also. I was the lucky one. I left before Slick crawled through my brain. You think the future cannot be foretold. But it can, much like weather prediction by your computers. Only better."

The message was there. Take one more drink, and …

"Thanks, brother—thanks, Michael." I had just learned to turn pain and suffering over to God, and I felt a tremendous weight being lifted, as I now understood the meaning of Step Three—*Made a decision to turn our will and our lives over to the care of God as we understood him.* I was doing better. Progress, not perfection, I guess.

My friends surrounded me, their eyes moist, murmuring and wondering if they had missed something. They had, but I had not. I began to get it.

I thought I was finished, yet the ghost would not depart. My head began to spin, my heart skipped beats, and white sound surrounded me. Michael just sat there waiting, waiting for … for what? I felt myself swaying, undulating. I was in a canoe, with Mike facing me, floating, bobbing on Namakan waters. *Again, I heard the waves slap, slap against the boat, tapping out some enigmatic message from above. Michael swiped at a mosquito above his scalp. Clumps of dry hair, now more gray than brown, flew into the air and drifted like snowflakes to the water.* But Mike's blue eyes danced with mirth. His hair was brown, shifting with the wind.

I was scared to ask, but I had to. "Mike, have you seen Stella since she ... since I ..."

"We have a surprise for you some day. I'll leave it at that."

"But ..." Suddenly my fishing line nearly jerked out of my hands, and before I knew it a Great Northern shot out of the water, my hook in its throat.

"Hey, bro, that's even bigger than the one I caught. What a beut! We've got to do this again, real soon!"

I found myself frantically reeling in the fish, my left hand gripping the pole, the right turning, turning, turning ...

"Ira ... *Ira?"* In the middle distance I heard Pascal calling my name. "What are you doing with your hands? Are you all right?"

Everything blurred and then pulled into focus. While I reached for a box of Kleenex, I turned toward Pascal. "Yeah, I am fine." *Maybe more all right than I have ever been in my life.*

He was silent for a hundred heartbeats. "Thanks for sharing with us, Ira. Questions or comments, anyone?"

Not a soul volunteered.

The preacher softly suggested, "Ira, describe your feelings for us."

"I'm sad, like every time I've thought on it." *But not as much as before.*

"You sound as if you have been lonely, as if you had found nobody to confide in. Perhaps two things just occurred. You found out that your AA group ... indeed, your buddies ... are willing to listen to you without sitting in judgment—" *Unlike Dad.* "And the dialogue between you and Mike melted part of that anguish."

"I guess."

Pascal waved his arm to include our circle. "As painful as this may seem, we alcoholics tend to hold on to our avalanche of misery. What better reason to drink?"

He walked back and forth, hands clasped behind his back, and then he continued. "Indeed, such unrelenting despondency can be a subconscious form of selfish thinking, rather like the unfolding physical and emotional pain many of us drug addicts refuse to abandon. The *'It's all about me'* syndrome—'Look at me, poor, poor, pitiful me. I hurt. Give me something to relieve my suffering.' We shall discover that when sadness and loneliness slip into our lives, we must go to an AA or NA meeting that very day. Otherwise drinking and drugging are just around the corner.

"Ira, in the next few days, write a letter to Charlene and one to Stella. Tell them ... well, you know what to say.

"Okay. Let's go on a break before Derrick takes his turn."

Strange. I feel so much better now. I don't feel the need for whiskey. The hurt in my gut is gone.

CHAPTER 31

The best thing about the future is that it only comes one day at a time.

Abraham Lincoln

Bursts of sunlight had warmed the outdoors, so after lunch we all assembled under an enormous pine tree. Simon ThunderHawk paced about on a carpet of green grass, a cool wind rippling his coal-black hair.

After we repeated the Serenity Prayer, ThunderHawk posed a query. "Sebastian, did alcohol or drugs solve the stressful problems in your life?"

"Seemed to at first. But only for a while. Then I found myself in deep shit."

"I dare say that strikes a chord in all of us," the Sioux responded. "And now?"

"Now I'll hit a meeting before the urge to drink or use becomes overwhelming ... I mean, as soon as it starts. Also say the Serenity Prayer.

"And call your sponsor, or at least another friend of Bill W. You will find that we recovering addicts have an advantage over nonaddicts. We have a built-in support group that costs each of us merely one dollar per meeting. It is amazing how our anger, sadness, and fear shrink and dissolve away when we face them with our friends.

"Medical science has discovered evidence that alcoholism and addiction are inherited diseases. They have not found a cure. MDs and

PhDs in psychiatry and addiction medicine have concluded that control of our sickness requires detoxification, often as an inpatient, for medical management of withdrawal, seizures, and depression. Continued treatment may include group therapy and psychiatric evaluation. Support meetings such as AA and NA, spiritual fellowship, and having a sponsor are required. Failure to attend to these may result in relapse, misery, and maybe a rendezvous with death, alcohol being a most notable executioner."

For us there were only two spheres of reality: drugs and an early demise or sobriety and a thankful life. There was no in-between where we could learn to drink and use socially and responsibly. Not with addicts like us.

That night I sat in the men's library, gazing outside. Memories of Steffi once more slipped their tether. It was at the recovery center that it dawned on me that Steffi was a methamphetamine addict. One might question why it took me so long to realize this, but I was blinded by infatuation and my own addiction. I wondered aloud if she could ever forgive me, a physician, for not helping her into a treatment center. I will always remember the one and only time Stephanie and I were at church. I watched as she approached the altar, knelt before the crucifix, and cried uncontrollably, begging God for … for something she never had. I saw, but I was blind.

Bright flashes from the Penn State operating room bloomed and then collapsed. *Our eyes locked briefly, and then she pressed the instruments into my hands and glanced down. I incised the dura mater, exposing Charlene's cortex.* I felt an adrenalin surge, even yet so many summers later. *In silence Steffi thrust the suction tube into my fingers. It was as if we were communicating by thought waves, as if we had worked together hand-and-glove for years.* I squeezed my eyelids closed. *"Here is the chart, sir. The orderlies are ready to take the body away. Do you wish to write your op note now?"* While handing over the patient's record, Stephanie gazed at me with glistening eyes. She appeared to be as disturbed as I in that unkind hour.

Yes, back then I strutted like a long-necked goose on the dance floor with Steffi, so many envious eyes upon us. But in the end, her kisses would suck out my vital juices, those spells leading to a heavenly bedding between those exceptional thighs, but the infernal coupling bound my infected soul as her long legs squeezed my sides. After all this time, Stephanie's once youthful and vibrant image haunted me even as my divided spirit continued to repair itself, her touch still echoing within.

In my mind I replayed a group session in which I had been required to recite the story of Stephanie DeLeon. Everyone listened, the room otherwise quiet. In the end I concluded that Steffi had brought to my universe an outer sparkle and an inner intensity, which drove my life and remodeled the world as I had once lived it. It had taken me thirty years—thirty fucking years to this very day!—to realize that her insane behavior was the work of Slick, a dungeon master feeding off her abusive childhood.

Christ, I was a physician, and even so I had failed to put two and two together. Marooned in ego-land, I was a husband smitten by fornication and alcohol. I guess Steffi never stood a chance. A big sigh blew from my lungs. We were both addicts, only our drug of choice differed back then.

Then "Luckenbach, Texas" came on for a split second, and I suddenly inhaled. *Where is little Mike now? Of course, he is not little anymore.*

Fletcher stepped into the silence. "When you first met Steffi, certainly you had no idea what had been going on with the woman. Her exciting and bubbly personality was infectious, addictive, even. That was all you needed to know back then, Ira. But her meth and effervescence, like the alcohol, had a hidden agenda, promising destruction of all that was near and dear to you."

She began to chew on her right cheek and grind her teeth, briefly picking at her forearm.

Then I said to the group, "In the 1970s, I could legally write a prescription for Quaalude and for methamphetamine, drugs on which Steffi had become hooked. I understand that now. I did not back then. I had ignored the fact that Stephanie had a poor appetite, irritability, paranoia, and sleeplessness, ignored at my peril. Indeed, at her peril. She required the Quaalude to soften those symptoms of meth addiction, to sleep, and to hide her demons. Rather like I used Valium ..."

I hesitated, struggling to wade through the swampy backwaters of time required to answer Fletcher's query. I did not want to lift another veil on my ignoble past, though it was difficult to ignore that lock of honey-blonde hair lying between the pages of memory. I had not known that meth-induced psychotic episodes lead to deadly violence upon one's self or an imagined foe. Methamphetamine, the Cerberus guarding her gates of hell.

Stephanie's cheeks were swollen, black and blue from hemorrhage. Her naked form was writhing, convulsing, snaking hard along the wall. Opaque liquid and small gouts of blood dripped from a scalp laceration and then pooled onto the floor beneath Steffi's head. Her swollen lips were silent except for ratchety respirations ... That image in Hershey still has a grip on me, the taste of her blood even yet with me.

I chewed on a pretzel while carrying out a mental autopsy on our fatal marriage. Steffi had been a human being, albeit an ill one. But two wrongs did not make a right, and two sick lovers did not make a healthy family. I still could not pull free from thoughts of Steffi, even sensing the shape of her presence. How the nurse had touched my arm that first day in the operating room—like a wisp of warm wind. I felt a tenderness that told more than words could express. A part of me yet cried out for her, for her caresses, or, perhaps, dreamed of the drama she once brought to my life. When I lost her, I was absolutely devastated. Time healed most of those feelings, though sometimes she came back like a phantom pain, a sliver of toxic shrapnel that couldn't be completely excised. I would still get a whiff of her perfume when no one was there—or at least my brain's Nucleus Accumbens did, or so says our counselor. *Panthere de Cartier.*

My goodness, Ira, I wonder how the IV line got disconnected? About the time I took a potty break, wasn't it?

Step Nine: amends. Amends to Stephanie? What would others do? My eyeballs focused on a telephone in the men's library. Michael Starling Senior earlier had located her address and phone number in Hershey, Pennsylvania. He strongly advised me not to contact her. But curiosity and the need to make amends got the better of me. Call? *No way.* But the telephone seemed to loom larger and larger, a magnet drawing me closer. *No!* My heart suddenly thumped wildly; my hands shook. *She's just human, Ira, and years have passed. What's stopping you? Are you chicken? Again?* My left fingers wrapped themselves around the receiver and lifted it. I dialed the area code. *Oh God, what if she actually answers?* Then the seven-digit number. I trembled so badly that I could hardly keep the phone against my ear. *Why open this can of worms, Ira?* Breathing became nearly impossible.

"Hello?"

Nearly in a state of shock, I swallowed. A man's voice. "Is ... Is ..."

"Yes. May I help ya?"

"I was ... ah ... looking for Steffi. May I speak with her?"

"Nobody's called her 'Steffi' fer years. Stella can't talk to no one, ya know."

"Stella?" My hand gripped the receiver as some form of venomous emotion tore through me.

"'At's right. Hello? Ya still there?"

"I ... I can call back later. When would be a good time?"

"In her condition, her being confused 'n all, she wouldn't know what ya was sayin' anyways. She's never been herself since that there surgery, Mister ... Mister ...?"

"Uh ... Jones. Did you say surgery?"

"She had that there blood clot taken from her brain a while back. Just stares off into space ever since, ya know. Keeps mumbling something about revenge from that there sister o' hers ... calls her Steffi now, but that there Stella lady's dead, been dead fer years, so that don't make no damn sense."

"Dear God! May I ask what happened?"

"A while back I came home from Pittsburgh, ya know, an' found her lying on the floor, beaten up terrible-like, bleedin', hair washed in some o' her blood—makin' it kinda red-like, unconscious 'n all. Police never found the guy what done this."

"Her hair?"

"Yup. Seems someone had cut her head an' took the bloody water in the wash bowl an' did up her hair with it. Water was still in the sink when we found her, ya know. Later she claimed she and her sister were in a fight, ya know, an' 'twas Steff what done this to her. But 'at's not possible."

A lump rose up in my throat. I could not breathe for nearly a minute.

"Hello, you still there? Hello?"

I cleared my throat. "Actually, sir, we are looking for her son, Michael. I'm calling from the high school alumni office."

"He don't live here no more, ya know. Haven't seen hide nor hair o' him since his teens."

"Thank you. Sorry to bother you. Good-bye."

About to pass out, I hung up.

*   *   *

Our home group filed in and sat in the usual circle. After Sebastian discussed a painful year in his past, Fletcher turned to me.

"Ira, do you plan on making amends to your wives in the near future? Steps Eight and Nine ask us to make amends to persons we have injured, even if the recipient is equally responsible. This is to help us in our own recovery, not necessarily to aid the recipient. Without admitting freely to our role in the carnage and making restitution, if possible, forgiving *ourselves* will be greatly hindered."

I took in a deep breath and explained my nerve-racking attempt to reach Stephanie. "Monica and I have already talked. I'll work on contacting Judi and Nadine. Just need to get over ... over that call to Steffi's home."

"In my own case I couldn't make amends to my ex early on, but I finally did a year later. Your feelings may also change as time goes by."

And what of Mikey Stone? For a number of years Mike Starling Senior and I tried without success to locate Mikey. He'd just disappeared from sight. I suspect a return to our world was too remote or too painful for him. I just prayed that he grew up more like his natural dad and stayed away from drugs. I wish that I could have done more for little Mike—the lad, who, if in college back then, would have been close to the age of my own youngest brother at the time of his death, both remaining forever engraved on my heart. Yet when I try to recall how they looked, the images became dimmer, like remembering candle flames after they had blown out.

EPILOGUE

He who goes out weeping, carrying seed to sow,
will return with songs of joy, carrying sheaves with him.

Psalm 126

Appleton rested on a hill. In that recovery center we were myopic caterpillars in a cocoon, departing as yet unseasoned butterflies. The trick was to *remain* a butterfly, not a moth drawn back to the flame of Pleasure Island. I took a risk by not staying the entire ninety days, but neither my department—if I still had a job—nor my medical insurance policy would help finance any recovery treatment expenses.

When I arrived at Appleton, I was one scared puppy. When the morning of departure arrived thirty days later, I found myself full of peace and a feeling of self-accomplishment. I was even sad at leaving my new buddies, all those men and women afflicted with one of nature's most lethal of diseases, an illness that presently could not be cured but only controlled, rather like diabetes. On the last day I was "gonged out" by all the men, who hugged me with warmth and kindness, and then I struck the large bell near the entrance of Appleton. I received my thirty-day coin with the AA symbol, a triangle within a circle, a gift I shall always cherish. I felt ready to embrace my future, to rush to meet it.

Luke was again my driver for the trip back to the airport. It felt so different this time. *"I was a patient in Appleton a few years back. They saved my life. Most of the medical people ... the therapists I mean ... are addicts themselves,"* he had said that misty night he delivered me to the rehab center. He was my friend now, a fellow alcoholic in recovery. I especially loved the man for ignoring my plea to turn back on that first of May. He was one of many the Lord had placed in my path.

"How's it feel to be heading home, my friend?" An unlit cigarette still bobbed up and down on one side of his mouth.

"Terrific. A bit nervous, though."

"Yeah. You'll do okay. I'm collecting another passenger from the airport after I leave you off. Another doc." He scanned a paper at his side. "An Alicia Chalmers from LA. Says here she's a neurologist for kids."

Sounds familiar. "Hope she sticks it out."

*   *   *

I returned home in June 2005, feeling a bit panicky over resuming my job and facing friends and family again. That nervousness disappeared when Monica met me at the airport and wrapped her arms around me. I was so happy, so thrilled, to be with Monica once more. My lips and heart reveled in the renewed taste of intimacy so long denied.

"I love you, I love you, I love you!" came first from my lips. I did not deserve her after all the isolation and emotional trauma I had caused. But she had waited for me. Thank God.

I returned to my AA and NA meetings—caduceus and others. Steps Eight and Nine required me to make of list of all persons I had harmed and then make direct amends to them where possible. And I continued doing so. It was not as onerous as I first thought, and accomplishing it lifted much weight from my shoulders. I only had to clean my side of the street, not theirs, as someone had said. (Street? It was a damn interstate!) The rusty links of guilt and shame, until then the parameters defining my very being, fell away as an inner happiness replaced self-righteousness, day by day. Upon my return, even my AA and NA buddies said that they had never seen me smile until then and that I appeared ten years younger.

As my counselor noted, God works in mysterious ways, often sending help in a form we refuse to recognize. In my own case it was Jocelyn, the sister against whom I had held a bitter hatred. Now I loved her even more for saving me from liver failure and perhaps a fate worse than death itself. She became the first of many to receive my phone call of apologies and amends. But I quietly thought to myself, *Michael—both of them in some way—was the messenger.* The fallout from my rehabilitation was even more awesome, as I was soon to learn.

There was a phenomenon quite strange but nevertheless true. Addicts seemed to have the uncanny ability to seek out and marry another addict, often unconsciously. Monica and I were no exception. Since the painful loss of her husband, Sam, she had become addicted to the prescription analgesic OxyContin, a hazardous mind-altering drug that makes Slick's mouth water. As I continued to maintain my sobriety by attending meetings, Monica took note of the remarkable changes in me—I did not drink, I joined in family gatherings, and I no longer hid out in the den. And my anger had abated.

One summer evening she turned to me and said, "Ira, I have been thinking. I desperately need to get off this narcotic." She wrung her hands, eyes tearing. "Do you think Appleton could help me? They certainly have changed you."

Yes! I silently agreed. "Monica, why don't you think it over? I will certainly support you should you decide to go." If there was one thing I learned, it was that the addict must *want* treatment and seek it out.

In October she left for San Francisco, just as I had six months before. She was terribly anxious, not knowing where it would lead. I knew the feeling. I visited her during family week, and our confrontation—addict and spouse—became an intense experience, with many drug abusers and their relatives in attendance.

Then my daughter, Alexandria, highly addicted to cocaine, had lost everything—her home, car, job, money, health, son, and self-respect. She saw what the rehab center did for Monica and me. Making the hardest decision of her life, Lexi left for Kellog, a recovery unit near Minneapolis, Minnesota. Both women returned home free from drugs, as well as the twin yokes of resentment and depression that had once foredoomed them to a short life. Following recovery I believed in a higher power, and I chose to call him God, a fixed star to steer by. He had worked through loved ones in my life. Every evening I got down on my own knees and thanked the Lord for what He did for me, my wife, and my second daughter, one after the other—the splash that still rippled from that precious stone Jocie cast.

The price tag? Appleton required each of us to calculate the financial losses from our addiction. We had to include the costs of alcohol and drug purchases, legal fees, court fines, personal income losses, alimony, and medical expenses. I had lost more wampum than most people acquired in a lifetime. The expense of rehabilitation paled before those figures, and the cost of ignoring treatment was incalculable—Uncle Barley, Joe Cooper, and Barfly had perished and Stephanie DeLeon had fallen into years of desolate grief.

What of my other spouses? Nadine, bone of my bones, flesh of my flesh, and the mother of my two girls, never remarried. We became good friends. I was screwing up my courage to make my amends to Nadine one day when I received a phone call from Alexandria. She was hysterical, crying uncontrollably.

"Daddy! Daddy, I … I'm in the hospital emergency room with Mommy."

"Alexandria, what's going on?"

"She's had a heart attack! The doctor says she is failing! They've … they've been working on her, but the heart isn't responding very well."

"I'll be there as soon as possible," I replied.

"She knows it doesn't look good. She wants to talk to you, Daddy. I'll hold the phone for her."

I could hear the erratic beeps of a cardiac monitor as Nadine came on the line. Her voice was soft and distant. "Ira, I know we … we have had our difficulties. I just want to say we're okay now." There was a long pause. "I love you, Ira."

I swallowed. "I love you, too, Nadine. I'll be right there. I'm praying for you, Nadine. Nadine? Are you there?"

Lexi answered, crying, "Oh, Daddy. Mommy just died."

I dropped to my knees. I knew that Lexi's very soul had just cracked at its core.

$*$ $*$ $*$

I was mind-boggled at my first statewide AA meeting. We laughed and cried at the stories told, but the most poignant minute was at the end, when one thousand men and women held hands and said the Lord's Prayer. I experienced a spiritual warmth and friendship such as I had never felt before. Where can one get that for the admission price of fifteen dollars? I couldn't wait to attend an international meeting.

I hadn't yet tried to contact Judi, but I knew I would in time. Through God I sent her my request for forgiveness, for the hurts I have caused. It is a strange and remarkable feeling—I just could not find any anger dwelling in my head those days, any resentment over the divorces or against my wives. I found that once Appleton had pulled away the bitterness, I still loved them. It was strange, though. I tried to remember how each had felt in my arms, but those memories mysteriously merged into one.

I no longer worshiped the purse and felt no distress over the loss of my hard-earned cash to my better halves. I ran the uninsured patient clinic, where I found contentment and joy in helping people less fortunate than I and in teaching young doctors the art and science of surgery. Two hundred million dollars could not buy that. What about the approach of five o'clock? I switched my watch to the right hand—just to fool Slick, that lethal internal committee of one. It worked.

Chapel Hill

One evening I attended a resident's graduation party, dinner and a cash bar. The doc sitting next to me was sipping a CC Manhattan, her third. I glanced at the lady's drink, her legs, and back to the Canadian whiskey.

My "opiate receptors" suddenly vibrated, grabbing hold of me. *The pure iridescence of dancing light beams reflecting off the inverted cone of a cocktail glass, a crystal standing seductively on her long slender leg, clear deep amber spirits chilled to perfection, an impeccable red cherry coasting in the depths—the answer to an immense desire ready to be slaked!* My nerves began to pirouette over the edge, my heart accelerating, pounding. *Oh heck. I can have just one.*

I walked, a bit too fast perhaps, toward the bar and bullied the bartender to construct the same. *Just one, dammit, that's all.* The bartender mixed the drink in his shaker, poured it over ice, shook again, and then filled my cocktail glass. I took a deep breath.

"Maybe this *is* better than sex," I whispered to no one in particular, though the woman looked up and smiled. My fingers wrapped themselves around the cold chalice, dormant cinders still smoldering in my brain, the past unfolding. *It felt good. Real good, burning as the lava settled in to singe my stomach, then spreading out, once more baptizing every fiber of my being.* Appleton faded for a minute and then resurfaced as I whispered to myself, "Do I really want to do this? *Just one.* But then I'll relapse into two, then three, and then …? Restart my sobriety date? More likely invite my liver to a slow death? Become a Jekyll and Hyde once again?"

That day, God and Appleton censored Slick and stayed my hand, which pulled away and threw down a ten dollar bill. My legs, having more brains than my head, steered me away and out the door. My barstool neighbor rotated and stared after me. Someday I will be able to safely sit next to another's Manhattan without the urge to drink, but not yet, not for many seasons.

Dubai, March 2007

Denni and her family had moved from England to Dubai, and I flew there for a visit. Yesterday, I gazed at her dresser mirror. The reflection revealed lines of age running playfully over my face, the frowns of anger and sags of depression no longer apparent. Next to me was a recent photo of one of my grandsons, the spitting image of me during my junior high school days. *Dear God*, I prayed, *don't let him inherit my disease.*

Today, the suffocating dominion of Grandma Stone and perilous charisma of Stephanie DeLeon are gone forever. I found myself perched on a bench in my firstborn's backyard. A honey bee playfully raced for my glass of Sprite. The fine desert dust of Dubai shadowed the blue sky into a basted sheen.

"Daddy, my husband has a new job. It looks like we are moving to

Hong Kong." Denise sat next to me, and I sensed a bit of fear. "No sooner do we get settled somewhere before we are on the move again. My whole life has been full of unnerving instability. Your grandsons and I need a nest that stays in one place," she sighed, on the verge of tears.

I also knew that feeling. If only there were a Movers Anonymous.

Denni's anger toward me had gradually dwindled, her carved and contorted emotions having surfaced after decades of enduring my alcoholism and her childhood separation. And our many moves. I made my amends to her, but forgiveness by offspring occurs by degrees, not overnight.

I explained to Denise Anne that Steffi had suffered from the evils of methamphetamine addiction when my daughters were little girls, when Stephanie had screamed her dire threats, the shrieks still echoing in both of my daughters' memory banks. Denni's child within was still quaking from the absence of her daddy's refuge, having listened to his footsteps disappearing from her life. Each day was better now, after she heard the soft tread of my boots coming back. Denise gave me a big hug today, bringing moisture to the corner of my eye.

Her sister, Alexandria Lee, and I had suffered each other's slings and arrows for years during our drinking and using days. Alexandria, especially, had endured life on the edge of hell itself. After we graduated from boot camp, clean and sober, we each found a new love for the other. We were addicts. We were in recovery. Only an addict can ever truly understand what has happened to another addict.

I looked up from my thoughts and spotted Denni's potted rose bush. The curious bee was fanning its wings.

*   *   *

Mike Starling Senior and I, having reestablished our friendship and the bond linking us, for years made numerous attempts to find our son, Mikey, through the postal service and Internet resources, without success. Letters to possible addresses came back unopened and labeled RETURN TO SENDER. I had nearly given up. One day I was checking my e-mail when I saw a communication from across the seas. It was from the United States Army, Department of Defense, Kabul, Afghanistan. For the longest time I sat and stared at the combat warrior's message, my heart pounding, knuckles white with tension. I burst out crying as I read.

> *Dear Dads, Your letter was forwarded to me by my wife in St. Paul, Minnesota ... am a Princeton graduate and now supervisor for coalition transport services in Afghanistan ... married to a librarian ... now blessed to be found by my two fathers ... You have a grandson! We named him Michael Jacob ... Had given up hope or just scared, but always wondered. I want to see you both when I return home!*
>
> *God Bless. Love, Michael*
>
> *Michael Starling Stone*
> *Lt Col US Army*